THE SCHOOL
for GOOD MOTHERS

THE SCHOOL
for GOOD MOTHERS

A NOVEL

JESSAMINE CHAN

**BLACK
STONE**
PUBLISHING

Copyright © 2022 by Jessamine Chan
Published in 2022 by Blackstone Publishing
Cover design by Grace Han
Interior book design by Carly Loman

The characters and events in this book are fictitious.
Any similarity to real persons, living or dead, is
coincidental and not intended by the author.

Printed in the United States of America

First large print edition: 2022
ISBN 979-8-200-91293-3
Fiction / Literary

Version 1

CIP data for this book is available
from the Library of Congress

Blackstone Publishing
31 Mistletoe Rd.
Ashland, OR 97520

www.BlackstonePublishing.com

For my parents

I wanted to find one law to cover all of living, I found fear. A list of my nightmares is the map of the way out of here.

—ANNE CARSON, **Plainwater**

1.

"WE HAVE YOUR DAUGHTER."

It's the first Tuesday in September, the afternoon of her one very bad day, and Frida is trying to stay on the road. On the voice mail, the officer tells her to come to the station immediately. She pauses the message, puts down her phone. It's 2:46 p.m. She meant to get home an hour and a half ago. She pulls onto the first side street off Grays Ferry and double-parks. She calls back and begins apologizing, explaining that she lost track of time.

"Is she okay?"

The officer says the child is safe. "Ma'am, we've been trying to reach you."

Frida hangs up and calls Gust, has to leave a message. He needs to meet her at the station at Eleventh and Wharton. "There's a problem. It's Harriet." Her voice catches. She repeats the officer's promise that their daughter is safe.

As she begins driving again, she reminds herself to stay under the speed limit, to avoid running red lights, to breathe. All through Labor Day weekend, she felt frantic. Last Friday and Saturday, she had her usual insomnia, sleeping two hours each night. On Sunday, when Gust dropped off Harriet for Frida's three and a half days of custody, Harriet was in the throes of an ear infection. That night, Frida slept ninety minutes. Last night, an hour. Harriet's crying has been relentless, too big for her body, too loud for the walls of their tiny house to absorb. Frida did what she could. She sang lullabies, rubbed Harriet's chest, gave her extra milk. She laid on the floor next to Harriet's crib, held her impossibly perfect hand through the bars, kissed her knuckles, her fingernails, feeling for the ones that needed to be trimmed, praying for Harriet's eyes to close.

The afternoon sun is burning as Frida pulls up to the station, located two blocks from her house in an old Italian neighborhood in South Philly. She parks and rushes to the reception desk, asks if the receptionist has seen her daughter, a toddler, eighteen months old; half Chinese, half white; big brown eyes, curly dark brown hair with bangs.

"You must be the mother," the receptionist says.

The receptionist, an elderly white woman wearing a smear of pink lipstick, emerges from behind the desk. Her eyes flick over Frida from head to toe, pausing at Frida's feet, her worn-out Birkenstocks.

The station seems to be mostly empty. The receptionist walks with halting steps, favoring her left leg. She leads Frida down the hall and deposits her in a windowless interrogation room where the walls are a cloying mint green. Frida sits. In crime movies she's seen, the lights are always flickering, but here the glare is steady. She has goose bumps, wishes for a jacket or scarf. Though she's often exhausted on the days she has Harriet, now there's a weight bearing down on her chest, an ache that has passed into her bones, numbing her.

She rubs her arms, her attention fading in and out. She retrieves her phone from the bottom of her purse, cursing herself for not seeing the officer's messages immediately, for having silenced her phone this morning after getting fed up with endless robocalls, for having forgotten to turn the ringer back on. In the past twenty minutes, Gust has called six times and sent a stream of worried texts.

Here, she writes finally. **Come soon**. She should call back, but she's afraid. During her half of the week, Gust calls every night to find out if Harriet has new words or motor skills. She hates the disappointment in his voice when she fails to deliver. But Harriet is changing in other ways: a stronger grip, noticing a new detail in a book, holding Frida's gaze longer when they kiss good night.

Resting her forearms on the metal table, Frida puts her head down and falls asleep for a split second. She looks up and spots a camera in the corner of the ceiling. Her mind returns to Harriet. She'll buy a carton of strawberry ice cream, Harriet's favorite. When they get home, she'll let Harriet play in the tub as long as she wants. She'll read Harriet extra books at bedtime. **I Am a Bunny**. **Corduroy**.

The officers enter without knocking. Officer Brunner, the one who called, is a burly white man in his twenties with acne at the corners of his mouth. Officer Harris is a middle-aged Black man with a perfectly groomed mustache and strong shoulders.

She stands and shakes hands with both of them. They ask to see her driver's license, confirm that she's Frida Liu.

"Where is my baby?"

"Sit down," Officer Brunner says, glancing at Frida's chest. He flips his notebook to a blank page. "Ma'am, what time did you leave the house?"

"Maybe noon. Twelve thirty? I went out for a coffee. And then I went to my office. I shouldn't have. I know. It was so stupid. I was exhausted. I'm sorry. I didn't mean to . . . Can you please tell me where she is?"

"Don't play dumb with us, Ms. Liu," Officer Harris says.

"I'm not. I can explain."

"You left your baby at home. Alone. Your neighbors heard her crying."

Frida spreads her palms on the table, needing to touch something cold and solid. "It was a mistake."

The officers arrived around two, entering through the breezeway. The sliding glass door between Frida's kitchen and backyard was open, with only the flimsy screen door protecting the child.

"So your toddler . . . Harriet is her name? Harriet was alone for two hours. Is that right, Ms. Liu?"

Frida sits on her hands. She's left her body, is now floating high above.

They tell her that Harriet is being examined at a crisis center for children. "Someone will bring her—"

"What do you mean, examining her? Look, it's not what you think. I wouldn't—"

"Ma'am, hold on," Officer Brunner says. "You seem like a smart lady. Let's back up. Why would you leave your kid alone in the first place?"

"I got a coffee, and then I went into work. I needed a file. A hard copy. I must have lost track of time. I was already on the way home when I saw that you called. I'm sorry. I haven't slept in days. I need to go get her. Can I go now?"

Officer Harris shakes his head. "We're not done here. Where were you supposed to be today? Who was in charge of the baby?"

"I was. Like I told you, I went to work. I work at Wharton."

She explains that she produces a faculty research digest, rewriting academic papers as short articles with takeaways for the business community. Like writing term papers on subjects she knows nothing about. She works from home Monday through Wednesday, when she has custody—a special arrangement. It's her first full-time job since Harriet was born. She's been there for only six months. It's been so hard to find a decent job, or any job, in Philly.

She tells them about her demanding boss, her deadline. The professor she's working with right now is eighty-one. He never sends his notes by email. She forgot to bring his notes home with her last Friday, needed them for the article she's finishing.

"I was going in to grab the file and then come right back. I got caught up with answering emails. I should have—"

"This is how you showed up to work?" Officer Harris nods at Frida's bare face, her chambray button-down, stained with toothpaste and peanut butter. Her long black hair tied in a messy bun. Her shorts. The blemish on her chin.

She swallows. "My boss knows I have a baby."

They scribble in their notebooks. They'll do a background check, but if she has any prior offenses, she should tell them now.

"Of course I don't have a record." Her chest is tight. She begins to cry. "It was a mistake. Please. You have to believe me. Am I under arrest?"

The officers say no. But they've called Child Protective Services. A social worker is on her way.

×

Alone in the mint-green room, Frida gnaws at her fingers. She remembers retrieving Harriet from her crib and changing her diaper. She remembers giving Harriet her morning bottle, feeding her yogurt and a banana, reading to her from a Berenstain Bears book, the one about a sleepover.

They'd been up off and on since 4:00 a.m. Frida's article was due last week. All morning, she went back and forth between Harriet's play corner and back to the living room sofa, where she had her notes spread out on the coffee table. She wrote the same paragraph over and over, trying to explain Bayesian modeling in layman's terms. Harriet kept screaming. She wanted to climb onto Frida's lap. She wanted to be held. She grabbed Frida's papers and threw them on the floor. She kept touching the keyboard.

Frida should have put on a show for Harriet to watch. She remembers thinking that if she couldn't finish the article, couldn't keep up, her boss would rescind work-from-home privileges and Harriet would have to go to day care, something Frida hoped to avoid. And she remembers that she then plopped Harriet in her ExerSaucer, a contraption that should have been retired months ago as soon as Harriet started walking. Later, Frida gave Harriet water and animal crackers. She checked Harriet's diaper. She kissed Harriet's head, which smelled oily. She squeezed Harriet's pudgy arms.

Harriet would be safe in the ExerSaucer, she thought. It couldn't go anywhere. What could happen in an hour?

Under the harsh lights of the interrogation room, Frida bites her cuticles, pulling off bits of skin. Her contacts are killing her. She takes a compact from her purse and examines the gray rings under her eyes. She used to be considered lovely. She is petite and slender, and with her round face and bangs and porcelain-doll features, people used to assume she was still in her twenties. But at thirty-nine, she has deep creases between her brows and bracketing her mouth, lines that appeared postpartum, becoming more pronounced after Gust left her for Susanna when Harriet was three months old.

This morning, she didn't shower or wash her face. She worried the neighbors would complain about the crying. She should have closed the back door. She should have come home right away. She should never have left. She should have remembered the file in the first place. Or gone in over the weekend to grab it. She should have met her original deadline.

She should have told the officers that she can't lose this job. That Gust hired a mediator to determine child support. He didn't want to waste money on legal fees. With Gust's rewarding but poorly paid position, his student-loan debt, and her earning potential, and the fact that custody would be shared, the mediator suggested that Gust give her $500 a month, not nearly enough to support her and Harriet, especially since she gave up her job in New York. She couldn't bring herself to ask him for more. She didn't ask for alimony. Her parents would help her if she asked, but she can't ask, would hate herself if she did. They already funded her entire life during the separation.

It's four fifteen. Hearing voices in the hall, she opens the door and finds Gust and Susanna conferring with the officers. Susanna approaches and embraces Frida, keeps holding on as Frida stiffens, enveloped in Susanna's lush red hair and sandalwood perfume.

Susanna rubs Frida's back as if they're friends. The girl is on a mission to nice her to death. A war of attrition. Susanna is only twenty-eight, a former dancer. Before Susanna appeared in her life, Frida hadn't understood that the gap between twenty-eight and thirty-nine could be so potent and deadly. The girl has a fine-boned elfin face, with huge blue eyes that give her a fragile, storybook quality. Even on days when she does nothing but childcare, she wears black winged eyeliner and dresses like a teenager, carrying herself with a confidence that Frida never possessed.

Gust is shaking hands with the other men. Frida stares at the ground and waits. Old Gust would yell. As he did on the nights she hid in the bathroom and wept instead of holding the baby. But this is New Gust, the one who hugs her tenderly despite her delinquency, who's been made placid by Susanna's love and toxin-free lifestyle.

"Gust, I'm so sorry."

He asks Susanna to wait outside, then takes Frida's arm and leads her back into the mint-green room, where he sits beside her, cradling her hands. It's been months since they were alone together. She feels ashamed for wanting a kiss even now. He's more beautiful than she ever deserved, tall and lean and muscular. At forty-two, his angular face is lined from too much sun, his sandy, graying waves grown longer to please Susanna. He now resembles the surfer he'd been in his youth.

Gust squeezes her hands tighter, hurting her. "Obviously, what happened today . . ."

"I haven't been sleeping. I wasn't thinking. I know that's no excuse. I thought she'd be fine for an hour. I was just going to go in and come right back."

"Why would you do that? That's not okay. You're not raising her alone, you know. You could have called me. Either of us. Susanna could have helped you." Gust grips her wrists. "She's coming home with us tonight. Look at me. Are you listening, Frida? This is serious. The cops said you might lose custody."

"No." She pulls her hands away. The room spins.

"Temporarily," he says. "Sweetie, you're not breathing." He shakes her shoulder and tells her to take a breath, but she can't. If she does, she might vomit.

On the other side of the door, she hears crying. "Can I?"

Gust nods.

Susanna is holding Harriet. She's given her some apple slices. It always kills Frida to see Harriet's ease with Susanna, her ease even now, after a day of illness and fear and strangers. This morning, Frida dressed Harriet in a purple dinosaur T-shirt and striped leggings and moccasins, but now she's in a raggedy pink sweater and jeans that are much too big, socks, but no shoes.

"Please," Frida says, taking Harriet from Susanna.

Harriet clutches Frida's neck. Now that they're together again, Frida's body relaxes.

"Are you hungry? Did they feed you?"

Harriet sniffles. Her eyes are red and swollen. The borrowed clothes smell sour. Frida pictures state workers taking off Harriet's clothes and diaper, inspecting her body. Did anyone touch her inappropriately? How will she ever make this up to her baby? Will it be the work of months or years or a lifetime?

"Mommy." Harriet's voice is hoarse.

Frida leans her temple against Harriet's. "Mommy is so sorry. You have to stay with Daddy and Sue-Sue for a while, okay? Bub, I'm so sorry. I really messed up." She kisses Harriet's ear. "Does it still hurt?"

Harriet nods.

"Daddy will give you the medicine. Promise you'll be good?" Frida starts to say they'll see each other soon but holds her tongue. She hooks Harriet's pinkie.

"Galaxies," she whispers. It's their favorite game,

a promise they say at bedtime. **I promise you the moon and stars. I love you more than galaxies**. She says it when she tucks Harriet in, this girl with her same moon face, same double eyelids, same pensive mouth.

Harriet begins falling asleep on her shoulder.

Gust tugs on Frida's arm. "We need to get her home for dinner."

"Not yet." She holds Harriet and rocks her, kissing her salty cheek. They need to change her out of these disgusting clothes. They need to give her a bath. "I'm going to miss you like crazy. Love you, bub. Love you, love you, love you."

Harriet stirs but doesn't answer. Frida takes a last look at Harriet, then closes her eyes as Gust takes her baby.

×

The social worker is stuck in rush-hour traffic. Frida waits in the mint-green room. Half an hour passes. She calls Gust.

"I forgot to tell you. I know you guys are cutting back on dairy, but please let her have dessert tonight. I was going to let her have some ice cream."

Gust says they've already eaten. Harriet was too tired to eat much. Susanna is giving her a bath now. Frida apologizes again, knows this might be the beginning of years of apologizing, that she's dug herself a hole from which she may never emerge.

"Stay calm when you talk to them," Gust says. "Don't freak out. I'm sure this will be over soon."

She resists saying **I love you**. Resists thanking him. She says good night and begins pacing. She should have asked the officers which neighbors called. If it was the elderly couple who have faded postcards of Pope John Paul II taped to their screen door. The woman who lives on the other side of the back fence, whose cats defecate in Frida's yard. The couple on the other side of her bedroom wall, whose luxurious moans make her lonelier than she is already.

She doesn't know any of their names. She's tried saying hello, but when she does, they ignore her or cross the street. Since last year, she's rented a three-bedroom row house near Passyunk Square. She's the only nonwhite resident on her block, the only one who hasn't lived there for decades, the only renter, the only yuppie, the only one with a baby. It was the largest space she could find on short notice. She had to have her parents cosign the lease; she hadn't found the job at Penn yet. West Philly was close to work but too expensive. Fishtown and Bella Vista and Queen Village and Graduate Hospital were too expensive. They'd moved here from Brooklyn when Gust, a landscape architect, was recruited by a prestigious green-roofing firm in Philly. His company's projects focus on sustainability: wetlands restoration, stormwater systems. Gust said that in Philly, they'd be able to save up and buy a house. They'd still be close enough to visit New York whenever they wanted. It would be a better place to raise children. She's stuck in the smallest city she's ever lived in, a toy city where she has no support network and only a few acquaintances, no real friends of her own. And now, because of joint custody, she has to stay until Harriet turns eighteen.

One of the overhead lights is buzzing. Frida wants to rest her head but can't shake the feeling of being watched. Susanna will tell her friends. Gust will tell his parents. She'll need to tell **her** parents. She's torn off most of the cuticle on her left thumb. She becomes aware of her headache, her dry mouth, her desire to leave this room immediately.

She opens the door and asks permission to use the

bathroom and get a snack. From the vending machine, she buys peanut butter cookies and a candy bar. She hasn't eaten since breakfast. Only coffee. All day, her hands have been trembling.

When she returns, the social worker is waiting for her. Frida drops the half-eaten candy bar and awkwardly retrieves it, getting a good look at the social worker's taut calves in black capri pants, her sneakers. The woman is young and striking, maybe in her midtwenties, has evidently come straight from the gym. She wears a spandex jacket over a tank top. A gold cross hangs low above her cleavage. Her arm muscles are visible through her clothes. Her dyed-blond hair is slicked into a ponytail that makes her wide-set eyes look reptilian. She has beautiful skin, but she's wearing a tremendous amount of foundation, her face made up with contours and highlights. When she smiles, Frida sees her gleaming white movie-star teeth.

They shake hands. The social worker, Ms. Torres, points out the bit of chocolate on Frida's lips. Before Frida can wipe it away, the social worker begins photographing her. She spots Frida's torn cuticles and asks her to display her hands.

"Why?"

"Do you have a problem, Ms. Liu?"

"No. It's fine."

She takes a close-up of Frida's hands, then her face. She studies the stains on Frida's shirt. She props up her tablet and begins typing.

"You can sit."

"My ex-husband said my custody might be suspended. Is that true?"

"Yes, the child will remain in her father's care."

"But it won't ever happen again. Gust knows that."

"Ms. Liu, this was an emergency removal because of imminent danger. You left your daughter unsupervised."

Frida flushes. She always feels like she's fucking up, but now there's evidence.

"We didn't find any signs of physical abuse, but your daughter was dehydrated. And hungry. According to the report, her diaper leaked. She'd been crying for a very long time. She was in distress." The social worker flips through her notes, raises an eyebrow. "And I'm told your house was dirty."

"I'm not normally like this. I meant to clean over the weekend. I would never harm her."

The social worker smiles coldly. "But you did

harm her. Tell me, why didn't you take her with you? What mother wouldn't realize, **If I want or need to leave the house, my baby comes with me**?"

She waits for Frida's response. Frida recalls this morning's mounting frustration and angst, the selfish desire for a moment of peace. Most days, she can talk herself down from that cliff. It's mortifying that they've started a file on her, as if she were beating Harriet or keeping her in squalor, as if she were one of those mothers who left their infant in the back seat of a car on a hot summer day.

"It was a mistake."

"Yes, you've said that. But I feel like there's something you're not telling me. Why would you decide all of a sudden to go into the office?"

"I went to get a coffee. Then I drove to Penn. There was a file I forgot to bring home. I only had a hard copy. I'm working on an article with one of the most senior professors in the business school. He's complained about me to the dean before. When I misquoted him. He tried to have me fired. And then when I got to the office, I started answering emails. I should have been keeping track of time. I know I shouldn't have left her at home. I know that. I screwed up."

Frida tugs at her hair, pulling it loose. "My

daughter hasn't been sleeping. She's supposed to take two naps a day, and she hasn't been napping at all. I've been sleeping on her floor. She won't fall asleep unless I'm holding her hand. And if I try to leave the room, she wakes up instantly and totally flips out. The past few days have been a blur. I've been overwhelmed. Don't you have days like that? I've been so tired I've had chest pains."

"All parents are tired."

"I intended to come right back."

"But you didn't. You got in your car and drove away. That's abandonment, Ms. Liu. If you want to leave the house whenever you feel like it, you get a dog, not a kid."

Frida blinks back tears. She wants to say she's not the same as those bad mothers in the news. She didn't set her house on fire. She didn't leave Harriet on a subway platform. She didn't strap Harriet into the back seat and drive into a lake.

"I know that I seriously messed up, but I didn't mean to do this. I understand that it was a crazy thing to do."

"Ms. Liu, do you have a history of mental illness?"

"I've had depression on and off. That's not what I meant. I'm not—"

"Should we assume that this was a psychotic break? A manic episode? Were you under the influence of any substances?"

"No. Absolutely not. And I'm not crazy. I'm not going to pretend I'm some perfect mother, but parents make mistakes. I'm sure you've seen much worse."

"But we're not talking about other parents. We're talking about you."

Frida tries to steady her voice. "I need to see her. How long will this take? She's never been away from me for more than four days."

"Nothing is resolved that quickly." The social worker explains the process as if she's rattling off a grocery list. Frida will undergo a psychological evaluation, as will Harriet. Harriet will receive therapy. There will be three supervised visits over the next sixty days. The state will collect data. CPS is rolling out a new program.

"I'll make my recommendation," the social worker says. "And the judge will decide what custody plan will be in the child's best interests."

When Frida tries to speak, the social worker stops her. "Ms. Liu, be glad the child's father is in the picture. If we didn't have the kinship option, we'd have to place her in emergency foster care."

×

Tonight, again, Frida can't sleep. She needs to tell the family court judge that Harriet was not abused, was not neglected, that her mother just had one very bad day. She needs to ask the judge if he's ever had a bad day. On her bad day, she needed to get out of the house of her mind, trapped in the house of her body, trapped in the house where Harriet sat in her ExerSaucer with a dish of animal crackers. Gust used to explain the whole world that way: the mind as a house living in the house of the body, living in the house of a house, living in the larger house of the town, in the larger house of the state, in the houses of America and society and the universe. He said these houses fit inside one another like the Russian nesting dolls they bought for Harriet.

What she can't explain, what she doesn't want to admit, what she's not sure she remembers correctly: how she felt a sudden pleasure when she shut the door and got in the car that took her away from her mind and body and house and child.

She hurried away when Harriet wasn't looking. She wonders now if that wasn't like shooting some-one in the back, the least fair thing she's ever done.

She bought an iced latte at the coffee shop down the block, then walked to her car. She swore she'd come home right away. But the ten-minute coffee run turned into thirty, which turned into an hour, which turned into two, then two and a half. The pleasure of the drive propelled her. It wasn't the pleasure of sex or love or sunsets, but the pleasure of forgetting her body, her life.

At 1:00 a.m., she gets out of bed. She hasn't cleaned in three weeks, can't believe the police saw her house this way. She picks up Harriet's toys, empties the recycling, vacuums her rugs, starts a load of laundry, cleans the soiled ExerSaucer, ashamed she didn't clean it earlier.

She cleans until five, becoming light-headed from the disinfectants and bleach. The sinks are scrubbed. The tub is scrubbed. The hardwood floors are mopped. The police aren't here to notice her clean stovetop. They can't see that her toilet bowl is pristine, that Harriet's clothes have been folded and put away, that the half-empty take-out containers have been discarded, that there's no longer dust on every surface. But as long as she keeps moving, she won't have to go to sleep without Harriet, won't expect to hear her calling.

She rests on her clean floor, her hair and night-shirt soaked with sweat, chilled by the breeze from the back door. Usually if she can't sleep and Harriet is here, she retrieves Harriet from her crib and holds her while Harriet sleeps on her shoulder. Her sweet girl. She misses her daughter's weight and warmth.

×

Frida wakes at ten with a runny nose and sore throat, eager to tell Harriet that Mommy finally slept, that Mommy can take her to the playground today. Then she realizes, with slow-blooming dread, that Harriet isn't home.

She sits up and rolls her aching shoulders, remembering the social worker and the mint-green room, being treated like a criminal. She pictures the officers entering this narrow dark house, finding frightened Harriet in the middle of the clutter. Perhaps they saw the mostly empty cupboards and refrigerator. Perhaps they saw crumbs on the countertop, balled-up paper towels, tea bags in the sink.

Frida and Gust each kept the furniture they'd brought into the marriage. Most of the nicer pieces were his. Most of the decor and artwork. They were in the process of redecorating their old place when he moved out. Her current house was painted in pastels by the owner, the living room pale yellow, the kitchen tangerine, the upstairs lavender and pale blue. Frida's furniture and decorations clash with the walls: her black photo frames, her plum-and-navy-blue Persian rug, her olive-green slipper chair.

She hasn't been able to keep any plants alive. The living room and kitchen walls are bare. In the upstairs hallway, she's only hung a few photos of her parents and grandmothers, an attempt to remind Harriet of her ancestry, though Frida doesn't know enough Mandarin to properly teach her the language. In Harriet's room, in addition to a string of brightly colored fabric flags, she's hung a photo of Gust from eight years ago. She's wanted Harriet to see her father here, if only his picture, though she knows Gust doesn't do the same. That is one of the terrible things about joint custody. A child should see her mother every day.

She checks her phone. She's missed a call from her boss, who wants to know why she hasn't responded to his emails. She calls back and apologizes, claims to have food poisoning. She requests another extension.

After showering, she calls her divorce lawyer, Renee. "I need you to squeeze me in today. Please. It's an emergency."

×

Frida's narrow street is empty this afternoon, though on sunny days, the elderly neighbors like to gather on lawn chairs on the block's tiny strip of sidewalk. She wishes they could see her now. She's wearing tailored trousers, a silk blouse, wedge heels. She's applied makeup, hidden her puffy eyelids behind thick tortoiseshell frames. The police officers and social worker should have seen her like this, competent and refined and trustworthy.

Renee's office is on the fifth floor of a building on Chestnut Street, two blocks north of Rittenhouse Square. For a time last year, this office felt like Frida's second home. Renee, like a big sister.

"Frida, come in. What happened? You look pale."

Frida thanks Renee for meeting on such short notice. She looks around, remembering the time when Harriet drooled on the leather couch and picked every piece of lint off the rug. Renee is a heavyset brunette in her late forties who favors cowl-neck sweaters and dramatic turquoise jewelry. Another New York transplant. They initially bonded over being outsiders in a city where it feels as if everyone has known each other since kindergarten.

Renee remains standing as Frida explains what happened, leaning against her desk with crossed arms. She's angrier than Gust and Susanna were, more shocked and disappointed. Frida feels as if she's talking to her parents.

"Why didn't you call me last night?"

"I didn't understand how much trouble I was in. I fucked up. I know that. But it was a mistake."

"You can't call it that," Renee says. "These people don't care about your intentions. CPS has been getting more aggressive." Two children died under their watch last year. The governor said there's no margin of error. New rules are being implemented. There was a referendum in the last local election.

"What are you talking about? This wasn't abuse. I'm not like those people. Harriet is a baby. She won't remember."

"Frida, leaving your baby home alone is no small thing. You understand that, don't you? I know moms get stressed out and walk out the door sometimes, but you got caught."

Frida looks down at her hands. She foolishly expected Renee to comfort her and offer encouragement, like she did during the divorce.

"We're going to call this a lapse in judgment," Renee says. "You can't call it a mistake anymore. You have to take responsibility."

Renee thinks getting custody back may take weeks. At worst, a few months. She's heard CPS is moving much faster now. There's some new focus on transparency and accountability, something about data collection, giving parents more opportunities to prove themselves. They're trying to streamline the process nationally, so there's less variation from state to state. The difference between states was always problematic. Still, so much depends on the judge.

"Why haven't I heard about this?" Frida asks.

"You probably didn't pay attention, because it didn't apply to you. Why would you? You were just living your life." Frida should focus on the long game: being reunited with Harriet, case file closed. Even when she regains custody, there will probably be a probation period with further monitoring, maybe a year. The judge may require Frida to complete a whole program—home inspection, parenting classes, therapy. Phone calls and supervised visits are better than nothing. Some parents get nothing. Even if she completes every step, there are unfortunately no guarantees. If, God forbid, worst-case scenario, the state finds her unfit and decides against reunification, they could terminate her parental rights.

"But that can't happen to us. Right? Why are you even telling me this?"

"Because you need to be very careful from now on. I'm not trying to scare you, Frida, but we're talking about the family court system. I want you to know the kind of people you're dealing with. Seriously, I don't want you joining one of those parents' rights message boards. This is not the time to advocate for yourself. You'll make yourself nuts. It's not like there's any privacy anymore. You have to remember that. They'll be watching you. And they haven't made any specifics of the new program public."

Renee sits down next to Frida. "I promise, we're going to get her back." She rests her hand on Frida's arm. "Listen, I'm so sorry, but I need to take my next appointment. I'll call you later, okay? We'll figure this out together."

When Frida tries to stand, she can't move. She takes off her glasses. The tears come suddenly.

×

At the end of the workday, Rittenhouse Square is crowded with joggers and skateboarders and med students and the homeless men and women who live there. It's Frida's favorite place in the city, a classically designed park with a fountain and animal sculptures and manicured flower beds, surrounded by shops and restaurants with sidewalk seating. The one landmark that reminds her of New York.

She finds an empty bench and calls Gust. He asks if she got any sleep. She tells him she just met with Renee, then asks to speak to Harriet. She tries to switch to FaceTime, but the connection is poor. As soon as she hears Harriet's voice, she begins crying again.

"I miss you. How are you, bub?"

Harriet's voice is still scratchy. She babbles a string of vowel sounds, none of which sound like "Mommy." In the background, Gust says that the ear infection is getting better. Susanna took her to the Please Touch Museum this morning.

Frida begins to ask about the museum, but Gust

says they're about to have dinner. She makes another pitch about ice cream.

"Frida, I know you mean well, but we don't want to teach her emotional eating. Come on, Hare-bear, say bye-bye now."

They hang up. Frida wipes her runny nose on the back of her hand. Though the walk home will take forty minutes and she'll surely develop blisters, she can't cry on the train and have everyone stare. She considers calling a car but doesn't want to make small talk with anyone. She stops in Starbucks to blow her nose and clean her glasses. People must think she's just been dumped or fired. No one would guess her crime. She looks too fancy. Too proper. Too Asian.

She walks south, passing pairs of young women carrying yoga mats, tattooed parents picking up their children from day care. The events of last night still feel like they happened to someone else. The judge will see that she's not an alcoholic, not an addict, that she has no criminal record. She's gainfully employed and a peaceful, committed co-parent. She has bachelor's and master's degrees in literature from Brown and Columbia, a 401(k) account, a college savings fund for Harriet.

She wants to believe that Harriet is too young to

remember. But there may be a faint, wounded feeling that could calcify as Harriet grows up. A sense memory of crying and receiving no answer.

×

The doorbell rings at 8:00 a.m. the following morning. Frida stays in bed, but after three rings, she grabs her robe and hurries downstairs.

The men from CPS are tall and white and barrel-chested. Both wear pale blue button-down shirts tucked into khakis. They have inscrutable expressions and Philly accents and close-cropped brown hair. One has a potbelly, the other a weak chin. Each carries a metal briefcase.

The one with a weak chin says, "Ma'am, we need to set up some cameras." He shows her the paperwork.

"This is the home inspection?"

"We have a new way of doing things."

Cameras will be installed in every room, Frida learns, except the bathroom. They'll also inspect the site of the incident. The man with a weak chin peers over her head at the living room. "Looks like you've cleaned. When did you do that?"

"The other night. Has this been discussed with my lawyer?"

"Ma'am, there's nothing your lawyer can do."

The woman who lives across the street opens her curtains. Frida bites the inside of her cheek. Never complain, Renee said. Be deferential. Cooperative. Don't ask too many questions. Every interaction with CPS will be documented. Everything can be used against her.

They explain that the state will collect footage from a live video feed. In each room, they'll mount a camera in the corner of the ceiling. They'll put a camera in the backyard. They'll track calls and texts and voice mails and Internet and app use.

They hand Frida a form to sign. She must consent to the surveillance.

Her neighbor is still watching. Frida closes the front door, wipes her damp palms on her robe. The goal is getting Harriet back, Renee said. Losing is losing everything. This misery may feel unbearable, but in a whole life, a few weeks or even a few months is short. Imagine the other misery, Renee said. Frida can't. If that happened, she wouldn't want to keep living.

She goes inside to find a pen, then signs the form.

As the men enter the house and unpack the surveillance equipment, she cautiously asks what they'll be measuring.

The man with the potbelly says, "We'll be getting to know you."

She asks if they'll be installing anything in her car, in her cubicle at work. They assure her that they're only focusing on her home life, as if knowing that they'll only watch her eat and sleep and breathe should make her feel better. When they have enough material, they say, they'll use the footage to **analyze her feelings**.

What does that mean? How is that possible? In the articles she found online, the CPS representative said the new program would eliminate human error. Decisions would be made more efficiently. They'd be able to correct for subjectivity or bias, implement a set of universal standards.

The men photograph each room, pausing occasionally to point and whisper. Frida calls in late to work. They check her cupboards and refrigerator, every drawer, every closet, the tiny backyard, the bathroom, the basement. They shine flashlights inside the washer and dryer.

They riffle through her clothes, lift the lid of her

jewelry box. They touch her pillows and bedding. They shake the bars of Harriet's crib and run their hands over the mattress and flip it over. They paw through Harriet's blankets and toys. Frida lingers in the doorway as they inspect each room, fighting the urge to protest the intrusion. It feels as if, at any moment, they'll ask to inspect her body. They might ask her to open her mouth, note the condition of her teeth. The state might need to know if she has any cavities.

The men carry in a stepladder. They clear cobwebs from the ceiling. After they finish installing the last camera, they call their home office and switch on the live feed.

2.

FRIDA IS TEMPTED NOT TO GO HOME TONIGHT, considers getting a room at the campus inn, finding a last-minute rental on Airbnb, taking an impromptu trip to visit long-neglected friends in Brooklyn. Sleeping in her cubicle is a possibility, though this afternoon, her boss noticed that the Harriet photos on her desk were turned facedown and started asking questions.

"I was trying to concentrate," she lied.

With her boss out of sight, she righted the photos and stroked them and apologized: Harriet as a tightly swaddled newborn; Harriet grabbing at her first-birthday cake; Harriet in heart-shaped sunglasses and a plaid romper at the beach. That face. The only thing she ever did right.

She stays until eleven, long after the building empties, until her fear of getting mugged on campus outweighs her fear of what awaits her at home. She called Renee throughout the day. Renee was alarmed to hear about the cameras but said, with a heavy sigh, that the rules are always changing. Avoiding the house isn't an option. Nor is arming herself with information. Not that Frida found much online. Only the usual think pieces about experiments using big data, social media addiction, the unholy relationship between the government and tech companies. The live-streaming of child-birth and violent crime. Controversies about infant influencers on YouTube. Whether secret nanny cams were a civil rights violation. Smart socks and blankets that measure a baby's heart rate and oxygen levels and the quality of their sleep. A smart bassi-net that sleep trains your baby for you.

Everyone has been observed through their de-vices for years. CCTV cameras have been installed in most American cities, the government inspired by lowered crime rates in London and Beijing. Who isn't using facial recognition software? At least, Renee said, these are cameras you can see. Frida should assume that they're listening. Anything a normal person might do could be interpreted as defiance. Don't leave too many footprints, Renee said. Stop it with the Google searches. They can tap into Frida's work computer too. She shouldn't be discussing her case on the phone.

Renee has heard rumors about CPS revamping its educational arm. They've been updating their parenting classes. Silicon Valley is supposedly contributing money and resources. CPS has been on a hiring spree. They're offering much higher salaries than before. Unfortunately, Frida lives in the test state, the test county.

"I wish I had more details," Renee went on. "If this had happened a year ago or even a few months ago, I'd be in a much better position to guide you." She paused. "Let's talk in person. Please, Frida, try to stay calm."

×

The house, which has never felt like hers, feels even less so tonight. After eating a microwave dinner, after straightening each room, mopping the dirt tracked in by CPS, closing drawers, folding Harriet's bedding, and rearranging the toys, Frida retreats to her cramped bathroom, wishing she could collapse her life into this room, sleep and eat here. She showers and scrubs her face, applies toners and moisturizers and antiaging serums. She combs her wet hair, clips and files her nails, bandages her torn cuticles. She tweezes her eyebrows. Sitting on the edge of the tub, she pokes through the bucket of bath toys: the wind-up walrus, the duckie, the orange octopus that's lost its eyeballs. She plays with Harriet's robe. She rubs Harriet's lotion on her hands so she can wear the coconut scent to sleep.

Though it's a warm evening, she layers a hooded sweatshirt over her nightgown. Cringing at the thought of the men touching her pillows, she decides to change her sheets.

She gets into bed and pulls up her hood and ties it under her chin, wishing she had a shroud. Soon, the state will discover that she rarely has visitors. She lost touch with her New York friends after the divorce, hasn't made new ones, hasn't been trying, spends most of her solo evenings in the company of her phone. She sometimes eats cereal for dinner. When she can't sleep, she does stomach crunches and leg lifts for hours. If the insomnia gets bad, she takes Unisom and drinks. If Harriet is here, just one shot of bourbon. If she's alone, three or four in quick succession. Thank God those men didn't find any empties. Each morning, before breakfast, she measures her waist. She pinches her flabby triceps and inner thighs. She smiles at herself in the mirror to remind herself that she used to be pretty. She needs to quit every bad habit, can't appear vain or selfish or unstable, as if she can't take care of herself, was perhaps unprepared, even at this age, to take care of a child.

She turns on her side and faces the window. She lifts a hand to her mouth, then stops. She looks up at the blinking red light. Is she giving them enough? Is she sorry enough? Afraid enough? In her twenties, she had a therapist who made her list her fears, a tedious process that only revealed that her fears were random and boundless. Whoever is watching now should know that she's afraid of forests and large bodies of water, stems and seaweed. Long-distance swimmers, people who know how to breathe underwater generally. She's afraid of people who know how to dance. She's afraid of nudists and Scandinavian furnishings. Television shows that begin with a dead girl. Too much sunlight and too little. Once, she was afraid of the baby growing inside her, afraid that it might stop growing, afraid that the dead baby would have to be suctioned out, that if this happened and she didn't want to try again, Gust might leave her. She was afraid that she might succumb to her second thoughts, take herself to a clinic, claim that the bleeding happened naturally.

Tonight she's afraid of the cameras, the social worker, the judge, the waiting. What Gust and Susanna might be telling people. The daughter who might love her less already. How devastated her parents will be when they find out.

In her head, she repeats the new fears, trying to leach the words of meaning. Her heart is beating too fast. Her back is coated with cold sweat. Perhaps, instead of being monitored, a bad mother should be thrown into a ravine.

×

Frida discovered the photos last year. It was early May, the middle of the night, insomnia striking again. She went to check the time, grabbed Gust's phone from the nightstand. There was a text sent just after 3:00 a.m. **Come over tomorrow.**

She found the girl in an album marked "Work."

There was Susanna in a sun-filled living room, holding a meringue pie. Susanna smashing the pie onto Gust's crotch. Susanna licking the pie off his body. The photos were taken that February, when Frida was nine months pregnant. She didn't understand how Gust had time to meet this girl, why he'd pursued her, but there were late nights at the office and weekends with friends, and she was on bed rest and trying not to be the kind of wife who dug her nails into his sleeve.

She sat in the kitchen for hours, studying Susanna's naughty grin, her messy face, Gust's penis in her hands, her little wet mouth. The girl had pre-Raphaelite coloring and a pale, freckled body with heavy breasts and boyish hips. Her arms and legs were finely muscled, her collarbones and ribs protruded. She thought Gust hated bony women. She thought he loved her pregnant body.

She didn't wake him or yell, just waited until sunrise, then took a selfie, however awful she looked, and texted it to the girl.

That morning, after nursing Harriet and settling her back into her crib, Frida crawled on top of Gust and rubbed her hips against him until he became hard. They'd only had sex twice since the doctor cleared her for intercourse, each time shockingly painful. She hoped he used condoms with the girl, that the girl was fickle. Maybe she wasn't deterred by wedding rings or infants, but the girl would surely tire of him. Frida had seen this happen with friends in New York who dated girls in their twenties. There would be a passionate affair, rekindled vigor, a sudden engagement followed by the girl deciding to flee to the Galápagos Islands. Adventure travel was often the excuse, as were spiritual awakenings.

After they made love, she told him, "Get rid of her."

He sobbed and apologized, and for a few weeks, it seemed as if they could save their marriage. But he refused to give her up. He claimed to be in love.

"I have to follow my heart," he said. He began talking about co-parenting before Frida was ready to concede.

He said, "I still love you. I'll always love you. We'll always be a family."

Frida came to understand that Susanna was the barnacle and Gust was the tall ship, though she never thought Susanna would win, not when Frida had the baby. If only she'd had the chance to prove herself as a mother, she likes to think. Harriet had just started smiling, was only sleeping for three-hour stretches. Frida's days were spent covered in spit-up and drool, rushing to clean the house or cook or do laundry between rounds of nursing and diaper changes. She wasn't done losing the baby weight. The wound on her belly still felt fresh.

She assumed that Susanna was feral, might have let Gust come on her face. Might have offered him anal. Frida said no to the face and no to anal, though she regrets it now. The thought that she should have opened her ass for Gust preoccupies her, as do all the things she should have done to make him stay.

If she'd been healthier. Easier to live with. If she'd stayed on Zoloft, hadn't relapsed. If he hadn't experienced her hysterical crying spells, her anxiety spirals. If she'd never shouted at him. But nothing was 100 percent safe, her doctor said. Did Frida really want to take that risk? Her OB warned her about links between maternal antidepressant use and adolescent depression in children, links with autism. The baby might be jittery. The baby might have trouble nursing. The baby might have a low birth weight, a lower Apgar score.

Gust was so proud of her for going off medication.

He seemed to respect her more. "Our baby should know the real you," he said.

Her need for antidepressants always made her parents feel like they'd failed her. She doesn't talk about it with them. Even now, she hasn't asked her doctor for a new prescription, hasn't tried to find a psychiatrist or therapist, doesn't want anyone to know how badly the house of her mind functions on its own.

She let Gust talk her into a no-fault divorce. He convinced her that having marital misconduct on the legal record would be damaging for Harriet. When Harriet is older, Gust said, they'll explain to her that Mommy and Daddy decided they're better off as friends.

Soon after claiming Gust, Susanna began voicing her opinions. She'd been a camp counselor in high school. In college, she'd nannied. She'd spent lots of time with her nieces and nephews. Emails began to appear, then texts. Frida should eliminate all plastic from her household. Exposure to plastics is linked to cancer. She should install a water filtration system so Harriet won't be exposed to heavy metals and chlorine in her drinking water or at bath time. She should make sure all of Harriet's clothing is made from organic cotton in factories that provide a living wage. She should buy organic skin care and diapers and burp cloths and bedding, chemical-free wipes. Would Frida consider switching to cloth diapers? Plenty of Susanna's sister's mom friends used cloth diapers. She should try elimination communication. Wasn't that how they did things in China? Frida should have some healing, grounding crystals in the nursery. Susanna would be happy to give Frida some rose quartz to start her off. The crib at Frida's house came from IKEA, and didn't Frida know that particle board was made of sawdust and formaldehyde? By the time Susanna began nagging her about the benefits of long-term breastfeeding and babywearing and co-sleeping, Frida was moved to pick up the phone and rail at Gust, who said: "Remember, it's coming from a good place."

She made him promise not to let Susanna experiment on their baby. No early potty learning, no crystals, no co-sleeping, no pre-chewing each bite of Harriet's food. In the past year, Susanna earned her certification as a nutritionist, intended to complement her occasional work as a Pilates instructor. Frida often worries that Susanna is mixing chlorella and spirulina into Harriet's food and treating Harriet with essential oils or detoxifying mud baths when she has a runny nose or ear infection. They've had heated arguments about vaccines and herd immunity. Gust has already removed his mercury fillings, and so has Susanna. Soon, they'll try for a baby of their own, but first they're going to heal their cavities through herbs and meditation and good intentions.

The women first met in June of last year when Frida was dropping Harriet off for the weekend. Gust had moved into Susanna's loft in Fishtown, while Frida still lived in their first house in Bella Vista. They'd been separated for only a few weeks. Nights she could keep Harriet for nursing, but Gust got the baby on Saturday and Sunday afternoons, and Frida had to deliver both the baby and bottles of pumped milk. That day, Susanna answered the door wearing only Gust's shirt. She had a proud and drowsy gaze that made Frida want to scratch her. Frida didn't want to hand her child to this just-fucked woman, but Gust came and took Harriet from her arms, and he looked happy, not happy like a man who'd found new love, but happy like a dog.

When Susanna reached for the cooler of milk, Frida snapped at her. Only the parents should handle the milk.

"Please, Frida, be reasonable," Gust said.

As they headed upstairs with Harriet, Frida hoped they wouldn't kiss in front of the baby, but as she walked away, she realized that they would kiss and rub and grab in front of Harriet, maybe even make love while the baby slept in the same room. In her father's home, Harriet would see love thrive and grow.

×

It's Saturday night. Early. Harriet's dinnertime. Frida sits at her kitchen table watching the minutes pass on the digital clock above the stove. She kicks at the leg of Harriet's high chair. Gust and Susanna might not be giving Harriet enough to eat. Susanna probably took her to the park today and chattered incessantly, narrating her every move. Susanna never stops talking. She read some book about how babies and toddlers need to hear ten thousand words a day, from birth until age five, in order to be prepared for kindergarten.

Though she eventually caved, Frida used to find American-mother babble pitiful. Other mothers shot her disapproving looks when she pushed Harriet on the swings silently, when she sat at the edge of the sandbox and tried to skim the **New Yorker** while Harriet played alone. She was sometimes assumed to be a distracted nanny. Once, when Harriet was seven months old, there was a mother who outright scolded her as Harriet crawled around the playground. Why wasn't she watching her baby? What if the baby picked up a rock and tried to swallow it and choked?

Frida didn't try to defend herself. She grabbed Harriet and hurried home, never returning to that playground, even though it was the closest and cleanest one.

The playground mothers frightened her. She couldn't match their fervor or skill, hadn't done enough research, stopped breastfeeding after five months when these women were still cheerfully nursing three-year-olds.

She thought that becoming a mother would mean joining a community, but the mothers she's met are as petty as newly minted sorority sisters, a self-appointed task force hewing to a maternal hard line. Women who only talk about their children bore her. She has little enthusiasm for the banal, repetitive world of toddlers but believes things will improve once Harriet goes to preschool, once they can converse. It wasn't that Frida didn't have ideas about child-rearing. She liked that book about French parenting, but Gust was horrified at the idea of sleep training Harriet at three months, the idea of prioritizing their adult needs. The ethos of that book was selfish.

"I'm ready to be unselfish," Gust said. "Aren't you?"

She hasn't been outside today. Renee told her to stop calling Gust and asking to FaceTime with Harriet, to wait to talk to the social worker. This morning, she wallowed in the nursery for hours, touching Harriet's toys and blankets. Everything needs to be washed. Maybe replaced, when she can afford it. The men didn't leave any marks, but they left bad luck. Harriet can never know that her nursery was treated like a crime scene.

Sitting in the rocking chair, Frida wept, angry that she had to fake it when she had no tears left. But no tears would suggest no remorse, and no remorse would suggest that she's an even worse mother than the state imagines. So she grabbed Harriet's pink bunny and squeezed it and pictured Harriet frightened and alone. She nursed her shame. Her parents always said she needed an audience.

She stands and walks over to the sliding glass

door. Opens it and peers into the neighbor's yard. The next-door neighbor on the north side is building a trellis. He's been hammering all day. She'd like to flick a lit match over the fence just to see what would happen, would like to burn down that tree that drips fuzzy brown tendrils into her yard, but she doesn't know if he was the Good Samaritan who called the police.

Her fridge is emptier than it was at the inspection. There's a container of sweet potato wedges starting to mold, a half-consumed jar of peanut butter, a carton of milk that expired three days ago, packets of ketchup stashed in the door. She snacks on some of Harriet's string cheese. She should prepare a nutritious dinner, show the state that she can cook, but when she considers walking to the grocery store, considers how the camera will note the time of her departure and return, her methods of food preparation and how gracefully she eats, she wants to roam further afield.

She'll leave her phone here so they can't track her. If they ask, she'll say she went to see a friend, though Will is more Gust's friend than hers. His best friend. Harriet's godfather. She hasn't seen him in months, but during the divorce, he said to call if she ever needed him.

The cameras shouldn't detect any suspicious behavior. She doesn't change into a dress or comb her hair or apply makeup or put on earrings. She has faint stubble on her legs and underarms. She's wearing a loose red T-shirt with holes and denim cutoffs. She slips on a green windbreaker and sandals. She looks like a woman who can't be bothered, a woman with little to offer. The last woman Will dated was a trapeze artist. But she doesn't want to date Will, she reminds herself, and she'll return at a decent hour. She just needs company.

×

By any reasonable estimate, he shouldn't be home on a Saturday night. Will is thirty-eight and single, an avid online dater in a city without many bachelors his age. Women adore his gentle demeanor; his tightly curled black hair, now flecked with gray; his thick beard; the pelt of chest hair that he jokingly claims is evidence of his virility. He wears his hair tall at the crown, and with his tiny wire glasses and long nose and deep-set eyes, he resembles a Viennese scientist from the turn of the twentieth century. He's not as handsome as Gust, has a softer body and a high voice, but Frida has always loved his attention. If he's not home, she'll consider herself lucky. She's not sure she remembers the cross street or the house number, somewhere on Osage between Forty-Fifth and Forty-Sixth, but desperation is its own beacon, leading her to the correct block, to a parking space a few doors down from Will's apartment in West Philly, where he rents the first floor of a crumbling Victorian in Spruce Hill. His lights are on.

They used to joke about his crush on her. The time he told her, in front of Gust, "If it doesn't work out with this guy . . ." She recalls his compliments as she climbs his front steps and rings the bell. The way he'd touch the small of her back. The way he flirted when she wore red lipstick. As she hears footsteps, she feels hope and despair and a surge of wildness, a terrible wildness that she thought was gone forever. There's nothing alluring about her except her sadness, but Will likes his women sad. She and Gust used to chastise him about his terrible taste. His broken birds. An aspiring mortician. A stripper with an abusive ex-boyfriend. The cutters and poets with their bottomless wells of need. He's trying to make better choices, but she hopes he's still capable of one last mistake.

He answers the door, smiles at her, bewildered.

"I can explain," she says.

They used to tell him that he'd never land a decent woman if he kept living like a college boy. There's a visible layer of dog hair on the couch and carpet, only one working lamp in the living room, piles of newspapers and mugs, shoes kicked off in the doorway, change strewn across the coffee table. Will is on his third advanced degree, a PhD in cultural anthropology, after master's degrees in education and sociology and a brief stint in Teach For America. He's been in the doctoral program at Penn for nine years, plans to stretch it to ten if he can get funding.

"I'm sorry about the mess," he says. "I would have—"

Frida tells him not to worry. Everyone's standards are different, and if she had standards or scruples, she wouldn't be here. She wouldn't say yes to a bowl of lentil stew or a glass of red wine, wouldn't sit down at his kitchen table and tell him, in rambling gushes, about her very bad day and the police station and losing custody and the men coming to her house and touching everything and installing cameras, how for the last few nights, she's hidden under the covers so she has some privacy when she cries.

She waits for him to get angry on her behalf, or if not, to judge her and ask how she could have been so stupid, but he remains silent.

"Frida, I know. Gust told me."

"What did he say? He must hate me."

"No one hates you. He's worried about you. I am too. I mean, he's definitely pissed, but he doesn't want these people messing with you. You need to tell him about this panopticon bullshit."

"No. Please. You can't tell him. I don't have a choice. These people are like the fucking Stasi. My lawyer said this could take months. You should have heard the way they talked to me the other night."

Will pours them more wine. "I'm glad you're here. I wanted to call you."

She didn't realize how good it would feel to see a familiar face. Will listens thoughtfully as she tells the story again. About Harriet's ear infection and uncontrollable sobbing. The forgotten file. The irrational decision to go to the office. How she couldn't cope, needed to get her work done, never meant to put Harriet in danger.

"As if I need someone else to punish me," she says. "I fucking hate myself." It's wrong to be here, wrong to burden him. She can tell he's struggling to find something supportive to say, but he can't. Instead, he brings his chair over to her side of the table and holds her.

Maybe if there was someone to hold her at night. She still misses Gust's smell. Warm. A temperature and feeling rather than a scent. Will's shirt smells like lentil stew and dog, but she wants to rest her face against his neck like she did with Gust. She should cherish his friendship and honor it, but she's imagining his body. Gust once told her about seeing Will in the locker room. Will supposedly has a huge penis, the source of his quiet confidence. She wonders if she can touch it, whether any of his broken birds have given him an incurable disease. She hasn't succumbed to this state since her twenties, when she would show up at the homes of men she found on the Internet and leave bruised and disoriented.

She stares at the tuft of chest hair peeking out of his collar, begins playing with it. "Can I kiss you?"

He sits back, blushing. "Sweetie, it's not a good idea." He runs his hands through his hair. "You'll feel terrible. I'm speaking from experience."

She keeps a hand on his knee. "Gust won't know."

"It's not like I've never thought about it. I have. A lot. But we shouldn't."

She doesn't reply, doesn't look at him. She's not ready to go home. She leans over and kisses him, keeps kissing him when he tries to pull away.

It's been more than a year since a man's touch felt decent. After Gust moved out, they continued fucking. When he dropped off Harriet, if Harriet was sleeping. Always with Gust declaring his love, saying he missed her, that he'd made a mistake, that he might come back. He fucked her on the morning of their appearance in divorce court, having just come from Susanna's bed.

It felt good to keep a secret from Susanna, to steal from her, though it meant that Gust left her over and over. She thought if she got pregnant, he'd change his mind. Some months she even tried to see him when she was ovulating. She still marvels at her own stupidity. She'll teach her daughter to be different. To be brave and wise. To have dignity. That fucking a man who doesn't love you, who decided he doesn't want you, even the father of your child, is no better than a fork in the eye.

Her therapists liked to blame her mother. Her mother had been too distant, they said. Frida never accepted this explanation. She never wanted to examine her behavior. It felt impossible to explain, too horrible to say out loud. When someone desired her, she simply felt more alive. Pulled into a different, better future. No longer alone. Before she met Gust, she would make herself anonymous and numb, convinced that all she wanted was a few hours of touching. She doesn't remember many names, but she remembers bodies, and the rare compliment, as well as the one who choked her. The one who played porn while she went down on him. The one who tied her wrists so tight she lost feeling in her hands. The one who called her timid when she refused to attend an orgy. She'd been proud of herself for saying no that time, for having limits.

She walks to the living room and shuts the curtains. What wildness was possible now, a decade later, after the divorce and the baby?

"Frida, seriously. I'm flattered."

Maybe he thinks she still belongs to Gust. Maybe he only sees her as a mother, a bad mother at that. She's nervous and dry as she approaches him. He doesn't protest when she begins unbuttoning his shirt.

One day, she'll teach Harriet never to behave this way. Never to offer her body like the lowliest cut of meat. She'll teach Harriet about integrity and self-respect, will give her enough love so she'll never go begging. Her mother never talked to her about sex, about bodies or feelings. Frida won't make that mistake.

"You're not seeing me at my best," Will says. He needs to lose twenty pounds. Needs to start working out. She touches the roll of fat at his waist and tells him he's beautiful, silently pleased that he has stretch marks too, on his sides and lower back.

She would leave if asked, but he hasn't asked, so she unhooks her bra and slips off her panties, hoping her sadness is radiant. Will's broken birds always emitted their own light, big-eyed and bony. At dinner parties, she wanted to touch their throats and play with their long, tangled hair, wondered what it was like to wear sadness so close to the skin and be loved for it.

She fidgets as he studies her, taking in her arms crossed over sagging breasts, the wavy pink scar above her pubic hair. She sucks in her stomach, looking down at her thighs, the hateful pucker above her left knee. He shouldn't see her with the lights on, without romance or ceremony. When she was younger, she could barrel through this awkwardness, but Will has seen her body grow huge, has felt Harriet kicking. **The alien invasion**, he'd say, laughing. **The creature.**

Gust and Susanna must be getting Harriet ready for bed now. When Frida has her, they do bath time and a book and a cuddle and turn down the lights and say good night to Harriet's whole world. **Good night, walls; good night, window; good night, curtains. Good night, chair. Good night, Lamby. Good night, blankie. Good night, jammies.** Good night to Harriet's eyes and nose and mouth. Good night to each toy in her crib until it's finally time for **Good night, Harriet** and a talk about galaxies.

Will's erection presses against Frida's stomach. She needs to know how Harriet has been sleeping. Frida hooks a finger into Will's belt loop but can't bring herself to touch his supposedly huge penis, not even over his jeans. If anyone found out she came here.

"I am a terrible person," she whispers. She picks up his shirt and covers her torso. "I'm so sorry."

"Oh, Frida, shhhhh. It's okay. It's okay." He pulls her to his chest. The hairs are rough against her cheek.

"I molested you," she says, her voice muffled. "What the fuck is wrong with me?" She didn't know it was possible for a grown woman to molest a grown man, but she's done it. What gave her the right to come here and undress?

"Frida, don't be so hard on yourself."

She makes him turn around while she gathers her clothes. When Gust decided to move out, she called his closest friends, hoping that someone might talk sense into him. Will was the only one who actually listened while she sobbed and ranted. By his pauses, she could tell that he knew about Susanna, had perhaps known for some time. He said he didn't approve of Gust leaving. He told Frida she was still young and beautiful. The sweetest lie.

She pulls her hair back into a ponytail. Her shirt is on inside out. She returns to the kitchen to fetch her purse. It's 8:17. "Promise you won't tell."

"Frida, don't freak out. You didn't do anything wrong."

"No, I did. You were trying to be nice to me. I didn't have to take it there. I swear I'm not some vulture." She wants to stay here. She could take the couch, the closet. If she could see one kind face each day.

At the door, Will kisses her cheek, then cups her chin in his hand. "I kinda liked seeing you naked."

"You don't have to say that to make me feel better."

"I mean it," he says. "Come back sometime, and maybe I'll show you mine." Laughing, he leans Frida against the door and kisses her.

×

The porcelain is cold against her tailbone. There are gray splotches on the top perimeter of the tub along the caulking, shadows from the mold that she scrubbed off a few days ago. Frida removes her glasses, rests flat on her back with her knees bent, hands clasped to her chest, nails digging into her palms. The family of yellers two doors down are outside smoking weed and clinking beer bottles. Loud white Americans taking up space. She never claimed her space. Gust used to tell her to stop apologizing, stop it with the Midwestern gosh-golly. But maybe some people weren't meant to claim their space. She claimed it for two and a half hours and lost her baby.

She lifts her nightgown, thinking of the way Will looked at her when they said goodbye. She and Gust used to tease him, would make him demonstrate that look over dinner. How he reeled them in. The fuck-me glance. She could never give Gust that look without laughing. With them, it was always Gust's hand on the back of her neck, Gust steering. She misses being a wife, being half of something. Mother and child isn't the same, though she remembers thinking, when Harriet was born, that she'd never be alone again.

She almost followed Will back inside. When was the last time anyone besides Gust kissed her properly?

She needs to return to her room, let them observe her. She's already been gone too long. But she wants a minute or two more. A minute to herself. Jump through the hoops, Renee said.

Frida runs her hands over her breasts and stomach. She pulls down her underwear and closes her eyes and rubs, making herself come again and again until she's dizzy and limp. Until her mind is empty.

3.

THE COURT-APPOINTED PSYCHOLOGIST LOOKS like a rich man gone to seed. Disheveled but aloof. Patrician features, no accent, probably from the Main Line. He has a double chin and broken blood vessels around his nose. A drinker. No wedding ring. He's taking forever to review Frida's file. He barely acknowledged her when she arrived, just ushered her to her seat and continued tapping on his phone. Frida expected a woman, doesn't know if it's better or worse to be evaluated by a fiftysomething white man. He doesn't seem like a parent, doesn't seem like he has a vested interest in child welfare. Then again, neither did the social worker or the men from CPS.

Frida hasn't spoken to Harriet in six days, hasn't seen or held her in a week, has been scrolling through photos, rewatching every video, smelling the teddy bear that still holds her scent. She should have taken more videos but had been wary of waving her phone in Harriet's face. Gust used to say taking photos was stealing someone's soul, but he has different standards for Susanna, whose 1,498 followers have seen Harriet in just a diaper, Harriet naked from the back, Harriet at the doctor's office, Harriet in the bath, Harriet on the changing table, Harriet first thing in the morning, groggy and vulnerable. Selfies: Harriet asleep on Susanna's shoulder, #bliss. Those people know what Harriet ate for breakfast this morning. Frida desperately wants to look, but Renee made her close her social media accounts.

The smell of mothballs is giving her a headache. She hasn't worn her black suit since her last round of job interviews. She's wearing extra blush and rosy lipstick, hair in a low bun, her grandmother's pearls. Disgraceful to wear them here. Her late grandmother's greatest wish had been for her to get married and have a baby.

On the psychologist's desk, a palm-size video camera on a tripod is balanced awkwardly on a stack of manila file folders.

"Ms. Liu, before we begin, is English your first language?"

Frida flinches. "I was born here."

"My mistake." The psychologist fumbles with the camera. "Ah, here it is." A red light goes on. He flips his legal pad open to a fresh page, uncaps his fountain pen. They begin with Frida's family history.

Her parents are retired economics professors. Immigrants. Her father from Guangzhou, her mother from Nanjing. They came to the States in their twenties and met in grad school. Married for forty-four years. Frida was born in Ann Arbor, grew up in Evanston, a suburb of Chicago. Their only child. Her family is comfortable now, but her parents came from nothing. Her father was dirt-poor. When she was a child, all her grandparents lived with them at various points. Her aunt too. Then another aunt. Cousins. Her parents supported all the relatives, sponsored their visas.

"Back when that was possible," she says.

The psychologist nods. "And how do they feel about the incident?"

"I haven't told them yet." She looks down at her nails, painted shell pink, the cuticles neatly trimmed and healing. She's been ignoring their calls. They think she's busy at work. A full week without speaking to Harriet must feel like torture. But Frida doesn't want to hear their questions, about Harriet, about anything. Every call begins with the same questions in Mandarin: **Have you eaten yet? Are you full?** Their way of saying, **I love you**. This morning, she had coffee and a fig bar. Her stomach is churning. If her parents knew what happened, they'd fly here. Try to fix things. But they can't see her empty house and the cameras, can't know that they escaped Communism and a daughter like her is all they get.

The child's father is white? Were there any cultural issues?

"I think, like all Chinese parents, they wanted me to go to Stanford and meet a nice neurosurgeon. Another ABC—you know, American-born Chinese—but they loved Gust. He got along well with them. They thought he was good for me. They were very upset about our divorce. Everyone was. We had a newborn."

Only tell them what's necessary, Renee said. The psychologist doesn't need to know that until Frida and Gust, there was only one divorce on either side of her family. That it was bad enough to marry a white man, let alone lose him, let alone lose custody of their child.

All the grandparents, she says, have a hard time with the distance. Gust's parents in Santa Cruz, California, hers in Evanston, watching Harriet grow up over FaceTime and Zoom.

"This country is too big," she says, recalling her last flight to Chicago, when she had Harriet sit on the tray table, facing the other passengers. The thought of her parents knowing makes her want to take a knife to her cheek, but she doesn't need to tell them yet. Daughters are allowed to have secrets in this new world.

Catching sight of the camera, she asks how today's footage will be used. Why is this being filmed if he's going to submit a report?

"Are you going to analyze my feelings?"

"There's no need to be paranoid, Ms. Liu."

"I'm not being paranoid. I'm just trying to understand . . . the rubrics by which I'm being judged."

"Rubrics?" The psychologist chuckles. "Aren't you a smart cookie."

Frida's shoulders creep upward as he continues to laugh.

"Let's talk about why you're here."

Renee told her to be contrite. She's a single working mother, normal and frazzled. Harmless.

She lists the combination of destabilizing forces: her insomnia, Harriet's ear infection, five sleepless nights, her frayed nerves. "I'm not trying to make excuses. I know what I did is completely unacceptable. Believe me, I couldn't be more ashamed. I know I put my daughter in danger. But what happened last week, what I did, doesn't represent who I am. What kind of mother I am."

The psychologist chews his pen.

"The last time I had to function on so little sleep was when she was a newborn. You know how delirious new parents are. And I wasn't working then. Taking care of her was my only job. And my husband, my ex-husband, was still with us. I was supposed to stay home with her for the first two years. That was our plan. I'm still figuring out how to juggle everything. I promise, this will never, ever happen again. It was a terrible lapse in judgment."

"What were you doing on the day of the incident, before you left the house?"

"Working. I write and edit a faculty publication. At Wharton."

"So you telecommute?"

"Only on the days I have Harriet. I took a lower-paying position so I could do this. So I could have more flex time. I wanted to be able to work from home more. How else am I going to see her? A lot of my job is stupid busywork. Emails. Nagging professors to approve drafts. Most of them treat me like a secretary. It's not ideal, but Harriet and I have a system. I work for a while, then take a break to feed her and play, work some more, put her down for a nap, get some stuff done during her nap. I work late after she goes to bed. She's good at playing by herself. She's not as needy as other toddlers."

"But aren't all children inherently needy? They are, after all, entirely dependent on caregivers for their survival. I take it you're letting her watch television?"

Frida finds a tear in her stocking behind the right knee. "There's some screen time, yes. I let her watch **Sesame Street** and Mister Rogers. Or **Daniel Tiger**. I'd rather spend the whole day playing with her, but I have to work. It's better than sending her to day care. I don't want strangers taking care of her. I see her so little as it is. If she went to day care, I'd only see her for maybe twelve waking hours a week. That's not enough."

"Do you often allow her to play alone?"

"Not often," she says, straining to keep the

bitterness out of her voice. "Sometimes she plays on her side of the living room, sometimes she plays next to me. At least we're together. Isn't that the most important thing?"

The psychologist scribbles in silence. Before the divorce, she argued with her mother about when she'd return to work, whether she'd work part-time or full-time, whether she'd freelance. They hadn't sent her to good schools so she could be a stay-at-home mom. The idea of living off Gust's salary was a fantasy, her mother said.

The psychologist asks whether Frida finds child-rearing overwhelming or stressful. He asks about her drug and alcohol consumption, whether she has a history of substance abuse.

"Ms. Torres's notes mention depression."

Frida pulls at the hole in her stocking. How did she forget that they have this strike against her? "I was diagnosed with depression in college." She grabs her knee to stop her leg from twitching. "But my symptoms were mild. I used to take Zoloft, but I went off it a long time ago. Before we started trying to conceive. I'd never expose my baby to those chemicals."

Did she relapse? Did she experience postpartum

depression or anxiety? Postpartum psychosis? Has she ever considered harming herself or her baby?

"No. Never. My baby healed me."

"Was she difficult?"

"She was perfect." This man doesn't need to know about the first month, those miserable weight checks at the pediatrician's office, when Harriet was taking too long to get back to her birth weight, when Frida wasn't producing enough milk. The pediatrician was having her pump after every feeding. How savagely she envied the mothers in the waiting room with their clean hair and well-rested faces. Their breasts were surely overflowing. Their babies' latches were perfect. Their babies purred with happiness. Harriet never purred with Frida, not even when she was first born. To Frida, Harriet seemed forlorn and not of this earth.

Questioned about physical affection, Frida admits that her parents rarely hugged her or said "I love you" in so many words, but they've become more affectionate as they've grown older. Chinese families are more reserved. She doesn't hold it against them. She hasn't repeated that pattern with Harriet, might hug and kiss Harriet **too** much.

"Your parents sound withholding."

"I don't think that's fair. Most of the day-to-day childcare was done by my maternal grandmother. My **popo**. She died twelve years ago. I still think about her all the time. I wish she could have met Harriet. We shared a room for most of my childhood. Popo was extremely affectionate. You have to understand, my parents had demanding careers. They were under serious pressure. Just because they were professors doesn't mean everything was easy. They weren't just taking care of us. They were responsible for their parents. And their siblings. They helped everyone get established. Some relatives had debt. My father had ulcers from all the stress. They didn't have time to hover over me. You can't judge them by American standards."

"Ms. Liu, I sense you getting defensive."

"My parents gave me a good life. They did everything for me. I'm the one who messed up. I don't want anyone blaming them."

The psychologist lets the subject drop. They discuss her response to Harriet's crying, whether she has fun taking care of Harriet, whether she initiates playtime, her use of praise. She answers as she imagines the playground mothers would, describing a life governed by patience and joy, her voice becoming high and girlish. If any of those mothers were in her position, she knows they'd blind themselves or drink bleach.

"You mentioned your husband leaving."

Frida stiffens. She tells him that she and Gust were together for eight years, married for three, introduced by mutual friends at a dinner party in Crown Heights.

"Gust said he knew right away. It took me a little longer."

The marriage was fulfilling. Happy. Gust was her best friend. He made her feel safe. She refrains from saying that they used to have more in common, that Gust used to have a sense of humor, that wanting to have **his** baby is what convinced her to have a baby at all, that he used to be a reasonable person who trusted science and medicine, that later, they fought over a birth plan. Her refusal to consider a homebirth or doula. Her blasé attitude about epidurals.

She explains the timeline of her pregnancy and Harriet's birth, her discovery of Susanna, the short-lived attempt at reconciliation.

"Harriet was two months old when I found out about the affair. We didn't get a chance to be

a family. I think if Gust had given us a chance—"
She looks out the window. "I was waking up three
times a night to breastfeed. I'm sorry, is that too
intimate?"

"Go on, Ms. Liu."

"We were in survival mode. The stress affected
my milk supply. I was recovering from a C-section.
We planned for this baby. Having a family is one of
the main reasons we moved here."

The psychologist hands her a tissue.

"I would have taken him back. I wanted us to
try counseling, but he wouldn't stop seeing her. It
was Gust's decision to get divorced. He didn't fight
for us. Gust is a good father—I knew he'd be a
good father—but he acts like the whole thing was
beyond his control, like he and Susanna were fated
to be together."

"Tell me about your relationship with the paramour."

"That's the term? **Paramour**? Well, I'd say the
paramour has some issues with boundaries. She
doesn't respect me. I've tried to establish boundaries, but nothing changes. My daughter is not a
project, and Susanna is not her mother. Susanna
is always coming in and imposing. Like with her

nutritionist work. It's not like she's even healthy. She was a dancer. You know how they are."

Is Frida dating? Has she introduced Harriet to any boyfriends?

"I'm not ready to date. And I wouldn't introduce any man to my daughter unless the relationship was very serious. As far as I'm concerned, Gust introduced Susanna to Harriet way too soon."

Prompted to say more, she grows agitated. "He moved in with her as soon as he left us, and suddenly I'm expected to bring my newborn to that girl's apartment and interact with her constantly. Seeing her with my baby . . ."

Frida pinches the skin between her brows. "I didn't want Harriet to be in the same room as Susanna. And then she had to go live there for half the week. Gust said he'd hire a nanny. I offered to find a nanny for him. He wasn't supposed to fob off the childcare on his girlfriend. I never agreed to that. I really don't care if she has a flexible schedule. I don't care if she **wants** to do the childcare. My daughter now spends more time with that girl than either of her real parents, and that's just not right."

×

Will's shoes are lined up in neat rows. The carpet has been vacuumed, the mail and loose change tidied away, the whole apartment dusted. His dog has been exiled to the backyard. Frida shouldn't have come here, eager for trouble on a Friday night, but what's one more wrong turn after so many?

Will has shaved off his beard, looks younger. Handsome. Frida has never seen him clean-shaven. The cleft is a surprise. With time, she could adore this face. Falling in love might help her. The social worker would see the tenderness in her eyes. Harriet would see it too.

Tomorrow morning is the first supervised visit. Sitting with Will, Frida confesses that she might be losing her mind. She keeps second-guessing her responses. She should have prepared better, deflected questions about Susanna, focused on Harriet, her love for Harriet.

"I only get an hour with her."

"You're going to do great," Will says. "You just have to play with her, right? And they observe you? Imagine the other moms they deal with."

"What if that doesn't help me?"

She met with the social worker yesterday. The social worker's office was decorated with children's drawings. Crayon and Magic Marker and pastels. Stick figures and trees. Some cats and dogs. The place felt haunted, like she'd entered the lair of a pedophile.

There was a camera embedded into the wall behind the social worker's desk. Someone had painted yellow petals around the lens, placing it into a mural of sunflowers, as if a child wouldn't notice.

They went over the same questions. Frida's motives. Her mental health. Whether she understands a parent's fundamental responsibilities. Her concept of safety. Her standards of cleanliness. The social worker asked about Harriet's diet. Frida's refrigerator contained take-out boxes, some sweet potatoes, one package of celery, two apples, some peanut butter, some string cheese, some condiments, only a day's worth of milk. The cupboards were nearly empty. Why wasn't she paying attention to Harriet's nutrition?

How restrictive is she? How does she enforce rules? What kind of limits does she consider appropriate? Has she ever threatened Harriet with corporal punishment?

Was Harriet being raised bilingual? What did Frida mean when she said her Mandarin is only proficient? That she speaks Chinglish with her parents? Wasn't that denying Harriet a crucial part of her heritage?

What about their favorite games? Playdates? How often does she hire babysitters and how closely does she vet them? How restrictive is she about nudity and exposure to adult sexuality? What is her attitude about interruption, manners, neatness, cleanliness, bedtime, noise, screen time, obedience, aggression?

The questions were more detailed than Renee anticipated. Again, Frida tried to emulate the playground mothers, but there was too much hesitation, too many inconsistencies. She didn't sound attentive enough, patient enough, committed enough, Chinese enough, American enough.

No one would call her a natural. In the social worker's office, her black skirt suit looked too severe. She shouldn't have carried her best handbag or worn her ruby earrings. She was the only mother in the waiting room who wasn't poor, who wasn't casually dressed.

The social worker needs to speak to her parents. Frida finally called them last night. She rushed her confession, asked them not to say too much, explained that the call was being recorded. They, like everyone else, wanted to know why. If she was tired, why didn't she take a nap? If she felt overwhelmed, why didn't she ask Gust for help? Or Susanna? Even if she hates Susanna. Why didn't she hire a babysitter?

"This didn't have to happen," her father said.

When will she see Harriet again? When can they see Harriet? They can't call Harriet? Why not? Who's deciding these things? Is this legal?

"What kind of trouble are you in?" her mother shouted. "Why didn't you tell us?"

Will asks Frida if she's hungry. They could order Thai food. Or Ethiopian. Watch a movie.

"You don't have to feed me."

Tomorrow her best mothering will be on display. She'll be trustworthy. She's still capable of such things. If she were truly reckless, she would've found a stranger. If she were truly reckless, Will wouldn't have cleaned. He wouldn't have shaved. If she were truly reckless, he'd fuck her on the floor instead of leading her to his now tidy bedroom. He wouldn't ask permission before undressing her.

He refuses to turn off the lights. "I want to see you," he says. She rakes her fingers through the dark hair on his stomach. His penis is huge and worrying.

She's never seen a penis of this size in person. Only the tip fits in her mouth.

After Will finds a condom, they begin the first of many attempts at fitting part to part. They try with Frida on top, Frida on her knees, Frida on her back, her feet on Will's shoulders. She's embarrassed by the limitations of her little-girl body. It takes another handful of lube and many deep exhales before he can enter her, his penis not a third leg but an arm, an entire arm digging up to the elbow.

"I feel like my dick is in your skull." Will marvels at his good fortune. "God, you're tight as fuck."

Built like a teenage girl, Gust used to say. Tighter than Susanna.

Frida wraps her legs around Will's waist. She remembers the hands at the hospital. Five different hands in thirty-four hours: three residents, two OBs. Her torturers. Their hands would go in and up and root around, checking the position of the baby's head. Against Gust's wishes, she had an epidural at hour fifteen. At hour thirty-two, she was cleared to push. Two hours later, the baby's head was in the exact same position. Failure to progress, they said. The baby's heart rate began dropping. More doctors and nurses appeared. Her body, still convulsing, was rushed to the operating room, where a dozen masked faces greeted her. Someone strapped her arms down. Someone else pinned up a blue curtain. Her body became a sterile field.

The lights were unbearably bright. The anesthetic made her teeth chatter. **Can you feel this?** A touch on the cheek. **Or this?** A touch on the belly. **No? Good.**

"Sweetie, are you okay?" Will asks.

"Keep going."

The doctors were chatting about movies they'd seen. She listened to their instruments clicking. Gust sat beside her head, mute with exhaustion, not looking at her. She told him she should have tried harder. She waited for him to say no, to call her brave. Someone placed his hands on her shoulders. She loved the man's gravelly voice, the calm weight of his hands. She would have done anything for that man. He kept touching her, smoothing her hair. He said, "You're going to feel some pressure."

×

Frida shields her eyes and looks up at Gust and Susanna's bay window. She's twenty minutes early. Last year, they bought a spacious condo in Fairmount, a few blocks from the art museum, on a newly gentrified stretch of Spring Garden. Susanna comes from an old-money Virginia family. Her parents paid for the condo in cash and give her a monthly allowance. Whenever Frida comes over, she can't help but compare. Their home has abundant natural light and high ceilings, Moroccan rugs in every room. A set of midnight-blue velvet couches. Plants on every windowsill, vases of fresh flowers on reclaimed wood tables. Paintings by Susanna's friends, furniture that's been passed down through two generations. She used to check Susanna's Instagram feed late at night to torment herself. There was her beautiful chubby baby nestled on sheepskin throws or cradling designer blankets, the perfect accessory.

The social worker is four minutes late, then five, then nine, then twelve. This morning, she'll see that Gust and Susanna's home is always spotless. She won't know that they have a cleaner come every week.

Gust texted last night to say that Susanna is sorry to be away. She's at a silent retreat in the Berkshires. She sends Frida her love and support. **You got this**, Susanna texted.

Frida checks her reflection in a car window. In movies she's seen about mothers seeking redemption, the bad mothers hide their wickedness beneath modest silk blouses tucked into dowdy skirts. They wear low-heeled pumps and nude hose. She's wearing her best approximation of this costume: a gray silk shell, a jewel-neck lavender cardigan, a knee-length black skirt, kitten heels. Her bangs are freshly trimmed, her makeup subdued, her hair pulled back in a low ponytail. She looks demure and inoffensive and middle-aged, like a kindergarten teacher or a stay-at-home mom who finds blow jobs a necessary evil.

Sustained face-to-face interaction, the social worker said. One hour of play and conversation. Frida can't be alone with Harriet, can't take her outside, can't bring presents. The social worker will ensure Harriet's physical and emotional safety.

There's a tap on her shoulder. "Good morning, Ms. Liu." The social worker takes off her mirrored aviators. She looks marvelously healthy. Her pale pink sheath shows off her copper skin and cut arms and narrow waist. She's wearing nude, patent-leather stilettos.

They exchange pleasantries about the weather,

which is sunny and dry, nearly eighty-five. The social worker has been circling for ages, had to park four blocks away. "I don't usually come to this neighborhood."

Frida asks if she and Harriet can have some extra time at the end, since they're starting late. "You said we'd get an hour."

"I can't change my other appointments."

Frida doesn't ask again. At the front door, she offers to use her key, but the social worker says no. She rings apartment 3F. Upstairs, the social worker asks Frida to wait in the hall while she speaks with Gust.

Frida checks her phone. They're eighteen minutes behind schedule. Hopefully Gust has prepped Harriet. It's not that Mommy doesn't want to stay longer. It's not that Mommy didn't want to bring presents. None of this is up to Mommy. None of this makes sense to Mommy. It probably doesn't make sense to Harriet either. Mommy is on time-out, Harriet's been told. The social worker asked Gust to explain the situation in child-friendly terms. It didn't matter, the social worker said, that Gust and Susanna don't do time-out. Harriet would get the gist.

Frida presses her ear to the door. She hears the social worker's shift into child register. Harriet is whimpering. Gust is trying to soothe her.

"There's nothing to be scared of. It's only Mommy. Ms. Torres and Mommy."

Frida doesn't want their names linked. She shouldn't have to be here with an escort. When Gust opens the door, the social worker is standing close behind him, already filming.

Gust hugs her.

"How is she?" Frida asks.

"A little clingy. Confused."

"Gust, I'm so sorry." She hopes he can't tell that she's been recently fucked. She made Will promise not to say anything. There was blood in her underwear last night. She's still sore.

"Ms. Liu, let's get started."

Gust says he'll be in his office. He gives Frida a chaste kiss on the cheek.

Harriet is hiding under the coffee table. Frida glances back at the social worker. They shouldn't begin like this. The social worker follows her into the living room, where she kneels next to Harriet's prone body and gingerly rubs her belly.

"I'm here, bub. Mommy's here." Frida's heart is

not in her throat, but in her eyes, her fingertips. **Please,** she thinks. **Please, baby.** Harriet peeks her head out and smiles, then rolls into a ball, covering her face with her hands. She won't budge.

"Mommy, come." Harriet beckons Frida to join her under the table.

When Frida tugs at her legs, she pulls them away.

"You have thirty-five minutes left, Ms. Liu. Why don't you two start playing? I need to see you play with her."

Frida tickles Harriet's bare feet. Gust and Susanna dress her in such drab colors. Harriet is wearing a gray blouse and brown leggings, like a child of the apocalypse. Soon she'll buy Harriet new dresses. Stripes and florals. They'll find a new house. A new neighborhood. No more bad memories.

"One, two, three!" She pulls Harriet by the legs. Harriet shrieks happily.

Frida picks her up. "Let me look at you, bub."

Harriet smiles, exposing her few chicklet teeth. She pats Frida's cardigan with her sticky hands. Frida smothers her with kisses. She runs her fingers along Harriet's eyelashes, lifts Harriet's blouse and blows raspberries on her stomach, making her cackle. This is the only pleasure that counts. Everything might depend on whether she can touch her child, whether she can see her.

"Mommy missed you so much."

"No whispering, Ms. Liu."

The social worker is two feet away. Frida can smell the woman's vanilla perfume.

"Ms. Liu, please don't block the child's face. Why don't you start playing? Does she have toys here somewhere?"

Frida shelters Harriet with her body. "Please give us a minute. We haven't seen each other in eleven days. She's not a seal."

"No one is comparing her to a seal. You're the one using that language. I'm telling you, it would be in your best interest to get started."

Gust and Susanna keep Harriet's toys in a wooden chest next to the couch. Harriet refuses to walk the few steps to her toy chest. She attaches herself to Frida's leg, then demands to be carried. With Harriet on her hip, Frida unpacks felt dolls and stuffed animals, wooden blocks with nursery rhymes. She tries to entice Harriet with stacking rings, a carved dinosaur on wheels.

Harriet won't let Frida put her down. She regards the social worker with fearful eyes, raised eyebrows.

Frida knows this look. She puts Harriet back on

the floor. "Bub, I'm sorry. We need to play. Can we play for the nice lady? Please, bub. Please. Let's play."

Harriet tries to climb back onto Frida's lap, and when Frida gives her only a quick hug and insists that she choose a toy, she begins wailing. Her sorrow spirals with alarming speed into a full-fledged meltdown. She flings herself facedown on the rug, drumming her hands and feet, emitting the cry of a loon, a cry that spans oceans.

Frida rolls her onto her back and kisses her, begging her to calm down.

Harriet is shaking, enraged. She points at the social worker. "Go way!" she shouts.

"That's not nice." Frida pulls her to standing and holds her by the shoulders. "You apologize to Ms. Torres right now. We do not talk that way."

Harriet hits Frida and scratches her face. Frida grabs Harriet's wrists. "Look at me. I don't like that. You do not hit Mommy. We do not hit. You need to apologize."

Harriet stomps her feet and screams. The social worker inches closer.

"Ms. Torres, could you please sit at the table? You're making her nervous. You can just zoom in, can't you?"

The social worker ignores the request. Harriet won't apologize. She wants more hugging. "C'mon, bub, we need to play. Ms. Torres needs to see us play. Mommy doesn't have much time left."

The social worker lowers her camera and sweetens her voice. "Harriet, can we see some playing? Play with your mother, okay?"

Harriet arches her back. She wriggles free from Frida's grasp. She charges. There's no time to catch her. Frida watches in horror as Harriet sinks her teeth into the social worker's forearm.

The social worker yelps. "Ms. Liu, control your child!"

Frida pulls Harriet away. "Apologize to Ms. Torres right now. You never bite. We do not bite anyone."

Harriet unleashes a stream of gibberish and vitriol. "No no no no no!"

Gust comes to check on them. The social worker informs him of Harriet's vicious attack.

"Gust, she was nervous," Frida says.

Gust asks to see the social worker's arm. He asks if she's in pain. Harriet has left teeth marks. He apologizes profusely. Harriet never behaves this way. "She's not a biter," he says.

He takes Harriet to the couch to have a talk. Frida

escapes to the kitchen to get a glass of water for the social worker. She packs a Ziploc bag with ice and wraps it in a towel. She feels mortified but proud. This is her demon child. Her ally. Her protector.

The social worker holds the ice to her injury. No apology is forthcoming from Harriet, despite her parents' best efforts.

"Ms. Liu, you have five more minutes. Let's try to finish."

Frida begs Harriet for one game, but Harriet only wants her father now. She won't let go of Gust. Every other word is **Daddy**.

Frida plants herself beside them and looks on helplessly as they play with Harriet's wooden pony set. Weren't they allies a moment ago? Is every child as fickle as hers? There are still two more visits. Gust will coach her next time. He'll explain how much these visits matter. The judge will understand that Harriet is not yet two. He'll see that Harriet loves her. That Harriet wants to be with her. He'll see her daughter's wild heart.

4.

It's a humid Friday afternoon in late September, six days since she last saw Harriet, nearly three weeks since her very bad day, and Frida is hiding in the ladies' room at work, listening to the social worker's maddeningly casual voice mail. Tomorrow morning's visitation has been postponed. The social worker has double-booked herself.

"It happens," Ms. Torres says. She'll call back with a new date and time when something opens up.

Frida plays the message again, thinking she missed an apology that never comes. She smacks her palm on the stall door. All week she's been using the visit to measure time. The days since Harriet, the days until Harriet. Another hour to win back her baby.

She should have known she'd be punished. When

they said goodbye last Saturday, she stole extra time, gave Harriet extra hugs and kisses. She can still feel the social worker gripping her elbow, can still hear the woman saying, "That's enough, Ms. Liu."

Once outside, the social worker lectured her about boundaries. The child was clearly ready to say goodbye. The child didn't want any more hugs.

"You have to recognize the difference between what you want and what she wants," the social worker said.

Frida's fists were clenched. Her toes curled inside her shoes. She kept her head bowed, stared at the rosary tattooed on the social worker's ankle. Had she looked the social worker in the eye, she might have delivered the first punch of her life.

The bathroom door opens. Two students begin gossiping at the sinks. One of them has a date tonight, met someone on that app that matches people by their pheromones.

Frida texts Renee about the cancellation. She wants to call Ms. Torres the sadist that she is, but her communications must be discreet. **Tomorrow is off**, she writes. **Second visitation = ???**

There's nowhere to speak freely. No, Renee said, she shouldn't buy a burner phone. She shouldn't set up new email accounts, shouldn't do research at the library, must watch what she says to her parents or friends or coworkers. Any of them could be questioned.

"You have nothing to hide," Renee said. "Repeat it back to me, Frida: **I have nothing to hide**."

Frida hears lipstick tubes and compacts being opened and closed. The girls discuss the merits of the app that matches people by voice. The one that matches people based on their commuting patterns, mimicking the likelihood of meeting a stranger on the train.

She could laugh. The idea of a normal weekend. She blots her eyes with a piece of toilet paper and returns to her desk.

Whatever relief she felt by coming here has faded, her cubicle simply a different place to miss Harriet and consider her mistakes. If she'd been more solicitous to Ms. Torres. If they'd had several hours, not one. If she'd never gone to Will's house. If she'd been able to convince Harriet to play. If there had been no tantrum and no bite. If it were just the two of them, without clocks or cameras or that woman telling them to **act normal**.

Corrected page proofs were due back to her boss

this morning. She spreads the pages out on her desk, checking for errant commas and misspelled faculty names and titles. She used to pride herself on her sharp eye, but now she can barely make sense of the words, couldn't care less about getting the files to the printer. She needs Gust to apologize on her behalf. Harriet needs to know that her mother is thinking about her every second. This isn't Mommy's choice. This isn't Mommy's fault. Ms. Torres could have canceled on that other family.

×

After dinner, Frida retreats to Harriet's nursery, as she has every night since the visitation. She faces the camera and kneels in the dark, her mind roaming to the past and future, unwilling to accept the unbearable present. Renee thinks the state should see her atoning. She should work or pray or exercise. She should clean. She shouldn't watch television or waste time on her computer or phone. She must show them that she's wrestling with her guilt. The more she suffers, the more she cries, the more they'll respect her.

The room smells of chemicals. Fake lemon verbena.

It doesn't smell like Harriet anymore, and for that and everything else, Frida is sorry. A few toys faded in the wash. The stuffing in one of the quilts was ruined. She's polished the crib and rocking chair. She's cleaned the baseboards and windowsill, washed the walls. Her hands are rough from scrubbing her bathroom and kitchen twice a week, always without gloves, her chapped palms and broken nails like a little hair shirt.

Renee is worried about how the bite will play in court. She's worried that the social worker didn't observe any playing. But she plans to say that Harriet was provoked, that Harriet's response was natural under the circumstances. They'd been apart for many days. Harriet's routine had been disrupted. She never plays with her mother at Gust and Susanna's, never on command, never with a timer.

Frida's legs are falling asleep. She wonders what shapes she should make with her body, whether there's a person watching her, or only a machine, if they're looking for certain expressions or postures. She could bow to them, press her palms and forehead to the ground three times, the way her family prayed to Buddha for protection.

Who will protect her now? She hopes the family court judge has feelings, that the judge, if he or she is childless, at least has a cat or dog, something with a soul and a face, that he or she has experienced unconditional love, knows regret. CPS should require this of their employees.

She moves so the camera is seeing her in profile. Her hips hurt. Her lower back hurts. Lately, she's been trying to remember the beginning. Bringing Harriet to the window in their hospital room and showing her daylight for the first time. Harriet's rosy skin, newly exposed to the air and beginning to peel. She couldn't stop touching Harriet's face, amazed by her daughter's huge cheeks and Western nose. How had she made a baby with blue eyes? At the beginning, it felt like they were taking care of a benevolent creature, not yet a human. Making a new human felt so grave.

Frida begins to weep. She needs to tell the judge about the house of her mind in the house of her body. Those houses are cleaner now and less afraid. She would never leave Harriet like that, not again.

×

The social worker keeps changing the date of the next visitation. September turns to October, and by the fourth postponement, Frida has dropped a dress size. She's been sleeping four hours a night, sometimes three, sometimes two. She has no appetite. Breakfast is coffee and a handful of almonds. Lunch is a green smoothie. Dinner is an apple and two slices of toast with butter and jam.

She's seen Will on campus twice, bumped into him once at the bookstore, once at the main food court. She asked him to stop calling, wouldn't let him hug her in public. Her work is slow and scattered. She sometimes shows up at her desk having obviously been crying in the bathroom. Emotion makes her boss uncomfortable. After another round of late articles, her boss rescinds her work-from-home days. He's sorry this will mean less time with Harriet, but the organization must come first.

"I don't want to have to speak to HR," her boss says.

"It won't happen again. I promise. There have been . . ." **Problems at home**, she wants to say.

She's thought about looking for another position, has considered quitting, but she needs health insurance. Penn has good benefits. Her father called in favors to help her get this job.

She's been lying to everyone at work. The professors

never ask her personal questions, but the support staff is mostly female, married with children. Convention dictates that they talk about their children at every opportunity. Never **How are you?**, but **How is Tommy? How is Sloan? How is Beverly?**

She told them, "Harriet's new word is **bubble**."

"Harriet has been asking to go to the zoo."

"Harriet is obsessed with butter cookies."

She doesn't tell them that Harriet is in therapy. That in the office of some court-appointed child psychologist, Harriet is supposedly being healed. Renee said the child psychologist would probably use a dollhouse, have Harriet act out her feelings with a mama doll and baby doll, have her draw and see how hard she presses down with the crayons. The psychologist would look for signs. There's a trauma checklist, but everyone responds to trauma differently. To Frida, it sounded an awful lot like guessing.

She doesn't tell anyone that her parents have wired her $10,000 for her legal fees, that they'll send more if she needs it, that they offered to take money from their retirement savings. Their generosity makes her feel even guiltier, unworthy of being their daughter or Harriet's mother or waking up in the morning.

They sent the money without her asking. Their interview with Ms. Torres was tense. She kept asking them to repeat things, to speak more slowly, as if she couldn't understand their accents. They said she didn't talk like a normal person. Her tone was fake friendly, but she was cold like a scientist. She made parenthood sound like fixing a car. The food part, the safety part, the education part, the discipline part, the love part. They told the social worker that Harriet is Frida's joy. Her **bao bei**. Her little treasure.

According to her mother, Frida is swallowing bitterness. **Chi ku**, a phrase Frida hadn't heard in years. To bear hardships. They used the phrase to describe what her paternal grandmother, her **ahma**, endured during the Cultural Revolution. Her father sometimes told the story of the night Ahma was almost killed. She was the widow of a landowner. Soldiers came to their village to find her. They made her kneel. Her sons hid beneath the wooden bed in the room that served as their house. That night, both children screamed until they tore their vocal cords. They watched as soldiers put a gun to their mother's head and threatened to shoot her.

Frida used to feel guilty whenever she heard that story. She felt spoiled and useless. She never learned

Ahma's dialect, could barely say more than **hello** and **good morning** to her. She had no way of asking her beloved **ahma** what happened. But Frida has no gun to her head, no soldier's boot on her neck. She brought this bitterness on herself.

×

The visitation is supposed to begin at five. It's the end of October, Tuesday night, eight weeks since they took Harriet, nearly six weeks since Frida last held her. The social worker gave them only an hour's notice.

Frida steps around puddles. Jack-o'-lanterns are waterlogged from last night's storm. Hurricane season lasts longer now. Fake cobwebs are drooping. Her coworkers have been asking about Harriet's costume. To one woman, she said lion. To another, she said ladybug.

At 4:58, she spots the social worker getting out of a taxi. She walks over and thanks her for the appointment. She didn't have time to return home to change. Fortunately, her weight loss is hidden under layers of wool—a gray-and-black-striped sweater dress, a purple scarf coiled high to obscure her newly sharp jawline.

The social worker doesn't apologize for the many cancellations. She doesn't apologize for interfering with Harriet's evening routine. They chat about traffic and last night's tornado warning.

Gust and Susanna's apartment is lit for romance and warmed by the oven and smells of cinnamon. They have a wreath of twigs and dried berries on their door, a bowl of gourds on the dining table.

Frida is alarmed to see that Susanna and the social worker are on hugging terms. With Frida, Susanna's hug is fierce and unyielding as ever. She kisses Frida on both cheeks, asks how she's been holding up.

"I'm surviving." Frida looks over at the social worker to make sure she's paying attention. "Thank you for taking her to the appointments. I know the schedule has been tough. I want you to know I appreciate—"

"It's nothing. I'm happy to do it." Gust is with Harriet in the nursery. "She's being fussy," Susanna says. "She only napped for twenty minutes today. We tried to give her dinner early, but she didn't eat much. You might need to give her something."

Susanna takes their coats and invites them to sit down. She offers them tea and dessert. She's made gluten-free apple crumble.

Frida says they don't have time, but the social worker happily accepts. Ten minutes are lost to sipping and eating and chitchat.

The apple crumble is delicious. Frida eats despite herself. She resents the friendly looks that pass between Susanna and the social worker, the way they're speaking in shorthand, discussing the jacket Harriet left behind at Ms. Torres's office, how Susanna should bring a snack for Harriet's next session with Ms. Goldberg. The social worker compliments Susanna's paisley silk peasant dress, her gold bracelets.

Susanna says they'll take Harriet trick-or-treating in West Philly on Thursday. The houses around Clark Park have the best decorations. There's a children's parade. A party on Little Osage. Harriet will be Dorothy. They're going to meet up with Will and some other friends.

At the mention of Will, Frida bristles. She gulps down more tea, scalding the top of her mouth. "You're going to let her have sugar?"

The social worker sets down her fork and begins taking notes.

"I don't know about sugar. It's more for the experience. I wish you could come with us." Susanna will be the Tin Man. Gust will be the Scarecrow. "It's too bad . . . ," she says. "You could have been . . . Excuse me, Janine. I should go check on them."

Frida pushes leftover crumble around her ramekin. She licks her fork. Her parents call Susanna the evil egg, the white ghost. When this is over, she'll ask them how to say **whore** in Mandarin, and that will be Susanna's name going forward.

When Harriet appears, only twenty-three minutes remain. Harriet rubs her eyes. There's a pause before she notices Frida, a split second into which Frida projects her nightmares. The social worker begins filming.

"Come here." Frida holds her arms wide. Harriet is both bigger and smaller than the Harriet of her daydreams. It feels like she's aged a year. She's grown more hair. It's darker and curlier, tangled. She's barefoot, wearing a sleeveless beige cotton dress that's too light for the season.

"Big girl," Frida says, her voice chirpy and strangled. "I missed you, I missed you." She kisses Harriet, touches the blotches of eczema on her cheeks. "Hello, beauty."

They press foreheads and noses. She apologizes for disrupting the evening routine. She asks if Harriet understands what's going to happen, why Mommy is here, what they're going to do, why they need to play for a little while.

"Visit," Harriet says, hitting the consonants hard.

She doesn't want her daughter to learn these words, not in this way.

"Miss Mommy," Harriet says.

Frida hugs her again, but their reverie is short-lived. The social worker has asked Gust and Susanna to leave them alone for a bit, to return at 6:00 p.m. sharp. When Harriet sees them heading toward the door, she takes off running and hurls herself at their legs.

She grabs Susanna by the ankles. The social worker suggests that Gust and Susanna leave quickly. As Harriet screams, they extricate themselves, promising to return soon, careful not to close the door on Harriet's fingers.

Harriet bangs on the door, demanding Daddy and Sue-Sue come back. Frida pleads for cooperation. She tries to carry Harriet back to the living room, looking like she's trying to catch a fish with her bare hands.

"Ms. Liu, she can walk," the social worker says. "You should let her walk."

This evening's sustained face-to-face interaction

consists of negotiation and refusal, chasing and begging, a steady uptick in Harriet's fury. The contents of her toy chest are strewn across the floor. Harriet behaves like a child who is secretly beaten, working herself into a frenzy that surges until it erupts in a nosebleed.

"Bub, please calm down. Please. Oh, please."

Harriet flails and chokes on her tears. She wipes blood across her face, then wipes her bloody hands on the ivory rug. The blood keeps coming. The social worker films Frida ministering to Harriet, twisting tissues and stuffing them into Harriet's nostrils. She presses one hand on Harriet's forehead to make sure she keeps her head back. She tries to remember what her parents and Popo used to do. This is Harriet's first nosebleed.

When the bleeding finally stops, Frida asks permission to take Harriet to the kitchen for some water.

"As long as she walks," the social worker says. The wobbling walk and searching for a sippy cup and filling it and coaxing Harriet to drink from it and wiping her wet chin consume more time. Harriet's dress is soaked. She's shivering.

Frida takes off her scarf and wraps it around

Harriet's shoulders. "No, bub, please don't do that." Harriet is licking the blood off her fingers. "You can go to bed so, so soon. No. No. Don't cry. Sit down with Mommy."

They're cross-legged on the kitchen floor, their backs against the oven, Frida sitting in a puddle of spilled water. The social worker tells them they have five minutes left. Time for one game.

"She's exhausted," Frida says. "Look at her."

"If that's how you'd like to use your visitation."

"Please, Ms. Torres, be reasonable. We're doing our best."

Frida asks Harriet if she's hungry. Harriet shakes her head. She babbles instead of using her words. She climbs onto Frida's lap. Frida has been dreaming of this moment, Harriet making her mother's arms a home, her body a home, like it was at the very beginning, mother and child going back in time together. She kisses Harriet's hot forehead. She wets her fingertip with saliva and tries to remove the rest of the dried blood. Harriet's eyes close.

"Ms. Liu, please wake her up. This isn't appropriate."

Frida ignores the warning. She loves feeling Harriet wriggle and make herself cozy. Harriet trusts her.

Harriet forgives her. She wouldn't fall asleep in her mother's arms if she didn't feel safe there.

×

As the days pass, Frida thinks of the social worker as much as she would a new lover. She carries her phone with her everywhere, has the ringer on the highest volume. Any day is a day the social worker might call, and then she does, and then she cancels.

The social worker claims to be swamped. There may not be time for a third visit. "Don't worry," she says. "They're taking good care of her."

Every night, Frida kneels in the dark nursery, thinking about the child who was cut out of her body, who should be beside her but who hasn't been beside her, not really, for eight weeks. Nine weeks. Ten. It is November, and Harriet is twenty months old.

×

On the morning of her hearing, Frida wakes up frozen. Her comforter has been kicked off the bed, the sheets are tangled around her legs. She slept with a window open, inviting the cold into the house of her mind and the house of her body, into the room where she's been waiting every night for her daughter to be returned. It's 5:14. She closes the window and puts on a robe and pads downstairs and forces herself to eat. An entire bagel with cream cheese. Ten flatbread crackers. A chocolate sea-salt protein bar. Coffee and green tea. Yesterday, she stocked her fridge with organic whole milk and string cheese, locally grown apples, organic chicken breasts, blueberries. She bought avocados and teething crackers and rice cereal.

Renee told her to be hopeful. Worst-case scenario is more supervised visits. But the judge is likely to approve unsupervised visits, overnight visits. Joint custody.

Frida takes a long shower and scrubs herself with a loofah until she's pink and tender. She dries her hair carefully and fluffs her bangs with a round brush. She practices smiling in the mirror. Renee said soft colors around the face, loose hair, small earrings. Frida has bought new clothes. Her tailored sheath is gray, not black. Her cardigan is not just ivory, but mohair.

After she finishes dressing, she throws up her

breakfast. She brushes her teeth and drinks a bottle of seltzer and reapplies her lipstick. Renee said that after the judge makes his decision, everything moves quickly. Harriet will stay home with Susanna while Gust attends the hearing, but Frida might be able to see Harriet tonight or tomorrow.

A good second visit was supposed to cancel out the bite, and a bite plus a nosebleed will require a leap of faith by the judge, and judges are not predisposed to leaping, but Renee said they can still win. She didn't want to be crass about it, but the judge probably won't see Frida as a person of color. She isn't Black or brown. She's not Vietnamese or Cambodian. She's not poor. Most of the judges are white, and white judges tend to give white mothers the benefit of the doubt, and Frida is pale enough.

She takes a car to Center City, where Renee and Gust are waiting for her in the lobby of the family court building, a new glass-and-steel construction that takes up half a city block, just past city hall and Dilworth Park, across the street from the fancy hotel Le Méridien.

They put their purses and wallets and phones through the scanner. They pass through the metal detector. She wishes Gust hadn't worn a suit. She hasn't seen him in a suit since their wedding, and today his beauty is distracting.

He looks tired though. She asks him how Harriet slept, how she behaved this morning, if they explained to her that today is important, that time-out will soon be over.

"I would have," Gust says. "But Janine told us not to promise anything."

Renee tells Frida to be quiet. It's not safe to talk here. On the elevator, they're shoulder to shoulder with weary state workers and unhappy parents. Gust tries to catch Frida's eye. She tries to remember where she is and why she's here, that she can't ask him for a hug no matter how badly she needs one. Renee was appalled that Gust held her hand in divorce court. Hand-holding clearly made him feel better and Frida feel worse, so why do it? Renee asked. Why absolve him?

The elevator opens on the fourth floor. Ms. Torres is waiting at the check-in desk. Frida signs in with her fingerprint. There are four courtrooms, each with its own waiting area, as well as smaller rooms next to each courtroom where lawyers and clients can meet in private. There are plastic display cases with pamphlets for counseling services, employment services, benefit offices, shelters. The floor has the feel of a high-end hospital, polished but grimy, with sorrow baked into the walls. There's morning light streaming in from a bank of windows, rows of orange bucket chairs bolted to the floor, televisions everywhere, all showing the home and garden network.

As far as Frida can tell, she's the only Asian. Gust is the only white man in a suit who isn't a lawyer. The televisions are showing a bathroom makeover program. A couple in California wants to add a Jacuzzi to their master bath.

Frida and Gust choose seats in the last row. The social worker and Renee sit on either side of them. Frida thanks Gust for taking the day off. She wants to ask for extra time with Harriet. They could switch holidays. Gust can let her have Harriet for Thanksgiving instead of Christmas, or maybe, in light of the last two months, he can let her have both.

On the screens above them, there are episodes about a landscaping project in New Mexico, a pool house at a Connecticut estate, commercials for erectile dysfunction remedies and homeowner's insurance and immersion blenders, a variety of pain medications whose side effects include death.

She watches workers in the hotel across the street

changing linens. As the morning passes, the rows fill. Parents are told to lower their voices. More social workers appear, more lawyers. Some parents seem to be meeting their lawyers for the first time. Some children climb over the seats, first talking to their mother, then their father. Their parents sit in separate rows.

Every hour, Frida goes to the bathroom to wash her hands and apply more powder to her forehead. She can't stop sweating. She feels certain she's developing an ulcer. Renee sometimes follows her into the bathroom and tells her to come back. They go across the street for lunch, eat greasy sandwiches that upset her stomach more.

The court-appointed child psychologist arrives. Ms. Goldberg is a pregnant white woman in her forties with a blonde pageboy haircut and a serene, perfectly oval face, like a Modigliani. She greets Frida warmly, saying how pleased she is to finally meet her.

"Harriet is a special one," she says.

Ms. Goldberg takes a seat in Frida and Gust's row, as do the state's attorneys. Frida regrets not letting her parents fly in. Renee didn't want them at the hearing. She plans to work the single-mother angle. The judge doesn't need to know that Frida has resources, that she could have asked her parents to pay for day care, that she could have asked them to help her with rent so she only had to work part-time.

But they'd already helped with grad school. They'd already helped with rent when she lived in Brooklyn. During the separation, they paid her attorney's fees, gave her money for a car, money for furniture. She's almost forty. By this age, her parents had tenure. They were homeowners. They were shouldering the responsibility for half a dozen relatives.

They're waiting for news. They'll come see Harriet as soon as it's allowed. Frida watches people leaving the courtrooms in tears. She hears shouting. A father is escorted out in handcuffs. Couples are arguing. Guards are rude to social workers; social workers are rude to parents; lawyers are texting.

It's getting dark outside. She watches her reflection emerge in the window. The room empties. Renee says it's possible they'll have to come back in the morning. Ms. Torres is called to testify several times on other cases. Gust brings Frida bottles of water and snacks from the vending machine, urges her to eat. He texts Susanna, finds out that Harriet didn't nap. He calls his boss and asks if he can take the day off tomorrow too.

"Yes, the situation with my daughter," he says.

Frida glances between the four sets of doors. She needs to know which courtroom she's been assigned, which judge she'll face, whether her judge will be strict or lenient, what Ms. Torres will say, what the child psychologist will say, what the state thinks they know about her. She needs to hold her daughter, needs to kiss her and tell her about the last two months. Her room is ready. The house is clean. The fridge is stocked. Soon, she won't have to meet any more strangers. Mommy won't miss any more days, any more weeks.

Frida continues to wait. She watches the clock. The building closes at five. At 4:17, the guard calls her name.

5.

WHEN FRIDA WAS A CHILD, SHE HAD NO SENSE of direction. North meant up, south meant down into the ground, and east and west barely registered. She developed a fraught relationship with roads, only relearned to drive at age thirty-six after two decades of excuses about her lack of spatial coordination and paralyzing fear of lane changes. Not having to drive was one of the reasons she loved New York. She never thought she'd miss it, but on this bus ride, she's been envying the drivers in the next lane: the woman with three screaming children, the texting teenager, the man in the delivery truck. It is late November, the Monday before Thanksgiving, four weeks since she last saw Harriet, twelve weeks since her very bad day, and Frida is about to change her life.

The family court judge said she has to.

The mothers departed before sunrise. They gathered at the family court building at 6:00 a.m., said goodbye to friends and relatives, surrendered their devices. With the exception of a single purse, they were instructed to show up empty-handed. No luggage or clothes or toiletries or makeup or jewelry or books or photos. No weapons or alcohol or cigarettes or drugs. They had their purses searched and bodies patted down. They passed through scanners. One mother had a bag of marijuana in her stomach. Another had swallowed a pouch of pills. Those two didn't make it on the bus.

The mother sitting next to Frida asks to look out the window. "How much fucking longer?"

Frida doesn't know. She's not wearing a watch, but it's light out now. She hasn't been paying attention to the road signs, too preoccupied by her hunger and thirst and chapped skin and runny nose. Her thoughts of Harriet.

The mother next to her is a white woman in her twenties, a weary brunette with skittish blue eyes. The woman's hands are tattooed with roses and spiderwebs. She's been diligently picking off her nail polish, leaving a pile of red flakes on the tray table.

Frida takes her to-do list out of her purse and checks it again. She finds a pen and begins to doodle spirals and hearts. It's her first time sitting still in days. In the past week, she's quit her job and broken her lease and packed her house, moved her and Harriet's belongings into storage, paid her bills, frozen her credit cards and bank accounts, given her jewelry and documents to Will for safe-keeping, lent her car to one of Will's friends, said goodbye to her parents.

Will accompanied her to the check-in this morning, held her until it was time to board the bus. She spent her last night of freedom on his couch, would have kissed him or slept in his bed if she'd been able to stop crying. She didn't want him to undress her, to see that she'd broken out in hives. He wants to visit her, wants to send letters and care packages. But none of those things are allowed.

Last night, he cooked her a fish stew, made her eat bread with butter, a slice of chocolate cake. As if she could regain her lost weight in one night.

The mother next to Frida takes off her down jacket and drapes it over her torso. Frida takes the armrest. Her seatmate begins to snore. Frida looks at the patterns on the woman's hands. It's too early to ask questions or make enemies, but she wants to ask about the woman's child. If she lost custody of one child, or more. She wants to ask the child's age, find out if the child is in foster care or with a relative. She wants to know what the mother did, if she had a very bad day or a bad week or a bad month or a bad life, if what she's accused of is true, or if the true things were twisted and exaggerated until they sounded like a pathology.

She wants to rant about her hearing, tell someone who'll understand about the Honorable Sheila Rogers, who said, "We're going to fix you, Ms. Liu."

She's surprised that she didn't burst a blood vessel, that she didn't faint, that Gust cried harder than she did.

"We're giving you the opportunity to participate in a new rehabilitation program," the judge said. "You'll undergo a year of instruction and training. At a live-in facility. With women like yourself."

The judge said it was her choice.

In order to get Harriet back, Frida must learn to be a better mother. She must demonstrate her capacity for genuine maternal feeling and attachment, hone her maternal instincts, show she can be trusted. Next November, the state will decide if she's made sufficient progress. If she hasn't, her parental rights will be terminated.

"You'll need to pass our tests," the judge said.

Judge Rogers's hair was gray and frizzy, pulled back with a plastic headband. Frida thought the headband was unprofessional, insulting. She remembers the beauty mark next to the judge's nose, her blue silk kerchief. She remembers watching the judge's mouth move.

The judge barely let Renee get a word in. The lawyer for the state said Frida's negligence was astounding. There was the damning police report, the fact that she'd decided her work was more important than her child's safety. Anything could have happened. Someone could have taken Harriet, molested her, killed her.

The men from CPS produced a report on Frida's character. They noted that she had no visitors in sixty days. Soon after the monitoring began, there was a sharp decrease in her nonwork-related emails and texts and phone calls. There were a few times when she seemed to leave her phone at home intentionally.

They expressed concern about her diet, weight loss, and sleep. They called her behavior erratic. The original claim of being overwhelmed was inconsistent with her conduct after the incident, when her house became spotless overnight. Analysis of her expressions suggested feelings of resentment and anger, a stunning lack of remorse, a tendency toward self-pity. Her emotional orientation was directed inward, rather than toward her child and the community.

"I didn't appreciate Ms. Liu's attitude," the social worker said. "With me, she was difficult. Abrasive. With Harriet, she was needy."

The social worker said Frida talked back. Frida couldn't follow directions. Frida kept asking for special treatment. She couldn't set boundaries. See the bite and the nosebleed and Harriet's regression: crawling instead of walking, losing her speech, wanting to be held, climbing into her mother's arms, acting more like a baby than a toddler. See also: the mother putting the child in an ExerSaucer on the day of the incident. Using developmentally inappropriate equipment to trap the child and keep her out of the way.

"I don't think we can completely rule out physical, emotional, or verbal abuse," the social worker said. "How do we know she never hit Harriet?

Maybe she didn't leave bruises. The neighbors told me they heard yelling."

In his report, the court-appointed psychologist found Frida insufficiently contrite. She was hostile toward her co-parents. She was a narcissist with anger-management issues and had poor impulse control. They had her medical records: a diagnosis of clinical depression at age nineteen, over seventeen years on antidepressants. A history of panic attacks and anxiety and insomnia. The mother was unstable. The mother lied about her mental health. What else might she be lying about?

The bus turns onto a bridge. There's traffic. The driver is tailgating. Frida looks down at the frozen river. It rarely gets this cold anymore. Last year, the cherry blossoms bloomed in January.

Next November, Harriet will be thirty-two months old. She'll have all her teeth. She'll be speaking in sentences. Frida will miss her second birthday, her first day of preschool. The judge said there would be weekly video calls, ten minutes every Sunday. "Believe me," the judge said, "I'm a mother. I have two kids and four grandkids. I know exactly what you're going through, Ms. Liu."

Frida leans her head against the window. Susanna

needs to make sure Harriet wears a hat today. She's too casual about dressing Harriet for cold weather. Blood rushes to Frida's face. She wants to know what time Harriet woke up this morning, what Harriet is doing right now, what Harriet ate for breakfast, whether Gust has been delivering messages every day as promised. **Mommy loves you. Mommy misses you. Mommy is so sorry she's not here. Mommy will be back soon.**

×

The mothers disembark. They squint and shiver. They stretch their legs and dab their eyes and blow their noses. More buses pull into the parking lot of a field house. How many mothers will there be? At the family court building, Frida counted eighty-six women. Renee promised her that real criminals—murderers and kidnappers and rapists and molesters and child traffickers and pornographers—are still being sent to prison. The majority of the parents CPS deals with, Renee said, will have been charged with neglect. That's how it's been for years.

"The surveillance might keep you safe," Renee told her. "Everyone will behave themselves, I hope."

Frida has peddled this line of thinking to her concerned parents.

Guards escort the mothers from the parking lot to an imposing walkway lined with bare oak trees. It feels like they're in France. An estate in the countryside. The walk takes ten minutes. Frida hears a guard say they're going to Pierce Hall. Up ahead is a gray stone building with windows edged in white, tall white columns, a gray domed roof.

At the entrance, a trim white woman in a pink lab coat stands before a set of doors, flanked by two guards.

Renee thought they'd be sent somewhere secluded, but the mothers have arrived at an old liberal arts college, one of the many that went bankrupt in the last decade. Frida visited this campus twenty-two years ago when she was touring colleges with her parents. She still remembers the details. Her parents repeated them often. This one had been their first choice for her. Four hundred acres for sixteen hundred students, two forests, a pond. An outdoor amphitheater. An arboretum. Hiking trails. A creek.

The college was founded by Quakers. The bike racks are still here. Recycling bins. Bulletin boards with staples. White Adirondack chairs. Blue emergency lights and call boxes. Frida supposes she should feel relieved. She's been picturing windowless rooms and underground bunkers and solitary confinement and beatings. But they're minutes from a major highway. A campus is a world she knows. The guards don't have guns, and the mothers aren't in handcuffs. They're still part of society.

The mothers are told to form a line. The woman in the pink lab coat asks for each mother's name and offense. Frida stands on her tiptoes and listens.

"Neglect."

"Neglect and abandonment."

"Neglect and verbal abuse."

"Neglect and malnutrition."

"Corporal punishment."

"Physical abuse."

"Abandonment."

"Abandonment."

"Neglect."

"Neglect."

"Neglect."

The line moves quickly. The woman in the pink lab coat has impeccable posture. She looks to be in her early thirties, wears her curly brown hair in a bob. She has freckled skin and small teeth, smiles with too much gum showing, seems oppressively cheerful. Her voice squeaks. She overenunciates in the manner of someone who works with non-native English speakers or small children. Her lab coat is the shade of palest blush pink worn by girl babies. Her name tag reads: MS. GIBSON, ASSISTANT DIRECTOR.

"Please take those off," Ms. Gibson tells Frida. "I need to scan your eye."

Frida removes her glasses. Ms. Gibson holds her by the chin, uses a pen-shaped device to scan her retina.

"Name and offense, please."

"Frida Liu. Neglect."

Ms. Gibson beams. "Welcome, Ms. Liu." She consults her tablet. "Actually, we have you down for neglect and abandonment."

"There must be a mistake."

"Oh, no. That's not possible. We don't make mistakes."

Ms. Gibson hands her a canvas sack, tells her to fill out the label and put her personal clothes inside once she's settled in her dorm room. The sack will be collected later. All the mothers will be living in Kemp House. Everyone will be wearing uniforms after today.

So it begins, Frida thinks. She is a bad mother among other bad mothers. She neglected and abandoned her child. She has no history, no other identity.

She enters Pierce Hall, passes through a carpeted lobby to a foyer with a gold chandelier and a huge circular glass table that must have once held floral arrangements. There are signs for the offices that used to be here: career services and financial aid, study abroad, the bursar's office, admissions.

In the foyer, she senses the cameras before she sees them, feels a faint tickle, like someone is drawing his fingers across the back of her neck. There are cameras mounted on the ceiling. She knows there will be cameras in every hallway, every room, on the outside of every building.

She finds a spot against the wall and counts heads and tries not to stare at faces. She fidgets with her scarf, doesn't know what to do with her hands, can't remember the last time she was among strangers without her phone.

She catalogs the mothers by age and race, as she imagines the state does, as she always does when she suspects she's the only. Gust used to make fun of her for counting how many Asians she saw in one week when they first moved to Philly.

The mothers eye one another warily. Some sit on the stairs leading to the old provost's office. Some clutch their purses and cross their arms and toss or pat their hair and pace in ferocious little circles. Frida feels like she's back in junior high. She surveys the new faces, hoping for another Asian, but none appear. Some Latina mothers have moved to one side of the foyer, some Black mothers to the other. Three middle-aged white women in fine wool coats huddle in the far corner next to the guards.

The trio of white women are getting dirty looks. Frida regrets her skinny jeans and ankle boots, her wool beanie and fur-trimmed parka and hipster glasses. Everything about her reads as bourgeois.

Once all the mothers have been checked in, women in pink lab coats herd them through Pierce and out a side exit. They pass a stone courtyard, a chapel with a bell tower, two- and three-story gray-stone classroom buildings. There are trees everywhere, acres of rolling lawn now bordered by a high fence topped with barbed wire.

The trees are labeled with English and Latin

names. Frida reads the signs. AMERICAN LINDEN. MOSSY-CUP OAK. JAPANESE MAPLE. NORTHERN CA-TALPA. HIMALAYAN PINE. TULIP POPLAR. EASTERN HEMLOCK.

If her parents could see this. If Gust could see this. If only she could tell Will. But she'll never be able to tell anyone. The mothers had to sign non-disclosure agreements. They're not allowed to talk about the school after they leave, can't say anything about the program during the weekly calls. If they do, regardless of the outcome of their cases, their names will be added to a Negligent Parent Registry. Their negligence will be revealed when they try to rent or buy a home, register their child for school, apply for credit cards or loans, apply for jobs or government benefits—the moment they do anything that requires their social security number. The registry will alert a community that a bad parent has moved into the neighborhood. Their names and photos will be posted online. Her very bad day would follow her. If she says anything. If she gets expelled. If she quits.

Last night, Will kept saying that Harriet won't remember, that, yes, this year will be horrible, but one day it will be a story. Like Frida went off to war.

Like she was kidnapped. He thinks Frida should count down the days until her reunion with Harriet rather than tallying lost time.

"She'll still be your baby," he said. "She won't forget you. Gust and Susanna won't let that happen."

They reach a rotunda that houses the college's old theater. The mothers grumble. They're freezing and hungry and tired and need to use the bathroom. Guards escort them to the ladies' room in groups of five.

Frida finds a seat in the second-to-last row of the auditorium. There's a podium at center stage. Behind it, a huge screen. She overhears someone say they'll probably have to wear ankle monitors. Another thinks they'll be identified by number instead of by name. Ms. Gibson seemed to be having way too much fun with the check-in.

Frida has needed to pee for the past hour, but she'll wait. She crosses her legs and starts tapping her foot, driven by the invisible metronome of Harriet memories and thoughts of the judge's patronizing tone, worries about her parents' blood pressure, visions of Susanna with Harriet.

The mother from the bus recognizes Frida and chooses a spot two seats away in the same row. She's cried off her makeup, looks much younger now. Frida shakes the woman's hand. "Sorry, I should have said hello earlier."

"It's okay. This isn't camp."

The woman's name is April. She has a teenager's hunched shoulders and a wide, elastic mouth. They make small talk about the freakish cold weather, how stupid they feel for desperately missing their phones.

Talk turns to their missing children. April is from Manayunk. "They caught me spanking my kid at the grocery store. Some old lady followed me to the parking lot and took down my license plate."

Frida nods. She's not sure what to say. There might be hidden devices recording them. She doesn't know anyone who spanks, wants to believe that spanking is worse than leaving, that she's different, better. But the judge said she'd traumatized Harriet. Harriet's brain, the judge said, may develop differently because of those **two-plus hours** alone.

Ms. Gibson enters the auditorium and climbs up to the stage. She taps the microphone. "Testing," she says. "Testing."

This morning, they meet the program's executive director, Ms. Knight, a towering blonde in a beige skirt suit who's unnaturally tan for November. Ms.

Knight removes her jacket, revealing a body that's been bullied into bone and gristle. She wears her hair long and fluffy, like an aging trophy wife.

The mothers fidget. Ms. Knight's diamond ring catches the light. She shows them charts that demonstrate the link between bad parenting and juvenile delinquency, bad parenting and school shooters, bad parenting and teen pregnancy, bad parenting and terrorism, not to mention high school and college graduation rates, not to mention expected earnings.

"Fix the home," she says, "and fix society."

Training centers are being developed all over the country, Ms. Knight reports, but these two are the first to be operational. This one for mothers, another for fathers across the river. Governor Warren won the first bid. There will be periods next year when the parents will train together. They're still working out the details for co-ed lessons.

"You're the lucky ones," she says. Only a few months ago, they would have been sent to parenting classes. They would have studied an outdated manual. But what good is learning about parenting in the abstract? Bad parents must be transformed from the inside out. The right instincts, the right feelings, the ability to make split-second, safe, nurturing, loving decisions.

"Now, repeat after me: **I am a bad mother, but I am learning to be good**."

A slide appears with the phrase in all caps. Pale pink letters on a black background. Frida sinks lower in her seat. April mimes shooting herself in the head.

Ms. Knight cups a hand to her ear. "I can't hear you, ladies. Let me hear you say it. It's important that we're all on the same page." She speaks slowly, enunciating each word. "**I am a bad mother, but I am learning to be good**."

Frida looks to see if others are playing along. This whole year may depend on playing along. Renee said to take a micro rather than macro approach. One day at a time, one week at a time. Closer and closer to Harriet.

Someone behind them says this must be a joke. She calls Ms. Knight "Dictator Barbie."

Ms. Knight tells them to chant louder. Frida cringes, but eventually, she too mouths the words.

Finally satisfied, Ms. Knight explains the rules of conduct. "You're expected to treat the state's property with care. You'll have to pay for any damaged equipment. Your rooms will be kept clean. You'll treat your roommates, classmates, and one another with the utmost respect and consideration. With empathy. Empathy is one of the cornerstones of our program."

She continues. "Drug or alcohol possession, consumption, or smoking will lead to automatic expulsion, and thus, the termination of your parental rights. There will be weekly check-ins with a counselor, who'll monitor your progress and help you process your feelings. We're all here for you, ladies. Drug and alcohol support groups will meet each evening after dinner. You'll have some grooming privileges, as well. We know you still need to feel like yourselves here."

Of course, Ms. Knight says, there will be no fighting, stealing, or emotional manipulation. "Now I realize we women can be competitive. There are a thousand little mental games we can play. But you should want your fellow mothers to succeed." They should think of the school as a sisterhood, get invested in each other.

"I don't want to hear about any bullying or rumor-mongering. If you spot one of your sisters engaged in an act of self-harm, you'll report her immediately. We have mental health professionals available to you twenty-four-seven. We have a hotline. There's a phone on each floor of Kemp House. You may find yourself discouraged. But you can't stay in that hopeless place. Remember, there's a light at the end of the tunnel, and that light is your child."

They'll train with a cohort of mothers based on their child's gender and age. It wouldn't do to have mothers of teenagers training with mothers of infants. Class sizes will be kept small, for the time being. Each mother will be assigned to a cohort based on the age of her youngest child. Mothers of girls and mothers of boys will train in different buildings. "Girls and boys have such different needs," Ms. Knight says. Mothers of both will report for extra training three evenings a week and every other weekend. Mothers who have multiple children, as well as addiction issues, will be extremely busy.

The work will be arduous, but the mothers must resist any thoughts of quitting. The state is investing in them. The fence, Ms. Knight notes, is electrified.

×

The size of the campus requires the mothers to be herded between buildings. Shepherded, Frida thinks. On the walk to the dining hall, she overhears someone talking about New Zealand. So much open space makes them think of New Zealand. Isn't that where all the rich people are buying land for the end of the world?

"My kid would love this place," the woman says wistfully.

The dining hall could hold a thousand. As it is, the mothers are able to spread out across the vast room. Some sit alone. Others cluster four or five to a table. The women in pink lab coats pass through the aisles, observing and taking notes on their devices.

The room has high ceilings and stained glass windows and outlines on the walls where portraits of college presidents once hung. The tables, scored with names and numbers and crosshatches, are sticky. Frida is careful not to let her elbows touch the wood. Her mind is filled with frivolous thoughts. She feels stupid for dwelling on dirt or communal showers, for craving her own face cream.

The mothers speak softly. Conversation proceeds in fits and starts, as if they're trying to speak a foreign language. There are long pauses, hesitations, retractions. They grow quiet and gaze off into the distance. Their eyes turn moist, the longing of these women enough to power a small town.

The mothers at Frida's table take turns introducing themselves. Some are from North Philly, some from West Philly, some from Brewerytown and Northern Liberties and Grays Ferry. Alice is originally from Trinidad. Her five-year-old daughter, Clarissa, began kindergarten without the required vaccinations. Another woman tested positive for marijuana. Another let her two-year-old son play in their backyard alone. A mom with purple streaks in her hair had three children removed because of inadequate child-proofing in her apartment. She lost custody of her one-year-old twin boys and five-year-old daughter. A woman named Melissa says her six-year-old son, Ramon, wandered out of their apartment while she was asleep, made it out of the building and walked fifteen minutes, was found at a bus stop. They all look so young. A mother named Carolyn, who looks closer to Frida's age, says her three-year-old daughter was removed after she posted a video of one of her tantrums on Facebook.

"I'm a stay-at-home mom," Carolyn says. "Of course I post stuff about my kid. That's my only adult contact. One of the other moms at her preschool saw my post and reported me. They went through everything I ever posted about her.

They said I complained about her too much on Twitter."

Frida pushes clumps of macaroni around her plate. If parents are being policed on social media, this campus will be at full capacity by next year. She pokes at a soggy piece of broccoli. She's not ready for institutional food or group sharing.

When it's her turn, she says, "Frida. Philly by way of Brooklyn by way of Chicago. Neglect and abandonment. I left her. Briefly. My daughter, Harriet. She's twenty months now. I left her for two and a half hours. I had a bad day."

The only white woman at the table touches Frida's arm. "No need to get defensive. We're not judging you."

Frida pulls her arm away.

"Helen," the white woman says. "Chestnut Hill by way of Idaho. Emotional abuse. Of my seventeen-year-old. Alexander. His therapist reported me for coddling. Apparently, coddling is a subset of emotional abuse."

Carolyn asks how one coddles a teenage boy. "Isn't he bigger than you?"

"I cut up his food for him," Helen admits.

Disapproving glances ricochet around the table.

"I zipped up his jackets. I liked tying his shoes for him. It was our special thing. I made him go over all his homework with me. Sometimes, I combed his hair. I helped him shave."

"Your husband was okay with that?" Carolyn asks.

"There's no husband. I thought Alexander liked our routines. But he told his therapist that I made him feel like a weirdo. He thought if he brought friends over, I'd try to spoon-feed him in front of them. He told his therapist that I was obsessed with him. He said he wanted to run away. I was planning to relocate to wherever he went to college. I still might."

Carolyn and the mother next to her snicker viciously. Frida averts her eyes.

After lunch, they receive their room assignments. Frida is paired with Helen, the coddler. Kemp House is on the other side of campus. Ms. Knight said they're being housed in a single building to make things easier for the cleaning staff. The other dorms are being prepared for future use.

Helen tries to chat with Frida on the way over. She complains about the mothers mocking her. "Every parent is different," Helen says. "Every child is different."

"I'm sure you had your reasons for babying him." Frida doesn't like how Helen is walking so close. She doesn't like Helen's aggressive eye contact. Helen seems like one of those friendship vampires who'll take and take if given the slightest opportunity. She can imagine Helen kissing her son on the mouth, holding hands with him, watching him shower.

She longs to be alone, to chew her fingers until they bleed, to call her parents and Will. In their report, the men from CPS noted her lack of friends. Had they asked, she would have explained that she lost touch with her college girlfriends years ago. Most had babies around thirty and disappeared from her life. She grew tired of trying to get them on the phone, weekend visits canceled at the last minute, conversations that were always interrupted. Baby comes first, they said. She swore it wouldn't be like that for her.

There's a pink satin ribbon wrapped around the light pole at the entrance to Kemp. The **K** in the sign has oxidized. The building is more civilized than Frida anticipated, made of the same shimmering gray stone as the rest of the campus. There are hydrangea bushes beneath the first-floor windows, the flowers now brittle and brown, a blemish on the school's otherwise immaculate landscaping. There's a fruit basket on a table inside the foyer, one pear remaining. Frida and Helen's room is on the third floor, overlooking a field. Frida tests the windows, relieved that they open. They each have a wooden desk and chair, a reading light, a chest with two sets of towels and two plaid wool blankets. The cupboard contains four navy blue cotton jumpsuits, two for each of them. The forms Frida filled out had asked for her dress size and shoe size, and though they've given her a pair of black boots in size seven, the jumpsuits are one-size-fits-all. There are plastic-wrapped packets of white bras and underwear, five bras and ten panties; three white cotton tank tops and two long-sleeve thermal shirts; seven pairs of socks; a kit containing a toothbrush, toothpaste, shower gel, lotion, and a comb.

Helen laughs as she opens her packet of government-issued underwear, happily noting that the garments seem to be new and don't have any stains.

Frida stuffs her coat and shoes into the canvas sack and fills out the tag. She's unreasonably attached to her things, would have liked to bring the wood Buddha from her dresser, her grandmother's gold bracelet, her wedding rings. She doesn't know how she'll fall asleep tonight if she can't look at Harriet's picture.

She turns her back to Helen and changes into a jumpsuit. She rolls up each pant leg three times. There are no mirrors. She must resemble a sack of potatoes with a head. In the cupboard, there's a scratchy gray wool cardigan that hangs to her knees, an oversize navy blue parka, a navy blue wool cap, and a gray acrylic scarf.

Please, she thinks, **let me not catch anything. Let there be no bugs, no lice, no airborne diseases**. She hopes they can wash their own underwear. She hopes they can bathe daily. Someone needs to give them dental floss and tweezers, razors and nail clippers.

There's a camera above the doorway, cameras trained on each bed. At least they have doors. At least there are no bars on the windows. At least they have blankets.

"Focus on the positives," Will said. She has a family. She is loved. She is alive. She knows where her child is living.

×

The mothers are free to roam the campus until dinnertime. Ms. Knight encouraged quiet reflection as well as contemplating the sky. The dinner bell will ring at six. A woman in a pink lab coat comes by to collect their personal items. Frida asks to take a last look at her things, sticks her hand back inside the sack and touches her scarf, likely the last soft thing she'll touch until next November.

"Can I walk with you?" Helen asks. "I'm feeling antsy."

"I'm sure we'll get plenty of quality time later." Frida runs downstairs before Helen can pressure her, taking off at a brisk pace.

Some mothers are walking together. A few are jogging. Others, like Frida, are guarding these last precious hours alone.

Frida has to slow down. The boots hit her instep at the wrong angle. They're too heavy. She keeps tripping on the hem of her jumpsuit, has to hold up the pant legs as she walks. The hat is too big; the parka is too big. The wind is picking up, and the jumpsuit is a wind tunnel. She may never be warm here. She needs another sweater, another undershirt, long underwear. She sticks her hands deep in her pockets, cursing the school for not providing any gloves.

What is the ratio of mothers to guards, mothers to women in pink lab coats? There are too many people working here. There's too much land. How many mothers are expected in the next round? How many more children will be taken?

She heads toward a stand of pine trees. Gust and Susanna and Harriet leave for Santa Cruz in the morning. Susanna's followers will see Harriet on the plane, Harriet on Gust's shoulders walking in the California redwoods, Harriet at Thanksgiving dinner, Harriet with her grandparents on the beach. Frida doesn't want to know what Gust's parents are saying about her, what they might say in front of Harriet, what they'll tell the rest of the family. The state could have chosen a less delicate time of year, though she supposes that every day is a delicate one for women who've lost their children.

She tears off a handful of pine needles and rubs them between her fingers. She told Will to ask Gust to take extra pictures of Harriet, film extra videos. She needs a record of every single day. So do her parents.

Renee tried to get her parents some phone privileges, but the judge thought that would be too confusing. Seeing the Lius would remind Harriet of Frida, and those reminders would interfere with her recovery.

Frida flops down on one of the Adirondack chairs. Her father loves visiting campuses. Even during trips to Paris and Bologna, they made time to tour at least one university in each city. When they visited this campus, her parents mused about teaching at this kind of college, living in a faculty house. It was a dream world, they said.

She needs to have Gust give them some updates. They'll be worried sick otherwise. Someone needs to make sure they're keeping up with their doctor's appointments and eating enough protein. He needs to remind her mother to take her blood pressure medicine and drink enough water. He needs to remind her father to wear sunscreen.

"Did you feel loved as a child?" the psychologist asked. She feels guilty for telling that man anything about them. She shouldn't have fought with them when they visited in July, shouldn't have scolded her father for not fastening Harriet's diaper tightly enough, shouldn't have yelled at her mother for breaking the cup holder on Harriet's stroller.

Frida's hands are frozen. She has a sore throat. It's already dark. From far away, the dinner bell rings.

Mothers emerge from the stone courtyard, the lacrosse field, the chapel. Some have ventured too far. They migrate toward the dining hall.

By the time Frida reaches the front of the dinner line, there isn't enough food left. She receives a tiny medallion of pork and three carrots.

Helen waves to her. She's found the trio of middle-aged white women. "This is my roommate, Frida," Helen says. "She's here for neglect and abandonment."

"Hi, Frida, Hi, Frida," the mothers say in unison.

×

The mothers shower furtively. As they wait their turn, they pass information in whispers. The numbers. Approximately two hundred women. Supposedly, if they get in trouble, they'll be sent to "talk circle." Every trip to talk circle will be added to their files.

On Frida's floor, there are twenty-six women and four shower stalls. Frida tries to feel grateful for her flip-flops, for her toiletries and clean towel and flannel pajamas. There are no flip-flops or pajamas in prison.

The hot water runs out during her turn. She

quickly rinses off, dries herself, and dresses, runs her hair under the hand dryers. The next mother screams. Frida leaves before anyone can blame her.

Helen returns to the room in just her towel. She begins applying lotion to every inch of her body, using up half the small bottle. Her breasts resemble deflated tube socks. Her thighs and belly have deep pockets of cellulite.

She catches Frida looking at her breasts and smiles. "Don't be embarrassed. We're all the same animal underneath."

"Sorry," Frida says. Helen seems like someone who's spent a lifetime feeling pleased with herself. Her body is soft and ruined and gleaming. She's still topless when Ms. Gibson knocks on the door.

"Ladies, thirty minutes until lights-out."

Frida climbs under the covers. At least the blankets are thick, at least she can make herself small and pull the blankets around her so that only her face is showing. She's hungry, and she thinks that if she makes herself warm and small, perhaps the hunger will dissipate. What little she knows about the lives of saints comes back to her now and she thinks, this year, she might become holy.

Helen beats on her pillows. "You still awake?"

"I'm trying to sleep."

"Aren't you curious what the dads are doing? I heard they don't have uniforms. They can wear their regular clothes." Helen thinks the fathers probably have fewer guards. Their minders probably don't wear lab coats. If their minders are female, the lab coats would be too sexually suggestive.

"They probably have better food," she says. "I bet they're allowed to keep their kids' pictures. Or have visitors. They probably don't have cameras."

"Everyone has cameras, Helen. Our phones have cameras. Our phones listen to us. Someone might be listening to us right now."

"Maybe they don't need cameras if there are only five dads."

"There are more than five. There have to be more."

"Doubt it," Helen says. "What about us? Who do you think will be the first to go?"

"Go like pass?"

"No, drop out."

Frida rolls over and stares at the wall. She's been wondering the same thing. Her money is on one of the middle-aged white ladies. Someone is probably placing bets on her. She says that everyone should get their kid back.

"Maybe some of them shouldn't."

"Helen, don't say that. Never say that again. I'd never wish this on anyone. You think anyone deserves to end up here? Shit. I'm sorry. I'm not complaining. Do not tell anyone I said that."

6.

THE MOTHERS ANNOUNCE THEMSELVES WITH A rustle of fabric. The jumpsuits are huge and sexless and infantilizing, inspiring a chorus of complaints on the way to breakfast. The mothers want better uniforms, more comfortable boots. They want softer towels, extra lotion, different roommates, no roommates, longer showers, curtains on the windows, locks on the doors. They want their children. They want to go home.

Floodlights switch on as they pass each building. Frida keeps her thoughts to herself. She shuffles into the dining hall, wondering if this is what it's like to land on a new planet. When the bell rang this morning, she had no idea where she was.

She fills her tray with a bowl of oatmeal, two

pieces of toast, a cup of coffee, a cup of milk, a Granny Smith apple. The food seems cleaner and fresher than it did last night. This will be her first real breakfast in ages. She'll make herself finish everything. Hopefully, the women in pink lab coats will notice. Perhaps if she'd eaten normally this fall. Cooked more. Kept her fridge stocked. It would have been easy to present a better picture. She pauses with her tray. To no one's surprise, the mothers have self-segregated. There are tables of Black mothers, tables of Latina mothers, white mothers in twos and threes, a few lone wolves.

Seeing Frida approaching an empty table, Ms. Gibson steers her toward a group of young Black mothers. "Mealtimes," she says, "should be used for community building."

The mothers look like cool girls. Several are remarkably attractive. They don't look as haggard and defeated as some of the older women. As Frida. Some cast withering glances in her direction. One whispers behind her hand.

Frida's cheeks burn. She sits and empties packets of sugar into her oatmeal. The mother across the table, a wiry young woman with a nearly shaved head, wide-set eyes, and an inquisitive manner, comes to

Frida's rescue. She's a dead ringer for early-career Lauryn Hill, though Frida doesn't mention the resemblance. She's probably too young to get it.

"Lucretia, endangerment."

"Frida, neglect and abandonment." They shake hands.

"Hi, Frida," the mothers mumble without looking up.

"Frida, like Frida Kahlo?" Lucretia asks. "She's one of my favorite painters. I love her style. I dressed as her for Halloween a few times."

"My mom picked it out of a baby-name book. It was either going to be Frida or Iris."

"You're not an Iris. I mean that as a compliment. I'm going to call you Frida Kahlo, okay? You can call me Lu."

Lucretia has an easy laugh that seems like it belongs to a bigger woman. She wears her uniform with the collar popped, touches the nape of her neck as she talks. She tells Frida that she cut off her twists just before coming here, figured it would be easier but feels naked with her hair so short. Short hair without earrings isn't cute.

"What did you do?" Frida asks.

"To my kid?"

"For work. Before this."

Lucretia's smile becomes strained. "I taught second grade. In Germantown."

"I'm sorry." Frida wants to ask if Lucretia will return to teaching next year, but the table has resumed gossiping. About the guards and the women in pink lab coats. Their roommates. How they miss their parents and sisters and boyfriends. The phone calls they wish they could make to their children. The stupid fancy plants around the campus.

If the school has money for landscaping, they should turn up the heat. They should let the mothers wear their contacts. They should be able to room by themselves.

Someone asks who's the worst of the worst, the baddest bitch. Lucretia points out a chubby, baby-faced Latina mother sitting alone near the exit. Linda. From Kensington. A friend of a friend of Lucretia's cousin used to fuck her. Lady stuffed her six kids into a hole in the floor. Found some secret passage to her building's basement. Their lungs got fucked up from black mold. They got bitten by rats.

"You should have seen them walking down the street," Lucretia says. Her kids are all different shades of brown. Different dads. Total freak show.

"I feel sorry for them," Lucretia says. The mothers stare and whisper. Linda is round all over and prettier than her transgressions would suggest. She has a high, clear forehead, a proud set to her shoulders, wears her hair scraped back into a tight bun, her eyebrows plucked into exaggerated arches.

"Used to be hot," Lucretia says. "That's how she got so many kids."

They gossip uncharitably about Linda's body, making crude circles with their hands. She must be like taffy down there. Like a water bed. Imagine her stretch marks. Her stripes.

Frida tears at her toast, feeling like a spy, an astronaut, an anthropologist, an intruder. Anything she could say now would be wrong. Tone-deaf. Offensive. She's never met anyone with six children from six different fathers, or anyone who'd put their kids in a hole. Some of her nastiest fights with Gust and Susanna were about brands of water filters.

×

Classroom assignments have been posted to a bulletin board outside the dining hall. Mothers push and jostle. Women in pink lab coats distribute campus maps. Buildings for training mothers of daughters are marked with pale pink dots; buildings for training mothers of sons are marked with baby blue. The majority of mothers have children under the age of five. There are four cohorts of mothers in the daughters, twelve to twenty-four months, category.

Frida runs her finger down the list. Liu. Morris Hall, Room 2D. Setting off alone, she soon encounters baddest bitch Linda, who follows her out of the building and shouts hello until she turns.

"You're Liu, right? Nice glasses."

"Thanks." They've been assigned to the same cohort. Frida forces a smile. They proceed in the direction of Morris, up Chapin Walk, noted on the map as the allée. They pass the bell tower and the stone courtyard.

Linda wants to know what got said about her at breakfast. "I saw you all looking."

"I don't know what you're talking about."

"Did that girl Lucretia say my kids got sick or something?"

Frida walks faster. Linda says Lucretia doesn't know what she's talking about. It wasn't every night. Only when her kids were fighting and stealing food from the pantry. She had to keep the pantry padlocked because they'd finish all the groceries in a day. It was her super who called CPS. He'd been trying to get rid of her for years. Her kids are now in six different foster homes.

"You don't have to justify anything to me."

"What'd they get you for?"

Frida doesn't answer. She waits out the awkward silence. Linda says Lucretia is a snob, that Lucretia thinks she's hot shit. She knows 'cause they're friends on Facebook.

They pass the music-and-dance library, the art gallery. Both buildings stand empty.

Frida tries to walk ahead, but Linda keeps pace.

Morris Hall is an imposing five-story stone building on the western edge of campus, one of the only classroom buildings above three stories. It's been remodeled with a set of modern glass doors that are nearly impossible to push open. The front of the building faces a quad, the back faces the woods. Behind the building, the electrified fence is visible.

Mothers dawdle on the steps leading from the foyer to the second floor but move aside for Linda, giving Frida quizzical, amused glances. Frida hangs back. She'd like to clarify that she's not Linda's bitch, that this isn't a women's prison. Let no one think that she's been made a bitch already.

They're in the old biology building. Classroom 2D, a former lab, still smells of formaldehyde, triggering memories of frogs and fetal pigs. There's a frosted-glass door marked EQUIPMENT, a dry-erase board, a teacher's desk, a clock, and wall-mounted cupboards, but no chairs or other furniture. The mothers deposit their coats in the back corner. They look up at the clock. There's a camera above the door, another above the dry-erase board. Four high, arched windows overlook the woods. Sunlight warms the room, warms the mothers, who've been told to sit cross-legged on the floor.

"Like preschool," Linda says, staying close to Frida.

The mothers form a circle. Their instructors are Ms. Russo and Ms. Khoury, both around Frida's age, both wearing pink lab coats over dark sweaters and tailored trousers and nurse's clogs. Ms. Russo, the taller of the two, is a plump, plummy-voiced white woman with a brunette pixie cut who talks with her hands. Ms. Khoury is petite and bony and Middle Eastern–looking, with sharp cheekbones and wavy salt-and-pepper shoulder-length hair, a lilting accent, and the bearing of an Eastern bloc ballet master.

They ask the mothers to introduce themselves by stating their names and offenses and a few pertinent details about how they harmed their children. There are five women, including Frida and Linda. Frida is pleased to see Lucretia, the friendly mom from breakfast. Lucretia goes first, tells the group that her daughter broke her arm after falling off a slide. Frida nods warmly. Lucretia and Linda exchange a hostile glance.

A white teenager, Meryl, is here for bruises on her daughter's arms and drug possession. A young white woman named Beth lost custody after she checked herself into the psych ward. Since she was a danger to herself, she couldn't be trusted with her daughter. Lucretia and Meryl were reported to CPS by ER doctors. Beth was reported by her ex-boyfriend.

At first glance, Frida thinks Meryl and Beth look alike, but there's no actual resemblance, only a similar petrified expression. Both girls have dark hair. Meryl's is wavy and dyed black, a blue-black that doesn't occur in nature and doesn't match her pale eyebrows. Beth's hair is straight and glossy, chestnut brown. Meryl seems like she shouldn't be messed with. Beth has the glittering haunted air of Will's broken birds, her black Irish coloring well-suited to blushing and tears.

Frida and Linda are the class elders, both here for neglect and abandonment. As Frida tells them about her very bad day, she notices Linda watching her, gloating.

Ms. Khoury thanks them for sharing. Ms. Russo excuses herself and slips inside the equipment room. There's movement behind the frosted glass, the sound of shuffling feet, peals of laughter, the high-pitched murmur of small children.

The mothers hold their breath and listen, hoping for the impossible. Lucretia pulls her knees to her chest and whispers, "Brynn? Are you in there?"

Frida looks away. These must be recordings designed to taunt them into submission, to keep them desperate and drooling during these months when they have no child to hold. The judge would never allow it. Gust would never allow it. Harriet is on the way to the airport. Frida doesn't want Harriet anywhere near this place or these people, but if, somehow, a fissure has opened in time and space and delivered her baby, she'll do anything they ask.

If she could hold Harriet right now. Holding Harriet for ten minutes could last her the long winter.

When Ms. Russo opens the equipment room door, she's trailed by five toddler girls of different races. There's one Black girl, one white girl, one Latina. Two of the girls are mixed: one looks to be half Black and half white; the other looks Eurasian. The girls are mirror images of the mothers, dressed in navy blue jumpsuits and sneakers.

The circle constricts. They sit close enough to touch shoulders, becoming, for a moment, one mother, a hydra of disappointed faces.

Harriet felt so close. Frida was imagining what she'd say, how she'd clutch the back of Harriet's head and stroke the downy hairs at the nape of her neck. Though the girls are the right age and the right size and the little half-Asian girl is looking right at her, she's not Harriet. Frida could punch herself in the face for hoping.

The instructors herd the girls into a single row at the front of the classroom. The children giggle and wave.

"Settle down," Ms. Russo says, guiding one of the wayward toddlers back in line. "Class, we want to start with a little surprise we prepared for you."

Ms. Khoury raises her arms. "On the count of three. Ready? One . . . two . . . three!"

"Hello, Mommy!" the children shout. "Welcome!"

×

The building fills with sound. Voices travel through the air vents. In other classrooms, there are older children, adolescents and teenagers. Except for the guards, all the voices are female.

Throughout the building, mothers are crying. There's a commotion in the hallway, a mother shouting at a guard, another being ordered back to her classroom, mothers arguing with instructors.

Frida's classmates shout questions. Beth demands to speak to Ms. Knight, the executive director. Lucretia wants to know where the children came from. Where are their parents?

"Ladies, be patient," Ms. Khoury says. She asks them to lower their voices, to please raise their hands and not speak unless called upon. "You're scaring the girls."

The instructors sort the mothers and toddlers into pairs, seeming to match them by the skin tone and ethnicity of their real children. Meryl's child must be biracial. The half-Asian girl belongs to Frida.

"You can hug her," Ms. Khoury says. "Go on. Give her a hug. She's been looking forward to meeting you."

"She has?" Frida holds the girl at arm's length. The girl could be half Chinese or Japanese or Korean. Like Harriet, it's impossible to tell. The girl steps closer. Her eyes and brows are perfectly symmetrical. There are no scratches on her skin, no birthmarks. She doesn't have a toddler's usual encrusted nostrils. Her eyes look more Asian than Harriet's. The rest of her face, her bone structure, is more Caucasian. Harriet's features are soft, her overall air is velvety. This girl has a freckled heart-shaped face and golden skin and narrow almond eyes, silky light brown hair, straighter and lighter than Harriet's, high cheekbones and a pointy chin. She's skinnier than Harriet, with sleek hands and long fingers.

She reminds Frida of a little wolf, a little fox. It's easy to imagine what she'll look like as a teenager, as an adult woman.

Since Harriet was a newborn, people have complimented her chubby cheeks. Her grandparents call Harriet **xiao long bao**, little soup dumpling. Growing up, Frida hated her own round face, but she takes such pride in her daughter's plumpness. She needs to remind Gust to feed Harriet enough fats, to have her drink cow's milk, not almond milk or soy milk or oat milk. If she returns to find Harriet as skinny as this girl, they'll never hear the end of it.

"What's your name?"

The girl stares at Frida blankly.

"Okay, you don't want to tell me. You don't have to. I'm Frida. Nice to meet you."

"Hi," the girl says, drawing out the syllable.

The girl drops to her hands and knees. She begins to inspect Frida's legs. She unrolls the hem of Frida's jumpsuit and runs her finger along the yellow stitching. If only Harriet had behaved this calmly at the visits. Frida touches the girl's cheek. Her skin feels strange. Waxy. Too perfect. Her lips are dry, whereas Harriet's are always wet. She sniffs the top of the girl's head, thinking it will smell oily like Harriet's, but her scent is rubbery, like the inside of a new car.

The instructors call them to attention. Ms. Russo asks for a volunteer. She selects Lucretia's toddler, who giggles as she's lifted onto the instructor's desk. Ms. Russo begins unbuttoning the girl's uniform.

"What are you doing?" Lucretia shouts. She looks alarmed as Ms. Russo pulls off the girl's undershirt.

Ms. Russo turns the girl around. The mothers

gasp. There's a blue plastic knob in the small of the girl's back. As Ms. Russo wriggles the girl's arms, there's a **glug-glug** of thick liquids shifting. She presses a finger into the girl's cheek, causing the left side of her face to droop. The girl shakes her head and returns to normal.

The mothers begin edging away from their assigned toddlers. Frida is thinking of outer space again, the part where astronauts leave the spaceship, where they die from lack of oxygen. She cycles through a list of improbable scenarios, certain that she's hallucinating. This might be the latest blip in an extended fever dream fueled by months of surveillance and too little sleep and separation from her daughter.

Once unscrewed, the knob reveals a hole of about four inches in diameter. Digging inside the hole with a spoon, Ms. Russo ladles out an electric-blue liquid that resembles antifreeze.

"Coolant," she says. "To prevent the girls from overheating."

Frida pinches her hands. Lucretia looks unwell. Ms. Russo replaces the blue liquid, dresses the girl, and returns her to a stricken Lucretia.

"Aren't they amazing?" These children—dolls,

Ms. Russo calls them—represent the latest advances in robotics and artificial intelligence. They can move and speak and smell and feel like real children. They can hear. They can think. They are sentient beings with age-appropriate brain development, memory, and knowledge. In terms of size and abilities, they resemble a child of about eighteen to twenty months.

Frida feels as if she's back in the mint-green room. She's floating outside her body and full of stupid questions.

"When your doll cries," Ms. Russo says, "those are real tears. She's expressing real pain, real need. Her emotions are not preprogrammed or random or designed to trick you."

The mothers must keep an eye on the blue liquid. If the liquid coagulates, the doll's face and body will dimple like cellulite, and the mothers will have to scrape out the blue mess. The liquid must be changed monthly. In addition to cooling properties, it helps their silicone skin remain supple and lifelike, gives their bodies the right texture and weight.

The doll pats Frida's face. She pulls Frida closer until Frida can feel the doll's hot breath on her cheek.

Her touch is so different from Harriet's, a blind groping. But the doll is warm and real, breathing, sighing. She has lifelines and fingerprints. Fingernails. Eyelashes. A full set of teeth. Saliva. How did they make saliva?

×

In the past, the instructors say, children were removed, then handed back to parents whose behavior hadn't been corrected. Mistakes were made. Children suffered. Some died. Here, the mothers' progress will be measured in a controlled environment. With this simulation model, their real children will be protected from further harm.

There's a camera inside each doll. "You can see her, and she can see you," Ms. Russo explains.

In addition to their role as proxy children, the dolls will collect data. They'll gauge the mothers' love. The mothers' heart rates will be monitored to judge anger. Their blinking patterns and expressions will be monitored to detect stress, fear, ingratitude, deception, boredom, ambivalence, and a host of other feelings, including whether her happiness mirrors her doll's. The doll will record where the mother's hands are placed, will detect tension in her body, her temperature and posture, how often she makes eye contact, the quality and authenticity of her emotions.

There will be nine units of study, each composed of a set of lessons. The first, Fundamentals of Care and Nurture, will cover basic, intermediate, and advanced bonding, as well as feeding and health. Each unit will conclude with an evaluation day, and scores from those days will determine the mothers' success.

It is assumed that, having kept their daughters alive this long, basic CPR training isn't necessary, but there will be refreshers. Future units will include Fundamentals of Play, Dangers Inside and Outside the Home, the Moral Universe. The instructors write these units on the board, telling the mothers not to think too far ahead. They're not providing the complete curriculum because the mothers must stay present, must put their faith in the program, trust that each unit will build on the one that came before, that with practice, they'll rise to meet the school's standards.

×

They begin the bonding process by naming the dolls. "With names come attachment," Ms. Russo says. "And with attachment comes love."

Frida smiles with her mouth, smiles with her eyes, makes her voice pleasant. She wipes her forehead, didn't realize she was sweating. When the sun hits the doll's face, she can see a metallic chip in each of the doll's pupils.

The doll plays with the Velcro tabs on her sneakers. They only have ten minutes to choose a name, not enough time to assess the doll's personality, if she has one, to find a name that suits her.

When she was pregnant, Frida kept a list of names in her desk drawer. Old-fashioned names. French names. She wanted Harriet to have a name she could grow into, might have named her after Marguerite Duras, her favorite author. She discussed these names with Gust on only one occasion, claimed that she wasn't picky, let him decide. She'd always envied her parents for choosing their own names when they came here. Davis and Lillian. She would have liked to be a Simone. A Juliana. Something elegant and musical.

"I'll call you Emmanuelle," she says, thinking of that film with Emmanuelle Riva where she played a woman who'd suffered a stroke.

As they practice saying her new name, the doll stammers and drops consonants. Frida has chosen the most complicated name in the class.

"Emannnnn," the doll trills. "Emmaaa-nana."

Frida supplies the rest.

The instructors say, "How creative."

And what would Frida like to be called? Mother, Mom, Mama, or Mommy?

"She can call me Mommy. Isn't that right? I'm your mommy."

×

The lunch bell rings at noon. The instructors freeze the dolls in place by entering a code on their tablets. Emmanuelle's cheek becomes cold to the touch and completely rigid. Meryl taps on her doll's head, squeezes her shoulders, pulls her ears. Her doll's eyes are still moving.

"What the fuck?" she shouts. In her head, Frida names the girl "Teen Mom." She seems too feisty to be a Meryl.

Teen Mom pokes her doll's forehead. She receives a warning for language and an unmotherly touch.

Emmanuelle's eyes dart wildly. She has the

trapped, terrified expression that Harriet would get whenever she had to have her nose suctioned.

Frida apologizes for leaving, promises to come back soon. She gazes intently at Emmanuelle, hoping to register her concern, which is genuine, as much as she'd feel for a dog tied to a post while its owner eats. Emmanuelle can be her pet child, her pet human. Hurrying to join the other women, she looks back at the trapped dolls, unnerved by the five pairs of frightened eyes.

Fear keeps the mothers quiet, keeps them moving. Now bonded by calamity, they no longer self-segregate. The cohorts sit together in the dining hall. Frida and Lucretia hug.

The mothers are sick of surprises. First the uniforms and the women in pink lab coats and Ms. Knight and the guards and the electrified fence and now this. The cohorts trade rumors about where the money might have come from, where the dolls came from.

"They must have come from the military," someone guesses.

Another mom suggests it was Google. "Everything creepy comes from Google."

Beth says, "It could have been a mad scientist."

THE SCHOOL FOR GOOD MOTHERS

Frida wonders if Beth met any in the psych ward.

Lucretia, still shaken from seeing her doll pucker, thinks it was an evil inventor. "Someone in South Korea. Or Japan. Or China." She looks over at Frida. "Sorry, no offense."

"What if we get electrocuted?" Beth asks. "I am seriously not good with technical stuff."

Lucretia worries the dolls will turn violent. She used to be a sci-fi nerd. She knows how these stories go. In movies, robots always rebel, dolls always turn out to be ax murderers.

"This isn't a movie," Linda snaps.

"It's not like you know any better."

Frida, Beth, and Teen Mom eat quickly while Lucretia and Linda bicker. Frida wants to know if the blue liquid is toxic, if it can burn them or blind them, if inhaling it will increase their risk of developing certain cancers. If Gust and Susanna knew about the blue liquid, they'd never allow her near Harriet again.

Yesterday's sadness gives way to anger. The mothers' complaining grows impassioned.

Lucretia shreds her napkin. "I would bet money the dads don't have to do this." They probably have workbooks and multiple-choice quizzes. All they have to do is show up. Isn't that always how it goes? They definitely don't have to deal with any robot babies or blue goo.

"Tell me they're going to make some dude stick a spoon in a kid's cavity," Lucretia says.

"Thanks for putting that image in my head," Beth mutters.

The women in pink lab coats tell them to lower their voices. Frida suggests they go outside. They turn in their trays and approach the dining hall guard. It's certainly starting to feel like prison. What she imagines of prison. Permission to leave the room. Permission to eat. Permission to use the bathroom. Activities monitored and preordained. Someone else deciding how her time will be spent and in what room and with what people.

Outside, near the bike racks, they run into a distraught Black mother who's sobbing on one of the benches. Today is her daughter's fourth birthday. They huddle around her and shield her from the cameras. They link arms. The mother is inconsolable. She sputters and wipes her wet face on her sleeve. Linda rubs her back. Lucretia hands her a half-torn napkin. Then it starts. Someone whispers her daughter's name. Someone else follows.

Carmen. Josephine. Ocean. Lorrie. Brynn. Harriet. As they say their daughters' names, it sounds like the roll call after an accident or a school shooting. A roster of victims.

7.

That afternoon, their class begins Unit 1: Fundamentals of Care and Nurture. The instructors introduce the concept of motherese: the delightful high-pitched patter that goes on all day between mother and child.

Using Linda's doll, Ms. Khoury narrates an imaginary trip to the grocery store. Her voice dips and curls, conveying a constant state of wonder.

"What kind of bottled water should we buy for Daddy? The still kind or the bubbly kind? Do you know what bubbles are? Bubbles go **pop-pop-pop**! **Fizz-fizz-fizz**! Bubbles are circles! Circles are shapes!"

The mothers must pay attention to both pitch and vocabulary. A component within the dolls will tally the number of words spoken each day, how many times the doll responded to questions, the amount of conversational give-and-take. The recordings will be analyzed for the number of encouraging phrases versus the amount of warning or scolding. Too many noes will cause the word counter to beep like a car alarm, and only the instructors can turn it off.

The mothers must narrate everything, impart wisdom, give their undivided attention, maintain eye contact at all times. When the dolls ask why, why, why, as toddlers are wont to do, the mothers must provide answers. Curiosity must be rewarded.

"The dolls have an off switch," Ms. Khoury says. "You do not."

The mothers practice like singers running through scales. If the dolls babble, the mothers must try to turn those sounds into words. Interpret, the instructors say. Affirm. Help her make meaning.

"Sky," Lucretia says, pointing out the window. "Clouds. Trees."

"Boots," Frida says. "Shoelaces." She names facial features. Body parts. She counts Emmanuelle's fingers and toes. What does the doll need to hear? At home, her conversations with Harriet revolve around feelings and tasks. The next nap, the next meal, how much she loves Harriet, how much she missed Harriet when she was at her father's. She mimics Harriet's babble. They make up words. "Gola-gola" for **granola**. "Goggy" for **dog**. "Blue-blue" for **blueberry**. "Cado" for **avocado**. Frida peppers their conversations with her rudimentary Mandarin. Harriet knows how to say **xie xie**, thank you. She knows the words for **father** and **mother**, **grandmother** and **grandfather**, **auntie** and **uncle**. She'll wave her hands and scream, "No **xie xie**! No **xie xie**!" when she wants Frida to switch to English.

Frida takes Emmanuelle's hand gently, lovingly. She relaxes her face and speaks in the soft, pleasing pitch of a customer service representative. There are so many questions she can't ask: **Who made you? How easy is it to break you? Are you wearing a diaper? Do you eat and drink? Can you get sick? Can you bleed? What happened during the lunch hour?** When Emmanuelle was unfrozen, she collapsed into Frida's arms as if she'd been holding her breath the whole time. That can't be good for her.

The instructors observe and give pointers.

"Relax your jaw," Ms. Khoury tells Lucretia.

"Use your imagination," Ms. Russo tells Beth, the broken bird.

"Your voice should be as light and lovely as a cloud," Ms. Russo says.

"What does a cloud sound like?" Beth asks, looking up at Ms. Russo through a curtain of glossy hair.

"Like a mother."

"But that makes no sense."

"Mothering isn't about sense, Beth. It's about feeling." Ms. Russo pats her heart.

Frida asks Emmanuelle if she's friends with the other girls. Emmanuelle shakes her head. Frida pitches her voice higher, extolling the virtues of female friendship. She never spoke to Harriet in such a thrilling fashion. No one ever spoke this way in her family. At the dinner table, her parents talked about work. She wasn't asked about her day or her feelings. With Harriet, motherese had felt no more natural than braces. The higher Frida's voice, the more suspicious Harriet became.

Frida glances at the clock. It's 2:43. They should have landed in San Francisco by now. She hopes Harriet behaved on the flight.

The lesson segues from motherese to physical affection. Both skills will be part of their daily mothering practice and will serve as the building blocks for more complex mothering tasks.

Hugs and kisses must communicate safety and security. Hugs and kisses should be plentiful but not smothering. The instructors demonstrate with Ms. Russo playing the mother, and Ms. Khoury the child. The mothers must first assess their child's needs: Hug or kiss or both? What kind of hug? What kind of kiss? Quick and gentle? One cheek, two cheeks, nose, or forehead?

The mothers must not kiss their dolls on the lips. On the lips is European, sets the wrong precedent, makes children vulnerable to molesters.

Ms. Khoury whimpers. Ms. Russo pulls Ms. Khoury to her breast stiffly. "One, two, three, let go. One, two, three. Release."

They shouldn't hold for more than three beats. Sometimes five or six beats is permissible if the child is injured or has experienced verbal, emotional, or physical trauma. Up to ten beats is permitted in extreme situations. Longer than that will hinder the child's burgeoning independence.

Remember, the instructors say, you're no longer dealing with an infant. The mothers can add some words of encouragement as they see fit. **I love you. It's going to be okay. There, there.**

Frida sees Emmanuelle watching her, cataloging

her. She tries to keep her expression neutral. Hiding her feelings has never been her strong suit. Her wide-open face was a dead giveaway whenever she traveled in Asia. Obviously an American. All her life, her mother has scolded her for frowning.

The instructors act as if a three-second hug is the most reasonable thing in the world. There are a few giggles, a few smirks and eye rolls, but for the most part, the five of them obey. Lucretia and Linda begin the one, two, three quick squeeze. Beth rocks from side to side, giving her hugs a personal flair. Frida and Teen Mom are on their knees, arms outstretched, trying to capture their elusive doll children.

Teen Mom is too aggressive. The instructors scold her for grabbing her doll by the wrist and making false promises.

"You can't offer treats," Ms. Khoury says. "We don't use a reward-based parenting strategy here."

Frida struggles for control. Emmanuelle wanders into the learning space of other mothers.

"Rein in your doll, Frida," Ms. Russo says.

Frida begs Emmanuelle to accept a hug. She thinks of the night before her very bad day, remembers how frustrated she felt when Harriet wouldn't hold still for her diaper change.

She catches Emmanuelle and counts to three, then stops counting. She should have let Harriet sleep with her that night. Every night. Why had she ever wanted Harriet to sleep in a different room? If she were holding Harriet now, she would caress Harriet's back, sniff her neck, squeeze her earlobes, kiss her knuckles.

Ms. Russo again calls Frida's name. She's been hugging Emmanuelle for three minutes.

"It's one-two-three, release, Frida. Which part are you having trouble with?"

×

Goodbye time comes promptly at five thirty. At the instructors' whistle, the dolls line up at the door to the equipment room. Frida hugs Emmanuelle goodbye. The doll holds her arms stiffly by her sides, acknowledges Frida with a curt nod.

Deprived of the naps their human counterparts enjoy, the dolls are tired, but they don't become fussy or hyper, instead becoming subdued in a way that would never happen with real children.

The mothers smile and wave. After the dolls are out of sight, their faces go slack. Frida's face hurts from smiling. She follows her classmates down the stairs. Lucretia is comforting a weeping Beth. Lucretia says maybe she's wrong about the robot stories. Maybe these robots are not evil in any way.

"I don't think you should ask for a different doll."

"But she doesn't like me," Beth says. "I can tell. What if that's her personality? What if they gave me a bad one? What if she's a bad seed?" She starts telling Lucretia how her mother once called her a bad seed, how that fucked up her whole childhood.

"Beth, seriously, pull it together," Lucretia tells her. "You're going to get all of us in trouble."

Frida feels her chest loosen once she gets outside. She longs for her narrow street and her tiny dark house.

×

Frida's roommate, Helen, is quitting. The whispers begin the next morning at the bathroom sinks. Some say her doll son spat in her face. Some say her instructors were too harsh. Some say she went into shock when the dolls appeared and never recovered. How old is she? Fifty? Fifty-two? The older mothers are having trouble adjusting.

All eyes are on Frida as she enters the dining hall. Mothers sidle up to her table, plying her with smiles and compliments, offering to bring her a fresh cup of coffee. Frida refuses to talk. She's desperate to gossip and would like to use her fleeting cachet to acquire some friends, but there are rules to consider and women in pink lab coats circling.

"We should respect her privacy," Frida tells them. The answer is too pat. The other mothers call her **cunt** and **bitch** and **pussy**. A white mother makes **ching-chong** noises in her ear. Another knocks her silverware to the ground. April, the tattooed mother from the bus, now points in her direction and whispers to the trio of middle-aged white women. Someone at the next table refers to her as the uptight Chinese bitch. She hears her name being whispered. The one who left her baby at home. The one who says she had a bad day.

"Ignore them," Lucretia says. "They'll forget about you by lunchtime."

Frida is too nervous to eat. She passes Lucretia the other half of her bagel.

Lucretia says only a white lady would quit on the second day. If a Black mother tried a stunt like this, they'd throw her ass in jail, maybe have her get shot on the way there and make it look like she killed herself. Several Black mothers at the next table overhear Lucretia and laugh knowingly.

Linda tells Frida, "Your roommate is weak as fuck."

"I don't think she actually loves her son," Beth says. "Imagine when he finds out his mom is a coddler **and** a quitter. The state **should** be paying for that kid's therapy."

Frida stirs her coffee. She wants to tell them about the tone Helen took with Ms. Gibson, how Helen called the dolls monsters. The school gave her a six-foot-tall doll son, built like a linebacker, far taller and stronger than her real boy. How could she be expected to control him? He refused to hug. He wouldn't answer to his new given name—Norman. He called Helen old and fat and ugly, demanded a different mother. Helen said the program was a mind-fuck. Psychological torture.

Ms. Gibson told Helen to modulate her aggression. Be more open-minded. Stop projecting. **Helen, you are a bad mother, but you are learning—**

Helen waved her finger in Ms. Gibson's face. What did changing the blue liquid have to do with parenting? What about the cameras inside the dolls, the sensors, the biometric nonsense, the insane curriculum? What were they being taught? Was it even possible to pass?

Ms. Gibson reminded Helen about the consequences of leaving. Did she really want to end up on the registry?

"I don't think the registry is real," Helen said. "My son is seventeen. We'll be apart for a year at most. Then he'll come find me. I should have thought harder about that before coming here. The judge made it seem like I had a choice, but **choice** and this place do not belong in the same sentence."

After lights-out, Helen tried to convince Frida to leave with her. Her niece is coming to pick her up. Frida could stay with her, join her in a lawsuit, take a stand. "We can stop them," Helen said.

Frida delivered the required platitudes about Helen's son as a beacon of hope, tried to convince Helen to give the program another chance, hated herself for feeling tempted. She imagined showing up at Gust and Susanna's door, making them promise not to tell Ms. Torres. But that was no solution. And Helen will never sue. She'll never go to the media. Helen said she wasn't afraid of the registry, if it even exists. That her lawyer can fight it. But Frida knows she's all talk.

After breakfast, the mothers gather on the steps of Pierce. They watch as Helen's niece pulls into the rose garden circle. Helen is escorted out by Ms. Gibson and one of the guards. Today, she takes the crown from Linda as the worst mother, the baddest bitch.

The mothers whisper, "Fuck her." "Fuck this."

Helen looks back at them and raises a fist. Some mothers wave. Others flick her off. The mother next to Frida sniffles. Helen and her niece hug and laugh. Frida is chastened, surprised that after only two days here, the sound of a car pulling away can break her heart.

×

Building upon the one, two, three release model, the mothers practice varieties of affection. The hug that conveys apology. The hug that conveys encouragement. The hug that soothes physical injury. The hug that soothes the spirit. Different cries require different hugs. The mothers must become discerning. Ms. Khoury and Ms. Russo demonstrate.

Lucretia raises her hand. "I swear I've been paying attention, but all those hugs look exactly the same."

The others agree. How are they supposed to tell which cry goes with which problem goes with which hug? What difference does it make? Why can't they ask their doll what's wrong?

Direct questioning puts too much pressure on young children, the instructors say. A mother shouldn't have to ask questions. She should intuit. She should know. In regards to differentiating between hug types, the mothers must consider intent. The invisible emotional work that parents must do all the time.

"You're speaking to your child through touch," Ms. Russo says. "Communicating heart to heart. What would you like to tell her? What does she need to hear from you?"

From the classroom next door, there's a crack, followed by screams and shouting. Ms. Russo says they don't want to remind the mothers of past abuse or encourage violent tendencies, but affection drills must be authentic. To practice the hug to soothe physical injury, they'll have to inflict some pain.

The instructors slap the dolls' hands. When a doll doesn't cry loud enough, they slap her face. Teen Mom shields her doll with her body. Lucretia begs them to stop.

The instructors work methodically, ignoring the mothers' protests, Ms. Russo restraining the doll while Ms. Khoury slaps. The hitting is real. The pain is real. Frida covers Emmanuelle's eyes. The instructors must be evil spinsters. Secret cat killers. If anyone ever did this to Harriet. Frida's never seen a toddler struck in the face before. Her father only ever spanked her over her clothes. Her mother only ever slapped her hand.

"Let go of her, Frida," Ms. Russo warns.

"Why are you doing this?"

"Because we have to train you."

Emmanuelle cowers behind Frida. "It's only going to hurt for a second," Frida says. "It's just pretend. I'm here. Mommy will take care of you. I'm sorry. I'm so sorry." She winces as Ms. Khoury slaps the doll across the face.

Emmanuelle's cries are sharper than Harriet's, more insistent and threatening. Frida increases her hugs to five seconds, then ten. For Harriet, she'll let the doll scream in her ear. For Harriet, she'll let the doll damage her hearing. She's amazed by the sheer volume of liquid issuing from the doll's eyes, nose, and mouth, a feedback loop with no obvious source, as if her body contains a secret fountain.

The collar and placket of Emmanuelle's uniform are soon soaked with tears. The dolls cry longer and louder than real children. They cry without pause. They don't get tired. Their voices don't become hoarse. They push themselves out of their mothers' embraces, discovering the basic animal pleasure of pure release. Cries of physical upset segue to cries of passion as they stretch their voices to full capacity, creating a dome of sound that makes Frida want to cry tears of blood.

Hours pass. The instructors wear headphones. At lunchtime, they pause the dolls mid-wail, their mouths stretched open, their throats red and wet and pulsing. They resume the same high pitch of grief when the mothers return.

The mothers aren't making their dolls feel safe. If the dolls felt safe, they'd stop crying. The instructors tell them to manage their frustration. By staying calm, they're showing their child that a mother can handle anything. A mother is always patient. A mother is always kind. A mother is always giving. A mother never falls apart. A mother is the buffer between her child and the cruel world.

Absorb it, the instructors say. Take it. Take it.

×

Each cohort thinks they have it the worst: the most badly behaved dolls, the harshest instructors. The tactics are inhumane. The explanations make no sense. Nothing they're learning relates to real life.

Beth thinks the school hired social workers who have the souls of Nazis. If the dolls can feel real feelings, they're going to feel real feelings about being abused.

"Social workers **are** Nazis," Lucretia says. "They're Nazi-adjacent. At least mine was." She thinks Ms. Khoury must be a fascist in a brown lady's body. There are more of those these days.

The infant dolls were made to cry just by setting them on the ground; the older dolls were slapped repeatedly by instructors. The teenage dolls yelled hateful phrases: "Rot in hell!" "Die, witch!" "You don't understand me!" "You're not my real mother! Why should I listen to you?" Helen's doll has been sent to storage.

At dinner, Frida and her classmates talked strategy. Pacifiers. Toys. Board books. Videos. Songs. Their real daughters need distractions when they're upset. Why can't they use pacifiers? They dared Lucretia to ask tomorrow.

Frida is exhausted from crouching and squatting and chasing and listening and giving and trying to channel frustration into love. She climbs into bed before lights-out, excited to have the room to herself. Then she remembers that Helen is home. Helen will sleep in her own bed tonight.

Ms. Gibson does final checks. The evening bell rings. The lights go off.

Aside from the business with Helen and the hitting and crying and her own desperate thoughts, the day started on a good note. The instructors said, "Find your mother," and Emmanuelle came to her right away. Most dolls couldn't do it. Teen Mom's doll went to Beth. Beth's to Lucretia. But Emmanuelle recognized Frida. She pointed at Frida's chest and said, "Mommy," and Frida felt a vague something. Tenderness, maybe. Pride. The doll is not Harriet. She can never be Harriet. She is simply a stepping-stone. Frida will step on the doll's head, her body, whatever is necessary.

×

For Thanksgiving dinner, the dining hall is lit with candles. The executive director, Ms. Knight, flits between tables, shaking hands and squeezing elbows, asking the mothers for their names and offenses.

"How are you enjoying the program? Have you settled in? Aren't the dolls fun?"

Once everyone is seated, Ms. Knight takes the microphone and leads the mothers in a moment of silence for their missing children.

The mothers don't appreciate the tribute. They know where they are and where they should be. The festive touches make them feel worse than if the school had done nothing. The candlesticks are wobbly, made of cheap plastic. Each table has a bowl of miniature pumpkins, which they've been warned not to use as weapons. There are paper garlands of Pilgrims and turkeys taped to the walls. They've been served dry, barely seasoned turkey, chalky stuffing, runny sweet potatoes.

Linda worries her children are going hungry. "You don't know the kind of people who sign up to be foster parents," she tells the group. "People do it for the money." She doesn't know where those foster parents live, doesn't know how many other kids they're fostering, if her kids are getting into fights with them, fights at school. For Sunday phone calls, she has to choose one kid to call each week. How's that going to sit with the others? She wanted her social worker to place the kids with Spanish speakers, wanted someone to take all six. The older kids take care of the younger ones.

Beth tells Linda about a lesbian couple who live near her in Mount Airy, who foster kids with special needs. "There are good foster parents too," Beth says.

"Unhelpful," Linda replies. "Un-helpful."

Frida is thinking about money. Private school and summer camps. Music lessons and tutors. Trips abroad. Everything her parents gave her. The more she hears about deprivation, the more she wants to give Harriet luxury.

Ms. Knight asks everyone to stand and give thanks. The first mothers to speak are shy. One mother thanks God. Another thanks America.

Frida's parents must be at her aunt and uncle's house in Burr Ridge. At least twenty relatives will be there. Frida is the eldest of the cousins on her mother's side, her late grandmother's favorite. She begged her parents not to tell the rest of the family, but her mother has probably broken down and told one sister, who told the three other siblings, who told their children. The aunts and uncles will blame her parents. Or her liberal arts degree or not finishing her PhD or waiting until she was thirty-seven to have a baby. Or marrying a white man, and what kind of name was Gust? She shouldn't have married someone handsome. Handsome men can't be trusted. She lived too far from home. If she'd moved home, her parents would have helped with the baby. The problem was Frida's choices. Her aunts and uncles will tell their children, **If you ever do something like this, I will throw myself in a river**.

Lost in her immigrant-daughter guilt spiral, she doesn't notice when Ms. Knight arrives at their table. Ms. Knight first passes the microphone to Linda, who gives thanks for the school.

"For all of you. My new sisters. You're beautiful. All of you, man."

They go around. There is gratitude for food, shelter, second chances.

Teen Mom doesn't look up from her plate. She hasn't said anything all night, has consumed only cranberry sauce. She asks to skip her turn. Undaunted, Ms. Knight presses the microphone into her hand.

"Lady, get that microphone out of my face. Aren't there enough fucking rules?"

"Meryl, language! One more incident like this and I'll make sure you get sent to talk circle."

Teen Mom takes the microphone and says, "I give thanks for the truth."

She hands the microphone to Frida, who hesitates, looking to Lucretia for guidance. Lucretia makes a heart with her hands.

"I give thanks for Emmanuelle," Frida says, taking the cue. "My doll. I mean, my daughter. My precious, beautiful daughter."

At the next table, the trio of middle-aged white women stand together. They pass the microphone, finish each other's sentences. They give thanks for Ms. Knight. For science, for progress. The instructors. Lucretia tells Frida to notice the way Ms. Knight is smiling at them. Maybe those three aren't even moms, Lucretia says. Maybe they work for the state. Maybe they're moles. There's talk of throwing dinner rolls their way, but before anyone can try, the ass-kissing of the middle-aged white women is cut short by a burst of flame. The room fills with the scent of burning plastic.

×

Mothers are interrogated. Surveillance footage is reviewed. Though no one can prove that the fire was intentional or identify who knocked over the candle, the next morning, there are dozens of new guards.

The new dining hall guard is a youthful, ruddy-faced blond with the soft, lumpy body of a drinker. It's their fifth day in the world of women, and even Linda, who declares the guard to be the whitest white man she's ever seen, gives the guard a coy glance.

The mothers stand a little straighter. They giggle and blush and point, the dining hall guard unruffled by their leering. Reasonable, Frida thinks, that a man wouldn't be aroused by a room of two hundred women who have mistreated their children.

It is Black Friday, and the mothers are grouchy and restless. They should be sleeping late and eating leftovers and spending money they don't have.

Lucretia says they should cause more trouble. Get themselves more guards. "A year is a long time," she says. Who knows when co-ed training is going to happen, if it's going to happen like Ms. Knight promised at orientation. They're not going to hang with those dads anyway.

"As if **bad father** is not the most pussy-drying phrase," Lucretia says, gesturing with her hand to mimic a flower opening and closing.

Someone could flood a bathroom in Kemp. Someone could mess with the instructors. Maybe some of the plants are poisonous.

Frida calls Lucretia crazy. Think of how they'll suffer, how their kids will suffer, if they lose their cases. Beth and Meryl scoff. Lucretia calls Frida a goody-goody. Linda calls her a fucking rule-following model minority.

They discuss whether they should blow the guard or have him go down on them. The table is divided on this question. Their intensity at this early hour, over this unappealing man, frightens Frida, who isn't immune to coarse thoughts. She's been missing Will, remembering his body, thinking of Gust and past lovers, the dirty-haired boy in college who chewed on her nipples, the chubby art director in New York who spoke too often of his dead father. But fantasy and desire belong to another life. She told Will not to wait for her. She leaves the table as her classmates continue their heated discussion of whether, for the sake of birth control, anal sex is the best option.

There's a new guard waiting inside the glass doors of Morris Hall, a slim and shy young Black man with green cat eyes and a short beard and a face as pretty as a girl's. He's not very tall, but the body beneath the uniform appears strong. Some mothers say hello to him on the way to class. Some toss their hair. Some brazenly look him up and down. The guard is blushing. The mothers place bets on how many women he'll fuck today. There can't be cameras in all the trees. There are plenty of empty buildings.

Frida wonders what kind of girl he likes. Sharp and funny like Lucretia. Haunted like Beth. She likes his green eyes and full mouth.

×

Counseling sessions are staggered throughout the day. At 10:45 a.m., Frida waits in the foyer of Pierce, where someone has placed an arrangement of silk poinsettias on the table beneath the chandelier.

She reminds herself not to ask questions, to only cry if it seems advantageous to do so, to refer to Emmanuelle as "her," rather than "it." The waiting mothers make small talk about going to bed hungry, how the turkey was not that bad, considering. Down the hall, behind one of the closed doors, a mother is sobbing with abandon. Frida worries for her, whoever she is, remembers how the men from CPS cataloged her crying episodes. They said Frida's grief seemed shallow. They told the family court judge that her crying postures—her habit of hiding her face with her hands, assuming the fetal position—suggested she was playing the victim.

She hasn't cried here yet, though the desire to weep is constant. At night, she struggles to keep her hands out of her mouth. She wants to pull out her eyelashes, bite the insides of her cheeks until they bleed. But she's learning to appreciate the dark. The solitude. Exhaustion has improved her sleep. In the last few nights, she's slept deep enough to remember her nightmares.

At eleven, Ms. Gibson escorts her to the college's old study abroad office. The counselor's office is dove gray and smells like antiseptic. There's a scale of justice on top of a filing cabinet, a dry-erase calendar with codes written in red, stacks of manila folders, assorted handheld devices. There's a camera mounted on the back wall, facing Frida, who takes her seat and crosses her legs and smiles.

The counselor, an elegant, middle-aged Black woman whose pink lab coat is snug across the shoulders, is named Jacinda, but Frida can call her Ms. Thompson. She has relaxed shoulder-length hair that's thinning at the temples and raised moles on her cheekbones. She speaks from the diaphragm and smiles like she cares, murmuring and nodding at the right moments as Frida answers questions about sleep and appetite and mood, if she's made any friends, if she feels safe here, how she's enduring the separation from Harriet. They spend the session reviewing Frida's shortcomings, starting with her very bad day and continuing through this morning. The counselor encourages her to say, "I am a bad mother because . . . ," and fill in the blanks.

She asks why Frida hasn't been able to comfort her doll. When Frida says no one has, the counselor says that doesn't matter.

"Frida, why do you have such low expectations of yourself?" she asks. Is the problem an insecure attachment? Some underlying resistance? To the program? To the dolls?

"Your instructors have told me that your hugs lack warmth. They said, I quote, 'Frida's kisses lack a fiery core of maternal love.' "

"I'm doing my best. No one told us we'd be working with robots. It's a lot to absorb."

"I'm sure Ms. Knight explained during orientation why the system has changed. Here, you practice with the dolls, and you take those skills back to your regular life. I encourage you not to overthink it."

The counselor sets goals. By next week, at least five successful hug sequences. More efficient articulation of shortcomings. Fewer shortcomings. More playful motherese. A higher pitch. Higher daily word count. Frida needs to relax. Her temperature and heart rate suggest an unsustainable level of stress. She needs to make more frequent and meaningful eye contact with Emmanuelle. Her touch should be gentler, more loving. Data collected from the doll has suggested substantial amounts of anger and ingratitude. Any negative feelings will impede her progress.

×

At dinner, they talk wants. Which guard, which day. Where. Empty classroom, broom closet, car, the woods. What they'd do if there were no cameras and no fence. They like the green-eyed guard best of all. Lucretia thinks Teen Mom has the best chance. The guard might only be twenty.

"He reminds me of my baby daddy," Teen Mom admits. "But my dude is taller. Way taller. And hotter. And he has nicer teeth."

"How do you know what his teeth look like?" Lucretia asks.

"He smiled at me."

Beth and Lucretia whistle and high-five each other. Teen Mom tells them to shut up.

Lucretia asks Frida which guard she wants. Fuck, marry, or kill?

Frida isn't thinking about the guards. She's still stewing over her counseling session. The school must be bringing them low to induce cooperation, the way that men she dated used to insult her until she hated herself enough to put out. Maybe they needed to feel that they were the lowest of the low in order to believe. To see that the only creature they deserve to mother is a doll. That they can't be trusted with a human of any age, can't even be trusted with an animal.

"Fuck any," she finally answers. "Marry none. Kill none."

"It's always the quiet ones." Lucretia pats her hand. She says fuck the dining hall guard, marry the green-eyed guard, kill none. "Ask me again in a few months," she says, giggling. She tells them she'd just been starting to date again when her daughter was taken.

They wonder if there have been any fires at the fathers' school. Frida tells them about Helen's idea of the pink lab coats fulfilling some kind of caretaker-nurse fantasy.

Beth thinks it's possible. When she was in the hospital, she developed a flirtation with one of the doctors. "He kissed me once," she confesses.

The normally sarcastic Lucretia becomes solemn. "And you told someone, right?"

"No. I didn't want to get him in trouble." The doctor was older. Married.

"But he's going to do it to someone else. You have to report him. When we get out. Promise me."

Beth tells Lucretia not to pressure her. She looks like she's about to cry. Linda tells Lucretia to back off.

To take the heat off Beth, Frida tells them about dating in New York, the various sociopaths she dated before Gust. The string of short, angry bald men during her first year of grad school. The stand-up comic who told jokes about Chinese restaurant workers while she was in the audience.

They wind up comparing histories, the age when they gave it up. Lucretia says sixteen. Linda says fifteen. Frida says twenty.

"Look at you, Frida Kahlo," Lucretia teases.

Linda asks if Frida married her first. Frida doesn't tell them she married her twenty-seventh. She calls herself a late bloomer.

Beth and Teen Mom haven't answered.

"Six," Teen Mom finally says. "I wouldn't say that I gave it."

Linda's smile fades. "I'm sorry, kid."

Beth admits it happened to her too. Twelve, her choir director. Her mother didn't believe her. Teen Mom says her mother didn't believe her either.

She hands Beth a dinner roll, looks up at the rest of her classmates. "Well, now you know. Is this enough fucking bonding for you?"

×

For Sunday phone privileges, the mothers report to the computer lab in Palmer Library, the building to the east of the rose garden. The computer lab is on the ground floor, a white-walled room with a vaulted forest-green ceiling and coffee-stained tables.

Mothers cycle in and out in ten-minute intervals. They line up in the hallway in alphabetical order.

Frida waits on the stairs. She stretches her arms, still sore from cleaning crew. Yesterday, Ms. Gibson came to her room before the morning bell and told her to dress warmly. This will be her new Saturday routine. She and Teen Mom and twelve others joined Ms. Gibson after breakfast. They were given gloves and sponges, mops and buckets and scrub brushes. Before they began, Ms. Gibson had them state their names and offenses and what was wrong with their homes. There were stories about rotting food and overflowing diaper pails, families of mice living in walls, mold infestations. The more innocuous offenders had sinks filled with dirty dishes, sticky high chairs, toys with food stains, odors that CPS deemed troubling or offensive. Frida confessed to dust and clutter and stale dry goods and a lone cockroach.

She was paired with Deirdre, a white mother from Pennsport whose five-year-old son, Jeffrey, is living with her sister. When Frida asked if it was only the state of the house that got her in trouble, Deirdre admitted that her son had some bruises. She might have hit him.

"In the face?" Frida asked, rushing to judgment.

"I am a bad mother," Deirdre said, "but I am learning to be good."

Cleaning crew, they soon realized, is ceremonial. Impossible for fourteen women to clean all the buildings currently in use and tend to the two hundred acres that aren't woodland. Frida and Deirdre were assigned to mop three of the classroom buildings. It took twenty minutes to walk there. A guard supervised them to make sure they didn't touch the dolls. They discovered that not all the dolls are kept in equipment rooms. A few classrooms are used for storage, with plexiglass partitions separating dolls of different ages. The dolls watched them work.

Now, Ms. Gibson directs Frida to a free computer. Frida wishes she'd written notes. She needs to remind Gust about flu shots. He should attend some preschool open houses, submit some applications. He needs to check in with her parents.

The connection is established. After a few seconds, Susanna's face comes into focus. She's wearing one of Gust's scratchy, ivory-colored fisherman sweaters, holding a steaming mug of tea, her mass of red hair piled on top of her head and secured with a pencil. Having seen women in uniform all week, her beauty is overwhelming.

Frida is embarrassed to have Susanna see her like this. "Where's Harriet?"

"I'm sorry, Frida. They're sleeping. She caught a tummy bug. She was puking all night. Gust went down too."

"Are they okay now? Could you wake them up? Please. I only get ten minutes."

Susanna apologizes again. She understands how important this call is for everyone, but Harriet just fell asleep. "She's really sick. I've been taking care of both of them. I'm pretty wrecked. Can you guys talk next week?"

"Please," Frida repeats. They go back and forth about the importance of Harriet's sleep versus the importance of this call, how many months it will be before Frida sees Harriet in person. Susanna finally agrees to get them.

Frida worries that she'll burst into tears before Harriet even comes on-screen. At seven minutes, she begins to pick at her cuticles. At six minutes, she holds her head in her hands. At five minutes, she tugs at her eyebrows. At four minutes, she hears Harriet's voice. Gust sits down at his computer, cradling Harriet in his lap. Harriet's cheeks are rosy. She's always at her most beautiful when she's just woken up.

Frida apologizes for disturbing them. She asks how they're feeling.

Gust says the whole place needs to be disinfected. Harriet vomited all over her crib.

"Did you call the doctor?"

"Frida, we know what we're doing. I can take care of my daughter."

"I'm not saying you can't. But you should call the doctor." She notices Harriet sniffling, the dark circles under her eyes. Harriet looks thinner. "I'm sorry I'm not there, bub. You can go right back to sleep. I just needed to see you." She wants to deliver streams of perfect motherese, but as she watches Harriet take in her new reality, mother in the computer, mother in uniform, mother she can't touch, as she watches Harriet's face crumple, it's her turn to cry.

Harriet tries to escape. She screams and windmills her arms. Ms. Gibson comes over and lowers the volume.

"Do you have to do that?"

"Frida, please be considerate of the others. You have a minute left."

Gust whispers in Harriet's ear.

Frida says, "I love you. I miss you."

She says, "Galaxies. Remember? Mommy loves you galaxies."

Ms. Gibson gives the mothers a five-second warning. "Say goodbye now, ladies."

Everyone leans toward their screens. Everyone's voice rises.

"It's going to be better next time," Gust says.

"I'm so sorry, bub. Mommy has to go. Feel better. Drink more water, please. Get healthy. I want you to be healthy. I want that so much." Frida leans close to the monitor and puckers.

Harriet stops crying. She opens her hand. She says, "Ma—"

The screen goes blank.

8.

SINCE SPEAKING TO HARRIET, EMMANUELLE has been harder to appreciate. Frida notices all the false parts: the new-car smell, the faint click when Emmanuelle turns her head, the chips in her eyes, the uniformity of her freckles, the lack of fuzz on her cheeks, her stubby eyelashes, her fingernails that never grow. Frida is a bad mother because her hugs convey anger. She is a bad mother because her affection is perfunctory. It is now December, and she has yet to complete a successful hug sequence.

The mothers have been in uniform for eleven days. Desire and mischief are being crushed out of them. Frida's classmates have stopped ogling guards. There's been bickering in the shower line, elbowing and shoulder-checking in the halls, tripping and name-calling, endless dirty looks.

A number of foster parents and grandparents and guardians missed their assigned call times. Some lacked computers or smartphones. Some lacked Wi-Fi. There were bad connections and misunderstandings, children who wouldn't talk.

Emmanuelle's new habit is running while crying. She's faster than Harriet was in September, though maybe not faster than Harriet is now. Frida feels like she's cheating Harriet with every embrace. More for Emmanuelle, less for Harriet, and how much of her is there to go around? She'd been so angry at Gust for his talk of divided loyalties—his family versus his new, glorious love. His divided heart. The difficulty of triangulation. She broke two wineglasses the night he used that term.

The sky this morning is overcast, with the kind of soft light that makes the dolls' skin look more real. The dolls run to the doors and windows. They bang on locked cabinets. They pull open drawers. Mothers pursue. Dolls collide. The crying gets louder.

Ms. Russo adjusts Frida's stance. Frida needs to kneel. She shouldn't bend over Emmanuelle or bend down to her. Children must be treated with respect.

"You have to meet them where they are," Ms. Russo says. She asks Frida to try her apology again. This time, with more feeling.

They're practicing the hug of contrition. This week, the instructors finally gave them toys—stacking rings and blocks and shape sorters and stuffed animals—but after an hour of playing, the dolls laughing, bonding seemingly within reach, the toys are snatched away, leaving the mothers to earn the dolls' forgiveness. The instructors have been doing this every morning, setting off tantrums that last the entire day.

Frida would not say that she is used to the place or the uniforms or the lessons or the mothers or the dolls, but she is growing used to the headaches. The throbbing behind her eyes is part of her life here, as is her dry skin and bleeding gums and aching knees and sore back, the sensation of never being clean, the tightness in her wrists and shoulders and jaw. She has a new roommate, Roxanne, a Black mother in her early twenties whose seven-month-old baby boy, Isaac, is in foster care. Roxanne let her twelve-year-old niece babysit Isaac when she got called into work on a Sunday. A passerby saw the girl wheeling Isaac in his stroller in front of Roxanne's apartment building and called the police. He was only five months old when they took him.

Roxanne is from North Philly, had been a student at Temple, was just beginning her senior year. Poli-sci major, with a minor in media studies. She doesn't talk about Isaac much, but she's asked Frida about the stages of development she's missing. Before all this happened, Isaac was just learning to sit up. He'll be crawling soon. Roxanne said Frida is lucky. She had a year and a half with Harriet. Harriet will know Frida's face. Her voice. What will Isaac remember about his mother? Nothing.

Roxanne has skeptical, inky almond-shaped eyes and a button nose and waist-length dreads that she plays with incessantly. She is compact and bosomy, with hips so narrow it's unclear how she birthed a baby. She changes her clothes quietly, makes her bed quietly, never wants to gossip, never lets Frida see her naked, but, unfortunately for Frida, she talks and laughs in her sleep. Her dream laughter is charmed and abundant. Her dreams, if Frida is interpreting them correctly, involve fragrant meadows and mountain streams, a gentleman caller.

Frida wishes she could laugh about it with Will. She wants to tell him about Roxanne rustling the sheets and smiling in the dark. She wants to tell him that these buildings are composed of pheromones and regret. Hostility. Longing. That it's possible to stop noticing sadness. That the sound of women crying now resembles white noise.

×

Some say the dolls needed time to get used to them. Some say all progress is due to the mothers. Some say the dolls' cooperation has been programmed to increase competition. Regardless of the reason, the impossible has happened. There have been breakthroughs. Trust has been established. Mothers are meeting their dolls' needs.

In Frida's cohort, the leader is Linda, who, on Friday morning, quiets her doll with an eight-second hug and a two-second bounce-bounce.

The instructors ask the class to observe. They silence the other dolls, then taunt Linda's doll with a teddy bear, which is then snatched away. Linda, who has birthed and allegedly neglected many, moves in swift and graceful. She presses her doll firmly to her shoulder, delivering affirmations in Spanish and English. She bounces the doll with jittery motions, as if she's preparing a cocktail. She pats and dips. Soon, the doll is calm.

Linda takes a long, satisfied look at her classmates, her gaze settling on Lucretia.

The mothers cross their arms and tilt their heads and bite their tongues. It had to be random. No child, not even a pretend one, is safe with Linda.

Ms. Russo has Linda explain her hug strategy.

"I have to think like an athlete," Linda says. "It's like we're at the Olympics. Every day, we're going for the gold. My family is the gold. I can't have my kids growing up without me. I don't want to just be some bitch—excuse me, some woman they hear stories about."

When the rest of the dolls are unfrozen, they all run to Linda. She is the pied piper. The shepherdess. Mother Goose. The instructors ask her to give her classmates pointers, a shift in power that results in a frosty lunch hour. Lucretia goes so far as to dump salt into Linda's coffee when her back is turned.

No one wants to take their cues from Linda, but with her success in mind, and the potential shame of being bested by the woman who supposedly put her six children in a hole, the mothers hug faster and faster. Some hugs resemble putting out a fire.

THE SCHOOL FOR GOOD MOTHERS

Others resemble wrestling moves. Eventually, Lucretia quiets her doll, then Beth.

After each breakthrough, they reflect as a group. The instructors say they should interrogate themselves every night. They should ask: "What did I learn today? Where is there room for improvement?"

"A mother is a shark," Ms. Russo says. "You're always moving. Always learning. Always trying to better yourself."

It's almost goodbye time. Frida counts to six, counts to eight, thinks of Harriet running on the playground, Harriet weak from vomiting, Harriet's nosebleed, the last time they touched. She says, "I love you. Please forgive me."

Emmanuelle stops crying. Frida can't believe it. She raises her hand, trying to catch Ms. Russo's attention. She checks the doll's face for moisture and dabs the remaining tears away. She kisses Emmanuelle's forehead. Their eyes meet in kinship. Contentment has been achieved. It feels better than she imagined.

×

Six inches of snow fall overnight. The campus turns stark and enchanted. Frida, Teen Mom, and two mothers from a different cohort are assigned to shovel the walkways from Pierce to the science buildings. The mothers have seen the regular maintenance staff use snowblowers, but questions about snowblowers are rebuffed. Snowblowers are shortcuts, Ms. Gibson says, and shortcuts are not what cleaning crew is about.

Only white mothers and Frida have been assigned to snow removal. The Black and Latina mothers on bathroom duty grumble. With the uptick in bad behavior, cleaning crew has expanded. There are now mothers on laundry duty, mothers cleaning the kitchen and dining hall. Mothers who have avoided Saturday punishment, and who don't have additional required training, must use the day for exercise and community building and writing in their atonement journals. Some staff members were hoping to start knitting and quilting groups, but the administrators decided that, after the Thanksgiving fire, the mothers can't be trusted with needles.

Teen Mom insists Frida shovel beside her. Teen Mom is from South Philly, far south, almost to the baseball stadium. She thinks Passyunk Square, where Frida lived, is full of posers with stupid haircuts and expensive bikes and tote bags and little dogs.

Frida is careful not to bad-mouth South Philly or the city in general. She's curious if having a mixed baby in a white part of South Philly caused any friction, but doesn't ask. They gossip about their roommates and instructors and Linda, every mother whom Teen Mom considers a basic bitch, whether anyone learned anything in class yesterday, whether anyone here is learning anything ever. Teen Mom thinks the instructors pick on her because she's the youngest. Her counselor says she has anger issues, trust issues, depression issues, sexual-abuse-survivor issues, marijuana issues, unwed-mother issues, high-school-dropout issues, white-mother-of-a-Black-child issues. The data suggests that Teen Mom hates her doll. She doesn't dispute this but clarifies that she hates everyone.

She asks Frida how it felt yesterday, doing something right. Teen Mom was the only one who couldn't get her doll to stop crying.

"It hasn't sunk in yet." Frida doesn't admit how much she enjoyed the instructors' praise, how proud she was that Emmanuelle was extra clingy. When they said goodbye, Emmanuelle sighed and rested her head on Frida's shoulder, a tender and surprising gesture that chipped away at Frida's resistance.

She says the dolls are unpredictable. She doesn't know how Emmanuelle will behave on Monday. The breakthrough came too late to count toward the week's goals. The counselor thinks she's falling behind. The counselor questioned her conduct during her Sunday call. She accused Frida of acting distant with Emmanuelle. Eye contact numbers were low. Affection ratings were inconsistent. Kisses were tepid. Motherese was stagnant.

Frida worries about being too candid with Teen Mom. She worries that she hasn't been supportive enough after Teen Mom's confession. Linda has been saying that she and Frida, the grown-ups here, need to keep an eye on Teen Mom and Beth.

"What you told us the other night," Frida begins. "Thank you for trusting us."

"Oh my God, barf. Beth won't stop bringing it up either. I didn't tell you so you could all ask me questions."

"I'm just saying you're brave. You're a survivor."

"That is the stupidest term. My mom uses that term. Well, now she does."

"I'm sorry she didn't believe you."

"Whatever. I'm over it."

"If you need someone to talk to—"

"Frida, seriously. Stand down. No more processing today. Okay? You swear?"

Frida apologizes. The snow is wet and heavy, like shoveling cement. They finish the four sets of Pierce steps, nodding at the mothers on their way to clean the classroom buildings. Their faces chap. Their backs and knees ache. Their eyes hurt from squinting at the snow. All day, Teen Mom hints she has a secret. She grows impatient with Frida's guesses.

"Come closer. No, don't look at me. Don't be so obvious. Listen, so, I fucked the guard. The cute one. You better not say anything, or I'll tell every single bitch here that you tried to kiss me."

"I promise." Frida tries not to appear concerned. Teen Mom and the green-eyed guard fucked in the parking lot. In his car. Frida asks how she got outside. Aren't there alarms? Floodlights? Cameras? Other guards?

"Lady, you seriously have no game."

"You used a condom, I hope."

"Really? You think I'm that stupid?" She only let him fuck her ass. The sex was nothing special. He came in two minutes. His dick is long and narrow. He kisses sloppy, but his hair smells nice.

Frida feels stupid and jealous and old. Teen Mom

has a body like Susanna's, thin and lanky, but with full breasts. She's pretty in the way that all teenagers are pretty, some baby fat on her cheeks; clear, shining brown eyes; poreless skin. Her hair is the only ugly part of her: fading to dark gray, blond at the roots. Of course the guard chose a teenager, a girl who is feral and gifted, infinitely resourceful.

She wants to ask if they kissed with tongue, if the guard fingered her while fucking her ass, if the guard was noisy, if they steamed up the windows. She would like to know these things, would like Teen Mom to know that she was once daring too, but asking would suggest that she hasn't changed, and change is essential, so she asks about Teen Mom's family, if she misses them. Not just her daughter, but her parents.

Teen Mom kicks at the snow. "I tell you one thing and now you're allowed to go in?"

She doesn't want to talk about them, says it's none of Frida's business, then admits that she misses her mom. They've never lived apart before. How old is Frida? Her mom is only thirty-five.

"Maybe you two can be friends," Teen Mom says, laughing. Her father left when she was three.

"Too bad they can't round him up and send him to dad jail."

Her daughter is named Ocean. Ocean's grandmother is taking care of her, but money for day care is running out. Ocean can be a little shit, likes eating soil from houseplants. They'd find her tooth marks on the soap. She started crawling at five months, started walking at nine months.

"She was like a little cockroach. I hit her a few times. But it's not what you think. I only did it when she was really bad." She points at Frida. "You better not repeat that. That shit is not in my file."

Frida promises, though she's alarmed. She and Roxanne have griped about hitters being grouped with non-hitters. Roxanne thinks that what she did, leaving Isaac with her niece, even what Frida did, wasn't on the same level.

"It's like the people with cancer are being treated the same as the people with diabetes," Roxanne said.

"I didn't want to keep her," Teen Mom tells Frida. "My mom made me. There was this couple who wanted to adopt her, but the dad looked at me weird. Some people just have that evil vibe, you know? And then, when I changed my mind, they went fucking nuts. People who want babies and can't have them lose their minds."

She asks what it was like getting pregnant as an

old lady. Is Frida's stuff all shriveled? "You can't have any more, right? Like you'll be forty, and then . . ." She makes a zipping sound.

"You mean, if . . . ? I guess not. You know, she'll be twenty-one months in a few days." Frida's eyes water. On her phone, there are videos for every month's milestone. The videos were partly for her, partly for her parents. She'd sit Harriet in her high chair, state the day and Harriet's age, then ask her for an update. The last one: "You're eighteen months today! How do you feel about it?"

Teen Mom notices Frida dabbing her eyes. She drops her shovel. She grabs Frida and delivers the hug to soothe the spirit, whispering, "There, there."

×

Ms. Khoury and Ms. Russo begin timing them. The mothers soothe their dolls in two hours, then one hour, then forty-five minutes, then thirty minutes. Ten minutes to silence is the goal.

Evaluation day arrives. The first unit, since it covers so much material, will have an additional evaluation in January. The mothers sit cross-legged in a circle, squirming dolls in their laps. Each pair will take a turn in the center. The instructors will evaluate the combination of hugs, kisses, and affirmations. The quality of the hugs: too long, too short, just right. How many were required. The mother's confidence and composure. How long it took to quiet the doll. Final scores and written assessments and video clips will be entered into their files. Anyone who goes over ten minutes will receive a zero.

Ms. Knight comes to observe, has so many more classes to visit before dinner. "If only I could clone myself," she says. The instructors laugh appreciatively.

The mothers give them the side-eye. The other day, Lucretia asked them if they have children, and the answer was no. Ms. Russo said that she mothers her three dogs. Ms. Khoury told them that she mothers her nephews.

"Not everyone is lucky enough to have children," Ms. Khoury said.

Lucretia's questioning of authority was added to her file. Outside of class, Lucretia called them imposters. She told Frida that it was like taking swim lessons from people who've never been underwater. How can anyone compare pets to children?

Being a mother is nothing like being an aunt. Only someone who doesn't have kids would say that.

The mothers wave at Ms. Knight, who looks yet more disturbing during the day. Parts of her face look eighteen, other parts look fifty. She has the round pink cheeks of a baby. Frida stares at her freckled, veiny hands, her diamond ring. At orientation, she told them that she has four daughters. One is an equestrian. Another is in medical school. Another is doing humanitarian-aid work in Niger. Another is studying law. She has plenty of experience raising good women.

Ms. Russo takes Lucretia's doll to the equipment room to be harmed. Frida, Beth, and Teen Mom wish Lucretia luck as she moves to the center of the circle.

Frida tells Emmanuelle that today is special. "Don't be scared," she says. Since their breakthrough last week, she's been thinking of Emmanuelle as her little friend. An orphan. A foundling. Perhaps she's not a pretend daughter but a temporary one. Emmanuelle came to be hers because of a war.

She wants to tell Emmanuelle that she's thinking about health. Harriet was too sick to talk last Sunday. The whole household had been ill. The promised flu shots didn't happen. Gust said this year's flu shot is only 20 percent effective. Susanna thinks exposure to germs will strengthen Harriet's immune system. She doesn't like washing Harriet's hands too often, doesn't want Harriet to miss all the good microbiomes. The school has Frida on record raising her voice, calling Gust irresponsible and Susanna crazy, referring to Susanna's reservations about the flu shot as "naturopath garbage."

The instructors let Ms. Knight call time. Diagnosing the source of the upset uses precious minutes. The waiting mothers cheer from the sidelines: "You can do this!" "Pick her up!" "Keep going!"

Lucretia finishes in nine minutes and thirty-seven seconds. Beth and Teen Mom go over ten minutes.

Ms. Russo takes Emmanuelle. Frida moves to the center. She tries to summon all the love she has to give, the love she would give Harriet. She unfurrows her brow. She hears Emmanuelle crying. She crouches. When they review the footage, her face should be beatific, like the Madonnas in Italy, their arms angled around their babies, their foreheads bathed in light.

×

The cohorts divide into cliques: those who passed, those who didn't. Frida squeaked by with a time of nine minutes and fifty-three seconds. Linda finished in first place. Six minutes and twenty-nine seconds, she tells anyone who asks. In exchange for extra food and toiletries, she dispenses tips during meals and talks strategy before bedtime. There's sometimes a line of mothers outside her dorm room.

An undecorated Christmas tree is wheeled into the entrance of the dining hall. The floor around the tree is littered with pine needles. Angry mothers have been stripping the branches.

The upcoming winter holidays provide fodder for lessons on intermediate and advanced motherese. Frida tells Emmanuelle about Chicago winters. Lake-effect snow. It's not like Philly, where the whole city shuts down after two inches.

"When I was little, the snow came up to my shoulder. We have pictures of my dad pulling me in a baby bathtub. He was supposed to use a sled."

"Sled?"

"It's this thing people use to go downhill. And people get in it with their kids or by themselves and they go **whoosh, whoosh**." She mimics the motion with her arms.

She teaches Emmanuelle about Christmas, explains the ritual of decorating trees and giving presents. She's not sure of the school's policy on Santa Claus, so she skips that part.

"My family celebrates on Christmas Eve. No one told my parents that you're supposed to open presents on Christmas morning, so the next day, we didn't have anything to do. We'd usually go to the theater to see a movie."

"Mov-ie?"

"A movie is a story. Something you watch on a screen. Make-believe. Entertainment. People watch movies to escape. Don't worry, I don't think you'll ever need to do that. You have Mommy to entertain you."

×

The next week, a sense of normalcy sets in. The mothers practice reading aloud from picture books on Christmas, Kwanzaa, and Hanukkah. Frida reads to Emmanuelle from a book about Rita the Reindeer.

"Pay attention to your vocal variation," Ms. Khoury says. Rita the Reindeer and her reindeer friends and Santa and Mrs. Claus all sound the same. "You have to treat each phrase as a burst of light, Frida."

She tells Frida to name the things and people on each page, point out shapes and colors. Frida should ask Emmanuelle to repeat the words back to her. She must stimulate Emmanuelle's curiosity with developmentally appropriate, loving, and insightful questions.

"Remember, you're building her mind," Ms. Khoury says.

Requiring the dolls to sit still during reading practice presents a major hurdle. As promised, too many noes cause the dolls to beep like a car alarm. Alarms are going off throughout the building, especially for mothers with younger dolls.

Frida has Emmanuelle point to the red things in the picture. The reindeer noses. Santa's outfit. The stripes on the candy canes. She would like to tell Emmanuelle that Harriet is in McLean, Virginia, that Harriet will wear a red dress at Susanna's parents' house.

Susanna took the last call from the car. She was sitting in back with Harriet while Gust drove. The connection was fuzzy. Harriet's face kept disappearing. Susanna prompted Harriet to say that she missed Mommy, that she loves Mommy. Harriet wouldn't do it, but there was one brief smile.

No one told Frida about the trip. No one asked her permission. They never discussed Harriet meeting Susanna's family. She'd never have agreed to it. Had they asked, she would have told Gust that one white family is enough.

×

As Christmas approaches, the dolls become surly. One doll's bad mood can spread through the group like a fever. Emmanuelle tears off a whole page of flaps from her lift-the-flap book. When Frida reminds her to be gentle with toys and books, Emmanuelle locks eyes with her and says, in a matter-of-fact tone, "Hate you." She hits the consonants extra hard. It's her first two-word sentence.

Though she knows it's not personal and Emmanuelle isn't human, the insult still stings. **Did it happen to you?** they ask at dinner.

Lucretia thinks the dolls have been programmed to be harder to manage around the holidays. "Like real kids," she says, but besides Linda, no one knows what toddlers are like at the holidays. Last year, their daughters were easily placated infants.

The mothers have been in uniform for four weeks. They're messing up each other's cycles. The women in pink lab coats dispense thick, hospital-grade maxi pads two at a time so the mothers are forced to keep asking. It's unclear what harm could be done to themselves or school property if they were given more. They have too much respect for the cleaning crew and janitorial staff to stuff anything down the toilets.

In the midst of the latest doll hostility, Frida's period arrives early and Emmanuelle begins to pucker. Dimples form on the doll's cheeks and the tops of her hands. Emmanuelle scratches at her mottled skin.

"Hurt," she says.

Frida carries her to the instructors.

"We're going to teach Mommy Frida how to clean you," Ms. Russo says. The doll looks terrified, her cry anticipating physical injury, emotional upset, and psychological harm all at once.

Frida stays behind during lunch. The other dolls watch in fright as Ms. Russo wheels an examination table from the equipment room and covers it with a tarp. Ms. Russo unbuttons Emmanuelle's uniform, places her facedown on the table, and holds her there. Frida kisses her head, remembering how scared Harriet would be before shots.

"It's going to be okay," she says. Ms. Russo directs Frida to unscrew the knob at the small of Emmanuelle's back.

Frida looks over at the four frozen dolls. She asks if they can do this somewhere else.

"It's nothing they haven't seen before." Ms. Khoury hands her a pair of elbow-length rubber gloves. Frida must be careful. If the blue liquid comes in contact with her skin, it will cause a rash.

If there's a hug of contrition, can there also be a touch? Frida is glad they don't have to reach inside a doll vagina or anus, but as she unscrews the cap, as Ms. Russo pins Emmanuelle down and tells her not to move, she feels like a rapist.

The blue liquid smells rotten and milky, but with a chemical brightness, as if curdled milk was layered with aerosol air freshener. Frida's stomach turns. Ms. Khoury gives her a speculum, tells her to widen the hole. The doll kicks her legs. She shrieks into the table.

"Can you turn her off?"

"We appreciate your concern, Frida, but we need the liquid to be the right temperature."

Ms. Khoury hands her a flashlight. Frida expects to see gears, wires, buttons, filaments, but whatever makes Emmanuelle run won't be revealed. The blue liquid is shiny and thick. Floating on top are several nuggets the size of golf balls.

Ms. Russo brings over four empty unmarked cans. She pops the lids open and finds a long metal spoon with a serrated edge. The liquid will be sent back to the doll factory and recycled for future use. Ms. Khoury finds a metal drum in which Frida can deposit the spoiled liquid.

Frida apologizes to Emmanuelle as she fishes out nuggets and deposits these in the waste drum, then ladles the blue liquid out one spoonful at a time, trying not to gag. Emmanuelle has settled into a trance. It's possible that Frida is inflicting upon her the worst pain she's ever known, forcing her to dissociate from her body.

As a child, Frida loved to stretch across her mother's lap and have her mother scratch her back while they watched television. Sometimes her mother would clean her ears with a bobby pin. She remembers the delight in her mother's voice—**Ah!**—when she scooped out an especially big piece of wax. The shadowy tumbling sound if she knocked a piece farther into Frida's ear canal. The feeling of the bobby pin scraping against her eardrum. She was willing to go deaf if it meant they could spend more time together.

Emmanuelle will have no such tender memories. Frida inspects the cleaned cavity, which is metal but flexible, moving with the doll's breath. The new liquid hisses on contact. Emmanuelle seizes. She opens her mouth in a silent scream. Frida unlatches the speculum. The cavity returns to its normal size.

"I think we're done now. Are you okay, sweetie?"

Emmanuelle won't look at her. She hangs limp as Frida fixes her uniform. Her face and hands are smooth again. The instructors catch Frida pressing her ear to the doll's chest, grabbing her wrist and feeling for a pulse. They smile and make a note on their devices.

×

Emmanuelle remains listless and withdrawn the next day. She refuses to speak. Stares off into space. No longer cries. Seems like a different child entirely.

Ms. Russo says this is natural. After a cleaning, the dolls can become shy.

The puckering is happening to the other dolls too. At meals, Frida's classmates speak in euphemisms, as if they're discussing sex. They refer to the serrated spoon as "the thing," call the blue liquid "the stuff," refer to the dolls' dimpled bodies as "the problem."

Everyone thinks it's evil to make the other dolls watch. Beth heard gasps.

"They should have told us about the side effects," Lucretia says. The zombie disposition.

This week's counseling sessions have been canceled. The mothers have no one in power with whom to discuss the strangeness of the procedure or their guilt. They have no one to ask, if by changing the doll's constitution, they're hurting their chances.

Linda has been making fun of them, saying this can't be any worse than cleaning up shit or vomit. When her doll finally dimples, the others rejoice.

"Hope there's mold," Lucretia says.

"Maybe she'll have to use her bare hands," Beth adds. She and Lucretia tap forks.

Linda shows up to dinner after the food has been packed away. The dining hall staff gives her one apple and three packets of crackers.

"Did anyone save me food?" she asks.

Her classmates make excuses.

×

Another weekend passes. Sunday calls are disrupted by Internet problems. On Monday, the dolls emerge from the equipment room with the glazed, faraway look of crash survivors. Teen Mom's doll has gone mute. Emmanuelle recoils from Frida's touch. The cohorts' motherese reaches an unbearably high pitch as they try to break through to the doll-children who now regard them as strangers.

Frida reads a picture book about two pigs who are best friends, but Emmanuelle pushes her away and crawls over to Lucretia and her doll. Frida and Lucretia watch dumbfounded as the dolls pat each other's hands and faces, looking for dimples.

"Boo-boo," Emmanuelle says.

"Hurt me is," Lucretia's doll replies, rubbing her belly.

"Help." Emmanuelle looks up at Frida. "Mommy. Help."

To cheer up the dolls, the instructors surprise the class with an hour of outdoor time. They distribute navy blue snowsuits and hats and mittens and boots. Much effort is expended in bundling the dolls.

Ms. Khoury leads them to a roped-off section of the quad. The first minutes of outdoor time are quiet as the dolls simply breathe, amazed to see their clouds of breath floating away. They stare into the sun. They slowly spin and fall. They see and touch snow for the first time, their faces filled with wonder. Frida remembers Harriet catching snowflakes, Harriet crying when they disappeared.

Emmanuelle points at the snow and asks, "Eat?"

"No, no." Frida prevents her from bringing the snow to her lips. "It's made of water. Frozen water. But you don't eat water. I do, but you don't. I'm pretty sure it would make your insides hurt."

"Me eat!"

"Please. Just play with it. Don't eat it. It's not good for you."

Linda and Beth and their dolls are making snowmen. Lucretia is teaching her doll how to make a snow angel. Her doll is being fussy, doesn't want to wear a hat or mittens. Every time Lucretia puts them on, the doll takes them off again. Lucretia tries to reason with her.

"Little bug, you need to wear these to stay warm."

"No! No want!"

"Sweetie, I'm telling you, you'll get cold. Listen to Mommy. I need you to cooperate. I'll be so proud of you if you can cooperate. I know you can do it."

The doll stamps her feet. She begins to cry, cries and screams until Lucretia gives up and lets her remove her hat and mittens. The doll throws herself down, then flips onto her back and wriggles, trying to make another angel. Lucretia shows her how to move her arms and legs at the same time in smooth arcs. The doll gets snow in her locks, snow on her neck.

"I wish we could do this every day," Teen Mom tells Frida.

Sunlight glints off the windows of the other classroom buildings. Teen Mom's hair falls into her face. Frida tucks it behind her ear. Teen Mom won't wear a hat either, no matter how often Frida reminds her. The other day, they were talking about their routines at home. Teen Mom admitted that she rarely took Ocean to the playground. Not even when the weather was nice. She couldn't stand the way other moms looked at her.

"Those looks," she said, grateful that Frida instantly knew what she meant.

With their bare hands, they show their dolls how to pack the snow tight to make a secure base for the snowman. Emmanuelle rubs snow on Frida's cheeks. The snow stings, and some falls inside her collar, but Frida accepts it gratefully. They're rekindling warmth and intimacy. She's happy to be here, happy to see Emmanuelle returning to normal. They're busy rolling the snowman's head when they hear a scream.

×

Playtime is over. The others wait in the hallway while the instructors try to revive Lucretia's doll. When they're allowed to enter, they find Lucretia's doll laid out on the instructors' desk, her face covered by Ms. Russo's pink lab coat. They hide their dolls' eyes. No one is prepared to explain the concept of death.

Lucretia sits on the floor, her back against the desk. She doesn't look up when her classmates enter. Ms. Khoury carries the dead doll away, the doll's head lolling at an authentic angle.

The other dolls point at Lucretia and ask what's wrong.

"Sad, why sad?" Emmanuelle asks.

"She's in shock." Frida has never heard an adult scream like that. She might have screamed even louder. If it had been her. If it had been Emmanuelle.

Ms. Russo leaves to help Ms. Khoury. Left unsupervised, the mothers surround Lucretia, each placing a hand on her. The dolls wedge themselves into the tangle of limbs. Even Linda asks Lucretia if she's okay.

"Lu, what happened?" Frida asks.

"We weren't playing for that long. She said she was hot. And we're supposed to listen to them, right? I wasn't going to let them ride me about the crying. I swear I'm not stupid. I wouldn't let my baby play like that, but they're not—" She stops herself before she says, **They're not real**.

Lucretia looks at the four doll faces. They've been listening. The dolls look at the desk. At childless Lucretia. They begin to cry.

×

Lucretia's doll won't be coming back. Her doll was sent to the technical department, which operates out of the college's former center for civic and social responsibility. The technicians found that essential components malfunctioned. The blue liquid froze. Lucretia will need to reimburse the school for damages. She'll have to start over with a new doll. The instructors will work with her during special evening sessions, weekends too. But there's no guarantee she'll catch up. Bonding may take weeks.

The instructors prompt Lucretia to begin her atonement. "I should have known better," Lucretia says. "I'd never let Brynn . . ." At the mention of her real daughter, she starts to cry.

The instructors tell her to control herself. They feed her the lines.

"I am a bad mother, because I let the snow touch Gabby's bare skin. I am a bad mother, because I prioritized my fear of my child's meltdown above her safety and well-being. I am a bad mother, because I looked away."

Ms. Russo interrupts. "If Lucretia hadn't looked away, she would have noticed that Gabby wasn't moving. If Lucretia hadn't looked away, Gabby could have been saved.

"A mother must never look away," she continues. She pauses and repeats herself, asks the mothers to repeat after her. They bow their heads in a moment of silence for the departed doll.

They hear about the state of Lucretia's finances at dinner. Student loans, credit card debt, legal fees. If she owes money to the school too, she'll have to declare bankruptcy. Who's going to give her custody after that? Maybe she should quit. Maybe she should allow the foster parents to adopt Brynn. Seems like that's going to happen anyway.

Linda says, "Stop talking like that. Think about your kid."

"Do not tell me what to do."

"What? You're going to be a quitter? Like Helen? You're going to let your baby get adopted by some white people?"

"I'm just talking. I didn't mean it."

"You said you'd give her up. I heard you say that. We all heard you."

"I was processing my feelings. Just drop it, Linda."

Mothers nearby are listening. Teen Mom tells Lucretia to calm the fuck down. Frida tells Linda to stop picking on Lucretia. She reaches for Lucretia's cutlery and moves it out of the way. If it was her, she'd be tempted.

Linda won't stop browbeating Lucretia.

"If you say one more word to me, I swear," Lucretia says. "Need I remind everyone that you're the one who put your kids in a fucking hole? **You** should be in real jail."

Frida touches Lucretia's arm. "Don't."

Linda pushes her chair back, comes to Lucretia's side of the table. She tells Lucretia to stand up. Mothers at surrounding tables go silent. Someone whistles.

Lucretia looks on in disbelief. "What? I am not fighting you. This isn't high school. What are we? Fourteen?"

Linda pulls Lucretia to standing. A tug-of-war ensues, with their classmates telling both of them to stop. Linda is nearly twice Lucretia's width and several inches taller, could win easily.

Mothers shout, "Go, Lu!"

As she resists, Lucretia pushes Linda away. The women in pink lab coats see the push. They see Linda fall.

All the guards and women in pink lab coats rush over. Frida, Beth, and Teen Mom shout. Lucretia was defending herself. They're willing to testify on her behalf. Lucretia tells them to watch the footage. If they watch the footage, they'll see that Linda started the whole thing.

Ms. Gibson takes Lucretia away while everyone is still arguing. Dinner ends early. The mothers wonder aloud what will happen, though they know. Violence leads to expulsion, expulsion leads to termination of parental rights.

Frida, Beth, and Teen Mom return to Kemp and look for Lucretia in her room. They search the other floors. Teen Mom thinks they should have stopped Linda from mouthing off. Beth thinks they should go to Ms. Gibson's office together. The instructors should have warned and corrected Lucretia when she took off her doll's hat. They notice every mistake. Why didn't they correct her?

They walk to Pierce and spend the next hour wandering the building, knocking on doors, trying to find Ms. Gibson. They head back outside. Beth spots Lucretia standing next to a security guard's SUV in the rose garden circle. Lucretia is dressed in her personal clothes, a green-and-white ski jacket over a pleated skirt and knee-high burgundy heeled boots, a fedora. She looks commanding and regal.

They run to her, catching snow in the cuffs of their uniforms. The guards tell them to leave.

Beth says, "We won't cause any trouble. We just want to say goodbye."

Linda is nowhere to be seen. More mothers arrive. For once, there's no gawking or whispering or rumormongering. Frida, Beth, and Teen Mom apologize to Lucretia and offer condolences as if her child has died. They blame themselves. They saw Gabby take off her hat. They should have said something.

"I'm so sorry," Frida says. "I should have helped you."

"Yeah, well." Lucretia shrugs.

Frida is surprised to find Lucretia calm, but she may be past tears. Tears will come later, when she thinks back on this one terrible day, following this one humiliating month, when all her life, she mourns her lost daughter.

Frida holds Lucretia for a good minute. It could have been any of them. She wants to ask where Lucretia will go tonight. "It wasn't your fault," she whispers.

"It doesn't matter. Listen, all of you better finish. Except Linda. I don't care what happens to her. But the rest of you. Don't you dare fuck this up. If I hear of any of you causing trouble—"

"Enough," Ms. Gibson says. She sends Frida and the others back to Kemp. Lights-out will be early tonight. Tomorrow is Christmas Eve.

9.

THEIR CLASS IS NOW KNOWN AS THE ONE WITH the dead doll. Other mothers keep their distance on the walk to Morris. Frida wishes she could tell Lucretia about the whispers, the staring. How they left her seat empty this morning as a tribute. How they banished Linda from the table. How some Black mothers took her expulsion personally. The ordeal has bonded Teen Mom and Beth. They've promised each other that if one gets expelled, the other will quit.

The instructors don't mention Lucretia or her doll Gabby by name, but begin class with a freestyle hug sequence, no counting necessary.

Emmanuelle points to the spot next to the window where Lucretia and Gabby usually sat. Frida says Gabby has gone to the equipment room in the sky, maybe to the equipment room in a doll factory in China.

"I won't let that happen to you," she says, trying to sound convincing. She turns away and yawns. Roxanne kept her up late with impossible questions. **Why isn't Linda being punished too? What if the foster parents don't want to keep Brynn? How will Lucretia find a job? Parents who get expelled are automatically added to the registry. She'll never be able to teach again. When does she have to start paying the school back? Does she still have to pay them back if they're taking her kid?**

"Lu should go get Brynn," Roxanne said. "Take her. There are ways. It doesn't have to end like this. I'd do it."

"Right," Frida said. "And then what? Your kid visits you in jail? Brilliant plan."

"And you wonder why I don't tell you things."

The instructors are wearing Santa hats with tinkling bells. They've set up the classroom with four mothering stations, each with a changing table, a diaper pail, a rag rug, and a basket of toys and books. Having honed their tenderness skills, the mothers will now incorporate this tenderness into basic child-care tasks. First diapering, then sleep.

Ms. Khoury shows them how to unfold a clean diaper with a flick of the wrist, how to roll the dirty diaper into a tidy cylindrical bundle so that it will take up less space in a landfill.

The dolls hate being on their backs. They can't lie flat because of their blue knobs. The instructors tell the mothers not to stare. The dolls' genitalia are remarkably lifelike. Blue liquid of different consistencies pours out of each hole. The make-believe urine and feces smell more pungent than the real thing. Beth and Teen Mom are caught saying "Ew." Linda doesn't seem bothered.

Emmanuelle's body is sleek and cheerless. It feels wrong to be looking at her labia. It feels wrong to part her vaginal folds to check for blue specks. Frida hates that Susanna knows Harriet's body this intimately. Harriet's diaper rashes sometimes lasted for days. Susanna thought Frida's preferred rash cream was full of chemicals that would increase Harriet's risk of Parkinson's and other degenerative diseases. She repeatedly suggested that both households use plant-based creams. Arguments about rash cream so often spiraled into fights about love and faith and what kind of person Harriet would become. It shocks

Frida to think she ever felt so passionately about consumer products.

Though there are now only four dolls, they make as much noise as a dozen toddlers. They grab at the diapers, the blue liquid, the rash cream, the wipes, their vaginas. Each diaper change is a battle. The dolls surprise the mothers with their strength and ingenuity. That afternoon, Teen Mom's doll picks up her jar of rash cream and hurls it at Ms. Russo while she's walking past. The jar hits Ms. Russo solidly in the chest. The doll laughs. Teen Mom laughs.

Linda's doll mimics her and strikes Ms. Russo in the back.

Frida covers her mouth. Her eyes are watering, she's laughing so hard. She looks up and sees Beth stifling giggles. Ms. Khoury is watching them. Ms. Russo tells Teen Mom and Linda to make their dolls apologize.

The dolls aren't sorry. They giggle and clap, their laughter coming from the back of their throats or somewhere deep inside their circuitry, as if they're being tickled.

Frida takes the jar out of Emmanuelle's hands. "We do not throw things."

The instructors could be stoned to death with jars of rash cream. If it were the mothers throwing, such force might be possible. They ought to do it for Lucretia.

Diapers are changed every half hour. After each change, the instructors freeze the dolls and carry them back to the equipment room to be refilled, carrying them two at a time horizontally, like they're lawn ornaments or loaves of bread. The imposition on the dolls is tremendous. Their bottoms turn pebbly and red. They wince as they walk. Motherese can barely be heard above the weeping.

Other classes are practicing potty training and bathroom hygiene and curing bedwetting. The mothers working on potty training sob during meals. Mothers with infant and toddler boy dolls have to wear face shields. Spraying is not just annoying but dangerous. One mother got blue liquid in her mouth and had to be taken to the infirmary.

×

The holiday is not without beauty. The next night, after an austere Christmas dinner, the mothers gather in the main stairwell of Kemp and listen to the trio of middle-aged white women sing carols. The trio's harmonizing suggests prior a cappella experience. "Silent Night" and "Little Drummer Boy" and "All I Want for Christmas Is You." Their rendition of "Edelweiss" is especially poignant.

Frida sits between Roxanne and Teen Mom. They hum and sway. Together, they sing the refrain, "Bless my homeland forever." That's the only line Frida knows. A music therapist played this song at Ahma's bedside when she was dying.

Frida looks down at the many faces, imagining them all as girls, shy and sad, wearing clothes they didn't choose, their hair braided, pin-curled, tied in kerchiefs. They are waiting, brimming, thinking themselves to freedom. Frida misses her mother's laugh, her father's cooking. Harriet. Gust had Harriet last Christmas too.

×

To give the dolls' bottoms time to heal, naptime practice begins early. Cribs and rocking chairs are moved into the classroom. The dolls need naps every hour. In beginning naptime, prep will be completed in ten minutes. By intermediate, the mothers should get their dolls down in five. By advanced, they should go down in two minutes or less.

"Out like a light," Ms. Russo says, snapping her fingers.

Naptime practice reminds Frida of a game of Whac-A-Mole. She asks Emmanuelle to notice what time it is. "It's naptime. What happens during naptime? Rest. You're so sleepy."

Emmanuelle begs to differ.

Frida is forgetting what Harriet's skin feels like. Her gurgling, wet laugh. The perfect curve of her forehead. The pattern of her curls.

It's New Year's Eve. Last year, Gust and Susanna dropped by unannounced on the way to a dinner party. Gust wanted to do bedtime.

Frida never denied these requests, which often came without warning. She remembers Susanna bending down to hug her while Gust was upstairs with Harriet, Susanna studying her bookshelves. Susanna wore a low-cut green satin dress that night, had a black velvet ribbon tied around her neck.

She suggested they get coffee sometime, just the two of them. "I'd like us to be friends. Gust speaks so highly of you. I just want you to know, Frida,

I think you're very brave. We've talked about it. I admire your strength."

Frida remembers staring at the ribbon, at Susanna's fine, pale throat. How she wanted that sinister story to be true. To pull on the ribbon and make Susanna lose her head.

×

The following week, Frida learns that Harriet has lost weight. Her cheeks have shrunk. Susanna has been reducing their carb intake, replacing carbs with vegetables and lean proteins and fats. They've gone gluten-free. The first thing Susanna does with all her clients is eliminate wheat. Everyone is a little intolerant of wheat. Wheat causes bloating. They were all so bloated after the holidays.

Visions of headless Susanna return. In early January, the school has Frida on record saying, "How dare you! She doesn't need to detox! She's just a toddler!" Had they consulted the pediatrician? How could Gust let this happen? But Gust was no help. He said Harriet was having tummy aches. Her digestion had improved. They all feel better now that they're eating clean.

The counselor thought Frida overreacted. Her tone was disrespectful. Her anger was unjustified. "Your daughter is changing," the counselor said. "It's a bittersweet experience for all parents. You need to accept it."

All children lose their chubby cheeks eventually. Harriet may be having a growth spurt. She may be more active. How can Frida use terms like **starvation**? Gust and Susanna would never harm Harriet. Frida only talks to Harriet for a few minutes every week.

"How much do you really know about her life right now?" the counselor asked.

Frida knows she's not imagining things. Harriet can digest wheat just fine, and the adorable-belly-and-jowls period is not supposed to be over yet. She wanted to tell the counselor that Harriet has had those cheeks since birth, that her round face defined her, made her look more Chinese. Like Frida. Like Frida's mother.

During intermediate naptime, her imagination goes wild. She pictures Harriet asking for bread and being denied. Harriet reduced to bones. Susanna will stunt Harriet's growth, will hinder Harriet's brain development, will give Harriet an eating disorder, will teach Harriet to hate herself before she can even speak a complete sentence. Self-loathing may lead preteen Harriet to suicidal ideation. Suicidal ideation may lead to cutting. Why was there no way for her to report Susanna? She is the one doing lasting damage.

Nap wars have all the mothers on edge. Frida is chewing her cuticles again and sleeping three hours a night. She's irritated by everything Emmanuelle does. She's dared to complain about Emmanuelle to Roxanne. She's risked these complaints being overheard in the shower line or on the walk to the dining hall.

After an especially trying day, she says, "Mommy doesn't want to play, not now. Now is naptime. Close your eyes, please."

When Emmanuelle talks back, saying, "No no no no no," Frida snaps. She reaches down into the crib and pinches Emmanuelle's arm, denting her silicone flesh.

"Oh my God." Frida steps back.

The instructors haven't noticed yet. Her classmates are occupied. Emmanuelle doesn't cry immediately. She looks from her arm to Frida's hands, from Frida's hands to Frida's face. Her mouth falls open in a stunned, heartbroken O.

×

Talk circle is for mothers whose classroom behavior falls on a continuum of aggression, from smaller outbursts—like Frida's—to mothers who threaten their dolls with the discipline they once meted out to their children. The group meets in the gymnasium after dinner. The numbers change every night depending on the day's infractions, usually going up around the holidays and children's birthdays, before evaluations, and when the mothers have PMS. There are seventeen women tonight, including Frida. In one lit corner, they sit on cold metal folding chairs, arranged in a circle. The effect of the overhead light amid all the darkness is garish. They could be stars of a slasher film or the world's saddest hip-hop video.

Ms. Gibson moderates. The mothers must state their names and offenses and discuss their troubled pasts and reflect on the harm they've done to their children and their dolls. Past behavior is the best indicator of future behavior. Presumably their transgressions are rooted in a troubled history. They may be succumbing to old patterns, which the school will help them break. After their confessions, the mothers must repeat the mantra of talk circle: "I am a narcissist. I am a danger to my child."

Some mothers confess to prostitution. Poverty. Drug addiction. Marijuana mostly, some opioids. Drug dealing. Homelessness. Several are alcoholics, including one of the middle-aged white women, Maura, a well-preserved brunette with a breathy voice, who started drinking at eleven. Stole money and booze. Would hang out with teenagers, wake up covered in dirt and blood. She has five children. She chuckles, says she does everything alcoholically. She's here for problems with her youngest: her thirteen-year-old daughter, Kylie.

"She called me a wasted old bitch. So I slapped her. She always threatened to report me, and one day, while I was at work, she called the hotline. CPS found cuts on her thighs. I didn't know she was cutting. She told them I drove her to it.

"I wasn't supposed to have her. I got pregnant after her father and I had already decided to split." Maura hesitates. "I burned her once when she was five. Dabbed my cigarette on her arm." She looks at the group, who are staring at her, aghast, and smiles warmly.

Ms. Gibson asks how Maura is feeling about the abuse now. The slapping, the burning.

"Burning her gently," Maura clarifies. "Let's not make it sound worse than it was."

Today, Maura and her doll were practicing bedtime negotiation. The preteen dolls had been given smartphones. Maura's doll was under the covers, playing with her device, so finally Maura pulled the covers off and threatened to smack her.

"That's all. I am a narcissist. I am a danger to my child."

The mothers thank her for sharing. Next, they hear from Evie, a daughter of Ethiopian immigrants, who has a narrow face and somber expression and delicate, child-size hands. Evie describes her childhood as happy. Her mistake was letting her daughter, Harper, walk home from the library alone. Her eight-year-old. "No, wait. She just turned nine." She gives the mothers a sad smile.

"It's about four blocks between our house and the library. Maybe ten minutes going at her pace. She wanted to walk by herself. Kids in our neighborhood do it all the time. People watch out for each other. If someone had a problem, they could have talked to me. They didn't have to call the police."

Evie stares at the floor. "She got picked up when she was a block from home."

Ms. Gibson thinks Evie isn't showing enough remorse. In what world is an eight-year-old allowed to go anywhere unsupervised?

"Lady," Evie says. She bites her lip. Her voice drops to a monotone. "I made a poor decision. I put her in danger."

"Excellent, Evie. Now what brings you here today?"

"My doll said I pushed her. But I didn't push her. She fell down. It was an accident."

"Evie, your instructors saw you push her."

"You can look at the footage. Don't you have footage of everything? I'm telling you, she's making it up."

They argue about whether the dolls are capable of lying, whether the dolls are manipulative like real children, whether if, by making this accusation against her doll, Evie is demonstrating the insecurity of their attachment and her lack of commitment to the program. Evie says she comforted her doll. Her hug to soothe physical injury worked within seconds. Her affection numbers have been good. On evaluation day, she came in first.

Why is Ms. Gibson giving her a hard time when all her daughter did was walk and all her doll did was fall? "It's not like I burned anyone," she says.

The mothers inhale sharply. Maura glares at Evie. Evie glares at Ms. Gibson. There is a flurry of tense leg crossing.

Ms. Gibson says, "Remember, ladies, this is a safe space."

One woman's boyfriend broke her daughter's arm. They told the hospital it was an accident. The boyfriend violated his parole, is now in jail. The mother is here for lying on his behalf and not protecting her daughter. Other mothers admit to fires. Belts. Curling irons, regular irons. One mother hit her ten-year-old son with a scale, giving him a black eye.

Frida lets the stories wash over her. The first time Harriet stayed at Gust and Susanna's apartment overnight, Frida wanted to take a hammer to her foot, a hammer to the wall. What was she supposed to do with that feeling? Today her anger consumed her.

She stares at the mothers' boots, noting the various ways of tying the laces, whose uniform cuffs are frayed, whose have mud on them. It is January 11. Harriet turned twenty-two months today.

When it's her turn, she tells them about her one very bad day, her depression, Susanna, the divorce. "I pinched my doll. During naptime drills. I've been distracted. My ex's girlfriend has my baby on a diet. They're cutting carbs. I know how incredibly stupid that sounds, but it's dangerous. Her cheeks . . ." Frida's voice trembles. She wipes away tears. "She should be **gaining** weight, not losing it. I lost my temper today. I didn't mean to take it out on my doll."

The mothers in talk circle welcome her as one of their own, murmur, "Hmmm, yes, Mama."

The woman who hit her son with a scale says, "That's how it started for me too."

The mother next to Frida, who burned her son with a curling iron, pats Frida's knee. Maura, the alcoholic mother of five, smiles kindly.

"And how did pinching Emmanuelle make you feel?" Ms. Gibson asks.

"Horrible. Like a monster. I'd never pinch Harriet. I'm not that kind of person." The mother next to Frida rolls her eyes.

"But?"

Frida purses her lips. "But I am a narcissist. I am a danger to my child."

×

Standing beside the instructors' desk, with Ms. Khoury guiding her, Frida articulates her shortcomings. She is a bad mother for fighting with her co-parents. She is a bad mother for wasting her Sunday phone privileges. She is a bad mother for not understanding the limits of her current role in her daughter's life.

"Anger is the most dangerous emotion," Ms. Khoury says. "There is no excuse for violence against children."

Frida's counselor thinks she's the architect of her own misery. She's dismayed by Frida's downward spiral: the pinching, talk circle. Ms. Gibson said Frida wasn't listening to the other women, that Frida seemed reluctant to participate in the hug chain.

Frida wanted to say that the hug chain was the stupidest part of the whole evening. At the end of the session, Ms. Gibson hugged the mother on her right, who passed the hug to the next woman. They joined hands and closed with the mantra of the school: **I am a bad mother, but I am learning to be good.** They repeated the phrase three times, as if they were Dorothy trying to get home.

Last night, she almost revealed more. Ms. Gibson wanted to hear about her childhood. Had Frida been abandoned as a child? Was abandoning Harriet the result of intergenerational trauma?

Though she and her mother are closer now, though her mother started softening in her fifties, as a child, Frida sometimes felt a chill. She made up her own explanations, blamed herself, thought her mother didn't want her. Her mother didn't like to spend time with her, didn't like to touch her. She had to beg for hugs. She felt like a nuisance. Her father and grandmother were always telling her to leave her mother alone.

She didn't find out about her mother's miscarriage until she was pregnant herself. The baby boy who died at six months. Frida had been two at the time, too young to remember her mother's growing belly. There were no photos of that pregnancy in the family albums.

She doesn't know if her parents yearned for a boy, if they named him, what they did with his remains, if they do anything to mark the date of his death, if they ever talk about him with each other. She knew better than to ask.

Her mother warned Frida not to exercise too much, not to lift anything heavy, to manage her stress. The doctors blamed her mother's miscarriage on stress, unfair as that was.

That phone call was only the third time Frida had ever heard her mother cry. When Frida finally found out about the miscarriage, she apologized for all the times she complained about being an only child. It had been a sore subject when she was in elementary school. She'd shout: "What's wrong with you?" Her classmates had mothers who gave them siblings. Frida thought that because she was a bad, ungrateful daughter, her mother didn't want to have another child like her. Ms. Gibson would have loved that story. But her mother didn't cause this. She did. Her mother's ghost child, her ghost brother, has no place in her file.

×

If Emmanuelle ever loved Frida, she doesn't anymore. The doll's arm is still dented. The instructors opted not to send her for repairs. The dent is only a surface wound, and the technical department is overtaxed, and leaving the dent will help Frida think about consequences.

Emmanuelle murmurs, "Hate you, hate you," as Frida sings lullabies.

Frida's temperature remains elevated. Her anger levels are rising. She remains woefully distracted. Harriet has been calling Susanna "Mommy." It slipped out during the last call. Mommy Sue-Sue.

Gust and Susanna were embarrassed. "It happens sometimes," Gust said. "I don't think we should make a big deal about it." Harriet hasn't seen Frida in person since November. She sees Susanna every day. "No one is trying to hurt you," he said.

Susanna took Harriet out of the room as her parents fought. Frida said it wasn't acceptable. They had an agreement. Susanna is Sue-Sue. Only she is Mommy.

"I don't want to put more restrictions on her," Gust said.

He asked Frida to calm down. Was it necessary to fight about terms? When Frida finds a new partner, down the line, he's fine with Harriet calling that man "Daddy."

×

While the dolls sleep, the mothers must meditate on their faults. For bedtime prep and nightmare management, the same protocol as naptime applies, but now, the dolls wake up twice within each four-hour cycle.

The mock bedtime sequences give Frida too much time to dwell on Harriet's weight loss, her daughter calling the wrong woman "Mommy," how many months remain.

The instructors detect false tenderness when Frida peers into the crib. Data from the doll backs them up. If Frida's performance doesn't improve, if she doesn't pass the next evaluation, the counselor will suspend phone privileges.

Ms. Russo thinks Frida's bedtime stories lack depth. "You can't just have the cow jump over the moon, Frida. You need to have the cow consider his place in society. If you're telling the Red Riding Hood story, you need to talk about the kind of woods, the kind of food in her basket."

She pantomimes Little Red Riding Hood's journey with her hands. "How was Little Red Riding Hood feeling as she made that journey? Ask Emmanuelle open-ended questions about that. Engage with her thinking. You're teaching her about being a girl. Remember, everything she'll learn about girlhood will come from you."

×

By late January, bedtime prep includes a diaper change, pajamas, a bottle of blue liquid, and tooth-brushing. When the doll wakes up, her mother must soothe her nightmare and put the doll back to sleep in ten minutes, then eight, then five.

Harriet hardly spoke during the last call. No Mommy Sue-Sue, but also no Mommy. She wouldn't look at the screen. Her cheeks were even smaller.

At the next call, Frida will tell Harriet that she's remembering. She tests herself every night. What changes happened during which months. When Harriet's eyes changed from slate-blue to blue-gray to hazel to brown. When her hair darkened and began to curl. At fourteen months, she started walking. At fifteen months, she learned to walk backward. She started speaking. Her first word was **hi**. At sixteen months, she started dancing. At seventeen months, she held a spoon. In Frida's memory, Harriet gains sound and sense. She becomes human.

×

On evaluation day, Frida, Beth, and Teen Mom wait in the hall while Linda is tested. Beth asks them to huddle.

"Today is for Lucretia," she says.

"For Lu." They each put a hand in.

Frida takes her turn after lunch. She hands Emmanuelle to Ms. Russo and sits down in the rocking chair. Ms. Russo returns with the crying doll. Ms. Khoury starts the timer. Emmanuelle arches her back and screams with abandon. It is a cry of lost love, families torn apart by war, a cry for the earth and its natural disasters. The falsehood of her body and how she must suffer without growing up.

The mothers have one hour. Frida's face reddens along with Emmanuelle's. She too feels despair welling up. Susanna now refers to Harriet as **our** daughter.

"You have to stop treating me like the enemy," Susanna said.

Frida calms Emmanuelle to a low, snotty gurgle. She completes the diaper change and pajama change. During the bedtime story, Emmanuelle flings her bottle to the ground. Frida forgets to clean the blue drips from her chin. When she has to brush Emmanuelle's teeth, the doll bites down on the toothbrush and refuses to let go for five agonizing minutes.

Frida can't get Emmanuelle to open her mouth. She thinks of the day before Christmas Eve. Lucretia running through the snow with her frozen doll. The instructors always tell them that motherhood is a marathon, not a sprint. Why, then, do they have to sprint?

Tooth-brushing finally completed, she rushes through the story of Hansel and Gretel. She sings "Three Blind Mice" and "London Bridge Is Falling Down" and "Row Row Row Your Boat." Emmanuelle won't stop whimpering.

Frida gives up on nursery songs, begins to sing "Killing Me Softly." The low tones of Roberta Flack's melody finally quiets the doll. She sets Emmanuelle in the crib. She takes her place in the rocking chair. She closes her eyes and waits for Emmanuelle to wake up.

10.

Gust and Susanna hosted last year. The
even-number birthdays were supposed to be hers.
Frida was going to make Harriet a flower crown
from pink tissue paper and ribbon. She was going
to throw a party and make flower crowns for all
the children. She wonders what her daughter is
learning about food and baths and nightmares.
When she considers her doll's dented arm and her
recent zero, she pictures herself taking a daring
leap off the roof of the school, imagines how she'd
smile as the pavement rose up, but knows that
with her luck, she'd just land in the bushes and
be deemed more self-involved, a danger to herself and others.

It is February, and she hasn't seen Harriet in

over three months. Her phone privileges have been revoked, punishment for failing the second care-and-nurture test. After the disastrous evaluation day, Frida begins spending more time with Meryl and Beth. All three have lost phone privileges. She's stopped thinking of Meryl as Teen Mom. She tries to be more tolerant of Beth's possessive behavior toward Meryl, her constant interrupting. The girls have been inseparable since the night of Lucretia's expulsion, affectionate as kittens.

She finds Beth's willingness to talk about her problems unseemly. Her mother would too. Only a white woman, an American, would be so indiscreet. Beth's favorite subject is her most recent attempt.

"I was being responsible," she said. She'd been hoarding her medication, planned to combine her pills with two bottles of vodka. Her first attempt was when she was thirteen. She tried again in high school and college. This time, the night she planned to do it, she dropped her daughter off with her ex and drove herself to the hospital.

Meryl often asks for details. She asks about the other patients, if they were actually crazy or medium-functional self-harming crazy like Beth, who has chunks of flesh gouged out of her forearms and pale crisscrossing scars on her legs that resemble winter birch trees.

Meryl has asked Beth how she started, whether she used knives or razors, how she prevented infections. Whenever she does this, Frida steers the conversation back to Ocean, sometimes also elbowing Meryl in the ribs.

The three of them mill outside the computer lab on Sunday, shuffling past the waiting mothers who still have phone privileges, trying not to make eye contact or brush shoulders or attract the attention of the guards or cameras or Ms. Gibson. Eavesdropping on the calls is morbid. They can hear children crying.

Meryl says, "It's like that thing people do on the highway."

"Rubbernecking," Frida replies.

"Yeah, that."

The buzzer rings. Twenty mothers file out. Another twenty enter. The mothers who just said goodbye weep silently. It's a technique Frida needs to learn. No wetness, no ugliness, just a brief face crumple and a sag of the shoulders, a dignified, private aching. The mothers hug and hold hands. They talk about how their children looked, if their children seemed healthy, whether their children were happy to see them, what they would have said if they'd had more time.

Frida needs Gust to check on her parents. She needs to know what's happening with Harriet's diet, if her second birthday party will have a theme or decorations in a particular color, if Harriet has a favorite color now, how Gust and Susanna will explain her absence.

Life has carried on without them. Relatives have had strokes. Children have responded to their mother's absence with aggression—with pushing, tantrums, even biting. Linda's oldest, her sixteen-year-old son, Gabriel, ran away from his foster home. He's been missing for five days. It's not his first time running away or the first time she's worried that he's dead, but it's the first time she can't look for him.

Though they haven't forgotten what Linda did to Lucretia, they've been trying to be nicer, given the circumstances. They say, **I understand**. They say, **I can't imagine**. Was Gabriel having problems at school? With his foster parents? Did he run off to be with a girl? Is he getting into drugs?

Linda covers her ears. She says, "Goddamn it, shut up!" Can't they leave her alone?

"Stop making this about you," she snaps when Beth tries to hug her.

Linda's sorrow makes their already tense meal-times unbearable. Others have been saying their class is cursed. Beth suggests a moratorium on news from home. They try not to discuss their children. No talk of babies or birth, their bodies, how long it's been since their children were taken away, no whining about phone calls, what they're permitted, whether they've forgotten their child's touch or smell. Instead, they talk about gas prices and the latest natural disaster, stories gleaned from the women in pink lab coats, who check their phones when they think the mothers aren't looking. They try to keep their conversation substantive and focused on real-world concerns. Thinking of themselves to the point of pathology is one reason they're here.

×

As in all institutions, germs are a problem. There have been cases of bronchitis. Stomach bugs. Colds. For a place claiming to simulate parenting, there's a distinct shortage of hand sanitizer.

This week, the mothers share the flu. It is, as

Frida imagines, how the plague worked in a board-inghouse. One cough, one sneeze, another mother goes down. Roommate infects roommate. Whole classes get sick. Roxanne's dream laughter has been replaced by hacking coughs. Frida finds that her entire brain has been reduced to thoughts of mucus. Linda proves to have a remarkably strong immune system.

With illness comes small rebellions. Some mothers try to cough on the women in pink lab coats, but after a few episodes of targeted coughing and malicious hand shaking, all punished with trips to talk circle, the staff starts wearing face masks and keeping their distance. No masks are provided for the mothers, who, even at their sickest, are not allowed to miss class. Beth unwisely asks about sick days and has the request added to her file.

"It's not like you can request sick days at home," Ms. Gibson says.

×

Unit 2 covers the Fundamentals of Food and Medicine. Cooking, the mothers learn, is one of the highest forms of love. The kitchen is the center, and the mother the heart, of the home. Like any other aspect of mothering, craft and attention to detail are paramount.

The dining hall chefs have the week off while the cohorts rotate through the kitchen, cooking children's meals for the whole school. Some nights, the mothers are served purees. Other nights, jam sandwiches with the crust removed, oatmeal with raisins arranged in a rainbow. They eat overcooked omelets, meat cut into child-size bites, mushy sautés, an array of bland vegetables and casseroles. They're only allowed to cook with a pinch of salt.

Several mothers sustain burns. One has a cast-iron pan dropped on her foot. One purposefully cuts her hand on a cheese grater. Allowing the mothers to handle sharp objects is risky, it's been decided. Before leaving the kitchen, they have to turn out their pockets and unroll their sleeves and pant legs. The guards wave metal detectors over their uniforms. They pat the mothers' hair and shine lights in their mouths. The known cutters in the community are taken to another room and subjected to cavity searches by the women in pink lab coats, a change in disciplinary procedure that dampens morale. Beth is searched twice a day.

The mothers go to bed hungry. They lose weight and become dizzy and irritable. When they're not on a cooking rotation, they report to the auditorium for lectures on kitchen safety, nutrition, and mindful eating. In the kitchen, they compete to see who can prepare the fastest, healthiest omelet, who can crack an egg with one hand, whose cake is the most moist and flavorful, who can juice an orange and butter toast at the same time. Beth impresses the instructors with her chocolate-chip banana pancakes, which are decorated with smiley faces and hearts. Linda tries to one-up her by whistling as she prepares batter.

Frida's father was the one who cooked. The family court judge should know this. Her father's specialty is seafood. Steamed fish. Red snapper. Halibut. He'd carve tomatoes and carrots into garnishes, plated every dish. Her grandmother cooked too, but her mother didn't have the time or inclination. Some women don't. Some families don't eat American food. Not once did her parents ever prepare pancakes.

She thinks herself forward and backward. To March, when she'll speak to Harriet again. To last August, when Harriet was still chubby and hers.

She is a bad mother because she hates cooking. She is a bad mother because her knife skills need work. Her grip is hostile.

"A hostile grip will lead to accidents," Ms. Khoury says, noting the bandages on Frida's left hand.

Observing Frida quartering grapes, Ms. Khoury shows her how to line up several grapes in a row and use a bigger knife to slice them at the same time, rather than cutting them individually. Frida lines up five grapes on the cutting board, and slices horizontally, then vertically. She collects the grapes into a bowl and hands the bowl to Ms. Khoury for inspection, wondering how much force is required to stab a person dead, what Ms. Khoury would look like with a knife in her neck or stomach, whether she would try, if all of them would try, if there were no cameras and no guards and no daughters.

×

Feeding Harriet had never been one of Frida's primary sources of delight. Gust and Susanna began baby-led weaning at six months. Frida continued to spoon-feed Harriet until ten months, relying heavily on organic food pouches. After they insisted that she was hindering Harriet's development, she began steaming vegetables, making pasta and eggs, serving solid fruit instead of purees. The laundry doubled. Feedings stretched to a full hour. After each meal, she had to clean up Harriet, then spend another twenty minutes cleaning the high chair and floor.

She tried serving food that was easy to grip, serving the same food she was eating, eating at the same time, scolding Harriet when she dropped food, praising her when she didn't, not reacting. She bought bowls that adhered to the high-chair tray. She placed food on the tray directly. She took photos of the messy floor and texted them to Gust with a string of question marks. She occasionally resorted to spoon-feeding, darting in with a spoonful of yogurt when Harriet was distracted. But when meals were peaceful, when she stopped to pay attention, she loved watching Harriet eat. Harriet would stare at new food—a piece of cucumber, a raspberry, a bit of doughnut—as if it were a gold coin. Her cheeks jiggled as she chewed.

Back in the classroom, they're feeding the dolls blue liquid molded into tiny pea-flavored balls. The food, the instructors explain, is made of a different substance than what's inside the dolls' cavities, but it's blue for the sake of consistency.

Each mothering station has a white plastic high chair on top of a circular splat mat. The dolls are wearing bibs. The mothers are wearing gloves and goggles. The dolls don't have functional digestive systems, but they have taste buds. They've been set to a high level of hunger and food curiosity.

One week has been allocated for feeding mastery. Demonstrating with Meryl's doll, Ms. Khoury places a single pea on the high-chair tray and asks the doll to notice it. "Can you try it? Can you taste it for me?" She tickles the doll's chin. "Auntie is so proud of you! Children who try new foods are curious and brave. They lead richer, more dynamic lives. Don't you want to lead a rich, dynamic life?"

Ms. Khoury describes the nutrients contained in peas, the effect of those nutrients on the doll's growth and development, the work that went into growing the peas and harvesting them and transporting them to this classroom.

"You're picking it up! You're opening your mouth. You're tasting it! Good, good! Taste is one of the five senses! Swallow for Auntie now, yes, swallow, yes yes

yes! I'm so proud of you! What a good girl you are! What a fulfilling life you'll lead!"

She cheers as the doll swallows a single blue pea, then repeats the process. As far as Frida can tell, the ratio is ten minutes of motherese to one pea. It takes the mothers even longer, with a lower success rate.

×

Winter is getting to everyone. There's been a second doll casualty. During outdoor activity time, one of the eleven-year-old-boy dolls ran for the tree line and threw himself against the electrified fence. His silicone skin melted, the burned patches making it look as if he was dipped in acid. His mother was blamed for the suicide. She was charged for the damaged equipment and received a new doll, who, her classmates say, won't even speak to her. Reunification with her real child seems doubtful.

Frida would like to tell the family court judge that last summer, Harriet's favorite food was strawberries. She remembers slicing strawberries and handing them to Harriet one piece at a time, Harriet casually

dropping the strawberries on the floor, Harriet examining and prodding and mashing every piece of
fruit until the juice ran down her arms.

Sometimes she let Harriet sit in her lap while
she ate, though that was even messier. Harriet once
draped individual noodles on her head like a headband. She loved wiping food in her hair. She ate so
much challah bread that Frida called her "the bread
monster."

They haven't spoken in four weeks. Chinese
New Year's Eve passes, then New Year's Day. There
are no oranges or incense, no Harriet in a padded
silk vest. Frida marks the occasion privately, saying
prayers for her parents and grandparents, for Harriet. For their health. Their well-being. She adds
a prayer for Emmanuelle. The prayer translates as
Preserve them.

×

The counselor checks Frida for signs of hopeless-
ness and despair. How long has it been since the
last call? Five weeks? Ms. Gibson has noticed her,
Beth, and Meryl hanging around the computer lab
on Sundays.

"We were just trying to support the others. We weren't bothering anyone."

"I know you miss Harriet very much. But why torture yourself?"

The mothers have been in uniform for almost three months. Frida tells the counselor that February has been different. The day Harriet turned twenty-three months old, there was zero pinching. She persuaded Emmanuelle to chew and swallow six pretend green beans. She doesn't mention that she's been gazing longingly at the bell tower, that she's wondered about using a bedsheet. If she tried to hang herself, she might only turn into a vegetable, kept alive at grave cost to her family.

What does she need to do to regain phone privileges? How high does she have to score on the next evaluation? Food and medicine skill sets are being tested separately. For cooking skills, she scored third out of four. Her counselor tells her to be more ambitious. Not last is not good enough. Try for the top two.

"And what if I can't do that?"

"I find your negativity very troubling, Frida. There is no can't. Do you ever hear us talking about can't? You have to tell yourself, **I can! I can!** Take

can't out of your vocabulary. A good mother can do anything."

×

Despite everyone's abysmal performance during feeding mastery, lessons proceed on schedule. High chairs and splat mats have been moved to storage. Rocking chairs and cribs have been moved back into the classroom. The mothers are learning to nurse a sick child back to health.

"A mother's love can cure most common illnesses," Ms. Khoury says.

They must heal their dolls with loving thoughts. The instructors will take the doll's temperature in the morning and at day's end. See who can get their doll down to 98.6 degrees. Break the fever.

Given the personal nature of this exercise, each mother's loving thoughts will be different, the instructors say. They should feel free to anthropomorphize the illness. Picture themselves doing battle with the infection.

Frida pursues the illness lessons with vigor. She was a sickly child. Asthma and allergies. Bronchitis every winter. Doctors, she knows. Medicine, she knows. The lessons make her think of Popo. The square of cloth her grandmother kept tucked into her cleavage because she always felt cold there. Her grandmother's lipstick and hair spray.

She used to help her grandmother dye her hair, touched up her roots with an old toothbrush. She sometimes helped her bathe. The only socks her grandmother wore were flesh-tone nylon knee-highs from the drugstore. Until the very end, she wore full-body girdles, even beneath velour pajamas. The texture of her grandmother's skin is as vivid in her memory as Harriet's, tight and shiny on her shoulders, on her hands, loose and silky like fabric. After her grandmother's lung cancer was diagnosed, Frida sometimes slept over. They shared a bed again as they'd done when she was a child. Her grandmother requested that someone sleep next to her, and the whole family took turns. She always scolded Frida for not taking better care of her hands. She'd startle Frida awake with a wet, cold plop of lotion.

Frida missed saying goodbye by twenty minutes. Her taxi was caught in traffic. She crawled into bed with her grandmother, held her as rigor mortis set in, felt the warmth leaving her body, saw the cancerous lump below her collarbone. It was hard as stone. The size of a child's fist.

Emmanuelle has a temperature of 103. Her hair is matted with sweat. She shivers. Frida takes a blanket from the crib and folds her inside it. "Mommy will make you better. We can do it. I can do it."

The counselor would tell her to stop thinking, stop doubting. It doesn't matter that love can't break a fever, that love can't be measured. Anything can be measured. They have the tools now.

Linda undresses. She holds her doll against her bare breasts. Meryl and Beth copy her. Frida doesn't want anyone to see her body. She's been eating three meals a day but can't keep the weight on. She's now smaller than she was in high school. She has the sharp jawline she always wanted, the cheekbones, the gap between her thighs.

The instructors nod approvingly at her classmates.

"Try it," Ms. Khoury tells her.

Frida sets Emmanuelle in the crib and unbuttons her uniform, reluctantly pulls off her T-shirt and bra. "Here, I'm ready for you. Come cuddle with Mommy."

Emmanuelle's heat against her bare skin is startling, uncomfortable. Harriet has never been this hot. When she first held Harriet, she worried she'd kill her just by sneezing nearby. She washed her hands incessantly. Each day, she searched Harriet's face for signs that death was imminent.

There must be people who thrive under pressure, but not Frida. Maybe she shouldn't be trusted with any kind of life. Maybe people should have to work up to children, from plants to pets to babies. Maybe they should all be given a five-year-old, then four, then three, then two, then one, and if the child is still alive at year's end, then they can have a baby. Why did they have to begin with a baby?

×

The classroom is quieter than it should be. From fevers, they've moved on to stomach viruses. Days of projectile vomiting has dampened their enthusiasm and slowed their motherese. The instructors want to know why no one is making progress. The mothers should know the correct sequence of embraces, kisses, and kind words to nurse their doll back to health. The love that awakens the spirit and heals an aching body.

Linda finds their current state of failure

unacceptable. At breakfast the next morning, she leads the four of them in a prayer. They join hands while Linda prays to Our Lord Jesus Christ for the strength to persevere. She prays for wisdom and the safe return of her son Gabriel. Beth prays for alcohol. Bourbon would have made this week easier.

Meryl prays for her doll. Look what happened to Lucretia's.

Frida goes last. She prays for love, for a full heart. "I pray for a miracle," she says.

Everyone nods. **Yes**, they say. **A miracle**.

×

Ceremonial snow removal continues. Frida and Meryl are asked to shovel the track, an especially insulting assignment since it's too cold to exercise outdoors.

Frida tells Meryl that her mother turned sixty-eight this week, that her cousin is getting married in Seattle today. Before her very bad day, there was talk of Harriet being the flower girl. Frida would have carried her down the aisle.

Meryl is twitchier than usual. Her counselor is threatening to suspend phone privileges for another month. Meryl wants to run. The school recently changed the rules about leaving voluntarily. Quitting is no longer an option.

Meryl turns nineteen in April, can't spend her birthday in this place. And Ocean turns two in May.

Frida reminds her that Lucretia would trade places with any of them. If Lucretia were here, she'd still have a chance to get Brynn back. She wouldn't be on the registry forever. If Lucretia were here, Linda would have actual competition.

"We're going to pass. They'll let us call home next weekend."

"You don't really believe that," Meryl says. "What, you think they're going to grade us on a curve? I don't think so. We are so totally fucked."

"No, we're not. You can't think that way."

Meryl says she and Ocean's father were going to find jobs on the Jersey Shore this summer. She was going to be a cocktail waitress, earn money for college. After she gets out of this place, she'll go to college to study computer shit. Maybe they'll move to Silicon Valley with Ocean and develop apps.

When she looks to Frida for affirmation, Frida says it's a great idea. Practical. She resists mentioning the cost of living in San Francisco. Or anywhere in the Bay Area. The cost of childcare. The many barriers to entry. Young people should be allowed to dream.

During a break, Meryl shows Frida a locket. A belated Valentine's gift from the green-eyed guard.

Frida tells her to get rid of it. The locket looks as if it cost $10.99 and came from CVS.

"No way, it's mine. He did something nice for me. What? Don't make that face. Why can't you let me enjoy this?"

"What if you get caught?"

"This is nothing. He's been taking pictures of me too. And videos."

"You've got to be kidding."

"Duh, my face isn't in them. I already thought of that. I'm not stupid."

"Tell him to delete them. And delete them from the cloud."

"You're paranoid. And jealous. Also, seriously middle-aged. Beth thinks it's cool that he got me something."

"And you're going to listen to her? Beth thinks it's cool to schedule her own overdose. How do you know he hasn't shown anyone?" She wants to tell Meryl that years ago, she'd drawn the line at photos, how she's grateful that there's no record. Someday, somehow, she'll raise Harriet so that she will not allow her naked body to be photographed, not her vagina, not her asshole. Harriet will never take naked selfies and send them to boys.

"He wouldn't do that," Meryl says.

"Everyone does that."

Meryl looks wounded. "Fine, Mom. I'll talk to him."

×

The mothers receive talking points for their Sunday calls, a change in procedure that's been rumored for weeks. They're supposed to ask open-ended questions about their child's education, home life, and friend-ships. They're not allowed to mention the subject of time or how long they've been here or when they'll go home. Drawing attention to parental absence may be triggering. Not everyone will pass. Not all families will be reunited. It's important not to make false promises. False promises will damage a child's ability to trust. They're not allowed to ask about their child's meetings with their social worker or experience in court-mandated therapy. They must praise their child's resilience. They must thank the child's guardian. They can say "I love you" once, and "I miss you" once.

"Make it count, ladies," Ms. Gibson says.

At the end of February, Linda's son Gabriel is still missing. He's been gone for a full month. The women in pink lab coats tell Linda to use the available resources: her counselor, the twenty-four-hour hotline, the other mothers. They urge her to sign up for extra counseling. They offer her meditative coloring books.

The night before the medicine evaluation, Linda gets sent to talk circle for shaking her doll. The class was working on seizure protocol. Linda claimed she was trying to bring her doll back to life. The instructors said she was being too aggressive. They thought she was on the verge of something worse, that she might hit her doll if they didn't intervene.

Linda breaks down at dinner. "I am not a hitter," she sobs.

Beth and Meryl pass her their napkins. Linda's cries are loud and shameful. Everyone is staring at their table. Frida pours Linda a glass of water. She says a secret prayer. For Gabriel. For his siblings. For their current and future parents. For their current and future homes.

11.

LINDA ISN'T EATING. SHE WANTS HER TRIP TO talk circle struck from her file. Same with her zero for Unit 2: Fundamentals of Food and Medicine. She wants to call her lawyer, her social worker, Gabriel's foster parents, the detectives. It's not her fault they lost her son.

It's Sunday dinner, the beginning of March, and Linda's list of demands is growing. The trio of middle-aged white women have joined her hunger strike in solidarity. The sight of them fawning over Linda offends most everyone. They sit with their empty trays in the center of the dining hall, sipping water and discussing objectives. Yesterday, Maura, the alcoholic mother of five who burned her daughter gently, spent all of breakfast stroking

Linda's arm and saying things like, "You are not invisible."

Linda's martyrdom has earned her new haters. The mothers feel for Linda, they really do, but they haven't forgotten how she fucked with Lucretia, and they're sick of listening to her cry. Some say the only reason she hasn't been punished is because of those white ladies. Some say Linda just wants attention. Some say all four strikers are secretly snacking at bedtime. Some say Gabriel is better off on the street than he ever was with her.

Frida should worry more about Gabriel, but she's too busy missing Harriet and imagining a fiery death for her counselor. It's been six months since Harriet was taken away, over four months since Frida last held her, a full season in uniform.

Frida has been shunning Beth all weekend, encouraged Meryl to do the same. Meryl accused her of being petty. Their fragile alliance fell apart after Beth finished first on evaluation day, Meryl placed a surprising second, and Frida finished third.

Beth hasn't been gracious about her success. She adopts some of the school's language even when they're alone. The arc of learning. Selfishness as a form of soul corruption. She said, "I can help you, Frida. I don't think this needs to be a competition."

Though the mothers were indeed graded on a curve and while Frida's maternal instincts have improved, both quantitative and qualitative measures kept Frida out of the top two. Anxiety remains a problem. "A lack of confidence," the counselor said. Moments of hesitation that, in aggregate, will impede a child's sense of security. Frida's motherese during the feeding test, though joyful, was insufficiently empowering. Other mistakes were more significant. She pressed too hard on Emmanuelle's breastbone as she delivered CPR, at first missing the spot where a real heart would have been.

"Harriet is doing fine," the counselor said. "I spoke to Ms. Torres a few days ago. She thinks having a break from calling you has been good for Harriet, and I agree. Have you ever considered that speaking to you, and seeing you like this, may be retraumatizing her? You're not looking well, Frida. You need to start taking better care of yourself."

×

The mothers are changing with the weather. Dozens more have lost phone privileges, and this weekend, amid the first signs of spring, there's been much gazing out of windows and talk of escape.

Frida listens to Meryl's escape talk during the day, and Roxanne's in the evening. Since Roxanne lost phone privileges, she's considered cozying up to a guard. She's considered the fence. It can't possibly go all the way around. Her latest ideas are about water. The river that separates them from the bad fathers, who are supposedly being trained in an old hospital ten miles away, won't lead anywhere useful. She's a strong swimmer, but after the woods, then what? Miles of red-state bullshit. Who's going to help a Black woman standing on the side of the road?

Frida worries that Roxanne might get shot. They've talked about this. And about whether Black fathers are dying at the other school. "Parenting while Black," Roxanne said. Like walking while Black. Waiting while Black. Driving while Black.

Tonight, Frida doesn't let Roxanne go there. "You can't say it, and you can't think it. Isaac is the light, remember? Go to sleep."

"I thought you were my friend."

"I am. I'm saying, you missed one call. I haven't talked to Harriet since January."

"Sometimes I really hate you." Roxanne flips onto her stomach, buries her face in her pillow, and begins crying herself to sleep.

Frida folds her pillow around her head to block out Roxanne's shudders. They had to change the blue liquid again last Friday. Instead of dissociating, Emmanuelle screamed the whole time. **No, no, no, no, no.** Ms. Russo held her arms. Ms. Khoury held her legs. They now perform the procedure in front of the whole class. The observing mothers had to narrate and comfort. Looking, the instructors said, will help the dolls understand their role here.

The instructors left bruises. The family court judge needs to know about those bruises and Emmanuelle's screams. The judge should know that Frida is learning to be a better mother. She'll keep believing that the doll's blue insides and the doll itself are real, because if she doesn't demonstrate her capacity for genuine maternal feeling and attachment, if she doesn't show she can be trusted, there will be no reunion with her real daughter, who is almost two years old, whose blood is not blue and doesn't turn soupy and thick, whose cavities she would never scrape with a knife.

×

"We have a surprise for you," Ms. Russo tells them the next morning. With a flourish, she and Ms. Khoury distribute smartphones and strollers. Each mother receives her phone with cupped palms, as if the devices are communion wafers. All four are truly thankful. Beth's and Meryl's faces approach a state of ecstasy.

Today, they can take their dolls outside, call their real children, their families. The new rules regarding talking points have been temporarily suspended. They can even use the Internet. However, they can't forget their responsibilities. They must maintain their daily word count and stay accountable to their dolls. Every hour on the hour, they must report back to the classroom for check-ins. It is the start of Unit 3: Reconditioning the Narcissist, eight weeks of lessons to strengthen their child-first orientation and ability to parent in the face of distraction.

"Think of this as a test of your impulse control," Ms. Russo says. No matter what, the mothers must provide the normal amount of attention and affection. She leads them in a call and repeat: "Who is my top priority?"

"My child!"

"What do I do when my child needs me?"

"I drop everything!"

Frida slips her phone into her pocket, alive with joy and anticipation.

Though the mothers are eager to go outside, the dolls, after their latest blue liquid trauma, are a fragile mess. Emmanuelle has to be carried. In the foyer, she refuses to get into her stroller. She and Frida make it only to the bench outside the building next door. Frida watches enviously as her classmates leave the quad. She can't remember Susanna's number. She calls Gust and gets his voice mail, asks him to have Susanna call her, or go home and call back with Harriet himself.

"I won't be able to talk to her again until the end of April. Please. I need to wish her a happy birthday. This is my only chance."

He's going to hear Emmanuelle yelling in the background. Frida isn't sure what she'll say if he asks. She makes the first check-in without incident, then the second, then the third.

"Excellent prioritizing, Frida," Ms. Khoury says. Her classmates have all been late.

The scene outside is chaotic. Mothers are searching for a decent Wi-Fi signal. Dolls of all ages are running. They explore garbage cans and bike racks, shrubbery, bricks, gravel. Some climb trees. Some try to scale light poles. Some grab handfuls of grass and rub it on their faces.

Frida ventures farther on each walk. She takes Emmanuelle to the amphitheater, where they run up and down the steps. She shows Emmanuelle the crocuses and budding trees. She reads Emmanuelle the names of plants.

"Rhododendron," she says. "Witch hazel." She asks Emmanuelle to repeat after her, but Emmanuelle has trouble with **h**'s.

"It's spring right now. And after spring comes summer. Then fall. Then winter. There are four seasons. Can you count my fingers? One-two-three-four. Most people like spring. I like it. Do you like spring?"

"No."

"Why not?"

"Spring scary. Scary, Mommy. Hate it."

"Hate is a big feeling. I think you need to experience it a little more. You know, by the time I'm old, spring will be different." She tells Emmanuelle about the warming earth, how Manhattan might be underwater in another generation, how humans need to stop eating meat, drive less, have fewer babies.

"There are too many people," Frida says.

"Too many?"

"Too many people like me. Not like you. You don't use as many resources."

They find a patch of sunlight and rest in the grass between the bell tower and Pierce. Did she ever rest in the sun with Harriet? She feels the heat on her closed eyelids. She turns and sees Emmanuelle staring directly into the sun. The chips in Emmanuelle's eyes sparkle. They play a blinking game, laughing each time they open their eyes in tandem.

"Cuddle," Frida says. "Let's have a family cuddle. Come here." She curves her body around Emmanuelle's, kisses the doll's head, rubs the nape of her neck as she used to do with Harriet. Over time, the doll's new-car smell has become comforting.

"Sweetie, do you ever get tired of living in the equipment room?"

Emmanuelle sighs. "Yeah."

"Where would you rather live?"

"With Mommy!"

"Oh, that's very sweet. You are my sweetest girl.

I want you to come live with me too. Where would we live?"

Emmanuelle sits up and points to the library. She points to the sky.

Frida tells her about nurseries and big-girl beds, night-lights and sleep sacks and security blankets. She's sorry she can't give Emmanuelle those things, that she only had blankets and toys during bedtime practice. Fleeting comforts. It's a shame she has to sleep standing up.

Emmanuelle grows excited at the prospect of her own room.

"We can pretend," Frida says.

They linger in the sun holding hands. Frida wants to stay here all day. If she ever tells Harriet about this place, she'll say that she had to store her devotion somewhere. Emmanuelle, a vessel for her hope and longing, the way people used to invest tablets and sacred trees with their faith and love.

×

In response to the day's emotional upheaval, the trio of middle-aged white women abandon Linda's cause and resume eating. Ms. Gibson descends on Linda with cans of protein shakes. She threatens Linda with a standing spot in talk circle. Extra counseling. An automatic zero for Unit 3. Expulsion. Ms. Gibson won't leave until Linda takes a first sip.

"Gabriel would want you to eat," Beth says. "I'm here if you ever want to talk." She passes Linda an apple, which Linda devours.

Linda looks sheepish, pitiful. Frida feels embarrassed for her. They've never seen Linda blush before.

Frida is the only one of her classmates who hasn't made contact yet. Calls were brief and unsatisfying. Goodbyes provoked meltdowns. The dolls kept interrupting. Mothers of infants had it easy. Baby dolls stayed in their carriers and they cried, but they couldn't move or say "Mommy" or grab the phone. Mothers of older dolls had to prevent death, accident, escape, and fraternization, all while connecting with their real children.

Rumor has it that some teen romances began in the doll factory. Frida saw a teenage girl doll rolling around at the base of a tree with one of the teenage boys. They had their hands down the front of each other's uniforms. They didn't seem to know how to kiss, were instead licking each other's faces. The boy bit the girl's shoulder. The girl stuck her finger in the boy's ear. The boy flipped the girl over and began stroking her blue knob through her uniform.

Their mothers were nowhere to be seen. Frida worried that the boy would undress the girl and unscrew her knob and try to enter her cavity. The opening is wide enough for a penis. She didn't know if the boy could become erect, if the activity was consensual. Emmanuelle thought the girl was hurt, that the boy was hurting her. The girl was moaning. Frida made Emmanuelle close her eyes as they passed.

After lunch, Frida is tempted to call Will but resists. She'd want to tell him the truth. She dials her parents' number, starts crying before they pick up. Her father asks to use FaceTime. Frida agrees, though she wishes they didn't have to see her. Her father's hair has thinned dramatically and gone completely white. Her mother looks frail. Her father cries for several minutes, though her mother, at first, remains stoic. But her expression soon changes. Frida knows her mother wants to comment on how different she looks. She was hoping that they'd never see her in uniform, worried about the memories it would trigger. On rare occasions, her father told her stories from his childhood—men in dunce caps who were paraded through his village, children pouring urine on their grandparents' heads, old people kneeling on glass during struggle sessions.

They talk over each other frantically. Her father has been writing her letters every day. Her mother has been buying clothes for Harriet to wear when she's three. Every day, they watch Harriet videos and look at her pictures. They have her photo on the dining table to keep them company during meals.

Frida holds the phone close, so they can only see her face. She asks about her mother's birthday, her cousin's wedding, their doctors' appointments.

"You're too skinny," her mother says. "What are they feeding you? Are they starving you? Has anyone hurt you?"

"Should we call Renee?" her father asks. "She should do something."

"Don't do that. Please!"

They ask if she's been able to talk to Harriet. Gust has sent them a few updates. They wish they could send Harriet a birthday gift. A card.

Between sobs, she tells them that she's fine. She has to go soon. "I'm sorry," she says, "for everything."

Who is the baby crying in the background?

"It's a recording," she says, giving Emmanuelle her free hand.

×

Frida is too excited to sleep. Everything will be different after she speaks to Harriet. If she ever tells Harriet about this year, she won't tell her how often she thought about death. Harriet doesn't need to know that her mother is lonely and scared. Harriet doesn't need to know that her mother thinks of rooftops and bell towers. Harriet doesn't need to know that her mother often wonders if this might be the best use of her life, the only real way to protest the system.

When she was a child, she thought she'd live only until thirty. She planned to wait until her grandmothers passed but didn't care about hurting her parents, wanted to punish them. She thought constantly about death when she was eleven, talked about it so often that her parents didn't take her seriously.

"Go ahead and kill yourself," her mother said, exasperated.

Gust cried when she told him about the year

she wanted to die, but she didn't admit that those thoughts returned when she was pregnant. She worried endlessly about the what-ifs of the genetic testing. The possibility that something might go wrong during labor, that anything that went wrong would be her fault.

But the tests were fine. Her baby was healthy. Her healthy baby will grow up to have a healthy mind. Better and purer than her mother's. She has Harriet's future to consider now. The girl she can become if her mother is living, the girl she'll never be if her mother takes her own life.

×

The air is still damp from last night's rain. Mist rises along Chapin Walk. Frida finds an empty bench beneath one of the magnolia trees in the stone courtyard. She and Emmanuelle talk about the flowers, identify the colors—pink and white. She asks Emmanuelle to notice how the colors blend.

Frida breaks off a leaf and hands it to her. "Don't eat it. Listen, sweetie, you're going to hear me talking to another little girl this morning. I'm going to talk to her a few times, and I need you to let me. It's confusing, I know. But don't worry. I am still your mother."

Emmanuelle flings the leaf away. She pulls at her stroller straps, then reaches for Frida, calling, "Up up!"

Gust answers on the third ring. He apologizes for not calling back yesterday. He couldn't leave work. Susanna misplaced her phone. By the time they tried Frida's number, it was evening, and there was no way to leave a message. He stayed home today so she'd be sure to reach them. Frida tells him it's fine. She thanks him and asks for Harriet.

They switch to FaceTime. As Harriet comes into view, Frida trembles, glancing from the screen to Emmanuelle. All these months, she thought they looked nothing alike, that there was something cruel in the set of Emmanuelle's mouth, that of course Harriet is more beautiful and Emmanuelle isn't real, but now that Harriet has lost weight, the resemblance between the girls is uncanny.

"Say hello, Hare-bear," Gust says. "You remember Mommy?"

"No." Harriet's voice is calm and definitive. Frida digs her fist into her lap. She is a bad mother because she's letting Harriet see her cry. She is a bad mother because Emmanuelle's face is the one that feels more familiar. She is a bad mother because the girl on-screen, with her bangs cut too short, with her sharp chin and darker, curlier hair, feels less and less like hers.

Harriet and Gust hear Emmanuelle calling, "Mommy Mommy!"

"Who dat?" Harriet asks.

"It's a recording." Frida turns away from Emmanuelle, trying to focus solely on Harriet. "Bub, it's me. It's Mommy. I'm so glad I get to talk to you before your birthday. Happy, happy birthday! Eight more days. You're my big girl! So big! I'm so sorry I haven't called. I wanted to. You know that, right? I'd call you every day if I could. I love you so much. I miss you. I miss you all the way to the moon. To Jupiter." She holds up a pinkie. "Remember?"

Harriet stares back at her, indifferent. Frida lets her tears run. "Remember, we say, I promise you the moon and stars. I love you more than galaxies. Then we hook pinkies."

"Gala-seas." Harriet sounds out the word.

"That's right, bub. And who am I?"

They test possibilities for several minutes. Frida is not a bubble. She's not an apple. She's not a spoon. She's not Daddy or Sue-Sue.

"I'm Mommy. I'm your mommy."

They talk for fifteen minutes at a time between check-ins, the longest Harriet can sit still, rushing through two months of news. They're going to have her party at home. They're getting a piñata. Susanna will bake the cake. They've bought Harriet a balance **b-i-k-e**. They're on the wait list for the Waldorf School in Germantown and the Montessori in Center City.

Susanna says hello. She and Gust both comment on Frida's weight loss, though they kindly resist saying anything about her gray hair. One hour is lost to the mothers' lunch break. Three more hours to Harriet's nap. Gust lets Frida watch Harriet play in the living room with Susanna.

Frida has to say goodbye whenever Emmanuelle gets unruly. It's an impossible choice—talk to Harriet, get penalized for ignoring Emmanuelle. Ignore Harriet, and maybe not live through the spring or summer. Frida feels guilty in every way. Guilty before her daughter, neglected on her mother's one very bad day, guilty before her doll, who looks at her reproachfully. Guilty before the instructors when she turns up late to the last check-in.

×

On Wednesday morning, she comes to class prepared to toggle between her daughters, but she doesn't have to toggle, because the test proved far too effective. All four of them neglected their dolls. They forgot their first priority. They gave in to distraction. Clearly, when given a basic freedom, this group will run wild, regress into selfishness and narcissism.

"We can't let your progress go to waste," Ms. Russo says. As quickly as the mothers were given a lifeline to the outside world, that lifeline is severed.

×

Frida and her classmates are bused to an off-site location. They reunite with their dolls in the parking lot of a warehouse by the side of the highway. Inside, there are four model homes, matching yellow bungalows with green awnings. The warehouse is freezing. The dolls have never seen a building of this size. They've never seen houses. They cling to their mothers' legs and scream, their voices echoing through the cavernous space.

The instructors call the lesson "Preventing Home Alone." To hone their supervision instincts, the mothers will be tested with distractions. At the sound of the whistle, the instructors will measure the time it takes them to notice their doll and carry her out the front door. As with the phone lessons, they'll be learning how to focus: to maintain eye contact with, and close physical proximity to, their child. To have their child's safety be their first desire and only priority.

The instructors make the mothers repeat after them: "An unsupervised child is a child in danger. I must never leave my child alone."

The building could host lessons for fifty mothers, maybe more. Emmanuelle strokes the goose bumps on Frida's cheeks. Frida could cry. She'll relive her one very bad day over and over, but now timed and filmed and scored, with phone privileges hanging in the balance. How often has she thought of Harriet home alone, how often has she considered every single thing she should have done differently?

The houses are equipped with phones and televisions and doorbells, all of which come into play during the drills, switching on at the same time at frightening volumes. The noises begin without warning, startling the mothers and dolls.

In between drills, Frida teaches Emmanuelle the words for **awning**, **front door**, **doorbell**, **curtains**, **sofa**, **armchair**, **ottoman**, **kitchen**, **mantel**, **television**, **remote control**, **coffee table**, **sink**. The inside of the model home is painted butter yellow and decorated with fake-wood knickknacks. Their house has a nautical theme, with anchors and rope accents. Every item smells as if the plastic wrap has just been removed.

Her very bad day had been stifling. It had been unbearably hot all weekend. Frida remembers being desperate to shower, remembers running the air conditioner, looking up at the dusty ceiling fans, thinking she should clean them. She remembers craving caffeine, something sweet and cold, stronger than she could make at home. She remembers wanting to walk outside with her arms free.

Had she come home an hour earlier. Forty-five minutes earlier. Talked to the neighbors herself. She would have offered them money. She would have pleaded with them. But Susanna would never leave. Gust would never leave. None of the grandparents would leave. No babysitter would leave. Only she would. Only she did. If Harriet hadn't been in the ExerSaucer, she could have walked to the basement door, opened it, tumbled down the stairs. She could have opened the front door and wandered into the street.

"Harriet isn't safe with you," the judge said.

×

In the days that follow, the instructors add distractions: sirens, appliances, European dance music. The noise gives Frida headaches, headaches make her dizzy, dizziness makes her forgetful.

She can't sleep for the ringing in her ears. The progress she's made falls away. Emmanuelle likes hiding behind furniture. She's crawled into kitchen cabinets. During some drills, Frida opens the door, then remembers to go back. Other times, she gets to the front porch before realizing what she's missing.

During drills, the dolls respond to the commotion by trying to destroy things. They tear at sofa cushions and jump on coffee tables and bang remote controls on every available surface. After Beth's doll begins leaking blue liquid from her ears, the dolls are given headphones. Still, they cry.

×

Ms. Knight warned them that birthdays would be painful. On March 11, the morning of Harriet's second birthday, Frida wakes at dawn. Roxanne gets up with her. It was Roxanne's idea to have a sunrise celebration. Roxanne's mother used to wake her super early on her birthday, would decorate the whole house while she slept. Roxanne will do the same for Isaac next year.

Frida opens her neglected atonement journal to her most recent entry: a wobbly line drawing of Harriet. She's drawn Harriet as she used to look, with cherub cheeks and a cap of dark curls. She props the journal on her desk. They whisper-sing "Happy Birthday" to the drawing.

Roxanne hugs her. "Eight months left."

"God." Frida rests her forehead on Roxanne's shoulder.

Roxanne speaks to the drawing. "Harriet, your mama misses you. She's a nice lady. A little bossy sometimes, but she's okay. We're taking care of each other." She holds out her hands to Frida, pretending she's shielding a piece of cake with a candle. "Make a wish."

Frida pretends to blow out the candle. "Thank you for humoring me." She tells Roxanne about Harriet's birth, how the doctors said "What a pretty baby" when they pulled her out. How she started weeping when she heard Harriet's first cry.

Frida tries to remember what Harriet looked like in the phone. She didn't say happy birthday enough times when she had the chance. She didn't deliver any wisdom. She should have told Harriet that they'll speak again in April. She needs to know if Harriet forgives her for not calling back, if Gust has explained why she can't.

Her body aches all day. She develops shooting pains in her left hip. She has trouble lifting Emmanuelle, running out the door with her. The fastest mother is the best mother, the instructors say.

At bedtime, Frida hides beneath the covers and chews off her cuticles. She has a doll that looks like Harriet, but Harriet should also have a doll that looks like her. Harriet should have a mother doll, sleep with it and tell it secrets, take it everywhere.

12.

MOTHERS ARE FALLING IN LOVE. INEVITABLE as the season. April, the sky an impossible blue. Giggling can be heard in the dining hall. New couples sit close, touching shoulders, elbows, hair, fingertips, blushing with pleasure.

Mothers in love live for the weekends. They stroll next to the fence or bring their atonement journals to the stone courtyard and write side by side on their bellies in the grass. They talk of pet peeves and hobbies. Parents. Past relationships. Money. Attitudes about monogamy. Whether they want more children. Whether they'll be able to find a job or a place to live after they leave.

They're supposed to be cultivating purity of mind and spirit, and if they're caught fraternizing, it will be added to their files. They could be expelled. But it's easy to hide burgeoning romances. The mothers can survive on so little. A hand on the cheek. A lingering glance. For most, nearness is enough. There are romances between classmates and roommates, mothers who've met via talk circle or cleaning crew, waiting in the Sunday phone line, or crying in the bathroom afterward.

There are perhaps only a dozen actual couples, but rumor and innuendo suggest more. Some crushes are unrequited. Some are ruined by gossip. There have been jealousies and love triangles. Roxanne says mothers in the showers have been using their hands. Frida asks how this is possible.

"Ladies move fast. There are some blind spots, you know. Someone pinched me last night. Tweaked my hip. While I was brushing my teeth. It was kind of funny."

"And?"

"And I thought about it. But I wouldn't. Not with her." She motions for Frida to join her by the window. They speak while staring straight ahead at the floodlights, backs turned to the cameras, barely moving their lips. Roxanne asks what Frida thinks of Meryl. Meryl is cute, Roxanne says.

"She's a kid."

"She's nineteen. I mean, she will be soon, right? That's three years younger than me."

"Nineteen is a kid. You're way more mature than she is. You've been to college. You've left Pennsylvania. She's been on a plane maybe twice. And she likes guys, you know."

"You have a such a one-dimensional view of this shit. Everyone my age is fluid. Put in a good word for me, okay?"

Frida is noncommittal. She wants to tell Roxanne that Meryl already has the green-eyed guard, that if Meryl were to choose a woman, she'd choose Beth. They might already be kissing in secret. Meryl calls Beth "babe." Beth calls her "darling." They've talked about getting matching tattoos. The girls are always casually touching in a way Frida has never done with anyone. She envies women who touch like that.

Lately, Frida and Roxanne have been talking more. They've bonded over being only children, shared stories about their pregnancies and labors and breastfeeding ordeals, connecting through stories of pain.

After Isaac was taken away, Roxanne had to go

to the ER because of mastitis. She'd been feeding on demand, had to have an abscess surgically removed.

Isaac would have been given to Roxanne's mother or aunt, but her mother is getting chemo for stage three breast cancer, and her aunt lives with a boyfriend whom no one trusts. Her mother had been putting her through college with little help from Roxanne's dad, who lives in Jersey with his new family. Her mother had been seriously pissed about her pregnancy, thought Roxanne would have been smarter, but it turns out she loves being a grandmother.

"She likes to say that every woman has a kid so she can have a grandkid one day," Roxanne said. "That's the reward. **She** needs Isaac too."

Frida only asked about Isaac's father once. Roxanne said they met at a party. They don't ever say his name out loud. When Isaac is older, she's going to tell him she used a sperm donor. "Of course my baby looks exactly like him," she admitted.

Roxanne asked Frida about New York, how New York compares to Philly. She was shocked by how little Frida knew about Black neighborhoods in Philly, that she'd never heard of the MOVE house, had never been to North Philly, had never been west of Fiftieth Street, had no idea that Sun Ra lived in Germantown, had never listened to Sun Ra, that she stopped listening to music once she moved to New York because the city was too noisy.

A guard comes by to do final checks. They hug good night.

Frida pictures Roxanne and Meryl in a closet, in the showers, outside, in the dark. She should be thinking about her daughter. The next phone call. Preschool. Potty training. What Harriet is eating. Whether Harriet is acquiring Susanna's mannerisms. When she gets home, she'll teach Harriet that the way Susanna touches people is rude, will make people assume the wrong things about her when she's older. But Harriet might grow up to be a flirt. She'll think her mother is the one who's cold and strange. She'll know that locked here with two hundred women, her mother could not start a lesbian affair if she tried.

This is the longest Frida has gone without a man's kiss or touch. She used to think she'd die without it. No mother has looked at her that way, and her interest in other women has always been purely theoretical, but she fears the day, or night, or furtive afternoon when loneliness will get the better of her, make her want to take risks. She'd like to be kissed again before she dies, and if she's going to die here, an idea that feels more real all the time, she might have to choose another mother. She'll insist that they keep their clothes on. She'll explain that this is not her normal self. She is dying; perhaps she should find another dying woman.

×

Nearly five months in, glitches still occur regularly. Instructors receive programming changes at the last minute. Lessons are skipped at random. Bath time lessons are hastily scheduled for April, then canceled. All the cohorts are given extra outdoor time while the instructors figure out what to do.

The dolls are supposed to be waterproof, but the infant cohorts had issues with loose blue knobs. When the dolls were submerged, water seeped into their cavities. Mold grew. The mold smelled like rotting broccoli. Moldy infants from Roxanne's class had to be sent to the technical department. One mother asked for her doll's cavity to be cleaned with bleach, but the instructor said that bleach was tested at the doll factory in China. It corroded the internal machinery and wore down their silicone skin. Noses and eyes disappeared. If that happened here, it would look very bad for their files.

×

Holidays that enhance the dolls' quality of life continue to be celebrated. On Easter Sunday, mothers with dolls eight and under participate in an egg hunt.

Emmanuelle insists on being carried to the toddler hunting grounds outside Pierce. Frida follows the procession to the lawn, her arms soon growing tired. Though she'd rather be calling home today, Emmanuelle is better company than she used to be. Her sentences are becoming more complex, her concerns more philosophical. The other day, she patted Frida's back, looking for a knob, became anxious when she couldn't find one. Frida explained that there are different kinds of families. Some children are born from your body, some are adopted, some come by marriage, some are grown in labs. Some, like Emmanuelle, were invented by scientists. The children invented by scientists are the most precious.

"It is a privilege to be your mother," Frida said.

At the top of the hill, they line up behind Beth

and Meryl and their dolls. Frida says hello. The younger women barely look up. They're talking about a restaurant Frida has never been to in South Philly. Easter services. How they dressed up their babies last year. Meryl confesses that she stuck one of those tacky satin headbands on Ocean and let her eat an entire marshmallow chick.

Frida carries Emmanuelle to the back of the line, refusing to feel jealous. These are not forever friendships. There's no point to these friendships besides survival. Meryl won't shut up about Beth during cleaning crew. Beth has been telling her to make the green-eyed guard break up with his girlfriend. She's been telling Meryl to get pregnant as a way of getting out early.

The beginning of the hunt is anticlimactic. The eggs are easy to spot in the short grass. Toddler dolls investigate the rope barriers and dart around their mothers' legs. Some take off running with their arms outstretched, feeling the wind in their hair. For a few beautiful minutes, no one is crying. Frida leads Emmanuelle down the hill. She directs Emmanuelle to a green egg, a white one.

There's shouting in the distance. Dolls fighting. Mothers arguing. Women in pink lab coats blowing whistles. Emmanuelle plunks herself in the grass. The morning is bright and cloudless. Frida plays with the part in Emmanuelle's hair. She wonders what the weather is like in the city, if Harriet is wearing pastels today, if Gust and Susanna will take Harriet to the zoo like they did last year, if Harriet is now old enough for face painting.

She would have dressed Harriet in yellow. She is a bad mother for never making Harriet a basket like the one the dolls were given. She is a bad mother for never taking Harriet to an egg hunt. Easter was one of the holidays when her parents tried hard to be American. There was a trip to St. Louis when she was in elementary school, a frilly pink dress. Her mother had her wear a white straw hat, even though white is the Chinese color of mourning.

One of the four-year-old boy dolls whizzes past them. He's not supposed to be in the toddler zone. He knocks over several younger dolls. Their mothers pull them to safety. The boy's mother follows close behind.

Frida leaps to her feet. She yells, "Stop!"

The boy is going for Emmanuelle's basket. Though she's expressed no interest in it until now, once Emmanuelle sees what the boy wants, she grabs hold of the basket and won't let go. They both pull as hard as they can. The boy wins. Emmanuelle scrambles to her feet and chases after him.

The boy turns around. He raises his arm. With Frida two steps away, he strikes Emmanuelle with the flat of his hand, hitting the top of her cheekbone.

Frida grabs Emmanuelle. She checks Emmanuelle's face, kisses her forehead. Within seconds, a bruise begins to form. Again, there's a delay before Emmanuelle realizes that she's hurt. Frida feels Emmanuelle's bruise in her stomach. She feels it between her eyes. She delivers the hug to soothe physical upset, the hug of encouragement, five more kisses.

"I'm so sorry, sweetie. I love you. I love you so much. It's going to be okay. There, there. There, there."

The other mother asks her son to apologize. "I think we need to check in with our friend," she says.

Her tone is timid. Deferential. Frida doesn't understand why the woman isn't shouting. Children like him need to be reprimanded. She carries Emmanuelle over to the boy and grabs his wrist.

"Look what you did! Look at her face. Do you see this bruise? You say sorry to my daughter right now!"

×

At talk circle that night, Frida counts fifty-three other women. Eighteen are here because of the egg hunt, including Tamara, the sour-faced white mother of the boy who hit Emmanuelle.

The guards pass out cups of bitter, lukewarm coffee. Confessions continue late into the night. The school is casting a wider net these days. Harm need not be intentional or malicious. All accidents can be prevented with close supervision, Ms. Gibson says.

Some mothers are talk-circle veterans, sent here at least once a week. Ms. Gibson lets the veterans describe their past transgressions in shorthand. There are now three guards every night, two to maintain order and one to protect Ms. Gibson. A mother lunged at her last week, got as far as wrapping her hands around Ms. Gibson's throat. That mother was expelled and added to the registry.

One mother let the doll use her first name instead of "Mommy." Some were rude to their children's guardians during Sunday calls. Some cried during meals. Two mothers were caught kissing behind the tennis courts. A guard overheard them plotting to run away together.

Everyone sits up. They're the first couple to be caught. One of the runners is Margaret, a gaunt young Latina woman with doleful eyes who seems to have pulled out most of her left eyebrow. Her original offense was letting her son wait in her parked car during a job interview.

Her beloved is Alicia, one of the slender, gorgeous, laughing young Black mothers whom Frida met on the first day. It seemed like she and Lucretia became good friends in the month before Lucretia's expulsion. Alicia has cut off her braids. She's lost so much weight that Frida barely recognized her. She had CPS called on her when her five-year-old was being disruptive at school. The teacher sent her daughter to the principal's office. The principal asked Alicia to come get her.

"I was ten minutes late," Alicia says. "They said I smelled like alcohol. I was working as a waitress then. Showed up in my uniform. Someone had spilled beer on me that day. They didn't believe me when I said I don't drink."

Ms. Gibson reminds Alicia to take responsibility.

"But—"

"No excuses."

"It was my fault," Alicia says through gritted teeth. "I am a narcissist. I am a danger to my child."

Alicia and Margaret are blushing so hard they could be glowing. Margaret sits on her hands. Alicia fidgets with her sleeves.

Frida remembers coming home from her boyfriend's house at one in the morning when she was seventeen, finding her parents waiting up for her. She and her boyfriend had fallen asleep watching a movie. Her parents didn't believe her. She remembers the way her mother looked at her, how her father didn't speak to her for days.

Ms. Gibson asks Alicia and Margaret to confess their degree of sexual contact. They answer questions about fondling, heavy petting, digital penetration, oral sex, whether they made each other climax.

The mothers avert their eyes. It's generally understood that the school finds lesbians unmotherly.

Alicia starts to cry. "We kissed a little. That's it. We didn't hurt anyone. I won't even talk to her anymore. Please! Please don't put this in my file."

"I appreciate that," Ms. Gibson says, "but what I'm not understanding is why you'd put your selfish desires before your mothering." Loneliness is a form of narcissism. A mother who is in harmony with her child, who understands her place in her child's life and her role in society, is never lonely. Through caring for her child, all her needs are fulfilled.

What problems can possibly be solved by running?

"You people are going to take my kid anyway," Margaret says. "Why don't you admit that instead of pretending like we have a chance? My kid's foster parents want to adopt him. They won't admit it, but I know they do. They're already looking at kindergartens. You'd love that, wouldn't you? You want us to fail so you can take them."

Frida tears at the rim of her coffee cup. She no longer cares about kissing. She's thinking about the bell tower, wondering how fast she could climb the steps, whether the tile roof is slippery, how the pavement would feel against her face.

When it's her turn, she speaks to Ms. Gibson like a penitent confessing to a priest. "I should have done a better job protecting her today. That's the part that upsets me the most. She was in pain. And I could have prevented it. I also regret my tone. But when I asked Tamara's son to apologize, he laughed at me. It was an evil laugh. A cackle. I found that very troubling. I don't know where he learned to behave like that. I'm sorry. I am a narcissist. I am a danger to my child." Frida pauses. "But so is she."

The mothers stare at Tamara.

"Frida, there's no need to be passive-aggressive," Ms. Gibson says.

Tamara is sitting opposite Frida in the second ring of the circle. Her original crime was spanking. Her ex-husband reported her. She admits that her doll has a hitting problem, but Frida should have been paying attention.

Tamara points at Frida. "I saw her looking away."

"I looked away for one second."

"One second is all it takes. Haven't you learned anything? You were letting your doll play by herself. If you'd been watching her—"

"Ladies!" Ms. Gibson says. "Control yourselves."

×

"Dude, you look awful." On the bus, Meryl drops her voice to a whisper, tells Frida that Tamara has been talking shit. "That lady is calling you a cunt."

Frida smiles. "I'm not a cunt, I'm a bad mother."

"Good one," Meryl says.

"I try," Frida replies. They bump fists. "I'm worried about her."

"Harriet?"

"Emmanuelle." The doll's bruise looks like a case of ringworm. A perfect circle, purple in the center with a ring of yellow, then green. The bruise pulses when she cries. This morning, the instructors found her crying in the equipment room. They didn't know crying in sleep mode was even possible. Frida asked if she needed to be repaired. Ms. Russo said the bruise would heal on its own.

"The more serious injury is here," she said, pointing to Emmanuelle's heart. "And here." She pointed to Emmanuelle's forehead.

Ms. Gibson said the way Frida spoke to Tamara's son was indefensible. Tamara made mistakes, but Frida yelled. Nothing justifies yelling at a child. Nothing justifies scaring him. Frida acted impulsively. She escalated. She didn't give Tamara space to mother.

The family court judge should know that yelling at Tamara's son is one of the most maternal things Frida has ever done. She'd always wanted her parents to yell on her behalf, remembers being pushed face-first into a chain-link fence when she was eight, telling her parents about it, her parents doing nothing.

The bus rides have lost their novelty. For the rest of the trip, Frida and Meryl play their usual game, trying to guess which drivers are cheaters, which are alcoholics, which are mean to animals, which are bad parents. Meryl undoes her ponytail and shows Frida the bald spot on the back of her head. It's the size of a quarter, perfectly smooth. When she can't sleep, she pulls. She scratches. She's given herself so many scabs. She's nervous about next month's brain scan.

"I don't want them looking into my head. It's so fucking creepy."

"It's going to be okay," Frida says, though she's nervous too. They haven't been told what the procedure will involve, only that the scan will be part of their mid-year evaluations, that their dolls will also be interviewed. Supposedly, the counselors will issue a prognosis for their child's return.

×

Having completed "Preventing Home Alone," this week's anti-abandonment lessons address the epidemic of children being left in hot cars. Four black minivans are staggered across the warehouse parking lot. The mothers are given headsets with a screen that fits over their right eye. No matter what distracting image is on-screen, they must rise above the distraction and stay focused on their doll. They will strap the dolls into car seats and load them in. Once that's complete, they'll have ten minutes to remove the car seat and run to the goalpost at the end of the parking lot.

The headset plays images of war, couples having sex, animals being tortured. The mothers stagger and weave. Linda trips and scrapes her hands. Beth collides with a side mirror. Meryl gets caught resting her head on the steering wheel.

Days later, practice continues in the rain. The mothers try not to slip on the wet asphalt. Frida is in the back seat tending to Emmanuelle when the video begins. Harriet's birthday party. Five children she doesn't recognize. Their parents.

Frida stops breathing. She stops hearing Emmanuelle's shrieks. The video was taken on someone's phone. Gust's. He's narrating.

"Frida, we miss you," he says. "Here's Will. Will, say hello."

Will waves. He's there with his arm around a

young woman. Susanna is holding the cake. Harriet appears in close-up wearing a paper party hat, white with rainbow stripes. The guests sing to her. Gust and Susanna help her blow out her number two candle.

The video switches to Gust and Harriet sitting in his office. On the bookshelf behind them, there's a 3D model of a green roof he worked on in Brooklyn. Harriet is rubbing her eyes. Seems to have just woken up from a nap. Gust asks Harriet to tell Frida about the cake. An almond cake with blueberries. Who came to the party? **Friends. Uncle Will**. Harriet received a balance bike from Daddy and Sue-Sue.

Frida returns to the driver's seat. Harriet looks thin and sullen. They've had her ears pierced. She's wearing gold studs. New clothes. Black and gray.

Gust shows Harriet a framed picture. "Who's this? This is Mommy. Remember we talked to her a few days ago? She looks a little different now."

"No," Harriet says. "Not Mommy. Not home. Mommy not come back! I want Sue-Sue! I want to play!" She slides off Gust's lap.

When the whistle blows, Frida remains seated. Even if the car were on fire, she wouldn't be able to move. Gust and Harriet disappear offscreen. Gust offers Harriet another piece of cake if she'll talk to Mommy. He asks her to please stop hitting him.

"I know you're upset," Gust says. "It's okay to be upset. I know this is hard for you. I don't like it either."

Frida ignores Emmanuelle's increasingly desperate flailing in the back seat. The video plays on a continuous loop. She notices new details each time. Harriet's eyes narrowing as she focuses on the candles, shutting them tight when Gust and Susanna show her how to make a wish. The adults laughing, the children reaching for pieces of cake. Their messy faces. The streamers. The balloons, gold this time. Will's new girl. Asian. Japanese, maybe. The girl's chic black dress. Susanna with her hair in braids. Harriet smiling at Susanna. The image blurring as Gust hands his phone to someone else. Gust and Susanna standing behind Harriet, kissing.

Several times, when Frida looks up, expecting to see her classmates racing in the rain, she finds them stuck in the driver's seats too.

×

Frida's was the only birthday party, but her class-mates watched their daughters brushing their teeth, eating breakfast, at the playground, playing with friends and foster parents. Linda's daughter cried as soon as Mommy was mentioned. Beth's daughter ran from the camera. Ocean wouldn't speak.

They want to know how the school obtained the videos, what their children's guardians were told, if they knew how the videos were to be used. Frida says Gust would never have consented if he'd known. "He wouldn't do that to me. They must have told him it would be a gift."

Roxanne's video showed Isaac standing by him-self. Isaac feeding himself steamed carrots and string beans. His first teeth have come in. His foster mom filmed him cruising along the furniture in her living room. He'll take his first steps any day now. Soon, he won't be a baby anymore.

Isaac's foster mother is a white woman, a Drexel professor in her fifties.

"She has him in full-time day care," Roxanne says. "What's the point of her having him at all if he's with other people for forty fucking hours a week? I wouldn't have had him in day care. I'd be taking care of him myself. How do I even know what kind of place she chose? He's probably the only Black boy."

Roxanne says she'll die if that lady keeps him.

"You don't mean that. She's not going to get him, okay?" Frida warns her to stop. Mothers who voice negative thoughts are placed on a watch list and required to attend extra counseling. Any hints of suicidal ideation are added to their files.

But soon after home video day, the watch list grows. Mothers in love become careless. A couple is caught cuddling in a supply closet. Another is caught holding hands. Weeks earlier, Margaret and Alicia's foiled escape attempt sent ripples through the other romances. Couples either grew closer or broke up. There are rumors that the school is developing an evening seminar on loneliness. How to manage it. How to avoid it. Why it has no place here, or anywhere, in the life of a mother.

×

Inside the warehouse, the drills are combined into obstacle courses. Frida and her classmates now carry their dolls from house to car to house to car. They must run and narrate, run and deliver affection.

Frida's counselor thinks she doesn't care anymore. Her best time is third place. The only reason she's not in fourth is because Meryl started having panic attacks.

"I'm not going to leave my daughter to die in a hot car," Frida says. "I'd never do that." And why is the school allowed to torture them? With videos of their own kids?

"**Torture** is not a word to use lightly," the counselor says. "We're putting you in high-pressure scenarios so we can see what kind of mother you are. Most people can be good parents if they have absolutely no stress. We have to know that you can handle conflict. Every day is an obstacle course for a parent."

×

Evaluation day for Unit 3 falls on the first Monday in May. In the warehouse parking lot, Frida, Meryl, Beth, and Linda unbutton their uniforms as low as decency allows and roll up the legs of their jumpsuits. They sit on the ground and lift their faces to the sun.

"I haven't been this pale since I was a baby," Linda says.

She begins telling them how she used to sunbathe on her parents' back porch but pauses when she sees Beth's legs. Her scars. Linda whistles. She asks when it started. She's afraid of knives.

Beth says she didn't use knives, she used razor blades. She now describes her cutting as an act of selfishness. "Had I known the pain I was causing my parents," Beth begins.

Meryl punches her in the arm. "You don't have to be fake with us."

"I'm repenting," Beth hisses.

Beth spots Frida's nearly hairless legs and exclaims. Since Frida stopped shaving, her leg hair has become sparse, though she still requests razor and tweezer privileges to manage her underarm stubble and upper lip. She hasn't cut her hair since November. Her ponytail hangs halfway down her back.

They take turns running their hands up Frida's calves, cursing the unfair advantages of Asians. Beth and Linda both have thick leg hair. Only Meryl's legs are shaved. Linda wants to know who she does it for—a man or a woman, a guard or another mom.

"None of your business," Meryl says.

Beyond the parking lot is more forest. A subdivision. A mall. Big-box stores. The highway is a major truck route. Several FedEx trucks pass. Some for Fresh Direct, UPS. The life in which Frida earned money and purchased goods on the Internet feels as far away as childhood.

She hasn't spoken to Harriet in nine weeks, doesn't know how Harriet is behaving with the social worker and child psychologist. It frightens her to think of the counselor interviewing Emmanuelle. There are days when the doll answers no to every question. Harriet was like that too. "No" came before "yeah," then "yes." Fifteen other words arrived before Harriet said "Mommy."

Linda is called into the warehouse. She hugs each of them before going inside, seems genuinely nervous. They wish her luck. "Run like someone is trying to kill you," Meryl says.

She and Beth choose to pass the time by braiding each other's hair.

"Frida, come sit with us," Beth says.

Frida takes her place in front of Beth. Meryl has been nagging her to be nicer, to stop calling Beth a bad influence.

"I'm allowed to have two friends here," Meryl told her.

As Beth begins braiding, Frida feels soothed. It's

been so long since another adult, a human, touched her head. That night at Will's, he played with the ends of her hair, compared the texture to paintbrush bristles. Gust used to stroke her head when she had trouble sleeping. She imagines his hands in Susanna's thick red mane, wonders if he always liked redheads, if she, the mother of his child, was the anomaly, the detour, when all along, he was looking for Susanna. They looked so happy at the birthday party.

They switch. Frida combs through Beth's sleek hair with her fingers. Beth asks Frida to rub her neck. When she woke up this morning, she couldn't turn her head. Soon, all three are braiding and massaging each other's necks and shoulders, sitting one behind the other.

If they were schoolgirls, they'd make clover chains. Frida remembers sitting alone at recess and tying the end of one flowering weed to the head of the next. She's never felt closer to them. A sisterhood based on shared incompetence. If this were another life, she'd take a picture now. Meryl resting her head on Beth's shoulder. Beth crinkling her nose. In this light, no one would be able to tell that they're losing hope. That they're dangerous women. Women who can't control themselves. Who don't know the right way to love.

13.

THE DOLLS MAKE THEIR BODIES HEAVY AND limp, like protestors resisting arrest. The instructors work together to carry each doll from the equipment room. Ms. Russo soon strains a muscle in her lower back.

Emmanuelle has a trail of dried tears below each eye. Frida cleans her face with spit. She chooses a station by the window and invites Emmanuelle to sit on her lap.

"We understand that yesterday was intense," Ms. Russo says. "Girls, you're allowed to feel scared. You're allowed to feel confused. It's very hard helping Mommy learn how to keep you safe. Thank you very much for your hard work." She leads the class in a round of applause.

The dolls remain aggrieved. Yesterday, Meryl broke her headset in anger. Beth vomited. Only Linda completed the full evaluation.

Emmanuelle's new word is **blue**. Also, **cheek**, as in, **I want a kiss**. After Frida kisses one cheek, Emmanuelle points to the other.

They're given time for freestyle hugs, a transition before they begin the next unit. Frida covers her eyes and leads Emmanuelle through a few rounds of peek-a-boo. They sing the ABC song. Frida sings "Twinkle Twinkle Little Star," explains that the songs have the same tune.

Emmanuelle pronounces **twinkle** as **winkle**. She waves her hands to approximate stars, following Frida's lead.

As they sing, Frida realizes that Emmanuelle has never seen stars. Harriet probably hasn't either. Not yet. Frida had noticed that during her first nights here. That they were far enough from the city to see stars. Constellations.

"I'm sorry I fell yesterday. You felt scared, didn't you?"

Emmanuelle nods.

Frida slipped a few yards short of the finish line. She is a bad mother for falling. She is a bad mother for swearing. She is a bad mother for finishing third, for missing another month of phone privileges.

"Do you know why Mommy had to do all that running?"

"Test."

"And why do the mommies have tests?"

"Learn." Emmanuelle pronounces the **r** and **n** with extra syllables, adds an **ah** at the end.

"Learn-ah," she repeats. She stands and kisses Frida on the forehead, placing her hands on either side of Frida's face.

She speaks slowly. "I know it's hard," Emmanuelle says. "I will help you."

×

Their classroom has been reconfigured with four mothering stations, each with a circular multicolor braided area rug. They receive a canvas bag containing half a dozen toys. It is the first day of Unit 4: Fundamentals of Play.

The dolls can have one toy, not all the toys, Ms. Khoury instructs.

The mothers will help the dolls make choices. Ms. Khoury demonstrates with Linda's doll. After she scoops up all six toys in her grabby hands, Ms. Khoury says, "Sweetie, that's too many." She gets down on the floor and speaks to the doll at eye level. "I notice you telling me that you want many things right now, but right now, we're only playing with one toy."

Ms. Khoury holds up a finger for emphasis. The doll continues to hoard all six. Ms. Khoury begins teaching her to sort, to determine her preferences. Which toy is calling to her? What does she need right now? Which toy will meet those needs?

In comparison, the rules for previous units almost made sense. The doll was crying, and her mother comforted her. The doll was sick, and her mother helped her get well. But there's no good reason, Frida knows, why the dolls can only play with one toy at a time.

×

The hardest part is staying cheerful and amazed. Speaking only in exclamations. Generating stories on the fly. Resisting boredom. Playing is harder than running. There's no numbered sequence of steps, no specific play protocol. Play requires creativity. Each mother must tap into her inner child.

Model the behavior you hope to achieve, the instructors say.

Frida and Roxanne now process every night after lights-out. Frida tells Roxanne that she grew up watching soap operas with her grandmother. There was no sitting and playing and setting a timer. She admits that she used to make out with her dolls, which Roxanne thinks is deeply weird. They list the toys they'll buy for Harriet and Isaac in November, reminisce about favorite toys from childhood. Roxanne made outfits for her Barbies using tissue. Ball gowns made of tissue and tape. She's going to let Isaac play with Barbies when he's older, wants him to develop his feminine side. She'll take him to dance classes. He'll learn to play the cello.

Back in the classroom, it takes Frida and Emmanuelle many days to deliver fifteen minutes of focused play with a single toy. Frida takes shortcuts. She promises Emmanuelle kisses if she cooperates.

"See how your friends are playing nicely? Don't you want to be nice like them?"

Ms. Khoury criticizes this approach. Frida isn't allowed to shame the doll into behaving. Shaming the child isn't loving.

"Maybe that worked in the cultures you and I grew up in, but this is America," Ms. Khoury says. An American mother should inspire feelings of hope, not regret.

×

In the gymnasium, there are twenty stations enclosed by black fabric partitions, each with a table and chair, a monitor, and a gray machine on wheels from which wires dangle. Frida looks into the camera above the screen. She expected an MRI machine or needles, a helmet, something powerful and futuristic. She closes her eyes as one of the women in pink lab coats swabs her face with an astringent-soaked cotton pad and tapes sensors to her forehead, brow, temples, cheeks, and neck. She unbuttons her uniform and allows the woman to tape a sensor to her heart.

"Let your thoughts come naturally," the woman says, handing Frida a set of headphones.

On-screen, it's the first day of class. The pairing of mothers and dolls. For the next half hour, Frida watches clips from the past six months. A highlight reel of her failures. The affection drills.

The first evaluation day. The first time changing the blue liquid. The pinching incident. Talk circle. The cooking classes where she kept cutting herself, the medicine she administered incorrectly. The warehouse. Easter. Talk circle again. Emmanuelle crying in the equipment room.

Her throat is parched. Her pulse races. Her stomach cramps. No one told them what the scans would involve. When she asked the counselor how to prepare, the counselor said preparation wasn't possible.

"Everything you need should already be inside you," the counselor said.

When Emmanuelle is pinched or hit, or particularly frightened or distraught, the camera zooms in on her face and shows her response in slow motion, giving Frida time to consider her suffering. Her anguish pierces Frida almost as much as Harriet's does. She feels responsible. Some clips are taken from the camera inside Emmanuelle, showing Frida exactly as the doll sees her. Frida watches herself age. She watches herself struggle.

The reel ends with a montage of affection, but even in scenes of them hugging or kissing or playing, Frida looks stricken and sad. She returns to class with imprints on her face from the sensors.

Emmanuelle loves Frida's "dot-dots." She presses her thumb into each circle, laughing.

By dinnertime, all the mothers have been marked.

×

On Mother's Day, phone privileges are canceled for everyone, a decision that's only announced at breakfast. Between meals, the mothers must remain in their rooms and write in their atonement journals. They're encouraged to reflect on their remaining shortcomings and their missing children, to remember last Mother's Day and think about next year's, as well as giving thanks to the women who raised them.

"I am a bad mother because," Frida writes. She quickly fills five pages.

She tries to visualize success. It is June and she's calling Harriet. It is December and she and Harriet have been reunited. Harriet is tugging on the flaps of Frida's fur hat. Harriet no longer likes owls, has moved on to penguins. She takes Harriet to get a flu shot. Gust lets Harriet spend two weeks with her. They fly to Chicago for the holidays to see Gong-gong and Popo. On the plane, Harriet's poise and good manners impress the flight attendants.

She tries to imagine what Harriet will look like in December, but the Harriet she imagines is the one from last summer, before her very bad day, when she had time to study Harriet's face. She doesn't know what Harriet looks like right at this moment, and this in itself seems the crime. She's not there to watch her daughter grow.

They have the windows open this morning. There's a breeze. The clear, dry day beckons. Some Sundays, she and Roxanne try to walk the length of the campus to see how far they can get. What will the family court judge do with her mistakes and her trips to talk circle and Emmanuelle's wounds? The doll's arm is still dented. Her bruise is still visible. The woman in the videos has nothing to do with how she parents Harriet. How can the school expect her to love Emmanuelle like her own? To behave naturally, when there's nothing natural about these circumstances?

Roxanne keeps tearing pages out of her journal and pushing them onto the floor. She's crying. Frida goes to the bathroom and gets a wad of toilet paper, leaves it on Roxanne's desk. Isaac turned one this week. Roxanne wanted to sing to him today.

"Don't cry," Frida whispers, hugging Roxanne around the shoulders.

Roxanne thanks her. Frida picks up the discarded papers and stacks the torn pages. When Roxanne tries to get back into bed, Frida won't let her.

In her atonement journal, Frida writes that Susanna deserves to be celebrated today, that she is Harriet's mother too.

Harriet can probably say her own name now. She might be speaking in complete sentences. **Mommy, I love you galaxies. Mommy, I love you best. Mommy, come home. You are my only mommy. You are my real mommy. Mommy, I miss you**.

×

The school reviewed Frida's brain scan to see which neural pathways lit up, looking for flickering in the pathways for empathy and care. Though they detected a few muted signals, results suggested that her capacity for maternal feeling and attachment is limited. Her word count remains one of the best in class, but analysis of her expressions, pulse, temperature, eye contact, blinking patterns, and touch indicated residual fear and anger. Guilt. Confusion. Anxiety. Ambivalence.

"Ambivalence at this stage is very troubling," the counselor said.

The counselor's interview with Emmanuelle was similarly inconclusive. When asked if she loves Mommy, Emmanuelle said yes, then no, then yes again, then no again. She stopped answering. The counselor asked if she feels safe with Mommy, if Mommy meets her needs, if she misses Mommy when she's in the equipment room. When pressed for an answer, the doll started crying.

The counselor said Frida possesses the intelligence to parent but maybe not the temperament.

"But I am a parent. I am Harriet's parent."

"But is it in Harriet's best interest to be parented by you?" the counselor asked.

The prognosis for return is fair to poor or just poor for almost everyone. Frida is in the former category. There are some exceptions, about sixteen in total, including Linda and Charisse, one of the middle-aged white women—the natural blonde with a smoker's rasp who's known to sing Wilson Phillips songs in the shower, "Hold On" being her favorite. Once everyone learns their names, the successful mothers begin to suffer. Someone shreds Linda's uniforms. Someone leaves ants in Charisse's bed. Charisse calls the hotline to report the ants. She becomes suspicious of her roommate, her hallmates.

352

THE SCHOOL FOR GOOD MOTHERS

She complains to Ms. Gibson and Ms. Knight. Her classmates begin referring to her as "the complainer," though supposedly none of her complaints have been added to her file.

The mothers imagine what they'd do if they had access to knives or scissors or chemicals. Not everyone came to the school a violent woman, but now, heading into month seven, they all might stab someone.

×

But fortunes can change, even here. After a surprise second-place finish for Unit 4, Frida begins Unit 5: Intermediate and Advanced Play in a state of blithe competence. Emmanuelle somehow decided to cooperate on evaluation day. She played with one toy at a time. She put them away when asked.

As June begins, Frida lavishes her with praise. Emmanuelle begins appearing in Frida's dreams as a living girl. In her dreams, Emmanuelle and Harriet roam the campus holding hands. The girls roll down hills. They chase each other around the stone courtyard. They wear matching blue dresses, matching shoes and barrettes. They run together through the woods.

Frida teaches Emmanuelle to say "I love you" in Mandarin. She teaches Emmanuelle to say **wawa**, little doll—a term of endearment she's never used with Harriet.

She begins sleeping normally, eating more, gains some weight back. Food has a taste again. When she showers, she's alive to the water hitting her face. In class, she's alive to her body next to Emmanuelle's body. She gives willingly, and what passes between them is love.

In the evenings, she prepares her talking points. She won't mention the birthday video, won't ask about carbs or sunscreen or sun hats, if Gust and Susanna have taken Harriet to the beach, if they've started swim lessons, where they'll go on vacation. She'll use her "I love you" judiciously.

They begin practicing in groups of four. Two dolls receive one toy. When the fighting begins, the mothers must separate the dolls and help them process their feelings. They practice sharing and turn-taking. They learn to manage toy-related aggression. They model reconciliation.

As the dolls fight over toys, Frida worries that Emmanuelle's passivity will be counted against her. She's disappointed to see that Emmanuelle conforms to racial stereotypes, a failure of imagination on the part of her makers. When Emmanuelle plays with other dolls, she's docile to the point of subservience. It's always her hair being pulled, her toy being stolen. When the other dolls wrong her, she responds by doing nothing.

Frida hates seeing Emmanuelle get hit. The battles bring back memories of her own childhood, when she didn't know how to defend herself, when a smart Chinese girl with a moon face felt like the worst thing to be. She often looked in the mirror and wished she'd been born a little white girl. Her parents sent her to her room for crying even though she was bullied daily. Not only did they push her against the chain-link fence, her classmates once chased her home from school, pelting her with cherry tomatoes. The juice dried in her hair. That night, when her mother bathed her, there was a layer of tomato seeds floating on the water. She doesn't remember any special hugs or kisses. She doesn't remember her mother denouncing the bullies. Life would have been different if her parents had held her, but she won't blame them. It wasn't a straight line from there to here.

She used to think it was a reason not to have a child. It seemed too painful to watch a son or daughter endure the cruelty of other children. But she told Gust that she'd be different. She'd be a mother who always said, "I love you." She'd never be cold. She'd never make Harriet stand against a wall for punishment. If Harriet were ever bullied, if she were ever pushed around or ridiculed, Frida would be there to tell her that things would get better. She'd call the other parents, confront the other children. But where is she now, and where is Harriet? It's been over nine months since she was removed.

×

The rules have changed again. Frida's phone privileges remain suspended. Before she can contact Harriet, she must finish in the top two for Unit 5. The school needs to see another set of results to make sure her performance was due to skill, not luck.

The night before evaluation day, the school has its first jumper. The mothers don't find out until the morning. The jumper was Margaret, one of the mothers caught kissing behind the tennis courts. Some say she tried to get back together with Alicia, that Alicia rejected her. Some say she was in trouble because her four-year-old doll hadn't learned to read yet. Some say her son's foster parents returned him because he stood on their biological baby, and the school wouldn't tell Margaret where he was moved.

Alicia and several of Margaret's classmates get in trouble for weeping at breakfast. Beth says she feels triggered. Linda says this is a bad omen. She asks them to hold hands. Together they pray. For Margaret and her soul, rest in peace. For Margaret's son, Robbie. For Margaret's parents, especially her mother. For her grandparents. For her siblings.

"For Alicia," Meryl says.

"For Margaret's doll," Beth adds. "That boy is going to be so confused."

Meryl says the doll will be erased.

"But she was his first mom," Frida says. "He's not going to forget her."

"Sure, tell yourself that."

Frida watches Alicia cry. Margaret was only twenty-five. Both she and Alicia were placed on the watch list weeks ago. Will Ms. Gibson be the one calling Margaret's family, or will it be the executive director, Ms. Knight? The thought of either of them delivering condolences makes Frida feel helpless and irate. She's imagined her parents getting that call, has wondered whether such a call would send them to the hospital. She's imagined them telling Gust, Gust telling Harriet. The danger has never felt so real. The boy who killed himself during freshman year was a stranger. The girl who hanged herself during grad school was someone she'd known only by name. She didn't realize that she and Margaret had anything in common besides their missing children.

×

Evaluations must be completed in pairs. There are three stations, one toy per rug. Station one has a frog puppet. Station two has a bag of DUPLO blocks. Station three has a toy laptop. The two dolls must complete ten consecutive minutes of peaceful play at each station. Their mothers must manage emotional upset, break up fights, set appropriate limits, impart wisdom about sharing, turn-taking, patience, generosity, and community values.

Beth is paired with Meryl, Frida with Linda. Frida can't let Linda win. Empathy will doom her chances. Gabriel was found a few days ago. He got himself arrested while shoplifting from a gas station. Linda is worried that he'll be tried as an adult, that he'll get into a fight in juvie and land in solitary, that he'll get moved to adult prison. That he'll keep fucking up and stay in the system forever.

Emmanuelle clings to Frida's leg. She's sensitive. A weather vane. A mood ring. She can sense Frida's nervousness.

Frida and Linda and their respective dolls move to the center. Ms. Khoury holds the frog puppet high so neither doll can reach it.

Frida tells Emmanuelle not to be afraid. She says, "Mommy believes in you. Mommy loves you."

She whispers, "I love you galaxies."

She looks away, horrified. She was supposed to guard this part of their life. How hard would it have been to honor their secret, their magic word? Even Gust and Susanna don't say it. If she could trade places with Margaret, she would. It should be her body hitting the pavement, her body being carted away from this place.

"Gala-seas?" Emmanuelle tries out the new word.

Ms. Russo asks if Frida is ready. Linda strokes her doll's head like she's preparing to unleash a pit bull. Meryl and Beth mouth words of encouragement.

Frida bows her head and holds Emmanuelle close. "I am a bad mother," she says. "But I am learning to be good."

14.

BENEATH WHITE TENTS ON THE LAWN OUTSIDE Pierce, there are long tables with red-and-white-checked tablecloths and folding chairs. One tent for doll food. One for human food. The school has set up activity stations: horseshoes, beanbags, Frisbees, Hula-Hoops.

They've been calling it the bad parents' picnic. Officially it's a Fourth of July barbecue. They'll finally meet the fathers, their comrades. Though the school couldn't have anticipated this sequence of events, the picnic is a well-timed morale boost after Margaret's suicide.

Supposedly, they can relax. They'll have a rare afternoon without lessons. They'll still be filmed, but words won't be counted, and the dolls' internal cameras will be switched off.

"Our gift to you," Ms. Khoury said this morning, noting that some mothers have responded to pressure in incredibly selfish ways. Today is only an icebreaker. Tomorrow, they'll be bused to the fathers' school to begin Unit 6: Socialization.

Everyone watches eagerly as buses pull into the parking lot on College Avenue. Frida is reminded of those MGM musicals from the 1950s. **Seven Brides for Seven Brothers**. But there are only two buses. They outnumber the fathers three to one. Like them, the fathers wear navy blue uniforms and work boots. Most fathers are Black and brown. Most look to be in their twenties and thirties. One is a teenager holding an infant.

They're younger than Frida expected. If she saw most of them on the street, she'd never guess that they had children. In New York, she once went on a blind date with a twenty-five-year-old grad student whose invitation she'd accepted on a whim. She'd been only six years older at the time, but men liked to tell her things, and as the boy told her about his dead twin and running away from home at fourteen, she wanted to put a blanket around the boy's shoulders and give him cookies. She feels the same protective impulse now.

"Who they?" Emmanuelle asks. Frida reminds her that they've seen fathers in books. Father raccoons and father bears and father bunnies. These are human fathers. She tells Emmanuelle about two-parent households.

Ms. Knight mills through the crowd in a stars-and-stripes dress. Her counterpart, Ms. Holmes, is also in attendance. The two executive directors hug and exchange air-kisses. From a distance, Ms. Holmes, also white, also statuesque, seems to have allowed herself to age naturally. She has a Susan Sontag–like white streak in her dark hair, wears no makeup, no jewelry, has her pink lab coat draped loosely over her shoulders. The fathers' minders are all female, all in pink lab coats. Some fathers and instructors look suspiciously close.

The younger mothers and fathers gravitate to one another. Parents line up at the doll food tent and cautiously begin mingling, everyone looking over their shoulders and whispering. Some parents introduce themselves by name and offense before realizing they don't have to.

No one mentions Margaret. Frida has been thinking about Margaret's son, wondering whether he's been told yet, who will bring him to the funeral, if he'll be allowed to attend, if the casket will be closed. She hasn't spoken to Harriet in four months. Someone needs to tell Harriet that Mommy will be calling soon—this weekend, if the counselor allows it. She finished second in yesterday's evaluation for Intermediate and Advanced Play, but she knows it's too soon to get excited.

She carries Emmanuelle to the doll food tent.

"Mommy, I feel nervous." Emmanuelle hides her face.

Frida tells her not to worry. To distract her, Frida waves to the boy doll in front of them in line, who's sitting on his father's shoulders.

They crane their necks.

"Up high," Emmanuelle says.

The father must be six-three or six-four. Emmanuelle asks if he's a giraffe. The father overhears them and laughs. He turns around, introduces himself. **Tucker**. Frida shakes his hand. Her voice cracks as she says hello. The man's palm is soft, much softer than hers. She hasn't met a man who isn't a guard since last November.

Tucker's doll son, Jeremy, is a pale, chubby brunette, a three-year-old with a bowl haircut and the stare of a serial killer. Tucker sets him down.

Emmanuelle waves. Jeremy pokes her arm. Emmanuelle touches his hand. Jeremy hugs her roughly, then tries to stick his entire fist in her mouth.

"Whoa, too rough," Frida says. Tucker asks Jeremy to be gentle. They make eye contact with each other instead of their dolls.

Frida looks and looks. Tucker is her age, maybe older, a fortysomething white man with the slouching body of a reader. His straight hair is mostly gray and flops over his forehead. It's been cut haphazardly. When he smiles, his eyes almost disappear. He smiles easily. He's thinner and less attractive than Will, more wrinkled than Gust, has enormous straight teeth that give his face an equine quality.

She checks for a wedding ring, remembers the jewelry rule, must find a way to ask. Emmanuelle notices her blushing.

"Why you hot, Mommy? You okay?"

"I'm fine."

Tucker is blushing too. A suitable response, she thinks, to meeting in uniform in a tent with blue food.

There are blue hot dogs, cookies, slices of watermelon, ice cream sandwiches, Popsicles. The dolls must be fed first. Frida and Tucker lead their dolls to an empty corner of the tent. The parents' self-segregation is dispiriting. Latino fathers hold court with Latina mothers. The lone fiftysomething white father has found the trio of middle-aged white women. His teenage doll daughter looks mortified.

Known lesbians in the community keep to themselves. Frida and the other mothers engaged in interracial socializing, especially the white mothers flirting with Black fathers, receive angry stares. Frida feels guilty, but if Roxanne or anyone else gets on her case, she'll say that Tucker was simply standing in line, that this isn't a manifestation of growing up with white culture. Most of the Black and Latino fathers are too young, most of the white fathers too creepy. There are no Asians.

Emmanuelle's and Jeremy's mouths are ringed with blue. Tucker and Frida talk about their dolls, whether their dolls are typically shy around strangers, how they behaved this morning, how they normally behave in class. Even chatting over blue food, she's surprised to find that she feels safe with him, enjoys his deep voice and the way he listens. She asks if the fathers have good food or more privacy, if they have Friday counseling and Saturday cleaning crew, how they celebrated Father's Day, if there have been romances or injuries or suicides or expulsions.

"We've had one. One suicide, I mean." She doesn't add that she could be next.

"None for us," Tucker says. "I'm sorry. You have my condolences."

"I didn't know her very well. I want to feel sadder. It's hard to feel anything here." She admits her detachment makes her feel selfish.

"You don't seem selfish."

Frida smiles. "You don't know me."

Tucker cheerfully answers her questions about the father's school: no cleaning crew, yes brain scans, counseling once a month, no talk circle, what's talk circle, some hand jobs, but no real romances, not that he knows of. A bunch of fistfights, but no expulsions. Some malfunctions, but no dead dolls. They get to call home for an hour every Sunday. No one has ever lost phone privileges. The counselors think it's important for them to stay in their children's lives. For the most part, it's been a supportive group.

Tucker has made friends. "From all walks of life," he says.

Frida regrets asking. She rolls and unrolls the

sleeves of her uniform, sighs deeply. If she'd been able to speak to Harriet every Sunday, as promised, how different this year apart would be.

She waits for him to ask about the mothers' program. When he doesn't, she says, "Don't you want to know about us?"

"Sorry. We haven't talked about you ladies very much. Do we have to talk about this? I don't want to talk about this place. We have the day off. Tell me about you."

"Really? Why?"

Tucker looks amused. "I'm interested in learning about the survival of the human spirit. Tell me about your spirit, Frida."

"I don't know if my spirit is allowed to talk to you."

"Is your spirit already taken?"

"Oh, definitely. Full dance card. I'm super popular."

"A girl like you," he says.

He wants to know about her old life. Where she grew up, where she went to college, where she lived in Philly, where she worked. His earnestness makes her wonder if he's Christian. She wants to know what's wrong with him. He seems like a natural with children. She'd once had the same feeling about Gust.

"I miss my books," he says.

"I miss reading the news. Remember how much time we used to spend doing that? Doesn't it seem ridiculous now? I can't wait to get my hair cut. I miss having bangs. They cover my frown lines. I have this horrid eyebrow crinkle. See? I can't cut them myself, it would look too crazy. I don't want to ask anyone here to cut them. I shouldn't have this much face showing."

"Why? You have a nice face."

Frida blushes again. She thanks him, insists she wasn't fishing for compliments. He didn't think she was. This is the longest conversation she's had with anyone besides Meryl or Roxanne. An hour passes. She enjoys talking to someone her age. She remembers telling friends about Gust after their first date. "He asked me questions," she said. "He listened to me." A rare experience in New York.

Emmanuelle and Jeremy play under the table while their parents eat human food and compare transgressions.

"I left my daughter alone for over two hours. When she was eighteen months. You?"

"My son fell out of a tree. On my watch."

"How old? How high?"

"Three. Very. He broke his leg. He was playing in his tree house. I was right there, but I had my back turned. I was texting. It happened in a minute. Silas decided that he wanted to fly. My wife. My ex-wife, told the hospital what happened."

"And now you're here."

"And now I'm here." Tucker raises his plastic cup.

She knows she should have higher standards, that she's perhaps attaching too much importance to his height, the feeling that if she were in danger, she could take refuge in his body, that all he'd have to do is wrap her in his arms and she could hide. She used to love how tiny she felt next to Gust.

She's not the only one who's found a favorite. All around them, conversations are hungry and rushed. Mothers are sauntering on the lawn. Fathers are weighing their options. Several older dolls are overheard calling their parents "embarrassing."

In his old life, Tucker was a scientist. He designed drug trials for a pharmaceutical firm. He owns a house in Germantown, had been remodeling one room at a time. A friend is staying there this year.

He's paying that friend to remodel the kitchen. Frida asks about his prognosis for return.

Tucker turns red. "Do we have to talk about that? I am a father learning to be a better man."

"Seriously? That's what they have you say? We have to say 'I am a narcissist. I am a danger to my child.' Does that mean you're getting him back?"

"If I don't blow it. My counselor said my chances are fair. What about you?"

"Fair to poor."

Tucker gives her a sympathetic look. The words don't hurt as much as they usually do. Loneliness clouds Frida's judgment. If there were no fence and no dolls and no consequences, she'd take him to the woods.

"Why did you do it?"

Startled by his candor, she begins telling him about her one very bad day, but her explanations sound especially pathetic after eight months in uniform. She tells him about leaving the house to buy a coffee, driving to work for the forgotten file, how she thought she'd return right away. She admits to wanting a break. He admits he left out some details. He was texting another woman when Silas fell.

"I know, I know. It's so cliché."

"It is."

She asks the woman's age, bracing herself, feels relieved when he says the woman is older, a colleague. That it was a flirtation, not an affair. They compare divorces. Tucker's hasn't been finalized. His ex-wife has custody. She's taken up with the father of one of their son's friends. A writer. A fucking stay-at-home dad. Tucker's expression turns ugly as he complains about the new man. His anger makes her nervous. This might be how she looks when she talks about Susanna. One minute reasonable, the next blinded by fury.

"I should go," she says. He touches her elbow, sending a shiver through her whole body. She remembers Will leading her to his room.

"You're judging," Tucker says.

"That's what we do here." She gets up and goes to look for Emmanuelle, asks Emmanuelle to say goodbye to Jeremy.

Tucker is still watching her. "Stay," he says. "I'm enjoying this. Aren't you?"

Frida returns to her chair. Tucker puts his arm around the back of her seat. She should be thinking about her daughter. She can't risk losing Harriet because of a man who let his son fall out of a tree.

×

The mothers compare notes at dinner: which fathers are creepy, which are fuckable, which are spoken for, which seem gay. Beth says Frida is practically married. Meryl says Tucker is old and super basic, but he has a full head of hair and seems like he might have money.

Frida shares what she learned about the fathers' program. Her classmates shake their heads. They're surprised, but not. They're angriest about the phone privileges. The rumors that the fathers' evaluations are easier. The rumors that the technical department handles all changes of blue liquid.

Frida tells them about Tucker's almost cheating on his ex. His son's broken leg. Linda says it's all relative. The trio of middle-aged white women are thirsting for an insurance salesman who hit his fourteen-year-old daughter and made her buy drugs for him. There are some truly harmless men, fathers whose only crime was poverty, but they met bad fathers who spanked, bad fathers who broke arms and dislocated shoulders, bad-father alcoholics, bad-father meth addicts, some ex-cons. One man, who might be mentally ill, said he doesn't want to leave. He'd do the course a second time. He told Beth that life at the school is better. Three meals a day, air-conditioning, a bed. He couldn't get over the size of the mothers' campus.

They tell Frida to stick with the distracted, neglectful tree house dad. At least he's not violent. At least he's not a drinker. At least he can get a job after he leaves.

"At least he's got big hands," Linda says. The whole table giggles.

×

The fathers' school is housed in an abandoned redbrick hospital. Built two hundred years ago, according to the plaque at the entrance. There seem to be more guards but fewer cameras. There's a long winding driveway lined with manicured rosebushes, a garden next to the entrance that's crowded with sunflowers.

Meryl says it looks like a place where they'd film a zombie movie. Frida reminds her about Helen's crazy nurse fantasy, the idea that men might find the pink lab coats erotic. Is it just her, or do the fathers' instructors seem to be younger and more attractive? They seem to be wearing more makeup. Several wear dresses beneath their pink lab coats. One is wearing heels.

They're led to the pediatric ward, to a room that must have been a playroom for sick children. All the furniture is child size. The walls are cream. There are sun and rainbow and cloud and teddy bear decals on the windows.

Several cohorts with dolls of the same age practice together. They're assigned to groups of six: two mothers with girl dolls, one father with a boy doll. Frida and Linda practice with a Latino father named George, who has an asymmetrical haircut and a tattoo of a winged beast on his forearm.

Emmanuelle rubs George's arm, trying to make the creature disappear. She asks for Jeremy. She asks for food. Why are there toys but no food? No outside.

"It sun." Emmanuelle points to the window. "Mommy walk!"

"Remember to say **please**. I'm sorry, sweetie. We're not playing with Jeremy today. We're making new friends. You're going to make so many new friends this month. We're going to play, and we're going to learn. Remember, you said you'd help me."

Emmanuelle wraps her arms over her belly and rocks herself. "Jer-my," she says softly. She's never been this fond of another doll.

Frida misses them too. At least the dolls can hug. Yesterday, Tucker asked if they could sit together in the cafeteria sometime. He tried to grab her hand, but she swatted him away, then hated herself for doing so. If he tries again, she'll let him. She doesn't want him to choose someone else. She's heard Charisse, the blond Wilson Phillips fan, might be interested.

She thinks of Tucker's hand on her elbow, imagines his hands on her wrists. She is a bad mother for thinking about him. She is a bad mother for wanting to see him. She is safer without him here. Sexual tension is interfering with everyone's parenting. The mothers sit with their backs arched. The fathers flex and gaze, their eyes panning up and down the mothers' uniforms, as if the body inside is still worth something.

Toy laptops are distributed, one for every three dolls. Once the laptop is in play, George's doll dives for it, knocking over both girls. He won't apologize. George hugs his doll from behind, trapping his limbs. He looks like he's delivering the Heimlich maneuver. It's the hug to soothe aggression, a move that's only been taught to parents of boys.

"Well done," Ms. Khoury tells George. She suggests that Frida and Linda watch and learn.

Frida provides the hug to soothe physical injury, the hug to soothe emotional upset. Emmanuelle asks why the boy is mean.

"He's not mean. He just likes you very much. That's how boys show their feelings." She tells Emmanuelle about Billy, the little blond boy who kissed her in kindergarten. Every day, Billy teased her mercilessly, called her ugly, pulled his eyes into slits and made **ching-chong** noises, rallied other children to make fun of her. Then, one afternoon, in the far-off time when children played unsupervised, when the playground was nearly empty, she heard someone running up behind her. She felt a kiss, such a hard kiss on the cheek that he almost knocked her over. She didn't realize who it was until he was halfway across the field.

"I didn't tell anyone until I was eight."

"Why?"

"He didn't want anyone to know that he liked me." Frida squeezes Emmanuelle's arm. "Boys are complicated."

After lunch, a coy hour filled with seductive napkin dropping and silverware twirling, the instructors assign them to new groups. Frida and Meryl practice with a young Black father named Colin, who co-slept with his toddler son and rolled over during a nap and broke the boy's wrist. They glean his background in bits and pieces as their dolls fight over a toy car. Colin is a baby-faced twenty-one-year-old, about five shades darker than the green-eyed guard and taller than him, with a short beard and a faint Southern accent. Speaking only to Meryl, as if Frida isn't even there, he describes himself as a people person. He was in college before this, a business major. No wife or girlfriend is mentioned. Meryl spends the afternoon with her lips gently parted and her head tilted to the side.

Frida nags Meryl to pay attention. She's being too obvious, risking too much. But her oblivion allows Frida to shine. Frida is quick to soothe Emmanuelle, quick to deliver talks about community values. Emmanuelle peacefully lets the others have a turn when Frida prompts her. She cries far less than the other two dolls.

Ms. Russo notices Emmanuelle's good behavior. Meryl and Colin ignore Frida's requests to focus.

Frida feels like their chaperone. She feels like she's glimpsing Meryl's past and Harriet's possible future. There are few things scarier than a desirous teenage girl. She only has eight or nine years before Harriet's body begins changing. The women in Gust's family are curvy. Boys will look at Harriet. Men will look at her too.

×

Co-ed training will continue for the whole month of July. Half the mothers land in talk circle that first week. Offenses include: flirtatious body language, speaking coyly, excessive eye contact, sexually suggestive touching, and neglecting their dolls. Meryl and Roxanne sit together one night, Roxanne having been caught touching a father's hand, Meryl having been caught hugging Colin too vigorously.

Roxanne tells Frida that when Meryl was supposed to confess, she claimed she wasn't flirting, said she wasn't distracting Colin from his parenting, and he wasn't distracting her. They were multitasking. Her sarcasm earned her some extra counseling and has been added to her file.

"What that girl gets away with," Roxanne says. She thinks Meryl is greedy. Meryl has a man at home and two men here. Some mothers have no one.

"We won't be here forever."

"Please, do not lecture me, Frida."

"I'm just saying that you're smart. You're young. You're beautiful. You'll meet someone normal after this. A grown-up. You should be with a grown-up."

They have this conversation all the time. Whenever Roxanne finds new gray hairs or when they talk about what they'll do after they leave.

"You're not thirty-nine," Frida says.

"So what? Who's going to want me after he finds out I had my kid taken away?"

"Someone will understand."

"Oh my God." Roxanne unleashes a luxurious eye roll.

Roxanne has given Tucker the code name "Beanstalk." She accuses Frida of thinking about Beanstalk whenever Frida's attention drifts or she doesn't remember the exact details of their last conversation. Roxanne has heard that a lot of fathers find Beanstalk annoying. He's a know-it-all who always tells stories about his one Black friend and being raised by a single mother and growing up poor and putting himself through college.

Roxanne said, "He pretends like he's woke, but he's just read a lot of stupid think pieces."

Frida hasn't tried to defend him. It would be better if they didn't speak about him, not even in code. She's never been good at resisting. She's been using sightings of him to measure time. At night, when she should be thinking about Harriet, she thinks about Tucker. To be desired again feels like a trick of the mind, but her classmates have noticed how he always searches the cafeteria for her. The other day, she allowed him to sit at their table. He whispered that she looked pretty.

She wonders if this is how romances begin in AA. An attraction based on shared deficiencies. If between the two of them they could make one trustworthy parent or if their weaknesses would cancel each other out. Whenever she considers her prognosis for return, which direction it might be tipping, she thinks of Tucker and imagines his house. The houses in Germantown are enormous. He might let her stay there for a few nights. She could live there while she looks for a job. There would be plenty of room for both her and Harriet.

×

On Friday, she walks into the counselor's office with her head held high. After her second-place finish, she should merit a call. But the rules have changed again. Denying phone privileges has been good for incentivizing everyone. Frida's phone privileges are suspended for another month. She must deliver another top-two finish for Unit 6.

Frida nearly shouts. "I did everything you asked. I need to talk to her. She's about to start preschool. I don't even know what school she's going to. I'm missing the first day. Do you understand that? I haven't spoken to her since March. It's July."

"Don't whine," the counselor says. She understands Frida's disappointment, but Frida needs to be realistic. Her training is what matters. Without the distraction of phone calls, her mothering may improve even more.

At this point in the program, the school needs to see synthesis, the counselor says. They need to know that if she gets Harriet back, she'll know exactly what to do in every situation.

Furious, Frida asks about her prognosis for return. She's improved. She hasn't been back to talk circle.

Emmanuelle's bruise has healed. Emmanuelle has been playing nicely with other children. Surely, her chances are now fair. Or even fair to good.

"The assessment is ongoing." The counselor refuses to answer Frida's questions about exactly how well she needs to perform to change her prognosis. Instead, the counselor wants to discuss temptation.

"Many of you have had problems with men in the past."

Frida worries that the counselor will bring up Tucker by name, but the counselor speaks generally about relating to the fathers in a nonsexual manner. When Tucker isn't mentioned, Frida decides to bluff.

"I haven't felt tempted. And I didn't have relationship problems. I was married. My daughter would have grown up in a stable two-parent household if my ex-husband hadn't . . ." She stops, composes herself. "I'm sorry. Please excuse me. Gust is an excellent father. I know he is. I'm trying to say I'd never jeopardize my case for some man. They're not exactly eligible bachelors."

×

Swing sets and jungle gyms have been erected on the Pierce lawn. The parents practice slide protocol. Swing protocol. Playground conversation. How to supervise children while chatting with adults.

Everyone's uniform has salt stains from perspiration. No hats or sunglasses are provided. Despite the trees, there's not enough shade. The sunscreen they're given is insufficient for the amount of time they're spending outside. Some parents succumb to heat stroke, others to dehydration and dizziness. During meals, they chug water. They can no longer drink any during class. One of the four-year-old girl dolls got her hands on some bottled water and malfunctioned.

The possibility of seeing Tucker distracts Frida from her thirst, as well as from her parenting. The instructors catch every mistake. She doesn't move fast enough when Emmanuelle runs in front of the swings. She pushes Emmanuelle too high. She isn't spotting attentively enough when Emmanuelle climbs the jungle gym. She's chatting too much with Tucker, preventing other mothers from working with him.

Tucker tells terrible, long-winded jokes, dares to make fun of the instructors and the program.

Emmanuelle likes going for rides on his shoulders. Frida spirals into the great beyond of November. She imagines introducing him to Harriet, introducing him to her parents, but not saying where they met.

"You need to find a man who loves you more than you love him," her mother once told her.

Gust wanted her to start dating again. Will has moved on. He'd want her to be happy. He'd like Tucker. There's a softness in both of them. A generosity. She always noticed this when she saw Will with his broken birds.

The counselor wants to know what happened. Last week Frida was doing fine. Now, her word counts have declined, as have her attachment levels. What happened to no eligible bachelors?

"He's only a friend," Frida says.

×

Someone found a dead section of the fence. One couple romped in the woods. Another broke into an empty cottage on the north side of campus. Another found a blind spot behind the art gallery. Another laid down next to the duck pond. The mud on their uniforms gave them away.

The explorers return with information for the rest: which cameras seem to be broken, which sections of campus seem to have no cameras at all, which women in pink lab coats and which guards are always checking their phones, the classes most likely to be visited by Ms. Gibson or Ms. Knight. Constant location changes make it hard to keep track of everyone. A mother and father are caught in the field house. Another couple is caught in the bushes. Another underneath a bus in the parking lot. The mothers lose phone privileges and are sent to talk circle. The fathers are assigned additional exercise on the weekends.

The next lessons are about consent. Ms. Khoury demonstrates with Colin's doll.

"Can I kiss you here?" she asks, pointing to the doll's cheek. The other doll must wait for Colin's doll to say yes. If the doll says no, then no kissing, hugging, or hand-holding.

They've returned to the pediatric wing. There are larger area rugs but no toys. The dolls have been programmed for body curiosity. The boy dolls unbutton their uniforms and grab their penises. The girl dolls rub against chairs. The dolls pet each other's blue knobs tenderly.

In instances of inappropriate touching, the parents must separate the dolls and teach them to say: "No! You do not have permission to touch me! My body is sacred."

The dolls have little patience for this exercise. Most can say "No!" and "You do not" but not the rest of the sentence. They repeat "body body body" ad nauseum so it sounds like a pop song.

Frida wants to know if anyone has been kissing Harriet, what Gust and Susanna do about these kisses, if Harriet has a playground boyfriend the way Emmanuelle has Jeremy.

It's becoming harder to ignore Tucker. She would like to tell him about the house of her mind, the house of her heart, the house of her body. Isn't the school teaching them that what they really need is a partner who earns the money? Aren't they being trained to be stay-at-home mothers? Where else is the money supposed to come from? The instructors have never mentioned jobs outside the home or day care or babysitters. She once heard Ms. Khoury say "babysitter" in the same tone as some people say "socialist."

What job can she find that would be worth the time lost? In grade school, she envied the classmates whose mothers baked and volunteered for field trips and threw them elaborate birthday parties. Having her grandmother there was lovely, but not the same. If she and Tucker were together, she might only have to work part-time. He'd provide them with health insurance. Harriet would go to preschool only on Gust's days. During her half of the week, she'd spend every minute with Harriet. They'd make up for their missing year.

×

Emmanuelle believes she's blue. "I'm blue" is her response to Frida's explanations about being biracial, how Mommy is Chinese and Emmanuelle is half Chinese.

"No, blue," she says. "Half blue I am."

They're three days into teaching racial difference, part of a subset of lessons on racism and sexism prevention. They've been using picture books to facilitate conversations about skin color, telling their dolls about the difference between inside and outside, how inside everyone is the same, how outside differences should be celebrated. However, harmony isn't the focus. Within a few days, the dolls are programmed to hate.

"Adversity," the instructors say, "is the most effective teaching tool."

The dolls take turns playing oppressor. They've been programmed to understand and speak derogatory language. White dolls have been programmed to hate dolls of color. Boy dolls have been programmed to hate girls. White parents of white boy dolls spend the week apologizing, ashamed. Some are cited for excessive reprimands. In classes with older dolls, there have been fistfights. The technical department has seen an influx of dolls with facial bruising and chunks of missing hair.

The parents practice comforting their dolls after they've experienced prejudice. Some parents of color are triggered. Some get emotional and scold the racist dolls. Some yell. Even Linda seems shaken. Stories of bullying and violence and microaggressions and police harassment are shared during meals.

Black parents don't appreciate having the entire issue framed in Black and white terms. Latinx parents don't appreciate having their dolls bullied in terrible singsong Spanish or being called "illegals." White parents don't appreciate having their dolls play the racists. Frida doesn't appreciate having Black, white, and Latinx dolls harass Emmanuelle.

At lunch, Tucker tells Frida that he's tired of playing the white devil. He's tired of hearing his doll use the N-word. His real son would never use that word. Silas's mother buys picture books depicting children from different backgrounds. They rotate these every few weeks, so Silas is never only looking at white faces.

"Studies have shown that even eighteen-month-olds can express racial bias," Tucker says.

"Don't let them catch you complaining." Frida resists asking if Silas has any Black friends. She's been over this with Gust and Susanna. What did playing with Black dolls matter if Harriet has no Black friends? When is Harriet ever going to meet another Chinese kid?

The dolls call Emmanuelle a chink. They pull their eyes into slits. Frida recalls people laughing when her parents spoke Mandarin, mimicking their accents. A long-buried memory. Two teenage Black girls laughing as her parents gossiped with the Chinese owner of the local ice cream shop. She was six or seven. She glared so hard at those girls, wanted to scream at them, but they didn't notice her and wouldn't stop snickering. The girls worked there, but they were making fun of their boss. That woman allowed them to laugh.

Maybe that hurt was less dangerous, maybe it wouldn't result in a child being killed, but when it happened in her childhood, she wanted to disappear. Sometimes she wanted to die. She hated the sight of her own face in the mirror.

Susanna won't know how to comfort Harriet if anything like that happens. She'll deliver platitudes about racial equality, but she won't be able to say, **It happened to me too. I survived. You'll survive**. She won't be able to say, **This is our family.** Everything Susanna knows about Chinese culture comes from books and movies. Without her real mother, Harriet may grow up hating the Chinese part of herself.

×

Racism practice has strained friendships. Roxanne has been telling Frida that she doesn't understand.

"You can't," Roxanne says. "I don't care how much you've read about intersectionality. You won't have to worry about Harriet getting shot. You can take her anywhere. She'll never get hassled."

When Isaac is older, Roxanne will have to teach him how to handle himself around the police. She can't ever let him play with toy guns or weapons or make gun shapes with his hands.

Frida has no room to argue. She is to Roxanne as Susanna is to her. The most palatable kind of Asian. Academic class, not business owner, not restaurant owner, not dry cleaner, not greengrocer, not salon worker, not refugee.

The lessons have made her feel ashamed for desiring another white man, but only white men have ever pursued her. She's moved in white worlds, has only had two Asian lovers, both of whom she attempted to turn into serious boyfriends to please her parents, one of whom thought she was too damaged, another who thought she was too negative, both of whom felt she wouldn't get along with their mothers or bear healthy children because of her depression. She shouldn't have told them about taking medication. Shouldn't have mentioned seeing a therapist. When she was younger, she used to think that if she ever had a child, she'd want that child to be entirely Chinese, but she didn't realize how difficult it would be to find a Chinese man who wanted her.

She's started fantasizing about another baby. A clean slate. Though she worries that a bad mother plus a bad father would produce a sociopath, that the new child would contain all their negligence and selfishness and bad instincts, the new child might also be just fine.

Loneliness has its own strange, insistent heat. She hasn't thought about the bell tower even once since meeting Tucker. She no longer dreams of murdering her counselor. She's regained her appetite. Watching her comfort Emmanuelle on the playground, Tucker said, "You know. I think you're a good mother, Frida. I really do."

×

July ends with joint evaluations at the mothers' school. In their classroom, Frida is paired with Colin. The fathers have to take several turns so all the mothers can have partners, though only their first turn will count.

After they shake hands, Ms. Russo starts the clock. At the first station, their dolls fight over a truck. Buoyed by her new happiness, Frida outtalks and outsoothes Colin. Emmanuelle outshares Colin's doll.

At the second station, Colin's doll kisses Emmanuelle on the cheek without first getting permission.

Frida and Colin deliver speeches on appropriate and inappropriate touching. After this month of playground fights and unwanted touching and racial bias, Emmanuelle has a short fuse. She smacks Colin's doll in the face. She apologizes for hitting, but only after eight prompts from Frida. Frida steels herself for another month without phone privileges.

Things get uglier at the race- and gender-sensitivity station. Emmanuelle calls the boy the N-word, he calls her a chink. He calls her a bitch, which he pronounces with a spray of spittle. The children are separated. They listen to lectures about respect and equality.

During his lecture, Colin forgets to mention the need for respecting women. Frida talks about the ramifications of slavery, the effects of institutional racism, how mass incarceration is an extension of slavery, how there aren't enough Black lawmakers and judges, how power begets power, what a difficult life the boy will have just trying to grow up, trying not to get shot by police or jailed for misdemeanors. She talks a good game, far better than Colin, who, though he speaks about the struggles of Asians in general, can't narrate a corresponding history of the Chinese in America. He doesn't know that Frida is Chinese. He's never asked.

When they're finished, Colin bursts into tears. "Thanks a lot, Miss Ivy League." He accuses Frida of fucking things up for him. He thinks the instructors programmed his doll to be extra aggressive today. The instructors tell him to collect himself but don't cite him for swearing.

Frida tries to apologize, but Colin cuts her off. "Save it," he says. He has to prepare for his next partner, Linda.

Parents who've completed their evaluations are allowed to take their dolls outside to the playground on the quad. Tucker is already there with Jeremy. Emmanuelle races ahead when she sees him. Jeremy races toward her. They miss their intended hug by several feet and continue running in opposite directions. Frida and Tucker laugh. Tucker waits until their dolls are out of earshot, then calls Frida's name.

Frida jogs over to Emmanuelle and takes her to the slide. They won't find out the results until tomorrow. What would she give to finish second? She'd say goodbye to all the other parts of her life to get her daughter back. No men. No dating. No romance. No other love.

Jeremy and Tucker are playing in the sand-box. Tucker sends Jeremy running to them with a message. "Daddy wants you to come play. Come play with us."

The dolls walk to the sandbox holding hands. Frida hesitates, then follows. She sits with Tucker at the edge. No other parents are nearby. The women in pink lab coats watch from a distance. Frida keeps her body language closed and chaste. She wants to grab Tucker's hand. She wants to sit in his lap.

"I know you like me."

Frida shoves her boots deeper into the sand. She watches Emmanuelle and Jeremy dig with plastic shovels. She secretly thrills when Tucker brings up the fall, but says, "We can't."

"I'm going to." Tucker nods toward Jeremy. "He's not listening. She's not listening."

He wants to talk about the places he'll take her when they get out. Has she ever eaten at Zahav? What about Barbuzzo? He loves Barbuzzo. He wants her to know that he loves cooking and hiking.

"The one good thing about this place is meeting you." He looks like he wants to kiss her. If they were anywhere else. If they already had their children.

"Frida, we're going to get them back," he says, his voice full of certainty.

15.

THE MOTHERS AREN'T SUPPOSED TO CELEBRATE their birthdays. They can only talk about themselves in relation to their children. When they first arrived, some got in trouble for making cards for their classmates or singing in the dining hall or discussing their birthdays with their dolls. In early August, on the day Frida turns forty, she doesn't tell anyone. Not Roxanne or Meryl. Not Emmanuelle.

Emmanuelle is playing under the table. If Frida could, she'd talk to Emmanuelle about time and aging, what it means to age, how her body would change if she were real, what society expects of mothers and daughters, how they're expected to fight, how she fought with her own mother and now regrets every cruel word. Last year, when she turned thirty-nine, she called her mother and finally said, "Thank you."

It's hard to hear over all the shouting in the fathers' cafeteria, a windowless room in the hospital basement with a linoleum floor and fluorescent lights. Unit 7: Communication Skills is underway. The first lessons are on mood regulation and anger management.

Frida opens her binder to the latest script. She and Linda are taking turns playing a mother demanding more child support. They're practicing with a white father named Eric, who has an adolescent's starter mustache and nails chewed down to painful-looking nubs.

"**B-I-T-C-H.** I'm not giving you any more money," Eric says.

"**M-O-T-H-E-R-F-U-C-K-E-R,** you are a lazy piece of crap," Frida replies.

Following the example set by the instructors, they continue in this fashion until they're red-faced and breathless. Then, after a minute of deep-breathing exercises, they begin again, practicing the same lines in a calmer tone, taking the aggression down down down until they're speaking in the lilting tones of yogis. They transition to scripts that model ideal interactions, with no name-calling or swearing. They speak to each other as they do their dolls: **I notice you're upset. I notice you're frustrated. Tell me what you need from me. How can I better support you?** Groups switch throughout the day. A fight becomes a discussion. Blame is diffused. Barbs lose their sting. Arguments become opportunities for empathy.

The shouting upsets and confuses the dolls. After each session, the parents must reflect with their group and discuss how it felt to respond to hostility with patience and love. Eric says it feels smooth. He's been imagining his anger as a piece of paper that he folds into a tiny square and hides in his pocket. Linda says she's been thinking of her dad. She takes after him. She doesn't want her kids to grow up hearing so much shouting. Frida says she and Gust don't speak this way, that they tend not to fight about money, that Gust's problem is avoiding confrontation, while hers is apologizing too much, but she appreciates knowing what to do if this dynamic ever changes.

She wants to make fun of the scripts with Tucker. Since the weekend, he's stopped shaving. He's even more appealing with stubble. She likes all the gray in his beard, wants to believe that he has pleasing chest hair, that his skin will feel good against hers, that he won't mind her bony body, that they'll enjoy sleeping side by side. After Gust left, it took months to learn to sleep alone. She watches Tucker from across the room, gets paired with him once that afternoon, but has to share him with Beth. The next day, they get a turn alone. Tucker nudges her boot under the table. He says, "I'd rather not yell at you, can we just talk?"

"We have to practice." Frida pulls her feet up and sits cross-legged. They've known each other for one month. At this point in her courtship with Gust, they'd already said "I love you." They were already spending entire weekends in bed.

All week she's been careful, refusing to sit with Tucker at lunch, walking in the other direction if she sees him in the hall.

Roxanne thinks catching feelings in this place is a matter of proximity. "It's like giving a starving person a piece of pizza," Roxanne said. "Beanstalk is your piece of pizza."

Is she his? Is he also starving for affection? Emmanuelle and Jeremy look up from their coloring books. They glance back and forth between their parents, alert to the excitement in their voices. The four of them look like a demented little family. Bad parents, false children. In the future, Frida thinks, there might be no other way.

Their hostile co-parenting scripts, as Tucker delivers them, sound more than a little like foreplay.

"**B-I-T-C-H**," he says slowly, his fingers dangerously close to Frida's. "I don't have any more money. We had an agreement."

Frida smiles despite herself. She's glad not to be touching Emmanuelle. Her hand would be too warm, her pulse too fast.

They giggle through the fury round. As they do their breathing exercises, his foot grazes her calf. Protected by the noise, he adds extra lines to the script. "You were supposed to pick him up at three thirty, why can't you ever remember anything?" becomes "You were supposed to pick him up at three thirty, why can't you ever remember anything? I think about you. I would definitely ask you out if we met under normal circumstances. Give yourself more credit. You're beautiful. You're a fox."

"Don't be ridiculous." She tells him to stick to the script. He's losing his mind if he thinks he can talk like this. It's not safe.

"No one can hear us."

Emmanuelle asks, "Mommy, what fox?"

"A furry animal. Mommy is not a fox. Daddy Tucker is just saying that because it's summer and summer is romantic and he's lonely. Mommy can't help him with that. Parents aren't supposed to feel lonely. I don't feel lonely. I have you."

To Tucker, she whispers, "Be reasonable. You should be thinking about your son."

"You'll meet him one day."

"I'm sure his mother would be delighted. Imagine telling her where you found me."

Ms. Khoury approaches. They practice two pages of hostile dialogue until she passes. Tucker reaches for Frida's arm.

"Unwanted physical contact," Frida says, pulling away. "Don't. The kids can see us."

At the end of the day, when they line up to return their dolls, Tucker takes greater liberties. His hand brushes Frida's. Their fingertips touch. The charge is sharp. Dazzling. More urgent than what she felt with Will.

Frida shoves her hands into her pockets, the happiest she's been since losing Harriet. They've played a whole history today, from total rage to a slow boil to begrudging respect to, finally, a serenity that makes them sound like they've both had lobotomies. She doesn't know what he sees in her. Surely they're too old for these games, too broken for romance. As she boards the bus, her thoughts are far away. Far from Harriet. Far from motherly. It's a fantasy that can be killed in a thousand ways. She's a fool for even thinking about him. But he could lift her so easily. Lift her heart, but also pin her to a wall and fuck her standing up.

×

Phone privileges are finally granted. Frida's prognosis has been upgraded to fair. When she returns to Kemp that night, she and Roxanne do a victory dance. They hop around the room and cheer. Roxanne bounces on her bed, makes Frida do the same, just for a minute. They laugh like little girls. Roxanne even tries teaching Frida the Cupid Shuffle, the dance she and her mother used to do around the house. They collapse in giggles when Frida keeps messing up the steps.

"I'm proud of you," the counselor said. Her words carry Frida through another day of anger-management drills, another Saturday cleaning crew. She asks for tweezer privileges and scissor privileges, irons her uniform, decides to wear her hair in a long braid, stays up late planning what she'll say to Harriet.

Sunday can't come soon enough, but when Gust, Susanna, and Harriet appear on-screen, Frida isn't ready for their news. Susanna is pregnant. Twenty-one weeks. They just had their anatomy scan. Gust and Susanna are engaged. They'll get married at city hall before the baby arrives in December, will have another ceremony and reception next spring.

"We hope you'll be there," Susanna says. "We'd like you to be part of the ceremony. You could do a reading." She shows Frida her ring, the two-carat solitaire that belonged to Gust's grandmother, the one Gust didn't think Frida should have because he didn't believe in diamonds.

Susanna tells Frida that her due date is December 20. They decided not to find out the gender. "There are so few real surprises in life," Susanna says.

In the background, Gust has been coaxing Harriet to say hello, reminding her that the woman on-screen is Mommy. He stands Harriet on his lap so Frida can see how tall she's grown. Three inches since March. Five pounds heavier. The pediatrician made them stop the low-carb diet.

Harriet's face has matured. Frida watches the seconds pass at the bottom of the screen. The computer lab is quieter than she remembers. No one is sniffling. No one is yelling. She tries to summon her lobotomy voice. The breathing exercises fail her. She wants to cry. Harriet's face remains slender. Her hair has been cut as short as a boy's. She looks elfin now, like Susanna.

Susanna potty trained Harriet a month ago, used the three-day method. They rolled up the carpets, did a whole naked weekend.

"She got it right away," Susanna says.

Within the first hour of having her diaper off, Harriet started talking more.

"The first thing she said on day one was 'Put a diaper on me. Put a diaper on my butt.' She's been cracking us up. It's like we unleashed her mind. She told me, 'I'm not a baby anymore! I'm a big kid!' I wish you could have been there. Harriet is so good at listening to her body."

"I'm **such** a big kid," Harriet says.

Frida grimaces. Gust and Susanna laugh. Two minutes remain. Frida looks down at her talking points. She manages to say, "Congratulations." Manages to thank Susanna for her efforts and refer to Harriet's pixie cut as "striking." She refrains from asking why Susanna thought she was allowed to cut it.

"Happy belated," Gust says. "Mommy turned four zero this week. Let's sing to her." Mindful of the time, they sing the song at double-tempo.

"Thank you." Reading from her notes, Frida praises Harriet's resilience, thanks Gust and Susanna for their time and care. The desperate look in her daughter's eyes makes her want to crawl into a hole.

Ms. Gibson gives everyone the thirty-second warning.

"Hare-bear, what else do you want to tell Mommy?" Gust asks.

Harriet shouts, "Mommy, you come back! Come back right now!"

She continues shouting "Now! Now!" as Frida speaks over her.

"I miss you. I miss you so much. I love you, baby. Mommy's heart actually aches. It feels like someone's squeezing it." She makes a fist and waves it at the screen.

Harriet mimics her. Before the call ends, the last

thing Frida sees is Harriet making a tiny fist and pretending to squeeze her heart.

×

For Frida, the following week's role-plays feel especially cruel. Peaceful communication with step-parents. Mother talking to stepmother. Father to stepfather. These strangers who have replaced them and now siphon off their child's love.

Whoever wrote the scripts understands women. The lines are passive-aggressive with a touch of birth mother as martyr. Frida's anger is authentic, but her cooldown lacks conviction. She didn't mean to talk about a heart being squeezed, hopes she won't be punished for it. They'll joke about it when Harriet is older. It will be their code for sorrow and longing. In truth, the sorrow barely touches her heart at all. She feels Susanna's pregnancy in her lower back, in her neck and shoulders, her teeth. The baby must have been conceived soon after Harriet's second birthday. She imagines Harriet rubbing Susanna's belly. Gust and Susanna talking to the baby while they're in bed. The three of them going to the doctor. Harriet seeing the ultrasounds, watching the baby move.

Susanna shouldn't be the one giving her daughter life lessons. The family court judge should know that Frida could give Harriet a sibling too. A sibling who looks like her. A Chinese sibling, a brunette. With Harriet's same eyes and skin tone. In Gust and Susanna's family, Harriet will always look like she's adopted. Strangers will always ask questions. If they're having their own baby, why do they need hers?

During class, Frida daydreams about another wedding. Tucker in a three-piece suit. Dark pinstripes, not a tuxedo. A pink gown for her. A secret tribute to where they met. A bouquet of anemones. They'll have the wedding in Chicago. She'll do everything her mother requested the first time. Invite more of her parents' friends and colleagues. Have a tea ceremony. Wear a veil. Pin up her hair. Wear a red **qipao** for the reception. Play music the older relatives can dance to. Allow more time for family portraits. Later, have a banquet for their baby's hundred days. Make her husband learn Mandarin.

The counselor is concerned about Frida's mental stamina. "I know how much you were looking forward to this call. It must be hard to see your ex-husband moving on."

"He moved on a long time ago. I'm aware of

that." Frida says she's glad Harriet will have a sibling, that she's happy for them.

"I'm just worried that my daughter won't get enough attention. After the baby arrives. Linda said the transition from one to two kids is the hardest. If I were home, I could help her. She's going through so many changes. We're going to be reunited in the same month that she gets a new sibling, aren't we? We didn't even get to talk about preschool. This was supposed to be my turn to talk to her, but Susanna—"

"Susanna has made plenty of sacrifices," the counselor says.

Frida should be mindful of Susanna's stress level. And she shouldn't make any assumptions about her case, not yet.

Before Frida leaves, they return to the subject of fraternizing. The instructors have noticed Tucker's interest in her. Frida reminds the counselor that she hasn't flirted, hasn't been accused of suggestive body language.

"I'm not saying you have. But you're all human. Feelings can develop. Remember, Frida, this is a man who let his child fall out of a tree. You left your baby girl home alone. Nothing good can come of this friendship."

×

Roses are wilting on the vine. There's a week of one-hundred-degree days. The cafeteria feels increasingly like a dungeon. Fans are brought into the fathers' school to augment the air-conditioning. Parents take cold showers and suck on ice cubes. Heat and mingling and boredom are contributing to high-risk behavior. Voices rise above whispers. Eye contact is brazen. Some parents refer to each other as boyfriend and girlfriend. Talk circle remains crowded. A father is abruptly expelled for allegedly leering at Charisse's teenage girl doll. Most parents think he's innocent.

"Her word against mine," he said. The doll was the one who complained to the instructors. She felt he was undressing her with his eyes, said he looked at her like she was a snack.

Charisse said, "Believe women."

Tucker has sent Frida messages via his doll Jeremy. He's asked Meryl to ask Frida to sit with him at lunch. She almost said yes. She almost told him about Susanna's pregnancy, Harriet's short hair, the counselor's latest warnings. She wants to thank him for treating her like she's worthy of love. If she'd known such kindness was possible, that she'd ever feel deserving of it, she might have been more careful when she was younger. She's imagined introducing him to Gust, has pictured them attending Gust and Susanna's wedding. She too has been thinking past November, wondering if she'll be able to get pregnant at forty or forty-one.

She knows she's getting away with more because she's yellow. Roxanne says they're coming down harder on the brown girls. It doesn't matter whether they're flirting back. Roxanne has no patience for Frida's problems with Beanstalk or Susanna. She tells Frida to get over her beef with Gust's girl.

"Do not talk to me about diamond rings," she says.

Roxanne's mom hasn't been staying hydrated, has developed another UTI. "I just want to wrap her in Bubble Wrap," Roxanne says. Neighbors and friends are helping, but it's not the same. Her mom is immunocompromised. Just an hour in a doctor's waiting room or a trip to the pharmacy could get her sick. What if her mom gets sicker and no one tells her? What if she has to go to the hospital?

Every day, Roxanne has been sitting with Meryl and Colin at lunch. Her crush on Meryl has grown more intense and irrational. Every night, she's been stubbornly asking if Frida thinks she still has a chance. Roxanne says Meryl has broken up with the green-eyed guard, will break up with Ocean's father once she can tell him in person.

"Meryl is not the right pizza for you," Frida says. "We only have three more months. You know this."

Frida has tried to warn Meryl about Colin, but the girl won't listen. Colin doesn't want Meryl to stay friends with Frida. He's still mad about evaluation day. He said that if Frida really cared about the fate of Black people in America, she would've let him win. Meryl said that she's truly happy for the first time in her life. She's happier than when Ocean was born. She's happier than when she met Ocean's father. This will be the story she and Colin tell their future children. Love in a hopeless place.

"Like that song," Meryl said.

Roxanne has stopped giggling and talking in her sleep.

"Are you there?" she asks, waking Frida throughout the night. Sometimes she sneaks out of bed and sits beside Frida.

They take turns scratching each other's backs. They talk about her mother, about Isaac, who's started walking. His foster mom has bought him his first pair of hard-soled shoes. When she tried to have him walk for Roxanne during the last Sunday call, he wouldn't do it.

"What cool shit is he going to do next?" Roxanne asks.

Frida tells her about Harriet's first steps and first words, the point at which Harriet could walk without falling. She's no longer sure what happened in which month.

×

The parents practice calm and friendly communication during disputes with teachers, pediatricians, coaches, and authority figures. Frida feels Tucker's eyes on her all day. Whenever he looks at her, she feels herself becoming more beautiful. She's sure the cameras can distinguish between this heat and the blush of mother love.

But she thrives on it. Wants more of it. She can't allow him to make her weak, but it happens despite her best intentions. At night, she imagines giving the house of her mind and the house of her body to the man who let his son fall out of a tree.

She pictures their bodies together in a room with no cameras.

She hasn't asked if he wants more children, can't ask him here. But her parents deserve another grandchild. Harriet's two families should be evenly matched. She'd love to feel the kicking again, should have appreciated those months when she and Harriet were always together, when she counted kicks twice a day, felt the drumming fists at bedtime, Harriet responding to her warm hands, their first secret codes.

One day at lunch, ignoring the counselor's warning, she sits with Tucker and tells him what's been happening at home.

"Do you still love him?" Tucker asks.

"No. I don't think so. I should be happy for him. I'm trying to be. If I was a good, unselfish person, I'd be happy. Do you still love your wife?"

"My ex-wife. You don't need to worry about her. She's my family. But, listen, I'm glad you're thinking about it."

He squeezes her shoulder. She removes his hand. He moves his right leg so it brushes her left. She becomes wet. She rearranges her silverware on her plate. She can't look at him. If she looks, she'll want to touch. If she touches, her life will be over.

"I can't get distracted," she says.

"Am I distracting you?"

"What else would you call this?"

He shrugs and says, "Maybe, a romance."

×

Gust and Susanna take the next Sunday call from the porch of their rented beach house in Cape May. Susanna is wearing a wide-brimmed sun hat and a black string bikini that shows off her freckled cleavage. Gust is tanned and shirtless.

Frida vows not to cry in front of the beautiful couple raising her daughter. She stares at Susanna's breasts. Susanna won't have any trouble nursing. Her baby will latch instantly. Her milk will be plentiful. She'll never have to use formula.

Their voices are garbled in the wind. Harriet's face is sunburned. Her hair sticks up in wet peaks. Gust asks her to say her latest funny sentence again for Mommy.

"The moon is a ball in the sky." Harriet pronounces each word emphatically.

After Frida finishes applauding, Harriet points at the screen.

"Mommy, you are bad."

Gust and Susanna tell her to be nice.

"You are bad! You are bad! Don't like you!"

Frida is devastated and impressed. "I notice you saying you're angry with me. Can you tell me more about that? I'm here. I'm listening."

"I'm upset. I'm upset because I'm upset."

Frida asks more open-ended questions, but Harriet won't answer. Frida raises her fist and squeezes, but Harriet has already forgotten their new game.

"I want beach. No Mommy."

"Just two more minutes," Gust says. "Tell Mommy you miss her."

"No, Mommy not home! I do **not** want to talk. That is **not** my plan!"

Frida wants to say she'll be home soon. Three more months. One, two, three. Numbers that Harriet knows. But three months is another season of waiting.

Harriet suddenly becomes very still.

"Oh no." Gust stares down at his lap. "Try to hold it. Remember, pee goes in the potty." He grabs Harriet by the armpits and rushes her back into the house without saying goodbye, leaving Frida with Susanna.

Susanna takes off her sunglasses. "She must be feeling stressed. We haven't had an accident in weeks. At least she didn't poop on him. The book said emotion causes the sphincter to open."

Before Frida can apologize, Susanna asks if Gust can get some of Harriet's things out of Frida's storage unit. They finally talk about preschool. She tells Frida about Harriet's first-day outfit, the backpack and lunch box she ordered, the galoshes and indoor shoes, the name labels, the family photo they've sent for Harriet's classroom wall. They'll have to take a new picture with all of them once Frida gets home. Harriet will attend the Montessori in Center City. A few days ago, two of her teachers came by for a home visit. They discussed separation anxiety, how Susanna should handle drop-offs, the possibility of an ease-in schedule. They asked if there were any special considerations, things they could do to support Harriet during the transition, things they should know about the family.

"And what did you tell them?" Frida asks.

"We told them everything. We had to."

×

The parents spend the last week of August practicing anger-management drills. Frida and Tucker are paired together Thursday afternoon. He refuses to take the drill seriously. He wants to use this opportunity, when they're enveloped by shouting and recrimination, to talk about the future. Where's Frida going to live? Does she have a place to stay?

"I could help you."

She wants to say yes. "Please. Give me your line. They're watching us. Don't go off script."

"You're killing me, Frida."

"I'm not killing you. Don't even talk like that. Think of your son."

"Guilt-tripping. Mommy one. Daddy zero."

"Just start. Yell at me. Let me have it."

"I'm a person with feelings."

"Please."

Tucker reluctantly begins the drill, playing the aggrieved ex-husband. They progress from initial outburst to quiet calm and compassion.

Frida drains all the hostility from her face and voice. Susanna said Harriet shouldn't feel ashamed. The teachers needed to know that Harriet will have to miss school for appointments with the social worker and child psychologist. Frida knows the teachers will watch out for Harriet the way they would a child who's been abused or molested. Susanna may tell the other parents, the other moms. The question will come up naturally. Gust's ex-wife. Harriet's mother. Where is she?

To Tucker, she says, "I hear you. I want you to know that I value your honesty."

Ms. Russo passes their table. They look tense and exhausted, a couple with a history.

Frida has tears in her eyes. She tries not to look at Emmanuelle, but the doll notices.

Emmanuelle climbs onto Frida's lap and throws her arms around Frida's neck. "Mommy, you okay?"

Ms. Russo places her hands on the back of Frida's chair. "Would you like to tell me what's really going on here?"

×

Frida's counselor is searching for an apt metaphor for the state of Frida's mind, the detritus within. The instructors have reported her as distracted. She hasn't been properly calibrating her emotions. Why isn't she striving for purity of mind and spirit? This friendship with a bad father can only harm her.

On Sunday night, the school will host an end-of-summer dance to keep spirits up as everyone heads into the final months of lessons. Since Margaret's suicide, the mothers have been required to attend extra counseling. At meals, the women in pink lab coats have been pulling mothers aside and conducting impromptu mood checks.

The fathers will be bused in on Sunday. "I suggest you stay far away from Tucker," the counselor says.

"I told you. He's only a friend."

"Frida, you are this close to getting sent back to talk circle. I have reports of unnecessary touching. Some flirtatious ad-libbing. Your instructors think they saw a note being passed."

Frida looks above the social worker's head to the camera. She looks down at her lap. If they had the note, they'd say so. If they have it, she'll blame Tucker. Yesterday, she slipped him her phone number as if they'd met as strangers in the real world. He promised to memorize it and destroy the paper. It thrilled her to break a rule.

"He's getting to you, Frida. How are you going to finish in the top two on Monday if you can't focus?"

"I am focusing. I promise I am. Harriet starts school next week. I need to speak to her."

"I don't know if that makes sense." The counselor says the calls have been disruptive. They don't seem to be benefitting Harriet either. The potty accident suggests that Frida is causing Harriet stress. Frida's classroom performance was better when she didn't have Sunday calls to think about. Without the calls or this dangerous friendship, she'll be able to concentrate. Phone privileges are therefore suspended until further notice.

"Don't think any of us take pleasure in punishing you," the counselor says.

×

Frida wants another house. In this new house, she'll be pregnant. This time, there will be no fear, no weeping, only gratitude. Their children will have been returned. Their children will have forgiven them. They'll live with their children in a house where the light comes in sideways. The light will blaze through the windows the way it only ever does in movies. Every room flooded with brightness. She'll learn to cook for a bigger family, learn how to raise a boy, how to mother someone else's boy, how to pack lunches, how to get two children out the door. Tucker's ex-wife will welcome her into the family. There will be no registry. No one will ask about the missing year.

She builds the house all day long. Imagines a garden and a swing set, a back porch where they'll share a drink after putting their children to bed. In the house where the light comes in sideways, she'll never want to be alone. There will be no boredom or anger. No yelling. No resentment. Harriet will be happy there. In both of Harriet's homes, with both her families, love will thrive and grow.

×

"Make a memory," Meryl says. It's Saturday morning, and cleaning crew is preparing the gymnasium for the dance.

"I don't want a memory."

"Bullshit. You'd suck his dick in a second if you were alone with him."

"No, I wouldn't. I can't have that in my file. I'm not getting expelled, and I'm not ending up on the registry. I told you. They're not even letting me call home anymore."

"You don't have to get caught." Meryl leads her

under the bleachers to investigate a possible blind spot. There's mildew, a family of mice. Meryl thinks it could work.

"Not in a thousand years," Frida says.

"Dumbass, you'd do it standing."

Frida wants to tell her about the alcoholic schoolteacher whose entire apartment was littered with bottles, the aspiring photographer who refused to kiss her because kissing was too intimate. She's no longer just a body. She'll no longer tolerate being just a body. She can wait. She and Tucker are people who've learned how to wait.

They set up folding tables, blow balloons until they're light-headed. Ms. Gibson lets them leave early to choose dresses, which have been donated by a committee established by Ms. Knight. The selection has been picked over. Most dresses are velvet or wool. Meryl tries on a black gown with silver sequins on the bodice. She pretends to hold a bouquet and does a pageant wave.

"Cute or lame?"

"Both," Frida says. "Cute in an ironic way."

Meryl has bruises on her back and hips, her thighs. Someone has been pinning her against sharp edges, maybe in a crawl space, maybe in a closet.

She catches Frida looking at her and says, "Don't be a les."

"Where did you do it? How?"

Meryl smirks. She and Colin have found a few unmonitored hallways and closets at the fathers' school. A lot can happen in five minutes.

×

A disco ball dangles from the basketball hoop. There are balloons and streamers. Bowls of nuts. Undecorated sheet cakes. There's a long line at the food table. Parents eat off paper plates. There are plastic spoons, but no forks, no knives. Several women in pink lab coats are bopping their heads to the music.

Frida enters the dimly lit gymnasium, wobbling in peep-toe slingbacks that are a half size too small. An hour ago, the mothers were desperate for hair spray and curling irons, perfume and makeup. The dresses don't look right with bare faces. They crowded into the Kemp bathrooms and helped each other get ready. For those whose dresses were too small, multiple hands pulling up a zipper. For those whose dresses were too big, experiments with tying sashes or folding waistbands. Some reminisced about their weddings. Some talked about their proms, imagined who'd be crowned king and queen here. Roxanne thought Ms. Knight would probably keep both crowns for herself.

Tonight, they wear silks and sequins, everyone tottering in heels after so many months in boots. Linda wears her curly hair down for the first time, looking lovely and carefree. Meryl has looped her hair into two buns. Frida is wearing a yellow cotton shirtdress with a Peter Pan collar and puffed sleeves, a full skirt. It's three sizes too big and ridiculously plain.

Tucker finds her, says he's been looking all over. "What's a girl like you . . ."

"A place like this. I know. Ha ha."

She does want to laugh. He's wearing a mismatched suit, the jacket much too big, the pants ending several inches above his ankles. His hair is parted on the side and neatly combed. He's clean-shaven again. From the neck up, he looks like an FBI agent. From the neck down, he looks like a vagrant.

They stand two feet apart. Frida clasps her hands behind her back.

"You look so pretty with your hair down."

She blushes. She can never control her blushing

around him. "We can't be seen together. They took away my phone privileges. Because of you."

"They can't do that."

"Of course they can. They can do anything."

He steps closer. "I would give you a hug."

"Don't." She makes herself walk away. She can't let him ask her to dance, doesn't want to dance with him in public. Dancing would lead to kissing. Kissing could lead to expulsion. Expulsion would lead her off a cliff. She'd be the next Margaret. The mothers have been talking this way. Whenever they hear about a mother indulging in nighttime or shower crying, they ask: **Will she be the next Margaret?**

Frida spots Roxanne, worries for her. Roxanne is trying to dance with Meryl, but Meryl won't leave Colin's side.

The trio of middle-aged white women find Tucker. Charisse pulls him to the dance floor and begins to shimmy. She spins fast and does a series of little kicks, making the sort of faces that Frida can only assume she makes during sex. Tucker is a terrible dancer. All wavy arms and nodding, like one of those blow-up balloon men at car dealerships. Frida should probably hold this against him, but she watches the dancing couples and yearns nonetheless.

Ms. Knight has outdone herself. She's wearing a satin cape with a jeweled clasp, elbow-length white opera gloves. The cape is pink, as is the gown, a narrow sheath that forces her to take tiny mouse steps. In a just world, Frida thinks, the mothers would have tomato sauce to throw on her. A bucket of pig's blood.

Ms. Knight gets on the microphone and tells the remaining stragglers to dance. It's seven thirty and the dance will end at eight forty-five sharp. The parents must get to bed early so they'll be ready for tomorrow's evaluation.

Frida had almost forgotten.

Ms. Gibson, the DJ for the night, plays the "Cupid Shuffle." Roxanne spots Frida and winks at her, miming the next steps. Only a few mothers dance with any grace. They flick their hips and wave their hands to indicate the situation is not getting the best of them the way it is getting the best of Frida.

A circle forms with Linda and Beth in the center. Briefly, they pretend to grind. Both are surprisingly limber. Beth slaps Linda on the butt. Linda does the running man.

Frida sways at the edge. Tucker is watching her.

What would she still be afraid of if they were together? Not forests. Not large bodies of water. Not dancing. Not aging. Not solitude. He'd help her take care of her parents. Help her raise Harriet.

Ms. Gibson is bouncing along to hip-hop, a disconcerting sight. When the song says to "throw your hands in the air," she does so with relish. Two intrepid fathers coax her away from her laptop. They lead her to the center of the circle and sandwich her between them. They get low. She gets low.

The mothers whistle. One of the fathers says, "Damn."

Seeing Ms. Gibson like this is regrettable. Frida would prefer not to think of the instructors or women in pink lab coats as real people, doesn't want to think of them in nightclubs or restaurants, as people who have fun.

Ms. Gibson resumes her DJ duties. She plays some disco. Some rap. "Groove Is in the Heart" is a popular selection.

The mothers take off their shoes. They return to the food table for second slices of cake. There are no slow songs, so they spin and bounce.

After six more songs, the lights come on abruptly. At first, parents think they're being punished for dancing too much. But through the open doors, they see floodlights sweeping the field. A few minutes later, the guards order everyone to divide up for a headcount.

Frida looks down the line of fathers, the line of mothers. She looks for Tucker.

Sirens begin to blare. Ms. Knight tells everyone to remain calm. Tucker appears at Frida's side. She's relieved that he's safe.

"I'll get in trouble for even standing near you," she says.

He holds her arm. "You'll see me after we leave, won't you?"

She doesn't answer. He pulls her closer. She rests her cheek on his chest, sniffing the musty fabric, winds her arms around his waist. His hands are in her hair.

"I'm serious about you, Frida."

She should be thinking about her daughter. Her daughter who starts preschool the day after tomorrow. Her daughter who's old enough to have her own backpack and talk about the moon. She lets go of him. Steps away.

He wants to meet under the bleachers. "I'll go first."

"I can't. We'll get caught. I always get caught."

"When are we going to get another chance to be alone? No one is paying attention to us." The instructors and all but one guard have left to begin the search. Parents are shouting. Frightened. Someone says Roxanne, Meryl, and Colin are missing.

"What?" She needs to find Beth.

Tucker asks her to meet him in five minutes.

She says, "I am a bad mother, but I am learning to be good."

"Frida, we don't have much time."

"I am a narcissist. I am a danger to my child."

His hand on the back of her neck is warm and confident. He's looking at her mouth. "I know you've thought about it."

She squeezes her fist, trying to stay focused on Harriet, her little girl who is learning about bitterness and longing and disappointment. And a mother who may disappoint her still.

16.

FRIDA HAS BEEN ADDED TO THE WATCH LIST. The school thinks she knew. Both girls told their counselors that they considered her a big sister. If they talked about running, she was obligated to report them.

The women in pink lab coats have been checking on her daily. Her sleep and food intake are being monitored. She now has three counseling sessions per week. She was questioned after the dance, again after the evaluation, again by her counselor. Roxanne's side of the room was ransacked. Frida's belongings were searched. Classroom, evening, weekend, mealtime, and cleaning crew footage was reviewed, as well as footage taken by Roxanne's and Meryl's dolls. The green-eyed guard who helped them escape was fired.

Some say they'll turn up dead. Others think they'll get caught. Linda thinks they'll eventually get pregnant again and get those babies taken away too. She blames Meryl. Beth blames Roxanne. Neither mentions Colin.

Linda says she misses Meryl's stank attitude. She liked how Meryl was always downing sugar packets, how she couldn't handle caffeine, turned every morning coffee into coffee-flavored milk.

"Remember she's not dead," Beth says. "Don't talk about her like she's dead."

Frida tells them both to be quiet. There's enough attention on their table. They're the only class with two mothers down, first Lucretia, now Meryl.

"Was it true about her and Roxanne?" Linda asks. "Were they, you know?" She makes fists and bumps them together.

Frida doesn't respond. She directs the question to Beth, who's been sulking about Meryl and Roxanne ever since the dance. Apparently Meryl never shared her escape fantasy with Beth. Frida's failure to report her suspicions about the girls has been added to her file. She won't risk further punishment by gossiping.

She never thought they'd actually do it. Roxanne had plenty of other ideas. She talked about hacking her classmates' dolls with a magnet. Finding some poison ivy and leaving it in the instructors' cars. No one will miss her more than Frida. Who will she count the days with? With whom will she whisper?

They've started Unit 8: Dangers Inside and Outside the Home. They're being taught a fear-based mothering practice designed to develop their safety reflexes and test their strength. This week, they've been practicing on the quad, sprinting while carrying their dolls, pretending to escape from a burning building.

Frida and Roxanne used to imagine what trials awaited them: running over hot coals, being shot out of cannons or thrown into snake pits, swallowing knives. She misses Roxanne's needy questions and dream giggling, talking about Isaac.

Roxanne would be angry at her for finishing third in Unit 7. Frida won't have phone privileges until October at the earliest, maybe not until they leave. The dance was only a week ago. She feels as if she's in mourning, ridiculous since they never kissed, let alone met under the bleachers. At night, she's been imagining Tucker holding her. She'd rest her head on his shoulder. On the shoulder of the man whose son fell out of a tree, she'd weep and he'd comfort her. They'd know how their children were sleeping.

×

It is early September, one year since Harriet was taken away, eleven months since Frida last held her, three weeks since their last phone call. Frida barely remembers what her life was like a year ago, doesn't remember the article she was writing, the elderly professor's name, the dean's name, why the deadline felt urgent, how she ever thought leaving the house without Harriet was possible.

In class, having covered fire and water safety, they learn how to rescue their dolls from oncoming cars. They practice in the parking lot beside the football field. Meryl would have enjoyed being outside with her doll, Frida thinks. She liked the campus more than she let on. Meryl often said she should've been born on the West Coast. She thought she would've become a different person if she'd grown up near mountains, believed that where you grew up determined your destiny, that growing up in South Philly doomed her.

"Why do you think I named my kid Ocean?" she said.

The driver starts his engine. Emmanuelle wants to know who the man is. She's unsatisfied with Frida's promises that the man won't hurt her.

The school has hired professional drivers. The instructors have marked the driver's target with an **X**, giving him room to accelerate across the parking lot.

"You have to pretend we're crossing the street," Frida tells her. "Streets are full of cars. Cars are dangerous. They can kill you. You have to hold my hand, okay?"

She tells Emmanuelle that crossing the street carefully was one of her father's great obsessions. "I have a father. And I had grandparents. My grandfather died when my dad was little. In a car accident. My dad was only nine. Isn't that sad?"

Emmanuelle nods.

"He still gets nervous when I cross the street. When we were traveling in China, he held my elbow at every single crosswalk. Like I was a kid. Parents always think their children are little kids, no matter how old they are."

She was twenty-one when he last did that. She was once a daughter who traveled, whose father worried about keeping her alive.

She tells Emmanuelle that her father turns seventy

tomorrow. Emmanuelle wants to know what China is, what seventy is, why Mommy looks sad.

"Because I wish I could see him," Frida says. "And because I should have been nicer to him. We're supposed to be nice to our parents. Seventy is a really big birthday."

Beth has been listening. "Be careful," she cautions. They're not supposed to burden their dolls with too much personal information.

Frida thanks her for the warning. She returns to the subject of pedestrian safety. She shouldn't have let her guard down. She must keep her real life separate, her real heart separate, must save her feelings for November.

×

In the house where the light comes in sideways, Frida adds rooms. In these rooms, the mothers will braid hair and tell stories. Tucker will serve them tea. Meryl will be there with Ocean. She'll be a terrible houseguest. Roxanne will be there with Isaac. Roxanne's mother will be healthy. Margaret will be alive. Lucretia will find them.

They should have a mother house. A mother

town. She remembers reading about an island off the coast of Estonia that was all women, where women did the farming and carpentry. Women served as the fishmongers and electricians. They wore different-colored aprons depending on their roles.

"Wait for me," she told Tucker at the dance. After November, she'll need a new term of endearment for him. The man who let his son fall out of a tree will become the man who got his son back. Her one very bad day will be in the past.

In class, they watch videos of plastic children being run over by cars. Frida teaches Emmanuelle about opposites: danger and safety. Safety is with Mommy. Danger is apart from Mommy.

They continue practicing in the parking lot. One afternoon, a storm sends them back to Morris. They change their dolls into dry clothes, but themselves remain soaked. Emmanuelle plays with Frida's wet hair. She laughs at Frida's fogged glasses.

The thunder and lightning continue for hours, scaring the dolls. Ms. Khoury tells them that a tropical storm is moving north from the Carolinas. The basement of Pierce floods that night. There are downed trees along Chapin Walk. On Saturday, after the sump pump has removed the water, cleaning crew is told to deal with the debris. They've never been down to this basement before. The storage area is disappointing, ordinary. They grumble about the smell as they remove damp boxes of papers, uniforms, shampoo, toothpaste.

They're nearly done for the day when Charisse gets lost, and during her attempts to rejoin the group, finds a locked room. The others wait for her at the base of the stairs. Frida tells Charisse to hurry up. Ever since Charisse joined cleaning crew, she's slowed them down.

Charisse shrieks. She calls to the group. After the mothers find her, they take turns peeking through the keyhole.

Someone says she's not sure what she's looking at. Frida is one of the last to look. She expects to see doll parts, rows of heads, maybe a pile of broken infants, the boy who threw himself against the fence and melted, Lucretia's doll, even the doll belonging to her first roommate, Helen. As her eye adjusts to the dark, she sees a body. The body is on a cot, the woman's face turned toward the door. One of the mothers.

Frida squints.

"Who is it?" Charisse asks.

While they're talking, the woman opens her eyes. She sits up and peers at them, then runs to the door and starts banging. Frida and Charisse jump back. The woman shouts. Frida recognizes her voice. It's Meryl.

Frida raises a hand to her mouth.

A guard hears the noise and tells the mothers to go upstairs. Meryl continues banging on the door and pleading.

Meryl has been gone for three weeks. In her head, Frida lists the reasons why she can't help. Harriet, Harriet, Harriet. Being the roommate of a quitter and a runaway. Two trips to talk circle. The watch list. The hug. But Meryl is afraid of the dark. She slept with teddy bears all through high school. The basement walls are damp. She could get sick.

Cleaning crew sits together at dinner. Charisse wants them to make a plan. "We need to talk to Ms. Knight. We can get Meryl out."

If they don't try, Charisse says, cleaning crew will be like the Germans who turned a blind eye when the Jews were rounded up. This line of argument is not well received. Everyone thinks it's unfair to bring up the Holocaust.

Charisse wants to call her lawyer, have her lawyer call the ACLU.

Frida warns her not to jeopardize her case. "I'm just as worried as you are, but we have to leave this alone."

Charisse gives her a long disapproving look. "That's pretty cold, Frida. She was your friend."

"She is my friend, but we have to think about our kids. The registry, remember?"

News of Meryl's confinement spreads quickly. Everyone is concerned about what's being done to her. They don't understand why the school brought her back. They worry Roxanne is being held somewhere else on campus.

Frida knows Roxanne would want her to do something. She'd want Meryl to be safe. She was so angry that they hadn't done more for Lucretia. Several times, when Frida sees Ms. Gibson or one of the women in pink lab coats, she wants to say something, wants to ask if they can at least move Meryl to a regular dorm, to one of the empty buildings. But then she thinks of Harriet and holds her tongue.

Charisse continues her campaign. She tells Frida to remember when she was nineteen, a college student probably, not locked in a dark, damp basement.

She brings up the case of Kitty Genovese and the innocent bystanders. Frida tells her that case has already been disproven.

At lunch the following day, Charisse makes a beeline toward Frida's table. Frida leaves before Charisse can shame her further, tells Charisse to ask Beth. Charisse follows Frida back to Kemp, follows Frida to her room.

"We have to take care of her," Charisse says.

Frida says, "Get out. Get out, or I'll tell the guards."

×

With Meryl in the basement, everyone is watching their table again. Beth spends all of Sunday sobbing. She says her parents used to lock her in the basement to punish her. She tells Linda to think about what happens to kids who get locked in dark places. What it does to their minds. Their souls. Linda responds by pouring water on Beth's food.

They don't have to worry about Meryl for long. The girl shows up at breakfast on Monday morning. Her hair has been cut into an unflattering shag, dyed a severe shade of auburn. There's a patch of hair missing above her left ear. Her hands shake. Her wan smile seems like a show for Charisse, who sits next to her and pets her arm and seems to expect continuous thanks for obtaining her release.

Meryl's mother reported her, refused to let her see Ocean when she showed up at their apartment after managing to stay away for her first two weeks of freedom. Meryl could hear Ocean crying through the door. She parked herself in the hallway and refused to leave.

The school is letting her finish her training. Linda says, "Of course they'd bend the rules for a white girl."

Charisse says the issue isn't rule-bending. Someone needs to make sure the school respects basic human rights.

"Lady, don't even," Linda says.

Meryl scowls at Linda, looking momentarily like her old self. "My mom told me I had to finish. She said she wouldn't consider me her daughter anymore if I didn't finish. You think I want to be back? She said she was ashamed of me for quitting. Said I was just like my loser dad."

Ms. Gibson came to collect her. Ms. Gibson and a guard. It was fucking weird to see the school's assistant director shake hands with her mother. Ms.

Gibson was wearing normal clothes. Jeans. Sneakers. So was the guard. They looked like normal people. They thanked her mother for respecting the rules.

"All our ladies should be so lucky to come from such a supportive family," Ms. Gibson said.

"What about the registry?" Until now, Frida has been afraid to speak, has avoided looking Meryl in the eye.

Meryl isn't sure. She doesn't want to think about it. They pester her for stories. Beth wants to know what's happening in the news. If details about the school have been leaked.

Meryl has no idea. That's not her problem. Linda asks whether she sealed the deal with Colin.

Meryl ignores Linda's question.

"I missed you, asshole," Beth says, trying to hug her.

Meryl pushes Beth away. "Give me a minute."

Frida asks about Roxanne.

"We split up when we got to the highway. No one would take all three of us. The uniforms didn't help, you know. We were going to meet in Atlantic City and hide in one of those abandoned buildings. Colin had a place picked out. But I wanted to see my kid. Stupid, stupid me."

On the walk to class, Frida asks if Roxanne will be allowed to return too. Meryl doesn't think so. She doesn't know where Roxanne might have gone.

"I hope she's with her mom," Frida says.

"Right, because a cancer ward is exactly where you want to go after this place."

"That's not what I meant. Anyway, I don't think her mom is in the hospital." Frida asks Meryl if anything happened in the basement, if anyone did things to her.

"They don't have to do things. They've already done plenty to us."

"I'm sorry." She tells Meryl about Charisse invoking the Holocaust. "It should have been me. Not Charisse . . . You know, you're in my file. So is Roxanne. I was supposed to report you." She puts an arm around Meryl's shoulders. The girl is different now. Thinner, more fragile.

Ms. Khoury and Ms. Russo look disappointed to have her back. She'll need to catch up, do extra training. Meryl's doll has been frozen for three weeks. When she leaves the equipment room, her legs are wobbly as a foal's.

The weather begins to cool. The mothers layer sweaters over their uniforms. They add extra blankets to their beds. In another few weeks, the trees will become splendid. Autumn, Frida recalls, is Roxanne's favorite season.

Frida and Beth stay close to Meryl at meals, trying to protect her from Charisse, who comes over with food and compliments, telling her that she's courageous.

A few Black mothers refer to Meryl as the girl who sank Colin. He might have gotten his kid back if not for her. Meryl has been tripped in the dining hall. She's been elbowed in the shower line. But with each day, she grows in confidence. Stories about Colin are replaced by stories about seeing Ocean's father, how many times she fucked him, how she ate fried chicken and pizza and doughnuts and candy, how good it felt to sleep in a real bed. To choose her own food. To smoke. "I didn't miss my doll one bit," she says.

×

Eight weeks remain. In October, the fathers return. Some say the school wants to prepare them to reenter the real world. Some say the school wants more fraternizing and expulsions so they can test out the registry. Some say the school wants to keep them

distracted so more mothers will fail. Maybe someone is making money off their failures.

The parents file into the gymnasium to watch
videos on stranger danger. Frida looks for Tucker.
She spots him in the first row of bleachers, wishes
he'd turn his head.

Time passes faster now that she might see him.
She gets her wish the following Monday, when
Tucker and another father join several cohorts of
mothers to practice hand-to-hand combat. Mats
have been laid out on the floor. A self-defense expert
comes to demonstrate basic techniques.

Tucker is the first to play kidnapper. The expert
shows Beth how to kick Tucker in the back of the
knee. She must then grab her doll, and strike Tucker
in the nose with the flat of her palm. A swift upward
motion will cause the most pain.

They're supposed to pantomime their motions,
but Beth accidentally kicks Tucker for real. The instructors remind the parents to be safe but otherwise
do nothing to discourage actual hitting.

When it's Frida's turn, she yells and lunges. She
lightly kicks the back of Tucker's knee. Emmanuelle curls into a ball, pretending she's a boulder, her
preferred method of surviving each round.

Tucker pretends to fall but grabs Frida's jumpsuit as he does, causing her to tumble. She pulls herself up, but he grabs her ankle and knocks her down again. They may never have more than this. She doesn't look him in the eye, ignores his hand on her ankle, his caress, the tingling in her stomach, the desire to slide beneath him.

×

It's better that Harriet can't see her. It's better that Roxanne isn't here. In the aftermath of kidnapping-prevention practice, Frida looks, in the words of Emmanuelle, like a "monster." Each day, they talk about colors, why Mommy's face is blue and purple, why it's puffy. They talk about Easter, the day Emmanuelle was hit by that mean little boy.

"It's Mommy's turn to fight now," Frida tells her. "It's Mommy's turn to be hit. I'd die for you. Mommies are willing to die for their babies."

Every night, the mothers line up at the infirmary, asking for aspirin and ice packs and bandages. Their faces resemble rotten fruit. Some have chipped teeth. Some have sprained wrists and ankles. Phone privileges are canceled to allow them time to heal.

Among themselves, they wonder what keeps the staff showing up, how much they're being paid, why none of the instructors have quit in protest, why no guard has talked, why none of the people here feel as deeply as the dolls.

Someone suggests the instructors are women who've had miscarriages. Others think they're women whose children have died. Beth thinks they're barren. Linda says all these ideas are coming from people who've read too many books, who've watched too much TV.

"Lots of people are all cold and heartless," Linda argues. "Who do you think works in a prison? Who do you think works on death row? It's a job."

×

Fear, they learn, is an asset that can be channeled into strength and speed. The parents watch videos of strangers leading small children into basements. A door closes, a child emerges with tangled clothes and dead eyes. They hear the statistics. Watch testimonials from survivors. Many blame their parents, their mothers especially. How different their life would have been if they were truly loved, if someone believed them when they spoke up.

Love is the first step, the instructors say. During molestation-prevention training, the parents learn that children who receive ample parental attention will be less susceptible to pedophiles.

Two mothers vomit during the testimonials. Some parents cry. Most are skeptical. Beth says this is never how it happens. What about fathers and stepfathers and uncles? Grandfathers. Family friends. Cousins. Brothers. Why does it have to be the mother's fault?

When the lights come up, Frida's neck and armpits are damp. She's cold all over. Last night, she dreamed that Harriet was hidden at the school, trapped in a dark room, surrounded by limbs. Someone was grabbing her wrist. Someone was ringing a bell. Frida followed the bell until she found the right room, but couldn't open the door. She stood on the other side screaming.

×

The walkways are sprinkled with gold leaves. Gust and Susanna are probably taking Harriet to see the fall colors. They'll take her to Fairmount Park, to the Wissahickon. They'll go apple picking. Frida intended to do that last year. She remembers eating Susanna's apple crumble and feeling envious, wanting to be the kind of person who made desserts from scratch.

They practice on the quad outside Morris. Swing sets serve as the pedophile's home base. The parent must prevent the pedophile from lingering too long at their doll's side. The pedophile must compliment the doll, saying things like, "What a beautiful little girl you are," and ask for a hug. The parent must then intercept the pedophile, reclaim possession, carry the doll to safety, then process the experience.

Meryl now speaks of her week in the basement in a nostalgic tone. She didn't know she'd be returning to a fucking fight club. At lunch, she says these lessons feel particularly stupid, cut-and-dried.

"Reductive," Frida says. "The word you're looking for is **reductive**."

One morning when it's Frida's turn to play the pedophile, she gets knocked down by Beth and hits her head on the base of the slide. She can't move. Her eyes won't focus. Beth has knocked off her glasses. Frida worries that she's paralyzed, that she'll leave on a stretcher. She hears Emmanuelle crying. Her classmates are asking if she's okay. Beth is kneeling beside her, patting her cheek and apologizing.

"Frida? Frida? Can you hear me?"

She wiggles her fingers, then her toes. She hears the instructors saying they should call the infirmary, hears Linda scolding Beth. Frida tries to move her legs, relieved that she can still bend them. She pats the ground, looking for her glasses. She hears Tucker's voice, feels his hands lifting her head, then her torso. He props her to sitting. He helps her put her glasses back on, resting his hand on her cheek.

Their heads are almost touching. Everyone can see them. She says she's fine. "I don't think you should do this."

He helps her stand. She tries to take a step and stumbles.

"Let me help you." He takes her arm and leads her back to the group. She can barely feel the pain. She needs his touch. His care. He sets her down in the grass, handling her like a treasure.

Tucker takes both Jeremy and Emmanuelle onto his lap, and begins processing with them. "Mommy Frida is okay. See? She's okay. When we fall, we get right back up. Mommy Frida is learning."

Frida feels dizzy and seasick. Happy. Chosen. She may never see his house. She may never meet Silas, may not become the boy's stepmother, may not have another baby. She may never kiss the man who let his son fall out of a tree, but today, she feels certain that she loves him. She tells him so when the group is shaking hands at the end of the day. She makes sure the instructors are occupied, then covers Emmanuelle's ears, tells him to cover Jeremy's.

She mouths the words.

"Yes," he says. "Me too. I told you. A romance."

×

Again, they pray. On the bus, Frida and her classmates bow their heads and whisper. They're heading to the evaluation day for Unit 8. Yesterday, several cohorts practiced together. Danger stations were set up in a zigzag formation inside the warehouse. One station represented a burning building, another had a swing set, another featured a van with blacked-out windows.

Between stations, they had to run with their dolls. There was only time for each parent to run the course once. The school had new people play the kidnappers and pedophiles, supposedly trainee instructors and guards who'll staff a school for mothers in California. They were stronger and faster than the parents themselves. When no one was able to finish, the instructors told them to expand their understanding of what's possible.

Ms. Khoury said, "It doesn't matter whether you're fighting one person or twelve. A parent should be able to lift a car. Lift a fallen tree. Fend off a bear." She stabbed at her chest. "You have to find that strength inside yourself."

"You can't let your bodies get in the way," Ms. Russo added.

Today, Frida finishes early, emerging in the late afternoon with a cut under her eye. She thinks she's broken a rib. She has trouble lifting Emmanuelle. When they walk outside, the cut throbs as the wind hits her cheek.

Emmanuelle is still crying. She touches Frida's cut, then rubs her face, getting Frida's blood on her. Frida tries to wipe the blood away. It seems to be staining Emmanuelle's skin.

Today's evaluation will be entered into her file as a zero. Parents deserve more than two chances, she'd like to tell the family court judge. They deserve more than this. The version of her future that includes Harriet now requires a miracle, and she's never considered herself lucky.

She leads Emmanuelle to the circle of parents standing in the parking lot. Everyone is finishing early. They stay close for warmth. There's frost on the ground. The dolls stand in the center, shivering and clinging to their parents' legs.

Frida has asked the counselor what comes next. If there will be a probationary period, if she'll need to check in with her social worker, Ms. Torres, if Harriet will still need to see the child psychologist, if there will be restrictions on her friendships or relationships, the kind of jobs she's allowed to do, if CPS will still track her, if she'll be able to leave the state, if she'll be able to travel with Harriet. The counselor said it depends if she gets Harriet back. If she does, there will be further monitoring. If she doesn't, no one will bother her. She won't be a concern to them.

"These are problems you want to have, people you want to see," the counselor said.

The counselor didn't say when further monitoring would stop.

It's fully dark when Frida senses Tucker beside

her. Jeremy is delighted to see Emmanuelle. They sit down and begin playing.

"I got clobbered at the first station," Tucker says.

"I made it to station two. Your prognosis is good. Maybe you'll be fine."

"That's not how this place works." Tucker looks at her tenderly. She never thanked him for taking care of her the other day, for soothing Emmanuelle.

Without another word, they take off their gloves and brush fingers. Frida glances behind her. They're not safe. There's light from the highway, other parents, guards.

Tucker notices the cut under her eye. He tries to touch her face, but she leans away.

"I wish I could protect you. When we get out, I'll protect you."

She wants to say she'll do the same. She wants to make promises. Three weeks remain. What then? She touches her fingers to her lips, then presses her fingers to his palm. He does the same. They pass three kisses this way before Emmanuelle asks what they're doing.

"Passing hope," Tucker says.

17.

BEFORE COMING HERE, SHE NEVER THOUGHT about trees much. Neither trees nor childhood nor weather. She used to make her father carry her over wet leaves. As a child, she found the texture of wet leaves disgusting. She'd stand on the sidewalk and reach up to him and make demands, cling to him as he struggled with his umbrella. He always said yes, though she was too old to be carried, must have been three or four.

How heavy is a three-year-old? A four-year-old? Outside, the trees are dripping. Frida has wet leaves stuck to her boots. As she watches the rain, she realizes that she won't have any more time with Emmanuelle outdoors. Emmanuelle has no idea about the season. She may never again experience daylight, not with Frida.

JESSAMINE CHAN

This morning, the instructors distribute plastic
robins with trickles of blood painted on their beaks
and daubs of red on their breasts. It is November,
and the mothers have returned to their classrooms
to begin Unit 9: The Moral Universe. Using these
props, they'll practice a morality-building protocol.
They'll have the doll notice the injured bird, then
ask the doll to help. They'll teach the doll to pick
up the bird and bring it to her mother.

The instructors will observe the depth of their
motherese, the depth of their wisdom, the quality of their knowledge cultivation, whether they're
situating this exercise in a larger framework of
moral responsibilities. During these final weeks,
they'll teach their dolls about altruism. Success
depends on their own moral fitness, the bond between mother and doll, whether they've given the
doll their values, whether these values are correct
and good.

Tucker has been added to Frida's file. So has a
third trip to talk circle. So have citations for flirtatious body language, sexually suggestive touching,
disobeying her counselor, and ignoring her doll.
The counselor thinks Frida is cracking. Besides suicide and self-harm, forming romantic attachments

during training is the height of selfishness. Pursuing a romantic attachment suggests a desire to fail.

In the first hours of morality training, birds are licked and bitten and thrown and pocketed. Emmanuelle drops her bird down the front of Frida's uniform. Frida retrieves it and cradles it in her hand. She asks Emmanuelle to notice the bird, notice the red.

"What does red mean? Red to the bird is like blue is to you." She reaches behind Emmanuelle and taps on her blue knob. She talks about big creatures helping small creatures, humans helping animals.

Though Frida is smiling, Emmanuelle senses something is wrong. She keeps asking if Mommy is okay.

"You sad." Emmanuelle presses on Frida's black eye and swollen cheek. "Mommy body hurt? Mommy body sad? Mommy big sad? Mommy tiny sad?"

So many things hurt. Every parent failed yesterday's evaluation. Frida claims to be fine though. She asks Emmanuelle to focus on the bird. The bird is more important than Mommy.

"Remember, we've seen birdies outside. This is a pretend birdie. Can we pretend? Do you think the birdie feels scared? What kind of feelings do you think birdies have? If you were the birdie, how would you feel?"

Emmanuelle thinks the birdie feels tiny sad. The birdie's chest has a boo-boo. The birdie needs a Band-Aid. The birdie needs to go outside.

"Up high. Birdie, you fly! Fly fly!" Emmanuelle tosses the bird in the air. She points to the window. "Mommy come!"

"I'm sorry, sweetie. We have to stay here. We have to practice."

"With Jeremy?"

"Remember, we said bye-bye to Jeremy last night." They talk about how the fathers won't be coming back, how Emmanuelle won't see Jeremy again, not until next year. Frida wants to tell Emmanuelle that he'll be different then. So will she. They'll have different names. Different parents. How long until they're loved?

Emmanuelle doesn't seem to remember Jeremy's outburst. The parking lot was full by that point. Every parent was injured. The dolls had been playing peacefully when Jeremy tried to throw a rock. Tucker snatched the rock from Jeremy's hand just in time. Frida delivered the hug to soothe emotional upset. Tucker delivered the hug to soothe aggression.

They talked about kindness and modeled reconciliation. When they hugged, they held each other for
too long.

They whispered, "I love you."

Tucker told her his address and phone number,
his email. She shared hers.

"Come find me," he said. "We'll celebrate when
this is over."

The school doesn't know about that conversation. She is a bad mother for hanging on those
words. She is a bad mother for missing him. She
is a bad mother for desiring him. She should have
known the darkness wouldn't protect them. She
should've known the hug wouldn't look innocent.
What will he cost her? Had she never met the man
who let his son fall out of a tree, her prognosis
might still be fair.

×

So far, Linda's doll is the only one who holds her bird
for more than a few seconds. Beth's doll throws her
bird alarming distances. Meryl's doll stuffs her bird
into her mouth. They're supposed to teach their dolls
about community, the necessity of helping others.

"Building good citizens begins at home," Ms. Khoury says.

Every mention of citizenship fills Frida with rage. She would like to tell the family court judge that her father is the most patriotic American she knows. There were family trips to Lincoln's birthplace, Lexington and Concord, Colonial Williamsburg. Her father visits the Liberty Bell and Independence Hall whenever he comes to Philadelphia.

"You've ruined America for him," she'd like to say. For her mother too. Perhaps they regret coming here.

Her father used to tell her about circles of responsibilities. First, his wife and daughter and parents. Then, his brother and his brother's children. Then, his neighbors. Then, his town. His city. Her parents never taught her about altruism, not explicitly. But she saw what they did for their family. For her. How hard they worked. How much they gave.

The school has turned back the clocks. It gets dark at four thirty now. The sky is azure, violet, periwinkle, a gem blue, bluest when it's about to rain.

When Harriet turns thirty-two months old, Frida marks the day alone, would have marked it with Roxanne. They would have imagined how much Harriet has grown, how much she weighs, what she might be saying, how she feels. Shaping a worldview used to seem like one of the hardest parts of parenting. What will she have left to teach Harriet when she gets home? Why should Harriet trust her?

She used to think she valued loyalty above all else, but during her third trip to talk circle, she betrayed her own mother. Ms. Gibson made them talk about their childhoods. She wanted details. Frida's behavior, Ms. Gibson said, was that of a damaged person. What made her latch on to Tucker? Only a very troubled woman would choose a man who harmed his child. Ms. Gibson pushed and pushed until Frida told the group about her mother's miscarriage. The grief she never discussed. How her mother perhaps wasn't done grieving. How sometimes her mother barely spoke to her or touched her. The times her mother said, "Get out of my sight."

After a fraught pause, Ms. Gibson said, "Maybe you would have turned out differently if you'd had a sibling. Clearly, you wanted something your mother couldn't give you."

Ms. Gibson said her mother should have sought help—seen a therapist, found a support group. Had she been a better mother, she would have taken better care of herself, and thus, been more available to her child.

Frida resisted saying those were American solutions. She hated having her mother analyzed. One small fact of her life being used to explain her character. Now her counselor will know. The social worker will know. The family court judge will know. She's never even told Gust.

When they finally talked about it, her mother said: "I put it out of my mind. Only you girls these days think and think and think. I didn't have time to do that. That is a luxury. I couldn't get emotional. I had to work."

In class, they've made thirty attempts to pick up the bird. Frida tells Emmanuelle about duty. Emmanuelle has a duty to be kind. She has a duty to care.

"Red stuff means the bird is hurting, and what do we do when we see a creature hurting?"

"Help."

"Good. Who helps? Does Mommy help? Does Emmanuelle help?"

Emmanuelle points to her chest. "Me help. My-self! My-self!" She jumps for emphasis.

"Yourself. Good job. Can you pick up that birdie and bring it to Mommy?"

Emmanuelle walks over to the bird and crouches.

She waves, saying, "Hello, bird! Hello! Hello!" She grabs the bird and tosses it at Frida, the first doll to complete the exercise.

×

One week remains. Even the mothers who've scored only zeros, the ones who've spent months in talk circle, believe their judge will give them a second chance. Supposedly they'll all have their final court dates within a week or two after they leave. They'll receive their personal clothes on the last morning, their purses and phones. The school will give them each sixty dollars. Buses will drop them off at points around the county. Their social workers and children's guardians will be contacted. Files and supporting materials will be sent.

Families have changed. Some husbands have filed for divorce. Boyfriends and girlfriends and baby daddies have started new relationships. There have been engagements and pregnancies. Sunday calls are bogged down by logistics. Who is staying with whom, who will pay the legal bills, whether there's anything left in the bank account, what to tell the children. The mothers look forward to long showers and haircuts, sleeping in their own beds, wearing their own clothes, driving, earning money, having money. Browsing the Internet, going shopping, getting a manicure. Speaking without a script. Seeing their children.

Tucker said the fathers were never given talking points. Sunday calls were never canceled due to technical difficulties. Frida wants to know if Tucker's ex-wife will allow her near their son, if Gust will allow Tucker near Harriet. She needs to be patient. Soon, she'll be free to have her own thoughts and feelings. She has a year of crying stored up. Sometimes it feels heavy in her body.

In the gymnasium, the mothers watch videos on poverty. There are segments on the global refugee crisis, homelessness in America, natural disasters. They must learn to speak to their children about world events. If they've had personal experience with poverty, they're encouraged to share these experiences with their doll.

Back in Morris, the instructors distribute tablets loaded with conscience-provoking imagery: homeless camps, refugees washing ashore on a rubber boat, children in third world slums. The mothers begin teaching their dolls new words. **Humanitarian crisis. Migration. Borders. Human rights.**

Frida narrates the images like a picture book: **Why is that man dirty? Why doesn't he have shoes? Why is he sleeping under a pile of garbage?**

"He bad," Emmanuelle says.

"No. It's because his life took a wrong turn and sometimes when people don't have anyone to help them, they end up on the street."

"Sad-sad."

"Yes, sad like the birdie. But big-sad, because he's a person."

Ms. Khoury praises Frida for making connections, the praise so rare it feels imaginary.

Frida teaches Emmanuelle about shelters and soup kitchens, halfway houses and rehab programs. She says, "Imagine what it's like to be homeless in winter, imagine when it's raining." She discusses the universal right to food and shelter.

Emmanuelle points to the door of the equipment room. "Home."

Frida says, "Not everyone is so lucky."

×

Frida is thinking about hearts and minds, towns and houses. Light that comes in sideways and not at all. Another house in another city. Seattle or Santa Fe. Denver. Chicago. Canada, always a fantasy. If Gust and Susanna would agree to relocate. If Tucker's ex-wife and her new partner would agree. And that man's ex-wife and her new partner.

More family data is added to Frida's file. Susanna's baby arrived early. Born at thirty-five weeks. A boy. Susanna needed an emergency C-section. Her placenta ruptured. She lost a significant amount of blood. Frida finds out from the counselor, who's impressed that Gust bothered to inform them.

"You haven't asked the baby's name," the counselor says.

"Please excuse me. What did they name him? I didn't know they were having a boy."

The baby's name is Henry Joseph. He was five pounds and one ounce. He has jaundice, will likely spend a month in the NICU. Susanna might be in the hospital for several weeks.

"But she's okay?"

"She's recovering. I suggest that you brainstorm ways to make your return easier on them."

Frida says she will. She wants to ask who's

watching Harriet. Gust must need to be at the hospital all the time. Have their parents flown in? Gust has arranged for Frida to stay with Will after she leaves, has given these instructions to the counselor.

Frida wants to tell Roxanne about the baby. Susanna might be swollen from a blood transfusion. Can she see Henry? Will she be able to nurse?

During their first week in the hospital, the nurses pressured them to give Harriet formula. Frida's milk was coming in too slowly after her C-section. Harriet had lost more than 10 percent of her birth weight. The nurses said they'd send her home without Harriet if Harriet didn't start gaining.

"It would be heartbreaking," the nurses said, "if you had to go home without her."

That's not what she wanted for Susanna.

×

To practice poverty awareness, one of the women in pink lab coats has been dressed to look like a beggar, with tattered clothes and dark eyeshadow rubbed on her cheeks. Each mother-doll pair must walk past the pretend beggar, who'll ask for money. The doll will be trained to notice the beggar and tug on her mother's hand, signaling altruistic intent. The mother will give the doll a coin, which she has to deliver, saying "Be well," or "Take care."

What follows is a day of confusion, negotiation, and tears. No altruistic intentions are signaled. No coins are delivered. The mothers can't undo two months of stranger-danger lessons in one day.

When the beggar asks for help, Emmanuelle shouts, "Go away!"

Frida corrects her, but Emmanuelle insists that the beggar is bad. Frida explains the difference between badness and misfortune, badness and suffering.

"What have we learned about suffering?"

Emmanuelle hangs her head. "We help. I help. Help bird. Help lady."

Frida explains the concept of charity. To Emmanuelle, charity is like baskets. Like Red Riding Hood. The story from months ago. Frida is surprised she remembers. Emmanuelle pretends to hop with her basket through the woods.

"Red Riding girl," she says. "Food food. Basket." The coin is a basket she'll give to the lady.

Emmanuelle listens to the beggar's plea and says, "Baskets. Bye-bye!"

Frida asks if they're allowed to substitute words. Ms. Khoury tells her to keep trying for the correct language. Emmanuelle drops the coin near the beggar's head and shouts, "My did it!"

Ms. Khoury says this isn't the time for cutting corners. If the child understands grace, she'll hand the beggar the coin and give her a kind word. They should be able to see the doll's humanity.

×

"You have to do this like a big girl," Frida says. It's the last day of training, and the classroom has been set up with two morality stations: injured bird and beggar. The doll must complete each drill without coaching.

Ms. Russo said Emmanuelle's behavior reflects everything she's learned this year. Whether she feels safe and loved. Whether she has the potential to become a caring and productive member of society. She is the clearest indicator of Frida's success or failure.

"Can you be smart and kind and brave for Mommy?"

Emmanuelle says yes.

"Thank you, sweetie. I love you."

They practice saying "Be well." Frida runs her hands through Emmanuelle's hair. She would like to know how soon Emmanuelle's memory will be erased, whether she'll go into storage until there's another Asian, who that woman will be, how long Emmanuelle will have to wait for her, what name she'll choose, what kind of relationship they'll have. The next mother needs to be careful. It helps, when changing the blue liquid, to massage Emmanuelle's back.

×

Only Frida's and Linda's dolls come close to completing the sequence. Linda's doll makes mistakes but finishes in five minutes. Emmanuelle finishes in six. With speed comes moral ambiguity. The dolls handle the birds roughly. Beth's and Meryl's dolls don't even take the coin.

Ms. Knight visits the mothers at dinner. "I know some of you thought you'd never get here, but I'm sure you've come to understand that a mother can do anything. After you leave, you'll have to assess the quality of your mothering every day. Our voices need to be inside you."

She asks the mothers to hold hands and leads them in the mantra. Their last evaluation is tomorrow. Their final brain scans are Wednesday.

"We're excited to see what you've learned."

×

At the evaluation for Unit 9, Meryl's doll drops the bird. Beth's doll sees the beggar and starts crying. Linda's doll pockets the coin.

Frida has a chance at first place. At station one, Emmanuelle touches the bird with her finger, saying, "I help, okay. You okay, you okay." She picks up the bird and delivers it to Frida.

Frida wants to kiss her. Emmanuelle once felt like her enemy, but today her movements are decisive and kind.

Frida leads her to the second station, where the beggar is moaning in pain. The judge should know that Emmanuelle is hers. Emmanuelle shouldn't be given to another woman. She shouldn't be erased. She shouldn't be renamed.

Emmanuelle finally notices the beggar and says, "Baskets."

Frida hands her the coin, which she drops next to the beggar's head.

She says, "Be well."

×

The technician's hands are cold. Frida closes her eyes and begins counting backward from one hundred. Emmanuelle is the focal point, the doll-child she's learned to believe in and love. Emmanuelle completed both drills yesterday. There were mistakes, but technically, Frida finished in first place.

The counselor said in the past, judges have sometimes made exceptions. An exception is the best Frida can hope for. She'll apologize for not reporting Roxanne and Meryl. She'll admit to knowing their plans, even if it's not true. She'll blame Tucker for pursuing her. She'll acknowledge the stress she caused Susanna during her pregnancy. She only earned two zeros. Emmanuelle was not as badly injured as other dolls. There were three trips to talk circle, not dozens. She was caught touching hands, not kissing.

On-screen, it's July. Emmanuelle is picking up toys. They're learning how to play. Frida is surprised to see that Emmanuelle has adopted many of her mannerisms. Her frown. Her habit of nodding when she listens. Her nervous blinking. They look like they belong together.

She feels hopeful, but a terrible variable appears in the next frame. She watches herself meeting Tucker at the picnic, trying to ignore the sweat running down her back, the temperature that will now mark her as guilty. Her forehead becomes damp. As she watches footage from the summer, she's warm with shame. At the dance, they stand close and whisper, obviously a couple. Desire so easy to read.

They've made it look like she and Tucker were always together. On evaluation day for the danger unit, she looks helpless, a woman who can't save any child, who can't save herself. There are close-ups of Emmanuelle screaming. A shot of Emmanuelle with Frida's blood on her. There's footage of Frida and Tucker in the parking lot, playing with each other's hands. They've shown her more scenes of fraternizing than parenting.

×

They receive their prognoses the following day. Frida scored high for tenderness, empathy, and care. Her maternal instincts have improved dramatically, but there were indicators of guilt and shame, certain spikes of desire when she watched footage of herself with Tucker.

"We never even kissed. I didn't cross that line."

"But you wanted to," the counselor says, "and wanting to distracted you from your training. I told you to stay away from that man, but you clearly invited his attention. You enjoyed it. How do we know that you won't pursue this relationship after you leave? You do realize you can't date him?"

"I promise I won't. You said that if I finished first this time, the judge might make an exception." Didn't she complete the hardest assignment? Didn't she teach Emmanuelle to be human?

"The judge will consider all the data. Remember, Frida, your scan was supposed to come back clean and maternal."

"My family needs me." Frida pleads her case once more. She can take care of Harriet while Susanna recovers. Someone needs to help them with Harriet. Gust and Susanna will be busy. Harriet can live with her while they get settled with the new baby.

She'll cook for them, babysit for them. Harriet needs her mother. She can give Harriet a good life. She'll always follow the school's teachings.

"My parents only have one grandchild."

"You should have thought of that before you left the house that day," the counselor says. "We invested in you, Frida. We've done everything we can."

Frida's prognosis is fair to poor. The counselor can't predict what the judge will do.

The counselor extends her hand, thanks Frida for participating in the program.

Frida has never asked if the counselor has children, though she's certainly wondered. None have ever been mentioned. What would she do in Frida's place? Frida shakes the counselor's hand and thanks her for her guidance. She atones for her shortcomings one last time.

The counselor prompts her. "You are a bad mother for desiring."

"I am a bad mother because I desired. I am a bad mother because I was weak."

Today is Thanksgiving. Her mother must be shopping for Harriet's Christmas present. She'll buy clothes as usual. When Frida was pregnant, her mother said that having a daughter would be like having her own real doll.

"Your daughter will be beautiful," her mother promised. "Even more beautiful. Like you are more beautiful than me."

For the rest of the morning, Frida paces the stone courtyard. She thinks of Harriet in winter, the house with sideways light, pulling her front door closed, driving away. Tucker's son stepping out of the tree house. The school needs to see that she's changed, but does survival count as progress? Harriet deserves more than a mother whose greatest achievement is keeping herself alive.

Once, she scratched Harriet's cheek by accident and drew blood. Once, she clipped Harriet's thumbnail too short.

"You are bad," Harriet said. When she's older, she'll say more: **Why did you do it? Why did you leave me?**

Frida hears screams coming from Pierce. Doors being slammed. She sees mothers marching down the hill. They continue across the lawn, past the amphitheater. When they reach the tree line, they begin howling. They're beginning to understand. Beginning to mourn. They sound like Lucretia on the day of her snow-angel disaster. Like the dolls on the day they were hit. The only word Frida can make out is **no**. She waits and listens, then decides to join them.

×

The alarm sounds at midnight. The mothers line up in the hallway for a headcount. As soon as the guard leaves and the lights go off, they start whispering. Meryl is missing again.

"No." Frida tries to shout, but her voice is ragged. She pushes her way through the group to find Meryl's roommate. Her roommate says there was a note, but she didn't get a chance to read it before it was confiscated. Ms. Gibson comes upstairs and tells everyone to return to their rooms.

That night in bed, Frida remains awake, praying there won't be an ambulance. Meryl might be hiding somewhere. She might have found another guard to help her.

When she went to the tree line to join the mourning mothers, she shouldn't have asked Meryl to come too. Meryl's prognosis was poor. Her social worker disapproved of Meryl's mother, didn't think she provided good care for Ocean, had already rejected Ocean's father as a possible guardian. After

Meryl's final hearing, Ocean would likely be placed in foster care.

Meryl screamed so hard she burst blood vessels on her neck. Many mothers screamed until they lost their voices. They held each other. Some knelt. Some prayed. Some bit their hands.

Frida thought of her father. Her father and uncle must have screamed like that on the night Ahma was almost shot. A body could produce pure fear. Pure sound. Sound that eclipsed thought. Meryl screamed louder still. Frida gripped Meryl's arm so she wouldn't pitch face-first into the snow, felt something lift from her as she howled, as if she were jumping out of her own skin.

She should have checked on Meryl after dinner, should have asked if Meryl could sleep in Roxanne's bed, just for tonight. Meryl wanted to teach Ocean to ride a bike next year. Not a tricycle. A bike. She said Ocean's love language was motion. She imagined Ocean growing as tall as her father, becoming a hurdler or high jumper, throwing a javelin. If her girl was a runner, she'd get a scholarship. If she got a scholarship, she wouldn't get pregnant.

"I can break the fucking cycle," Meryl said.

×

They leave her seat empty at breakfast. As mothers pass their table, they deposit bagels and muffins and packs of saltines in front of the empty chair. They build a bread shrine. Frida makes a pile of sugar packets in Meryl's honor. Beth refuses to eat. She's scratched open a scab on her cheek, continues scratching it all through breakfast.

Linda takes Beth's hand. She dips her napkin into a glass of water and cleans Beth's face. Ms. Gibson gets on the microphone and says grief counseling services are available. She asks the mothers to bow their heads and observe a moment of silence. Someone is sobbing loudly. Frida looks up and sees Charisse in the far corner. Even from this distance, she can tell the tears are fake.

In class, it's Goodbye Day, one last day of playing and bonding before the dolls are switched off. Frida and Beth get in trouble for crying and upsetting their dolls. Meryl's doll remains in the equipment room. She looked forlorn as the others exited without her.

"Why she there?" Emmanuelle asks. "Where Mommy Meryl?"

Frida tells Emmanuelle about time and maturity and impulses. Mommy Meryl was very young. She was still learning how to make good decisions. She wasn't thinking about how sad she'd make everyone. Sometimes people do things because that thing will make them feel good in the moment. Because they just want to feel better.

At breakfast, they learned that Meryl jumped from the bell tower. Emmanuelle presses on Frida's brow and says, "No sad, Mommy. You happy."

They talk about why Mommy's voice sounds scratchy. Frida explains that she felt big feelings yesterday. Sometimes when mommies feel big feelings, they get very loud.

They lie side by side on their stomachs, inching a rainbow snake along a pretend road. As they play, Frida asks, "Do you love me?"

Emmanuelle nods.

"Have I been a good mommy to you?"

Emmanuelle pokes Frida's cheek. "You okay."

Frida should thank Emmanuelle for her suffering, for becoming real enough. She tucks the doll's hair behind her ears, memorizing the curve of her eyebrows, her freckles. The next mother needs to keep her safe. She needs to protect Emmanuelle from the instructors and other dolls. She can't let Emmanuelle get hit. She should know that Emmanuelle prefers carrots to peas. She should find Jeremy and allow the dolls to spend time together.

They play all morning, stop for lunch, then continue. In the late afternoon, the mothers are photographed with their dolls. They pose at the dry-erase board, at the window, in front of the equipment room door.

Ms. Khoury hands Frida the stack of Polaroids. "Show them to her. She'll enjoy them."

They spread the photos on the rug and watch their faces emerge. Frida hasn't seen a photograph of herself in a year. Emmanuelle perhaps never. There are six Polaroids. Frida is blinking in five of them. Her face is tiny. Her hair is more gray than black. Her features are washed-out. Emmanuelle's features are vivid, her expression delighted. The love between them is obvious.

"Let me see," Emmanuelle says. "Again! Again!" She leaves fingerprints all over the pictures.

At the end of the day, the dolls know something is amiss. It's time to return the photos. Time to say goodbye. Linda's doll throws herself on the floor. Beth's doll has an accident.

Frida sees Linda slip a photo into her sleeve as Ms. Khoury finds Beth some wipes.

Ms. Russo is busy typing on her tablet. Ms. Khoury takes the photos back from Linda without counting them. When Ms. Khoury approaches her, Frida returns five photos. The one with her eyes open, she pockets.

Ms. Russo tells the mothers to deliver their final hugs.

Frida holds Emmanuelle around the shoulders, resting her chin on the doll's head. She'll commit Emmanuelle's scent to memory. She'll remember her clicks.

Emmanuelle digs in her pocket. She still has the coin from evaluation day.

"Mommy basket," she says. "Tiny basket." She drops the coin into Frida's hand and says, "Be well."

Frida begins to cry. She holds Emmanuelle again and thanks her. She tells Emmanuelle that the equipment room isn't an equipment room. It's a forest with a castle. She's going to sleep a special sleep. Like that story about the princess under glass.

Emmanuelle pouts. "Mommy, don't want sleep. Not tired."

Linda's and Beth's dolls are already inside, with Meryl's.

Frida doesn't say, "Goodbye." She gives Emmanuelle a final kiss and says, "I love you, baby. I'll miss you."

Ms. Russo leads her away. At the equipment room door, Emmanuelle looks back at Frida. She waves and shouts, "Love you, Mommy! Take care! Take care!"

18.

THE SOCIAL WORKER'S OFFICE HAS BEEN PAINTED blue, a shade of robin's egg that was once Frida's favorite color. There are new drawings on the walls, trees made of hands, monsters and stick figures, a framed poster-size photo of a little blond girl shedding a single tear.

The tear offends Frida, as does the daisy in the girl's hand, as does the fact that it's a black-and-white stock image. Whoever took the photo didn't intend for it to be used this way. Frida's temperature is rising. Her blinking is rapid. Her heartbeat is a hard, fast tap. She's never been here in the morning. While she waits, she answers questions about her transition, admits that she's living out of suitcases. She's retrieved some clothes from storage, reopened her bank accounts, has her car back, has been getting used to driving again, is lucky to be staying with her friend Will. She hasn't started looking for work yet, hasn't looked for an apartment, hasn't had time, was busy preparing for court. She has to get through today. She doesn't know what happens after today.

It's the first Tuesday in December, fifteen months since Harriet was taken away, fourteen months since Frida last held her, four months since their last phone call. They're about to have their final visit. Yesterday, the judge terminated her parental rights.

She hasn't been added to the registry, doesn't have to be if she has no child. The judge promised her thirty minutes this morning. Frida checks her phone. Gust hasn't texted. It's 10:07. She didn't think he could possibly be late. She asks if his tardiness will be held against her. Twenty-three minutes isn't enough.

"Don't worry," Ms. Torres says. Going five or ten minutes over won't be a problem. She smiles, seems to have softened, looks at Frida with pity. Ms. Torres says she understands that today is important. They can take care of paperwork in the meantime. She hands Frida a clipboard. By signing the forms, Frida grants the state permission to release her information when Harriet turns eighteen.

The judge's decision is final. Parents can't appeal. Frida asks if she can contact Harriet then, or if she has to wait for Harriet to contact her.

"She'll need to look for you. Have confidence, Ms. Liu. Most children want to find their birth mothers."

Frida nods. She hopes the next parent sitting in this chair will become violent. Someone should throw the social worker against the wall, strangle her, push her out the window. The body count should be equal. As many women in pink lab coats and instructors and counselors and social workers and family court judges as the mothers who've died, as the ones who'll die in the next round, at the next school.

For her permanent contact information, she lists her parents' address and phone number, adds her own cell phone number and email. She signs her name. When Harriet is eighteen, she'll be fifty-five. She doesn't know where she'll be living, if she'll be able to survive until then. It feels wrong to be alive, to be sitting here dressed up and wearing makeup. Her hair has been dyed black and cut into a blunt bob with bangs, a style Renee suggested. Her nails have been manicured. Her teeth have been whitened. She's wearing the same sweater set and pencil skirt she wore to the first supervised visit. The clothes are baggy on her now. She looks conservative and tidy, not the mother she was before, not the mother she became, but a mother from a manual, blank and interchangeable.

Her hearing took two hours. The judge had already reviewed classroom and evaluation and Sunday-call footage, considered data from Frida's brain scans and taken from Emmanuelle, read the recommendations of Ms. Khoury and Ms. Russo and Frida's counselor, Ms. Thompson.

The judge said, "I've learned so much about you, Ms. Liu. You're a complicated woman." What made the program so special was having the child's perspective. Even if Emmanuelle didn't have all the language to describe Frida's mothering, even if the instructors couldn't watch Frida at every moment, with the rest of the data, with the technology, the court had a full picture of Frida's abilities. Her character.

"We're able to extrapolate," the judge said.

Frida thought she'd go blind. Renee spoke. The state's lawyers spoke. The social worker and court-appointed child psychologist and Gust and Susanna testified. Susanna was only two days out of the hospital. Gust and Susanna, who weren't permitted to hear anything about the program, each only spoke for a few minutes before leaving the courtroom and returning to the NICU to be with Henry.

"We've all forgiven Frida," Gust said. "It would traumatize our daughter to keep them apart. Harriet has been through so much already. I want her to have a normal childhood. A normal life. You can make that possible for our family."

Susanna said, "Harriet asks about Frida all the time. She says things like, 'Mommy come back. Mommy miss me.' For us, it's not a question of trust. I know Frida can do it. She's a good person."

When it was Frida's turn to testify, she atoned for her poor judgment regarding the runaways and Tucker. She answered the judge's questions about her three trips to talk circle, the pinching incident, her zeros, her arguments with the counselor. She described her relationship with Emmanuelle as beautiful and rich. She learned from the doll as much as the doll learned from her. "We were a team," she said.

She told the judge that motherhood gave her life

purpose and meaning. She said, "I never knew what was missing until I had my baby."

Frida checks the time again. Where is Gust? She returns the clipboard and takes a box from her purse, asks permission to give Harriet some family heirlooms.

"Ms. Liu, you can't give—"

"They're not presents. Here. Take a look. They're for when she's older. I want her to have them. In case . . . in case she doesn't look for me."

The social worker inspects the contents. There are family pictures and jewelry, Frida's grandmother's pearl earrings and jade bracelet, her own wedding rings, family photos, a gold locket in which she's coiled strands of her hair. This morning, she became breathless as she pulled hair out, picturing Harriet at five and seven, as a teenager, as a young woman. She wants Harriet to have a piece of her mother as she grows.

Ms. Torres agrees to make an exception. Frida thanks her. As she puts the jewelry away, she hears voices. Gust and Harriet are on the other side of the door.

"C'mon, you can walk. Walk like a big girl. We're going to see Mommy now. Sweetie, c'mon. She's waiting for us. Mommy is right in there. We have to go in now."

Frida takes a mirror from her purse and checks her lipstick, then wipes it off. She tries to breathe.

When they enter, the social worker starts the timer on her phone. They begin their goodbye at 10:18. Frida and Gust embrace while Harriet clutches the doorframe. People in the waiting room crane their necks. Frida crouches beside Harriet, but Harriet won't look at her.

Turn, Frida thinks.

Gust asks how she's getting home. Yesterday, he and Renee were worried that she'd walk in front of a bus. He called every hour, made Will go home early to take care of her.

Will won't be home until five. He asks if she can wait for Will somewhere in public. What's her plan for today? Did she get any sleep last night?

"I need to know that you'll be safe," he says.

"We can't talk about this now." They've used up three minutes. She remembers to ask about Henry. Gust tells her that Henry's bilirubin level is getting better.

She wants to tell Gust that she loves him, give him directions for the next sixteen years, tell him how Harriet should be raised. Today she's saying goodbye to Gust, too.

She rubs Harriet's back, out of habit touching the spot where Emmanuelle had her blue knob. Harriet pushes Frida's hand away.

"My body," Harriet says, moving from the doorframe to Gust's leg.

Frida pushes the door closed and tries again. "I hear you saying that's your body. That's true. Can you look at me? It's Mommy. Mommy Frida. I can't believe how tall you are. Can I give you a hug? I'm so happy to see you, bub. I've been waiting to see you. Can I see you?"

Harriet looks up. She remains the most beautiful child Frida has ever seen. Her daughter's beauty stuns and silences her. They hold hands and stare. Frida feels the social worker's eyes on them, the weight of the camera and the clock, a year of expectations.

Harriet is tall and lean, about eight inches taller than Emmanuelle. Her face is now heart-shaped. Her eyes look more Chinese. They've kept her hair short. It curls around her ears. She's carrying a Black plastic baby doll with its own bottle. Gust has dressed her in earth tones: a charcoal cardigan with white flowers, a brown jumper, loden-green tights, tiny brown boots.

"Hello, Mommy." Harriet points to Frida's bangs. "What happened to your hair?"

Gust and the social worker laugh. Frida can't believe how clearly Harriet speaks now. If they had more time, if they were alone, they could have real conversations.

"Do you like it?" Frida asks. Harriet nods. She steps toward Frida, holding her arms out. As they hug, Frida feels unsteady. Dazed. She kisses Harriet's hands, cups her face, looks into her real eyes, strokes her real skin.

Gust tries to leave, but Harriet begs him to stay. Their negotiations use up another five minutes. Gust reminds Harriet what's going to happen. She's not going to see Mommy for a long time. Mommy is staying on time-out. They have to say goodbye today.

"No time-out! No! I don't want to do that!"

Gust kisses Frida on the head, kisses Harriet on the cheek, says he'll be in the waiting room. The social worker asks Frida and Harriet to move away from the door. She directs them to sit on the couch. Frida holds Harriet on her lap, shifting beneath Harriet's weight. She's considerably heavier than Emmanuelle. Between sobs, Harriet asks why today is goodbye.

"Why Mommy on time-out? Why time-out a long time?"

Frida tells Harriet about their life a year ago, how Mommy had a very bad day, how because of her very bad day, she went to a school, where there were lots of mommies and lots of lessons. There were tests that Mommy was supposed to pass.

She kneads Harriet's hands. "I tried so hard. I want you to know that I tried my best. This wasn't my decision. I am still your mother. I'll always be your mother. Those lawyers were calling me your biological mother, but I'm not your biological mother, I'm your mother. Period. It's not fair—"

"Ms. Liu, please refrain from criticizing the program."

"My criticism doesn't matter anymore, does it?" Frida snaps.

"Ms. Liu—"

"Mommy, I feel bad. My tummy hurts. I want a pack-pack."

The social worker explains that Harriet's school gives the children ice packs when they get boo-boos. Frida begins sobbing. This is her last chance to make

JESSAMINE CHAN

requests, to share secrets, but what secret, what story, would explain her whole life to her daughter?

The instructors would tell her to speak at a higher pitch. They'd tell her she's hugging for too long and giving too many kisses. She says, "I love you," over and over.

Harriet says, "I love you too, Mommy." The sentence Frida has been waiting for. "I love you so much."

Harriet's face is nestled against Frida's neck. They talk about what saying goodbye today means, that goodbye today isn't goodbye forever, that Harriet will grow tall and strong and smart and brave, and even if Mommy can't visit, she'll be thinking of Harriet all the time. Every day. Every second.

Harriet scoots off Frida's lap and pats the space beside her on the couch. "Mommy, sit right here. Sit right here and let me talk with you." She shows Frida her doll. "Mommy, say bye-bye to Baby Betty too."

Frida smiles and says, "Bye-bye, Baby Betty. I love you galaxies, Baby Betty. I love you to the moon and stars."

"To Jupiter. Love Baby Betty to Jupiter."

"You remember. Thank you for remembering. I love you to Jupiter. I love Baby Betty to Jupiter." She holds up her fist and reminds Harriet about aching hearts. They practice the gesture and teach it to Baby Betty. Whenever Harriet is missing Mommy, she can give her heart a squeeze.

"Ten more minutes," the social worker says.

Frida sets Harriet down and grabs the box of heirlooms. She shows Harriet photos of her grandparents and great-grandparents. They look at a sheet of calligraphy written by Frida's father when Harriet was a newborn, the individual strokes numbered so that Harriet can learn to write her Chinese name. Liu Tong Yun. Red clouds before snowfall. Vermillion. Her grandmother named her. Frida teaches her how to say it.

They open the box containing the locket. Frida shows her the coil of hair. "This is a piece of Mommy. Please don't lose it. I want you to have this even when you're old."

"I'm not old. I'm two. I'm almost three." Harriet holds up three fingers. "I'm a big kid. Mommy, come to my three birthday. My birthday is tomorrow!"

"No it's not, bub. You're being silly. I'm sorry, Mommy won't be able to come. But Mommy will be there in your heart."

"In the necklace too?"

"In the necklace too."

Six minutes remain. It's time to take pictures. The social worker has them pose beside a miniature Christmas tree, then loads her Polaroid camera and asks them to smile. Harriet weeps. Frida asks her to be kind to Daddy and Susanna, to be a good sister to Henry.

"Let's take some more by the window," the social worker says.

Frida props Harriet on her hip. "Remember you never did anything wrong. You're perfect. Mommy loves you so much. Mommy loves you galaxies. Remember Gonggong and Popo. They'll always love you. They'll miss you every day."

She whispers in Harriet's ear, "Please be happy. I want you to be so, so happy. I want you to come find me when you grow up. Please look for me. I'll be waiting for you."

"Okay, Mommy, I will look." They hook pinkies.

One minute remains. Frida hugs Harriet tight, trying to deliver every kind of hug—not varieties of affection, but an entire world. She pretends she's holding Emmanuelle, that this is just a drill.

The judge said she wasn't ready for the responsibility. Maybe she wouldn't leave Harriet alone again, but she might do something else. If she pinched her doll, what might she do to Harriet? If she couldn't protect her doll from danger, how could she be counted on to protect her daughter? If she couldn't make good decisions about friendships and relationships in a controlled environment, with so much at stake, why would she be able to do so in the real world?

"I simply don't trust you," the judge said. "Someone like you should know better."

The social worker's phone begins beeping.

"No!" Frida shouts. "We need more time."

"I'm sorry, Ms. Liu. You've had your full half hour. Harriet, Harriet, honey, you need to say goodbye to Mommy Frida. Daddy will take you home now."

"Please! You can't do this."

"Mommy!" Harriet shrieks. "I want to stay with you! I want to stay with you!"

The social worker leaves to get Gust. Frida is on her knees. She and Harriet cling and cry. Harriet holds tight to Frida's collar. She continues screaming. Frida fled from these screams on her very bad day, but now she takes the screams into her body, feeling the vibration, the longing. She needs to remember this sound. She needs to remember Harriet's voice, her smell, her touch, how much Harriet wants her now, how much Harriet loves her. She kisses Harriet's wet cheeks, gazes at her again. They press foreheads as they used to. She says "I love you" in English and Mandarin, calls Harriet her treasure, her little beauty. When Gust and the social worker return, she refuses to let go.

×

From the living room window, Frida watches Will's neighbors arrive home with their children. The neighbors on the other side of the wall are a white family with a son and a daughter, both in elementary school. The boy fights with his parents about getting dressed. The girl fights with them about tooth-brushing. A white man across the street smokes on his front porch in his pajamas. A Black woman across the street plays guitar in the evenings. A Black family down the block has twin baby boys. She's seen the mother carrying two car seats, one slung over each arm.

She never thought of herself as living in a city full of children, but maybe every city and every neighborhood is full of children when you've lost your own. West Philly is its own particular brand of torture, friendly and wholesome, a small town within the city, with wide, tree-lined streets and houses decorated for the holidays. She and Gust once looked at this neighborhood. They visited five-bedroom Victorians they couldn't afford in the catchment for the city's one good public school. Had they bought one of those houses, she likes to think. Had they lived in a different community.

If she could get herself to leave the house, she'd buy medicine. Benadryl from the pharmacy on Baltimore, Unisom from the CVS on Forty-Third. NyQuil from the Rite Aid on Fifty-First. Too much medicine from one store would invite questions. She doesn't want to answer questions from strangers ever again.

When she imagines it, it's always pills. Pills and bourbon. Never a razor blade and a bathtub. Her body feels like it's filled with electricity. Her hands tingle. It's Friday afternoon. In the three days since the final visit, she's consumed all the liquor in Will's apartment. She's run out of Unisom. Will won't buy her more.

Will had office hours today. Otherwise, he's been staying home to grade papers. He's been cooking for her. She's overheard him talking to Gust. They've discussed whether they need to enlist other friends to watch her. He's hidden the knives. He's given her his bedroom. For the first few nights here, he slept on the couch, but at Frida's request, he now sleeps beside her. He's still keeping his apartment clean, easier now that his dog lives with his ex. The girl from Harriet's birthday video wasn't serious, he said.

Frida feels guilty for constantly comparing him to Tucker, but she likes having Will's hand on her waist every night and listening to him sleep. She thanks him too often but doesn't say much else. Will thinks she doesn't trust him anymore. He wants her to feel free to cry with him. He's given up asking about the school. They have the same conversations every day. Whether she's taken a shower, what she's eaten, whether she needs to eat, the dangers of mixing pills and alcohol.

The Polaroids from the final visit are still in her purse. She's not ready to look at them. She hasn't looked at the photo of Emmanuelle either, hidden in the same place. She hasn't read the news. She spends most of her waking hours scrolling through Harriet photos and watching old videos. The first time Harriet clapped. Her first steps. The time Frida's father recited the Gettysburg Address to Harriet when she was a newborn.

Will let her look at Susanna's Instagram on his phone. She watched Harriet grow up across the squares, saw photos of Harriet's friends and teachers, Susanna's baby bump, Harriet's first dentist appointment, potty training photos, family selfies. She's not allowed to follow them on social media. She's not allowed to stalk them online. If she sees Harriet on the street, she's not allowed to approach. Legally, she's a stranger.

Christmas is in less than three weeks. She hasn't been answering her parents' calls, let Gust give them the news. Renee said the old policies allowed grandparents to stay in contact. Under the old system, Gust could have allowed her to see Harriet, even if Harriet couldn't live with her. But things have changed.

Her parents said goodbye to Harriet over Zoom. They've wired Frida money, though they want her to consider moving home. It may not be healthy to stay. This city has too many memories, her mother wrote.

Frida returns to Will's room and gets under the covers. She needs everything around her to be soft. She wants to know how much Harriet remembers, whether she remembers the social worker prying them apart, whether she remembers biting her father's hand.

"Mommy, you come back!" Harriet screamed. "I want my mommy! I want you! I want you!"

Harriet wet herself. There was a puddle on the social worker's carpet. After they left, Frida screamed as if she was at the tree line. The social worker called security and had her escorted out of the building. She continued screaming in the elevator, collapsed when she reached the sidewalk, woke to a stranger patting her cheek. People were standing over her, asking what happened. Someone helped her stand. Someone put her in a taxi.

She should have tried to make Harriet laugh. She would have liked to hear Harriet laugh, see her smile more. At the school, they had the electrified fence, the guards and the women in pink lab coats. It's dangerous to be in the same city, three miles from her daughter.

×

Will makes Frida get dressed. They walk to the Saturday farmers market in Clark Park, arriving as soon as it opens. Frida asks to turn back. There are too many people. Will reassures her, keeps his arm around her and leads her through the crowd.

Shoppers are buying wreaths. Some are placing orders for turkeys and pies. Will asks Frida to choose apples. They line up to buy bread. Will runs into friends from Penn, who greet Frida as if she's his new girlfriend.

She doesn't want to meet anyone, doesn't want to see anyone with their children. They move aside for parents with strollers. They're a block from a toddler playground. She feels like everyone is watching her, that they know where she's been and what she's done.

The family court judge should know that she's resisting. Tucker has called four times. He's texted and emailed. He won. Silas is living with him. His ex-wife is letting them have extra time together over the holidays.

Germantown is only thirty minutes away. Tucker has assumed that Harriet has been returned. He's asked her to pick a date when they can all meet, suggested ice-skating in Dilworth Park. He's invited them over for an early dinner.

If they'd both lost, she would have gone to him.

But there should never have been a house with side-ways light, not in her mind, not in her heart. Harriet must never know about him. Gust and Susanna can't know. Will can't know. Her parents can't know. The judge said she has problems with willpower, that she's susceptible to temptation, a fantasist, unstable. She is a bad mother for still thinking about him. She is a bad mother for still wanting him. She is a bad mother because she can't bear to see him with his son.

×

Back at Will's apartment, Frida finally calls home. Her father answers, and she agrees to use FaceTime so they can see her. They cry. She begins apologizing. She's a coward for making Gust tell them.

"You're so thin," her mother says.

They are too. They tell her to call a doctor. To eat more meat. They speak in English. Frida resists asking how Harriet seemed during their call, how Gust seemed.

Her parents want her to come home. If she's home, they'll be able to take care of her.

"I'll cook for you," her father says. She doesn't have to look for a job right away. She can find work in Chicago. Live with them. Save money. How nice that would be, to all be together again. If she doesn't feel up to traveling alone right now, they can come get her.

They wanted to fly in for the final court date. She should have let them. She should have taken Harriet to see them more, invited them to visit more often. How many visits have there been? How many days has Harriet actually spent with them? They wanted more branches on the family tree and there's only Harriet to absorb their joy and expectation. She used to think that pressure would burst her baby's heart.

She thanks them for sending money. She should tell them that they don't have to forgive her. She doesn't deserve their forgiveness, doesn't deserve a family.

"I long to hold a grandchild in my arms," her father once said.

When Harriet is eighteen, Frida's mother will be eighty-four, her father will be eighty-five. Frida will be taking care of them. They'll be living with her. She thought they'd move here eventually. Three generations living in one household, the way she grew up.

×

After another few days of discussions, she agrees to fly to Chicago on a one-way ticket. She'll stay for a month or two, maybe longer. Her father offers to come to Philly and rent a truck, drive home her belongings, but Frida isn't ready to make the move permanent. She doesn't know where she should live. She may want to stay close to her daughter.

Her parents want to get the family together to welcome her home. Her father will cook lobster with black bean sauce, her favorite dish. He'll go to Chinatown to shop for ingredients, will buy pastries too—coconut tarts, baked pork buns.

She craves these flavors. Craves salt. Her father says they'll drink champagne. They received a bottle last Christmas that they've been saving for her.

The happiness in her parents' voices makes her nervous. She wonders how soon she'll disappoint them, whether it will take days or only hours. It's been one week since the final visit. Yesterday, she looked up the address of Harriet's school. She thought about driving past Gust and Susanna's building, considered waiting there, learning their routines.

After she hangs up, she calls Renee and leaves

a message saying she's moving home temporarily. She curls up on the couch and falls asleep for a few hours, waking only when Will returns. Will lets her rest her head in his lap. He plays with her hair.

She imagines it's Tucker touching her, thinks of the dance, how he took care of her when she hit her head on the slide.

She tells Will about the plan.

"I'll miss you," he says. "But this makes sense. Then you'll come back. Right?"

"I think so. I don't know what I'm doing. I don't know what I want. This is what my parents want."

Thinking about returning to Evanston, she gets up abruptly and shuts herself in the bedroom. If she's halfway across the country, she won't be able to look for Harriet in every park or playground. Harriet won't be able to hear her signal. What can she do over the next sixteen years to make Harriet proud, to signal to her, to tell her that her mother is still yearning?

×

Her parents want her to fly home immediately, but Frida needs more time. She books a ticket for

December 22. She drives to her storage unit and collects more clothes and papers, a bin of Harriet's baby clothes, the baby memory book, photo albums. When she gets to her parents' house, she'll build a shrine for Harriet, keep it next to her bed so she can look at Harriet's picture as she's falling asleep. If she keeps the memory of Harriet alive, she might be able to endure. She'll count down the months like she did at the school.

She's surprised by how keenly she misses the mothers and the dolls. She wants to tell Roxanne what happened to Meryl. She wants to know if the dolls are being taken care of in storage. Emmanuelle must be lonely. She must need her blue liquid changed. If she hasn't been erased yet, is she thinking of her mother? Does she expect Frida to return?

Until now, Frida didn't realize how much she relied on Emmanuelle for a daily dose of affection. In the future, if they lose their real children, maybe parents will be given their dolls. Some mothers said they wanted to take their dolls home with them.

It's a shame, she thinks, that no one has invented grafts or transplants. The school could have replaced the faulty parts of their characters with mother instincts, mother mind, mother heart.

×

Frida begins going outside more. She stops spending the whole day in pajamas. She takes walks up and down Baltimore Avenue, watching mothers with their children, the parade of families on their way to Clark Park. But nothing feels true without her daughter, neither time nor space nor her body.

She's been free for three weeks when the call comes. It's Saturday morning, mid-December. Will takes a call from Gust. Frida pieces together information from Will's side of the conversation. How Gust and Harriet just got home from the ER. How Susanna is still there with Henry. They brought him in because he can't keep anything down. He's been vomiting all night. The doctors did an ultrasound on his stomach a few hours ago. Henry has pyloric stenosis. He'll have surgery this afternoon. Gust needs to return to the hospital, stay overnight with Susanna. He asks if Will can watch Harriet. Will hasn't done bedtime before, but Gust thinks he can manage it. He'll leave Will detailed instructions. Harriet is used to him. They can't have someone new watch her. Gust's mother has returned to California. Susanna's mother has returned to Virginia. They never had a reason to find a regular sitter.

Will says yes, and Frida begins to dream. After he gets off the phone, she asks if he could take some pictures of Harriet. Will thinks pictures will make her feel worse.

"I need to see her."

"I understand that, but I thought you weren't supposed to—"

"Just a picture or two. Maybe a video. Please. Don't tell her it's for me."

×

For most of the morning, she keeps busy. Will leaves to run errands, has to get to Gust's place by noon. Frida calls Renee to say goodbye, apologizes for bothering her on the weekend. Renee commends her decision to go home.

"Maybe when Harriet is older . . . ," Renee says. Her voice trails off, allowing Frida to fill that silence with hopes and fantasies.

She asks if Frida would like the video of the final visit. The social worker sent it the other day. Frida isn't ready. They agree to connect in January, wish each other happy holidays in advance. Renee suggests she take up some soothing hobbies like knitting or baking.

"I can't think about hobbies right now."

"You're going to be okay, Frida. You're tougher than you think."

Frida mutters a small thank-you. She can't believe she's deceived anyone into thinking that she's good. There may be no part of her that remains pure and unselfish and motherly. If they scanned her brain now, they'd find only dangerous thoughts. The first, that Harriet is a deep sleeper. The second, that Will can let her in.

×

Before Will leaves, Frida asks for another favor. Tonight, after Harriet falls asleep, she wants to come over. "I won't wake her up. I won't touch her. I won't talk to her. I just want to see her."

"Frida, please." He wants to help her, doesn't think what happened is fair, doesn't think the program, whatever it was, was fair, not to her, or anyone, but she could get arrested. She could get Gust in trouble.

"They have enough going on right now."

"I'll text you, and you can buzz me in. Their building is full of old people. No one will be awake. I'll never have this chance again. No one else would do this for me. I need to see her. I didn't get to say goodbye to her properly. You realize they only gave us half an hour."

"Frida, you shouldn't put me in this position. You know I'm not good at saying no to you." He hugs her, whispers in her ear, "Are you going to be okay by yourself? I need to go."

She asks him to think about it. If he agrees, he can just text her **yes**.

That afternoon, as she waits for Will's answer, she tries to clean her mind. She thinks of the day they found Meryl, what she was like afterward. Meryl said she never slept in the basement. She thought if she fell asleep, someone would come in and attack her. She felt like an animal, jumped at the smallest noise. She was so fucking scared. It was worse than the brain scans, worse than any of the evaluations. The panic never went away. She said nothing was worth that week in the basement, not food, not sex, not freedom, but Frida's grasp on what things are worth anymore is tenuous.

Her bank is still open. She drives to the branch

on Thirty-Sixth Street and withdraws $8,000, has to answer questions from the bank manager about why she needs such a large sum. He tells her that she should have called ahead. She nods. She knows that any transactions over $10,000 will be reported, researched this before coming in, then deleted her search history.

She apologizes, says she's going to a family wedding tonight, that it's Chinese custom to give red envelopes with cash. Her cousin is getting married. Her parents asked her to take care of the **hong baos**.

She receives the cash in hundreds and buries the envelope at the bottom of her purse. She drives to Target and uses the cash to buy a car seat, remembers to choose a front-facing one for a taller, heavier Harriet. She shops for groceries, snacks Harriet might like, nonperishables, juice boxes, fruit and veggie pouches, bottled water. Will might make the decision for her. He might refuse. Even if he says yes, she might lose her nerve. But the other night, he said he loved her. That he's always loved her. That he'd do anything for her. He said when Frida is ready, maybe, if she feels the same, they can start over.

At Will's apartment, she packs her clothes and

papers. She loads her suitcases into her car. She calls her parents, hoping that hearing their voices will stop her. She prints a list of hotels in New Jersey, then packs her computer. There will be an Amber Alert. They'll announce her name on the news. They'll show her picture. Harriet's. They'll retrace her movements. She doesn't know how to steal a car or change a license plate or assume a new identity. She doesn't have a gun. She won't be able to fly. She can't put Harriet in danger. There's nowhere in this country where a mother and daughter who look like them can be invisible. She's not sure if she's willing to spend years in the basement, but what will the punishment matter if the alternative is nothing?

She spends the evening cleaning the apartment. She does Will's laundry and changes his sheets and towels. At 10:23 p.m., he texts. **Yes.**

Frida's hands are shaking as she puts on her coat and turns off the lights and locks the door. During the drive, she tells herself that she could still avoid the basement. Meryl said that, in the dark, she thought about Ocean, surviving for Ocean.

"I knew she'd want me to try," Meryl said.

Will might change his mind when she gets there. Harriet might wake up. But she would take the basement for a few hours, a night, a few days, a week with her daughter.

At each stoplight, Frida considers turning back.

Tonight, it's easy to find street parking. She parks a few steps from Gust and Susanna's front door. She texts Will and asks him to buzz her in. This might be how Meryl felt when she reached the top of the bell tower. No matter what happens, there will be comfort and pleasure. A moment with her daughter where she makes the rules. A different ending.

As she climbs the stairs to the second floor, Frida thinks of her parents. They can't wait to see her. They've never gone this long without seeing her. Her father still calls her his baby. They've prepared her room. They've been getting the house ready. She could simply take a look at Harriet and fly home as scheduled. Despite her mistakes, everyone is excited to see her at the family party on Christmas Eve.

Will has left the door ajar. The living room is strewn with Harriet's toys. There are new pictures of the three of them on the walls, Harriet's preschool watercolors hung with pink tape, photos of Henry on the refrigerator, a Moses basket in the hallway, stacks of cloth diapers, a pile of onesies on hangers.

Frida has never seen their place messy. She refuses

to think about the new baby or his surgery or Gust and Susanna in the hospital. She sits down beside Will and takes his hand. She needs one more favor. She'd like an hour with Harriet alone. There's a bar a few blocks away. He can wait there. She'll text him when she's done.

"I don't think you should. What if she wakes up?"

"She won't. Gust said she sleeps well now. They made a big thing about that at my court date. How well she sleeps. She only has trouble sleeping when she's sick. Please. I need this. It's only an hour. I'm not asking to stay all night. I'll never ask this of you again." She promises to be quiet. She promises not to turn the lights on. She just wants to watch her baby sleep.

"No one will find out." She tells him about the social worker timing them, making them pose for pictures, being dragged out of the building. Didn't he say that what happened to her was barbaric? Didn't he say he wanted them to have more time? They had thirty minutes after a year apart. "You don't know what they did to us. At that place. If I told you, you wouldn't believe me."

They argue for another ten minutes. Frida watches the clock as Will asks her again what happened. To her, to the other mothers. Why can't she tell him?

"I'll tell you later. I promise. But I need you to do this for me. Please. You said you'd do anything for me. This is anything. If I have to say goodbye to her, I want some privacy. They didn't give me any privacy. I just want more time."

Will relents. "Okay." He goes to get his jacket.

Frida follows him. She stands on her tiptoes and kisses him on the lips. Gives him the kiss she would have given Tucker. Will is a good man. One day he'll be a good husband. A good father.

"What was that about?" He tries to kiss her again.

"Nothing." She pulls away. "I love you. Thank you."

"I love you too. Be careful, okay? Call me if you need anything."

Once he leaves, Frida moves quickly. She finds a duffel bag in the front closet. She finds Harriet's winter coat, her hat and mittens, her shoes. She goes to the bathroom and grabs Harriet's toothbrush and toothpaste, a bottle of baby shampoo, one of her hooded towels, some washcloths. She enters the nursery and opens Harriet's dresser drawers, grabs sweaters and pants and T-shirts, socks and under-wear, pajamas, some blankets.

Harriet is sleeping the sleep of the dead. Frida

grabs a few stuffed animals from the rocking chair. She hasn't taken a good look at Harriet yet, knows that if she stops to consider what she's doing, she'll unpack the bag and put the room back in order, she'll think of her parents and Will, Gust and Susanna and Baby Henry, everyone she's hurting.

In an hour's time, she'll be at least sixty miles outside the city. She doesn't know what happens after that, only that she has to get Harriet out of bed quickly and quietly. She sinks to the floor and bows her head to the carpet. She whispers, "I'm sorry."

The instructors would be proud. She moves faster tonight than she ever did at the school. She harnesses her fear for strength and speed. She resists the urge to kiss Harriet as she lifts her up. She stuffs Baby Betty into her purse and covers Harriet with her winter coat. She slings the duffel bag over her shoulder.

She still has forty minutes to undo this, to respect the rules of the state, to save herself from the basement, save her parents from losing their daughter, too. But as she descends the stairs, trying not to disturb Harriet, she feels happy and whole. They're together, as they should be.

No one sees them leave the building. No one

sees her strap Harriet into the new car seat or layer blankets up to Harriet's chin. She turns up the heat, then pulls away from the curb carefully. She's on the highway heading north when Harriet wakes up.

"Mommy."

Harriet's voice startles her. Harriet didn't used to wake up speaking words. For a second, Frida feels proud, then realizes that Harriet is calling for Susanna.

She pulls over onto the shoulder of the highway, puts on her hazards, and joins Harriet in the back seat. "It's me," she says. She gives Harriet her doll. She kisses Harriet's forehead and speaks in perfect motherese. "Don't be scared, bub. I'm here. Mommy is here."

Harriet's eyes are still half-closed. "Why? Why you here?"

"I came back for you. We're going on a trip. A vacation."

It takes several minutes to calm her, to tell her not to worry about Daddy and Mommy Sue-Sue and Uncle Will and Baby Henry, to explain that she'll spend a little time with Mommy, that this time will never be enough.

"I couldn't let you go like that. Not with that

mean lady. Not in that office. I'm not going to let you go."

Harriet rubs her eyes. She looks out the window. "It's dark, Mommy. I'm scared. I'm scared. Mommy, where we going?"

Frida holds Harriet's hands, then kisses her knuckles and fingertips. "I don't know yet."

"Can we see the moon?"

Frida laughs. "We can look at the moon later, sure. Maybe we'll even see some stars tonight. You're never up this late, are you? We're going to have a nice time, bub. For as long as we can. Go back to sleep, okay? Don't be scared. I'll take care of you. I love you so much. I came back, see? I'm going to stay with you."

She begins to hum. She strokes Harriet's cheek. Harriet grabs Frida's hand and holds it to her face, leaning into it like it's a pillow.

"Mommy, stay with me. You going to put me to bed?"

"I will. We're going to find a nice comfy place to sleep. You can sleep next to me, okay? Remember, you used to like that. We can do that every night. I'll hold you." Frida thinks of Emmanuelle in the grass. The doll staring at the sun. Her other daughter, vessel for her hope. For her love.

"We can have a family cuddle."

She waits until Harriet's eyes close. If she'd been able to comfort Harriet like this last fall. If she'd been a better mother.

She returns to the driver's seat, remembering the lessons at the warehouse, watching Harriet's birthday video while Emmanuelle screamed. As she pulls back onto the highway, she checks the rearview mirror. Harriet is perfectly still. Soon, in hours, or days if she's lucky, there will be sirens. There will be more guards, more women, a different kind of uniform.

Frida has the photos in her purse. When they get to the first rest stop, she'll slip the Polaroid of herself and Emmanuelle into Harriet's inside coat pocket, where only Gust and Susanna will ever look. When they find it, they'll ask questions. They'll bring the photo to Renee. Renee will ask questions. When she's older, Harriet will ask questions. Frida will give her a photo from their final visit, too.

Harriet will learn a different story. One day, Frida will tell Harriet the story herself. About Emmanuelle and the blue liquid. How Harriet once had a sister, how her mother wanted to save that sister. How her mother loved both girls so much. She'll tell Harriet about Roxanne and Meryl. She'll tell Harriet about the mother she was, the mistakes she made. She'll tell Harriet about making a new person in her body, how the making of this person defies language and logic. That bond, she'll tell Harriet, can't be measured. That love can't be measured. She'd like to know if Harriet will ever make a new person, if she'll be back in Harriet's life by that time. She'd like to tell Harriet that she can help raise that person. She can be careful. She'll convince her daughter to trust her. **I am a bad mother**, she'll say. **But I have learned to be good.**

ACKNOWLEDGMENTS

For as long as I've been working on this novel and dreaming of its publication, I've also been looking forward to saying thanks. My deepest gratitude to the people and institutions that have been instrumental in the creation of this book and sustaining my writing life:

Team Frida. To Meredith Kaffel Simonoff, my fierce and dazzling agent, for our collaboration and literary partnership. To my brilliant editors, who understood this book's heart and purpose and showed me how to get there. Dawn Davis, for loving, elegant problem-solving and guidance, making my manuscript leaner and meaner, and mentoring me on book, career, and motherhood. Jocasta Hamilton, for abundant wisdom, magic, and humor. Marysue

Rucci, Charlotte Cray, and Ailah Ahmed, for taking the reins with such warmth and panache. Working with you has been a dream come true.

The Simon & Schuster team. Jonathan Karp, Dana Canedy, and Richard Rhorer championed this book. Brittany Adames, Hana Park, and Chelcee Johns steered the ship. Morgan Hart, Erica Ferguson, and Andrea Monagle corrected my timeline and fixed so much. Jackie Seow, Grace Han, and Carly Loman designed the most beautiful house for my words. Julia Prosser, Anne Pearce, Elizabeth Breeden, Kassandra Rhoads, and Chonise Bass connected this book with readers.

The Hutchinson Heinemann team. Laura Brooke, Sarah Ridley, Olivia Allen, Henry Petrides, Linda Mohamed, Claire Bush, Rose Waddilove, Emma Grey Gelder, Mat Watterson, and Cara Conquest, thank you for your passion and vision.

At CAA and DeFiore & Company, much gratitude to the intrepid Michelle Weiner and Jiah Shin; their assistants Zachary Roberge and Kellyn Morris; Jacey Mitziga; Dana Bryan; Emma Haviland-Blunk; and Linda Kaplan for tireless work on my behalf.

Diane Cook and Catherine Chung, my novel-writing mentors and dear friends, for draft reading and pep talks. Diane's short story "Moving On," from her acclaimed collection, **Man V. Nature**, was also an early inspiration for the school.

Keith S. Wilson and Yvonne Woon, for enthusiastically reading and discussing one revised chapter at a time and always demanding the next installment. Additional thanks to Keith for serving as informal tech consultant.

Friends who generously read the entire manuscript or parts: Naomi Jackson, Annie Liontas, Sarah Marshall, Lizzy Seitel, Chaney Kwak, Sean Casey, and Lindsay Sproul. Special thanks to Lydia Conklin and Hilary Leichter for reading and cheering at all stages.

For life-changing gifts of time, space, and financial support: the Elizabeth George Foundation, the Anderson Center, the Jentel Foundation, the Kimmel Harding Nelson Center, the Helene Wurlitzer Foundation, and the Virginia Center for the Creative Arts. Special thanks to the Ragdale Foundation for first taking a chance on me in 2007.

The Bread Loaf Writers' Conference has meant so much to me. This project would have remained a complicated short story if not for a crucial push from Percival Everett. Thank you, Percival, for seeing a novel within the pages I submitted for your workshop. To Lan Samantha Chang and Helena María Viramontes, for excellent advice and big dreams. To Michael Collier, Jennifer Grotz, and Noreen Cargill, for the early vote of confidence.

My teachers at Brown and Columbia: Robert Coover, Robert Arellano, Ben Marcus, Rebecca Curtis, Victor LaValle, David Ebershoff (joy and wonder!), Sam Lipsyte, Stacey D'Erasmo, and Gary Shteyngart. Thank you for teaching me about craft, literature, and perseverance. I wrote my first stories in Jane Unrue's beginning fiction workshop at Brown in 1997. Thank you, Jane, for setting me on this path.

Thomas Ross and Rob Spillman at **Tin House**, Michael Koch at **Epoch**, and their colleagues, for publishing my first stories.

My **Publishers Weekly** family, for the opportunity to learn about the industry while working with the nicest bookworms imaginable.

Beowulf Sheehan, for your kindness and artistry.

Carmen Maria Machado; Diane Cook (again); Robert Jones, Jr.; Leni Zumas; and Liz Moore for your words.

Erin Hadley, for emotional support and key backstory. Erin O'Brien, Brieanna Wheeland, Samuel

Loren, and Bridget Sullivan, for advice about family court and pediatric medicine.

The journalists and scholars whose work influenced the development of this fictional world in tangible and intangible ways. From the **New Yorker**, "Where Is Your Mother?" by Rachel Aviv and "The Talking Cure" by Margaret Talbot sparked early interest. Ms. Talbot's article also inspired the dolls' word counters and introduced me to motherese. Highlights of additional reading include: "Foster Care as Punishment: The New Reality of 'Jane Crow'" by Stephanie Clifford and Jessica Silver-Greenberg in **The New York Times**; **What's Wrong with Children's Rights** by Martin Guggenheim; **Nobody's Children** by Elizabeth Bartholet; **Beyond the Best Interests of the Child** by Joseph Goldstein, Anna Freud, and Albert J. Solnit; **Small Animals** by Kim Brooks; **To the End of June** by Cris Beam; **Perfect Madness** by Judith Warner; **All Joy and No Fun** by Jennifer Senior.

The teachers and staff of the Children's Community School of West Philadelphia and my daughter's loving nannies—Pica, Alex, Angel, Madeleine, Daniella, and Teacher Alex—whose hard work allowed me to finish this book.

ACKNOWLEDGMENTS

My cherished friend, Bridget Potter, at whose idyllic Log House I began writing Frida's story in February 2014.

Friends who listened and encouraged: Sara Faye Green, Emma Copley Eisenberg, Jamey Hatley, Meghan Dunn, Crystal Hana Kim, Vanessa Hartmann, Steven Kleinman, Gabrielle Mandel, Shane Scott, Rui Dong-Scott, CLAW and GPP comrades, my Brooklyn writing group, residency pals, and the 2013–2015 Bread Loaf waiters and social staff. The late Jane Juska. Dorit Avganim, Ellen Moscoe, and Jordan Foley, my West Philly mom crew. Muriel Jean-Jacques, Kristin Awsumb Liu, Maya Bradstreet, Nellie Hermann, and Jenny Tromski, believers for over two decades.

My godmother Joyce Fecske, and the Chan, Soong, Wang, Kao, Diller, Hodges, and Sethbhakdi families, thank you for your love and support. My beloved sister, Audrey Chan, and brother-in-law, Jason Pierre, for solidarity and Chan factory steam. To the loving memory of my grandparents, especially my grandmothers, Chin-Li Soong and Soolsin Chan-Ling.

My parents, James and Susy Chan, for boundless love, a childhood full of books and art, patience, generosity, devoted parenting and grandparenting, and your good example. I cannot ever thank you enough for all you've done to make this book, my writing, and my family possible. Thank you for always believing in me.

My husband, Adam Diller, for your love and care and heavy lifting, for this happiness, our family, and our bird. I'm able to write because of the life we've made together.

My daughter, Lulu. When you were three and a half, you asked me to include your name in my book. Here it is. I love being your mother and I will try to be good.